Legends of Havenport

Emma Kaye
Lita Harris
Nicole S. Patrick
Ruth A. Casie

Timeless Scribes
Publishing

Timeless Scribes Publishing LLC

Print ISBN-10: 1-945679-39-5
Print ISBN-13: 978-1-945679-39-1

Digital ISBN-10: 1-945679-38-7
Digital ISBN-13: 978-1-945679-38-4

Edited by Deserie Comfort of Comfort Editing
Copy Edited by Michael Mandarano

This edition published by arrangement with Timeless Scribes Publishing LLC.

www.TimelessScribes.com

Havenport Herald

*** Special Edition ***   *** Volume 05 Issue 01 ***

Get the latest with Candy Apples.
Gossip with a snarky, tart bite…

LET THE HOSTILITIES BEGIN!

Well, the reenactment, anyway. Havenport is all revved up over the 250th anniversary of the Havenport Hostilities. Our proud history and local legends are the name of the game around here these days.

♥♥♥

Speaking of local legends, anyone seen the cutie running around town with our favorite single mom and closet witch? Rumor has it he's the spitting image of one of our very own "Lovers of Havenport." You know the story — the star-crossed lovers who disappeared in the roaring twenties never to be heard from again, with only an old photograph to remember them by. But my sources say we don't have the story straight and there's a beast to go along with his beauty. Now the photo's missing. Some say coincidence, but I'm not convinced. Let's just hope our friends are successful in **Tricking the Beast**.

♥♥♥

Is our neighborhood Gal Friday finally giving in to temptation? A certain someone's been hanging around her place quite a lot lately. He'll claim he's helping her fix up the place and laying to rest a long-lost scandal while he's at it, but the twinkle in his eye says he's looking for something more. I sure hope the untimely arrival of his ex-wife doesn't throw a wrench in their plans. Our very favorite workaholic deserves a little happiness.

And who knows, maybe she'll realize that sometimes our doubts are better left **In Days Past**.

♥ ♥ ♥

A little birdie told me the hunky Marine hanging out with one of my colleagues here at the *Havenport Herald* is fulfilling his late mother's last request and is itching to leave the second he's done. But I hear he's more connected to this town than he knows. In fact, his mother's something of a local legend. With our intrepid journalist on the case, his wanderlust doesn't stand a chance. Before you know it, I'll bet he's whispering **Make Me Stay** in her ear. And she's just the one to make it happen.

♥ ♥ ♥

Did you hear about the Senate-hopeful's sister? After her boyfriend, our beloved police chief, asked her to look into some documents he recovered from a murdered ex-con, all hell broke loose. She's supposed to be authenticating the diary of one of our proud Havenport ancestors, but instead she's dodging bad guys and solving crimes with eerie **Echoes of Betrayal** from that very same diary.

♥ ♥ ♥

I hope you all soak up as much gossip — um, history — as I did. Enjoy the festivities!

~Candy Apples

Contents

Tricking the Beast

by Emma Kaye

♥ ♥ ♥

Reina Mills has always admired the Lovers of Havenport legend—and not only because the hero is drop-dead gorgeous. But when her daughter's emerging magick pulls him from his portrait, she can't let her feelings interfere with returning him to where he belongs. Someone's going to notice the famous photograph is missing a key player, and Reina isn't about to let her daughter get in trouble for it.

Keenan O'Connell can't remember anything after rejecting a spoiled socialite's advances, until he wakes up almost one hundred years in the future. At first he's determined to return home, but the more he gets to know the woman who saved him, the less he wants to go anywhere without her.

When an evil witch from Keenan's past threatens Reina and her daughter, Keenan will sacrifice himself to defend the family he's come to love. With help from the Havenport coven, can Reina save her daughter *and* the man she loves? Or is their attempt to trick the beast destined to fail?

Dedication to ~

My family for their love and support.

Lita, Ruth, Nicole, and Desi for making Havenport so much fun.

Chapter One

"Mom," Mia's exasperated, embarrassed whisper carried across the museum to where Reina stood admiring the portrait of *The Lovers of Havenport*. Several of Mia's friends giggled. The group of teen girls, with skirts that flirted with dress-code regulations and attitudes that could try the patience of a saint, locked arms while whispering to one another and keeping one eye on the teacher. No one wanted to get caught not paying attention to the tour guide, though they didn't seem to mind ticking off the chaperones.

Reina Mills rolled her eyes and stuck her tongue out at her daughter but crossed the room to a painting of the Havenport marina circa the 1920s. So what if Mia had a point. Reina might have been drooling the tiniest bit, but who could blame her? The hero of the painting—Keenan O'Connell—was smoking hot. With his rolled sleeves showcasing the sinewy muscles of his forearms, and his pants pulled tight across his tight rear end, he was obviously in great shape. But there was something about his eyes that always drew Reina in whenever she came to Havenport's tiny maritime museum. And while she normally wasn't crazy about beards, he looked damned good with facial hair. Rugged, dangerous…she could definitely see why the heroine of the picture had been willing to throw away her cushy life to be with a man like him.

When Mia's teacher asked for parent chaperones for the trip, Reina jumped at the chance. Part of the reason she worked nights at Heartbreakers strip club was to be available for events such as this. When she managed to land a daytime job, she would miss these things.

The docent explained the legend of the star-crossed lovers, but Reina had heard it before and continued to admire the old photograph she loved so much. Only now, she did it from across the room while feigning interest in a bunch of boats.

The story usually drew her in, but not today.

"Abigail Ashford was engaged to a man old enough to be her father," the docent droned on. "An arranged marriage typical of the Havenport upper class at the time. But young Abigail had already fallen in love with a young man who worked for her father's shipping company. Recently returned from fighting in World War I, Keenan O'Connell got a job at the docks and met Abigail that same day. Knowing their relationship would be frowned upon by Abigail's parents and the rest of Havenport society, they kept their liaison secret until Abigail's betrothal was announced. This proved too much for Keenan, who declared his love for Abigail and stole her away from her bedroom in the dark of night. Neither was ever heard from again. Some say they successfully made their way out of Havenport, married, and lived happily ever after. Others suspect foul play. Abigail's fiancé was not one to take no for an answer. Some believe he discovered the pair's plans to escape and murdered them with…"

This particular volunteer was not one of Reina's favorites. She somehow managed to make the romantic story of *The Lovers of Havenport* sound boring.

Reina had heard the tale a hundred times and read the museum literature even more. She sighed. What must it be like to have a man love you enough to risk everything—job, reputation, even his life—in order to be with you?

Mia's father had failed spectacularly in *his* first test as a lover. Harold took off running the minute Reina told him she was pregnant. Couldn't risk his family finding out he'd impregnated the poor white-trash, Southern slut he'd fooled around with the summer of his senior year in high school. His charmed life wasn't about to be ruined for someone like Reina.

So he'd dumped her. *Thank the goddess.* She couldn't imagine being married to the dick. That should have been the end of it, but a week ago he showed up asking questions about Mia.

Reina forced her hands to unclench. She still didn't know what to do about his sudden interest in their daughter. She'd never asked for a penny in child support. His name wasn't even on the birth certificate, for heaven's sake.

If she thought for even a moment he was actually interested in Mia, she'd work on some kind of visitation arrangement. Much as it would break her heart to spend less time with her daughter, Mia had the right to get to know her father.

But Reina was under no such illusion. His attitude made it perfectly clear he still didn't give a shit about Mia. Was he just using her as a pawn in some sick, twisted power play with his parents? Pretend interest so they would get off his back? Thank goodness he was moving to California in a few months so they wouldn't have to suffer through his games for too long.

She didn't pretend to understand what he really wanted, but since it obviously wasn't Mia, Reina was going to fight him tooth and nail to keep their daughter from getting hurt in whatever drama he planned to enact.

She just didn't know how…yet.

Another frantic hiss made Reina turn her concentration back to her daughter.

Mia blushed a fiery red while pretending she hadn't a care in the world. She flipped her long, blue-streaked hair over her shoulders and turned her back on her mother. Reina was used to it. Ever since Mia had turned fourteen she'd become a sullen, sour-faced, stereotypical teenager.

Reina was losing her mind over it.

What happened to her sweet, innocent, happy little girl?

And the power that poured off her when they least expected it? Yeah, that would be an even bigger challenge than having a teenager in the house.

Reina simply became more attuned to the supernatural when she turned fourteen. Mia had power sparking out at the most inopportune moments, creating havoc wherever she went. Thank goodness no one made the connection between Mia and the fire in the chemistry lab. After all, Mia had been clear across the room. Who would suspect the fire started because Noah was making crude gestures in Mia's direction? No one was hurt, and the teacher assumed Noah was careless with his Bunsen burner.

Served the little shit right for messing with Reina's baby.

A ripple of movement behind her daughter and a skittering of magickal power along her skin caught her attention.

Mia.

Reina swiveled her head in the direction of the photo. Mia now stood with her gaggle of friends in front of the portrait. But it wasn't the girls' movements that sparked the prickle of trepidation down her spine.

Nope.

The photograph itself had changed. The lovers were no longer in the heated embrace that brought sighs of longing to all the women who viewed it. Instead, Keenan held Abigail at arm's length. Almost as if he were pushing her away while she clung to him.

The magick Reina sensed flowed off Mia.

Damn.

Reina approached the girls from behind. Luckily, the docent had moved on to the next room, which featured various relics from the Havenport Hostilities and the Scottish highlander who sounded the alarm and lost his love as a consequence. Another great story. For a sleepy little town, Havenport had quite a history.

"Move along, girls. History awaits." She made a shooing gesture to usher the girls along. She wanted them gone before someone noticed the change in the painting.

♥ ♥ ♥

Keenan O'Connell pushed away from Miss Ashford's embrace.

"What the hell?"

Yellow, gray, and brown hues dominated the world around him, the colors muted and not quite right. Was it from the approaching storm? He glanced up at the sepia-toned sky. Something was amiss. The ocean waves lay perfectly still behind him. Silence reined over the world. Instead of the salty brine of the ocean, his nose tickled from the sour scent of the acetic acid he used in his darkroom.

"Keenan," Abigail whined. She clutched at his arm, refusing to let go.

"Enough, Miss Ashford. I'm not falling for your hokum. I do not love you. Nor are you stuck on me, despite what you proclaim." He brushed off her pinching grip. "Return to your fiancé. He can provide for you as I never could." He couldn't understand the woman's obsession. She was a spoiled, rich debutant. She would never accept the type of life he could provide for them. Nor did he care to convince her otherwise. She was beautiful, yes, but he'd quickly seen past her pretty face. Her heart was as black as jet. The initial spark of desire quickly faded when he recognized her true nature.

A bright light flashed to his right. They both swung in that direction.

Abigail gasped. "No. How can this be? We were supposed to remain together forever." She stomped her foot in a distinctly unladylike way. Childish and spoiled down to her very bones.

Keenan squinted against the brilliant glare and held up a hand to shield his eyes. "I don't understand. What's going on, Miss Ashford? What have you done?" Memories returned, slow and foggy. "When did you get here?" How had they come to be on the docks together? He had sought his solitude on the docks. After confronting Abigail about her manipulations, he needed a moment of peace to calm his raging temper.

Yes, he'd picked up his camera, intent on capturing the waves in all their fury. A storm had been brewing and the ocean was sure to respond to the turmoil in the air.

Her nails dug into his arm, and his anger surged. She thought him an easy target for seduction when he could barely stand the sight of her. His stomach turned at the thought of becoming a patsy in her plot to deceive her father and fiancé.

The light increased in intensity. Abigail released his arm with a gasp. A tugging sensation began at the base of his spine. What magick was this? "What are you doing to me, witch?"

She screamed. "No. He's mine. He's supposed to love me! He'll always be mine."

The light flashed. Everything went black. Abigail's angry scream echoed in his ears.

♥ ♥ ♥

Mia hesitated at the doorway into the next room.

Reina made a shooing gesture. "Move along. Lots to see." She didn't want Mia to know the havoc her magick created any more than she wanted the other teenagers to notice. If Mia panicked, the problem would only get worse. Any mention of her out-of-control powers had a tendency to cause Mia's anxiety to soar.

"What are you up to?" Mia asked.

"Nothing, sweetie. Why?" Reina crossed her fingers behind her back. She hated lying to her daughter, but desperate times…

"Your fingers are crossed behind your back, aren't they." It wasn't a question. "Why are you lying? What are you up to?"

Reina rolled her eyes. Damn, Mia knew her too well. "Fine." She peeked through the door to make sure the docent had all the kids' attention before continuing. "There's a slight issue with the *Lovers* portrait I don't want to call attention to."

Mia ran to the portrait and gasped. Her hand shook as she pointed one black painted nail at the image.

Reina followed suit. The image had changed again. Keenan not only stood several feet away from Abigail, but now faced toward them. One hand shaded his eyes, his mouth turned down in a confused frown. Abigail's hands clenched into tight fists, her mouth open in a scream of rage. She looked deranged. No longer the sweetly innocent high-society miss in love with a World War I veteran.

The museum lights flickered overhead, then brightened way past their wattage.

The figures in the portrait continued to move. Keenan edged closer, loomed larger, while Abigail remained in the background.

"Oh, shit." She grabbed Mia's arm. "We have to go." Mia didn't budge, so she tugged harder. "Now, Mia." They had to leave before it was too late. Reina didn't know how this was happening, but somehow Mia's magick was drawing Keenan out of the portrait.

Chapter Two

Keenan stumbled into a small room. Colors returned to normal and the familiar buzz of life hummed in his ears.

A beautiful woman stared at him with her mouth open in horror. Her arm flung out defensively, pushing a young lady partially behind her. Both were dressed in the oddest fashion. Scandalous. The beauty wore pants and a top that hugged her breasts, revealing a tantalizing view of cleavage.

He shook his head, not to be distracted by the vision before him. "What witchcraft is this?" he asked, his voice hoarse and throat sore, as if he hadn't used it in a while. Yet a moment ago, speaking with Miss Ashford had brought no such discomfort.

The woman gasped and lurched forward. "Hush now, sugar. No need to go about making such vile accusations." She cast a glance over her shoulder into another room he spied through an adjoining door.

His head spun. He slammed into the wall, right next to a photograph of Abigail screaming. Just as he'd last seen her.

"We've gotta get you outta here, sugar."

The woman rushed to his side and propped him up. She smelled like fresh-baked apple pie. The scent calmed his frayed nerves. There was something familiar about her. Her voice, perhaps? He trusted her, odd as it seemed to trust a stranger.

He nodded and allowed the woman to assist him out of the building. The girl followed until the woman turned to her and said, "Go back to your class. Try to act like everything's okay."

"But, Mom—"

Mom? She didn't look old enough to be the girl's mother.

"Do it, Mia. I'll take care of Keenan. But I don't want anyone associating you with the change to the *Lovers* picture. We've had enough strange shit going on lately. We don't need this now."

Mia rolled her eyes, shot daggers at her mom, then stormed out of the room.

"Your daughter?" he asked. Stupid. Obviously Mia was her daughter. Why the hell had he asked such an inane question?

"Yeah. Teenager. Still figuring out how to deal."

He tried his best not to lean too hard on her shoulder, but his legs were weak, as if he hadn't used them in days. They staggered outside and stopped at a strange-looking vehicle.

"Get in."

He was shoved into the front passenger seat, his knees tucked practically to his chin in the tiny space. He flew back with a *bang!* as his lovely temptress pulled a lever between his legs and sent his seat crashing backward.

"Sorry. Should have warned you."

Before he had a chance to respond, she slammed the car door, then circled around to the driver's side. She slid into the seat. After taking several deep breaths, she turned to him. "Now, sugar, I'm in the middle of something, so I'd appreciate it if you'd wait right here. I should only be another half hour or so."

Keenan nodded. He didn't trust his voice. Besides, he would likely tell her the truth.

He had no intention of following her orders.

♥ ♥ ♥

Reina's hands shook as she paused before going back into the museum. The kids would hop back on the bus to the junior high school in about—she checked her watch—half an hour. *Please, please let Keenan stay in my car.*

After a deep breath, she entered the building and caught up to the group. Mia's face was deathly pale, but she appeared to be doing a good job of pretending nothing was wrong. Her pallor could be attributed to the contrast between her skin and the god-awful black lipstick she wore. Reina shot her daughter a reassuring wink, then pretended great interest in the docent's boring lecture.

It felt like forever before the teacher clapped her hands to get everyone's attention. "Okay, everyone. Time to go." Once all the kids were on the bus, she turned to the parents. "Thanks for coming. They'll head home on their regular buses."

Reina lingered a moment after saying goodbye to everyone. She hoped no one would spot Keenan in her car if she didn't bring attention to him.

After everyone else cleared out, she made her way to her little yellow Bug. She loved her car. She'd bought it shortly after Harold had dumped her and her mother had kicked her out of the house, calling her a slut and a host of other names because she *got herself* pregnant. Yeah, right. Immaculate conception Mia was not.

But Reina had a stash of cash she'd been hoarding for a rainy day. Or for the day she gathered up her courage and left the hellhole she called home. That day came sooner than anticipated when she confessed her pregnancy to her mother.

Her stepfather surprised her with an account he'd set up in her name. He'd been putting money aside for her since he'd married her mom. Thank God for Jerry. He was a better parent than her birth mother had ever been. Her biological father had never been in the picture.

A car wasn't the first thing on her priority list when she'd suddenly found herself homeless, but she quickly realized she needed a mode of transportation for any job she managed to score. The only apartments she'd found in her price range were not even close to walking distance from town.

The car door was open. *Shit.* She ran the last few steps. "Keenan?"

Empty. She slammed the door and spun in a circle. Where did he go?

A path led down to the water. If she recalled correctly, which she did, Keenan used to work on the docks. She remembered everything about him. Oh, man, she was screwed.

The gate leading toward the dock stood slightly ajar. She couldn't see anyone, but the path went around the museum, the view of the ocean blocked by the building.

She took a deep breath and walked. Maybe Keenan wanted a good look at the ocean or to spy something familiar. She picked up her pace.

He stood at the end of the pier, his back to her.

"Keenan?" she called. Shoot. She whipped around to make sure no one heard her. A lone woman, skirt fluttering around her thighs in the wind, strode away from the museum in the opposite direction. Too far away to have heard anything.

How was she going to explain this? There were only a few people who would believe her. Most of them members of the Havenport coven, or their men.

The dock was mostly empty, the museum dark and locked up tight. The docent had left, along with the school group. She nodded to Ralph Tanner, a ghost that haunted the dock where he'd drowned fifty years ago. He was a nice enough spirit, just not ready to move on. She'd tried to help him, but he'd refused. Someday she'd figure out what he needed. But not today.

She slowed, then stopped a foot behind the man she *was* here to see. "Keenan?" she said again, quieter this time. "Are you all right?"

His shoulders were hunched about his ears, his head tilted down. Rather than staring out toward the horizon, his gaze trained down into the water. "I hated working the docks. Gutting fish, hauling crates. The smell permeated my clothes and wouldn't wash out." He lifted his arm and sniffed the sleeve of his jacket. "But I always loved the ocean. The play of the sun's setting rays across the water, the sound of the waves crashing on the shore. I would come out here at the end of the day and wait for hours for the perfect lighting."

Reina shook her head. "I—I don't understand, sugar." She stepped up beside him and leaned against the railing. She kept her head tilted toward the water, but studied him out of her peripheral vision. He wasn't making any sense. Where was he going with this?

"That's the last I remember. I had come down here to take some photographs of the sunset." His brows scrunched. "Then all of a sudden, the colors are muted. Strange. Like a photograph. I found myself in Miss Ashford's arms, and she's screaming nonsense about being together forever. What did that witch do to me?"

Witch. There was that word again. And the inflection in his tone made it perfectly clear he was not a fan.

"I don't rightly know." She put a hand on his arm. His bicep clenched, rock hard under her fingers, the fabric pulled taught against some mighty fine muscles. *Good Lord.* "But maybe I can help? Speaking of helping…why don't you come home with me for now? We can figure out what's going on and make a plan for what to do next." She snuck a quick peek at the museum and what little was visible of the parking lot beyond. "We should get away from here, though. You're *kinda* recognizable around these parts."

♥ ♥ ♥

Keenan turned to get a good look at this woman who was so determined to hide him from view. They sped down the road in her strange vehicle, his knees uncomfortably crushed in the small space. Everything was so strange; he couldn't take it all in. He hadn't even questioned when this beautiful stranger led him to her car. "I'm sorry, miss. Do I know you?" He was certain he did not, and yet there was something familiar about her. His memory was foggy. Had he somehow forgot their introduction?

"Oh, gosh. Sorry, no. We've never met. I'm Reina." She thrust out her hand like they were two men meeting up at a sporting event.

He took her hand gently in his. Warmth spread from where they'd touched. Her hands were soft, delicate. The urge to lift her knuckles to his lips was strong, but he got the impression she wouldn't expect, or appreciate, such a gesture. "Yet you know my name?"

A pink tinge blossomed on her cheeks, setting off her perfect complexion.

"The museum's one of my favorite places. I've, um, heard your story once or twice."

"My story?" Her words confused him. Not much of a story. He wasn't any different than hundreds of other soldiers returned from the Great War. And less than so many of them. He unclenched his fists and flattened them against his thighs, pleased to see they weren't shaking. Provided he didn't hear any loud noises, they might stay steady.

He lifted his head to stare out the window at the passing scenery.

His jaw dropped. Had they left Havenport? Minutes from the marina and nothing was as he remembered. Not even the automobiles.

Reina's auto had been easy to dismiss. He wasn't an expert by any means, so not recognizing her vehicle was unsurprising. The street full of unidentifiable autos was another story. The usual Cadillacs and Model Ts were nowhere to be found.

And the people. He'd already noted Reina's strange manner of dress. Who could blame him for being sidetracked by the way she looked in them rather than noting he'd never seen their like?

The clothing of those they passed was just as odd. Not nearly as eye-catching in most cases, but strange nonetheless. Scandalously, at least half of the women wore pants. He knew the trend was building, but hadn't seen quite so many women flaunting this latest form of fashion rebellion. And almost no one wore a proper hat.

He slapped a hand to his head. Nothing. He must have taken it off in order to snap a picture. The brim of his fedora interfered with his efforts, so he often found a place to stash it while he worked.

His hands itched to pick up his camera. Taking photographs calmed his nerves, and with the questions screaming in his brain as he took in all the peculiar sights, he could use some soothing.

A structure he recognized finally came into view. "When did they finish the gazebo? I was speaking with Joseph just yesterday and he predicted it would not be complete for at least another two weeks."

Reina's eyes widened, but she didn't look his way. Her knuckles whitened on the steering wheel she gripped it so tight. "Oh, dear. I don't know how to tell you this." A tear leaked from her eye. "This isn't your world. You're not real."

"The hell I'm not." What was she talking about? Had she lost her mind? He ran a hand through his hair, feeling indecent out in public without his hat. This conversation wasn't helping.

She sighed. "We're almost there. We'll grab a drink and I'll explain."

"I could go for a bit of the brown plaid about now."

A minute later, they pulled up before a large building along the water on Main Street. Darn, but everything looked different. "Royce's Tavern? This is Tilly's Inn. I've been here a time or two. But it looks nothing like...are you sure it's open?" He climbed out onto the sidewalk, a headache forming behind his eyes. Tilly's didn't usually open until much later. "Where are the lookouts?"

Reina stepped up beside him and placed a hand on his arm. "Lookouts?" She shook her head. "I'm sure this is very disconcerting. I promise I'll clear everything all up. Let's go in. Are you hungry? We can get something to eat. I want to talk to Jane. She and her husband own the place."

He resisted her tug. "Perhaps having a meal together is not a wise idea. Your husband might object." And perhaps she was unaware that Tilly's was a speakeasy. They hadn't been raided in months. They were due. Stupid not to have someone on the lookout for the coppers.

"No husband. Don't worry about it."

A widow then. "The war took many of our best men and left so many young wives on their own. I'm sorry for your loss."

Frown lines creased her forehead and she bit her lip. "No husband. Just an asshole who suddenly discovered he was too good for me when I told him I was pregnant."

Keenan's jaw dropped. "Was there no one to see him do right by you? Had he no honor?"

"None at all, sugar. I dodged a bullet, that's for sure. And I ended up with Mia and not tied down to some asshole, so I got the better end of the deal. Make no mistake, I wouldn't have it any other way. We're better off on our own."

"You hardly look old enough to be her mother."

Reina rolled her eyes. "Are we back to this? Yes, she's my daughter, and yes, I had her young. Sixteen, to be exact." She tugged on his arm. "Come on. Let's go in."

Chapter Three

Once they settled into a booth in Royce's Tavern, Reina excused herself to go to the bathroom. She needed a moment.

What in the Sam Hill was she going to do? How do you convince someone they aren't real? And that as soon as you can, you're going to turn them back into nothing more than a photograph? That's *if* he didn't simply revert to his natural state at some unforeseeable time. She placed her palms on the sink and leaned forward, her forehead almost touching the mirror. The contents of her stomach threatened to spill.

God, how she hated confrontation. At least when it was personal. Let a guy get handsy with her at Heartbreakers and she'd tell him a thing or two. But that was different. Assholes she could deal with. Telling a decent person she was going to end what semblance of life he had was a different story.

Could she do it? Could she look Keenan in the eye and tell him his life was a fake and could be over at any second?

How could she not? Eventually, the museum would open again and someone would notice the portrait of *The*

Lovers of Havenport was missing a crucial aspect. One of the lovers.

And it wouldn't take long before someone mentioned that Reina and Mia were the last people in the room. Which normally wouldn't worry her. They'd only been alone in the room for a few minutes, not enough time to switch photographs. Reina obviously hadn't been hauling around a sixteen-by-twenty framed photo waiting for her moment. People didn't usually jump to magick as an answer to inexplicable occurrences.

If only Heather Besares hadn't been one of the chaperones.

Damn, she couldn't stand that woman. And the feeling was mutual. Had been ever since high school. Reina would probably never know what she'd done to tick the harpy off, but she must have done *something* because Heather certainly had it in for her and Mia.

That she was now the counselor in Mia's school made everything worse. If anything unusual happened while Mia was in the room, Heather gave her the stink eye, even if Mia had nothing to do with it.

Mia felt the pressure, though she had ceased telling her mother about it. Teenagers.

Which was exactly why Reina had to put everything back to rights. And as quickly as possible. The museum was closed for a week while the outside was painted in preparation for all the tourists expected to flock to the small town for the Havenport Hostilities Revolutionary War reenactment. That gave her a little leeway.

But not much. Reina couldn't take the chance someone would connect Mia to Keenan's disappearance. Especially now that Harold had put in a reappearance.

The cold water she splashed on her face did little to calm her nerves. After patting her face dry, she took a few deep breaths, did a quick makeup fix, and headed for the door. She grabbed the handle, then stepped back to hold the door for another woman exiting at the same time.

The door slammed open with a *bang*, clipping her arm. The other woman grabbed the door right before it would have smacked Reina in the face. She gasped in surprise and massaged her wrist.

"Hey," the other woman exclaimed. "Jeez." She turned to Reina. "You okay?"

Reina gave a shaky laugh. "I'm fine. Thanks. That would have hurt." A bloody nose and concussion were definitely not on her to-do list for the day. She had enough to deal with.

"And that bitch just ran away. She could have at least said sorry." She shook her head. "What is wrong with people these days?"

Reina overheard her telling the story to her friend at the bar when she walked by on the way back to the table to face Keenan. The slight sting on her wrist had already faded, so she put the incident out of her mind as her thoughts drifted back to her current problems. What was she going to do?

Whatever she had to. Mia was, and always would be, her top priority. Reina couldn't let personal sensibilities get in the way of protecting her daughter. She made her way back to the table.

A ridiculously tall figure leaned against her side of the booth, blocking Keenan from her view.

Adam Royce.

Jane's husband liked to visit with customers whenever he could find the time. Right now, business was light so he'd obviously settled in for a long chat with a stranger.

"Hey, Adam," she said before she slipped into a bench seat across from Keenan. "Is Jane around?"

"Hello, Miss Reina." He gave a perfunctory bow. "What brings you here this afternoon? I am unaccustomed to seeing you outside coven meetings."

She hid her grimace at Adam's choice of words and from the corner of her eye, watched the blood drain from Keenan's face. Shit. Everyone around here knew about the coven. Most assumed they were Wiccan, not actual *magickal* witches. Only a few, like Heather, suspected they might be something more. And Adam, of course, knew the truth. His wife was instrumental in bringing the group of Havenport witches together.

"Is Jane around? Keenan and I could use a little help with something." Adam would understand her predicament more than most. Jane had pulled him forward in time with a careless spell about four years ago, so magick was nothing new to the nineteenth-century sailor turned tavern owner. But while he would be a sympathetic ear, he didn't understand how magick worked like his wife did, so Reina was eager to speak with Jane.

She wasn't as optimistic for Keenan. If he were a real person, rather than a manifestation of teenage magick gone wild, then maybe.

"School will let out soon." He glanced at his watch. "I expect she will arrive here within the hour."

Duh. Reina forgot school was still in session. The high school got out much earlier than the lower grades. Jane taught art at the elementary school, so of course she wouldn't be here yet. "Mind if we stick around for a while? It's pretty urgent."

"That would be quite acceptable. Let me get you a menu. We have a few new items from which to choose."

She had bypassed being seated by selecting a booth within the bar area and hadn't thought to grab a menu. Her head was preoccupied with Keenan's situation.

Adam placed the menus on the table before them. "Here you are."

The leather-bound menu folder was the same as always, but when opened contained a different look with new options. "Wow, these are lovely. When did you decide to upgrade?" She admired the creamy paper and the font that was all so much nicer to look at than what Adam had used from the beginning. Classier.

"Our new manager suggested a few changes. We've been quite pleased."

"New manager?"

"Miss Elizabeth Taggart."

Reina raised her eyebrows in surprise. *Liz Trailer?* She immediately cursed herself for using the slur people so often used for the hardworking woman. Reina should know better than to judge people. Shit, she was an unwed mother who worked at a strip joint. People jumped to all sorts of conclusions about her. The fact she hadn't dated anyone in over a year and had a strict rule not to sleep with anyone until they dated for at least six months would shock the ever-lovin'…well, she should know better.

Liz worked practically every part-time job in Havenport. Waitress, dog walker—if there was a job opening, Liz was there. Reina had even seen her answering phones at the police station at one point. "Full-time? When did that happen?" Must have been within the past two weeks. The coven had met here three weeks ago and Jane hadn't mentioned promoting their part-time waitress.

"I asked her to take over the position a little over a week ago. We were discussing business one night when Miss Annie called in sick. Miss Elizabeth came to our rescue and did an exemplary job, as per usual. I had been looking to relieve myself of some of the day-to-day responsibilities of the tavern. Her hire was quite fortuitous."

"That's great."

"Can I start you with something to quench your thirst?"

Keenan cleared his throat. "Are you not worried the coppers might raid you?" He gestured toward the bar where bottles lined up behind the bar.

"Coppers?" Adam frowned.

Reina smacked herself in the forehead, suddenly realizing what he was so concerned about. "Oh, I'm an idiot. I didn't think…Prohibition is over, sugar."

At Adam's confused look, she said, "Keenan's not from this time. You remember how confusing that can be?"

Keenan's eyes were going to pop out of his head if they got any bigger. She patted his hand. "I'll explain everything. Just be patient." She turned to Adam. "Can you just bring us a couple beers? We have a lot to talk about."

Adam nodded. "Yes, I can see that." He turned to Keenan. "Mr. O'Connell, please feel free to seek me out should you have any difficulty adjusting to this new reality. I, also, am not from this time. It can be quite disconcerting in the beginning." The two men shook hands and Adam left.

"I'm sure you have a lot of questions. I'll do my best to answer all of them." Except, maybe, the whole *how did I get here* part. Because there was no way she'd admit to Mia's part in all this. He could condemn her for being a witch, but she'd be damned if her daughter got dragged into it.

♥ ♥ ♥

Keenan had followed the conversation between Reina and the large gentleman with great interest. Any questions? Damn straight. He had a million of them.

"Not from this time? What do you mean by that?" He asked the question he knew to be true. The cars, the buildings…Havenport was nothing like the town he lived in. Yet he recognized many of the buildings they passed along the way. The building they were in now was familiar, if different.

"It's not nineteen twenty-three anymore. Y'all are in the twenty-first century now. Just about one hundred years in the future."

Was she a witch of some sort? She had all but admitted to it with mention of her coven. "Did you bring me here?"

Her face blazed bright red. "Yes. I'm so sorry. It was completely unintentional." She tilted her head down, her shoulders hunched forward. The hand that still lay on top of his twitched. The way she chewed on her bottom lip…

No, he couldn't be distracted by her beauty. "And will you be sending me back?"

Tears sparkled in her gorgeous blue eyes. "Not exactly."

He used his thumb to wipe up a tear that had spilled onto her cheek. "Your distress is apparent and seems out of proportion to the situation. If you brought me here, surely you can send me back? Tell me what's upsetting you." Ridiculous that his instincts hollered to comfort her when he was the one ripped out of his time.

"I'm so sorry, sugar. I don't know that I can."

He sat straight, head touching the booth, his eyes closed, hands pressed tight against the table in front of him. He couldn't look at her. Anger at being pulled from his home, his time, should be paramount, but when he looked at her, his urge was to comfort. "Why?" Was he stranded in this time, this place?

Would that be so bad if it meant he'd have the chance to get to know her more?

The warmth of her hand on his distracted him. This infernal attraction would be the death of him. He wanted to turn his hand over and link his fingers to hers. This touching was completely inappropriate, yet he wanted more.

Her unwed state had come as a shock. A most welcome one.

He startled when she spoke. His mind had taken him so far afield.

"I'll do what I can. But…" She hesitated. "Magick drew you out of a picture from the nineteen twenties. If I put you back…"

A picture? The colors, the utter silence of the world when he first woke, suddenly began to make sense. The world had looked as it did in one of his photographs.

"God, what am I saying? I have to put you back. I don't see any way around it. You don't belong here. I'm so, so sorry. But you're not real. The real you disappeared from Havenport in nineteen twenty-three with the love of your life. Legend has it you, um, ran off and lived happily ever after."

"That's not the first time you've accused me of not being real." He leaned across the table, and she moved forward to meet him. His hand slid under her silky hair to the back of her neck. Their lips met in a featherlight kiss that sent a wave of passion surging through his veins. It took all he had to restrain his desire to press forward, but he did. "I *feel* real."

"You sure do," she said, her voice breathy with a sexy tone of longing that did nothing to ease the tightening of his trousers.

He gulped. They remained less than an inch apart. He traced the lines of her jaw with his thumb. Her breasts strained against the tight confines of her blouse. He forced his eyes up, but the image was seared on his brain. Lord help him.

The scent of apples and cinnamon brought thoughts of home.

But he hadn't been home for years. Long before he found himself in Havenport.

He backed away.

But not quick enough to miss her sigh. She cleared her throat, sat tall, and plucked at the neckline of her top. "*Ah-hem.* As I was saying, you come from a photograph. I don't know how it happened, but I have to put things right."

"What you're saying makes no sense. If I were merely the manifestation of a photograph, I would have no history. I wouldn't remember my parents, or where I went to school, or…the war." He took a large drink from the water in front of him. His throat tightened, the air suddenly dry. Nothing could make him forget.

He only wished he could.

♥ ♥ ♥

Reina's heart nearly broke for him. He seemed so *real*. And in so much pain. She could all but feel his headache when he winced and rubbed his temples. The tight set of his shoulders had her stretching her neck in sympathy.

She sifted through all she knew about the real Keenan's history. The museum program usually focused on his involvement with Miss Ashford, but they did have a few sketchy details about his time in the war. Mainly that he served his time honorably and was known as an amateur photographer. A few years after he disappeared, some of those photographs surfaced, originally attributed to an unknown soldier. Eventually, Keenan's name was discovered when his father published a book of his photography. He was connected to the photos from then on. They still appeared in books today. His work was hailed as some of the best photography of its time for capturing the emotion and horror he and his fellow soldiers faced. They even had a few reproduction postcards at the museum gift shop.

Some of his photographs were seriously heartbreaking. She wouldn't be the least bit surprised to find out that Keenan suffered from PTSD, although as far as she knew they didn't call it that back then. What was it, shell shock?

But he was a photo. He shouldn't be able to feel anything. Yet he certainly acted like he felt it all.

"I don't know why you remember anything. Maybe it's part of the magick that woke you." *Please don't ask about that magick.*

"Your magick," he said, his voice flat and emotionless. Completely at odds with the strained expression on his face.

She hesitated just a fraction of a second before lying. "Yes."

His eyes narrowed. "You don't seem convinced."

"I'm a bit nervous, to be sure. You, uh, don't seem to have a good opinion of witches."

"Is that what you are? A witch?"

She shrugged. "Yes. Although my magick tends more toward communing with the spirits."

"Am I a spirit then?"

"No. I don't know what happened, exactly. That's why we're here."

"To see this Jane person." He leaned forward, elbows on the table. "Can she send me back to my own time?"

Here we go again. "Sugar, you can't go back because you've never been there. Not as anything more than a photo. There's nothing to go back to."

"Nothing?" He slammed his hand on the table. The glasses jumped and silverware rattled.

She flinched. Shit, she'd really pissed him off now.

"What about my family—my father, my brother?" His nostrils flared and his face reddened. "What are they going to think when they never hear from me again?" He dropped his head into his hands, threaded his fingers into his dark hair. "Do you know? Are there stories about my family?"

"I've never heard what happened to your family. The story focused on you and Miss Ashford." He grimaced when his love's name was mentioned. Damn, he must miss her. But why didn't he list her among those he left behind? Was there more to the story, or was that just wishful thinking? He had called Miss Ashford a witch earlier. Not exactly lovers' talk. "We can look it up, though. We'll Google it when we get back to my place, okay?"

"Google? What's a google?"

Ugh, now she had to explain the Internet? Better to show than tell. "That could take some explaining. I'll show you when we get home."

Adam brought their meals. He placed two plates of burgers and fries on the table. She inhaled the delicious scent. "Mmm. This looks incredible, thanks." She smiled up at him. "All on your own today?"

Adam tilted his head toward the bar where a young woman cleaned glasses. "Miss Annie is here and I shall have plenty of help for the evening rush, but this time is typically quite slow so my needs are not great. Besides, I wished to inform you that Jane will not be in this afternoon."

Reina's stomach sank. "Is she okay?"

"Yes, she's quite well, thank you. Bastian asked us to watch the children while he and Winnie attend school conferences for the girls. I will be heading there directly after my evening shift arrives. Shall I have her call you on the…telephone?"

She hid her smile. He'd been in this century for a few years now, yet he still struggled with modern conveniences. The lightening of her mood quickly died when she glanced at Keenan. Small lines wrinkled his forehead. His mouth was turned down in a fierce frown. How strange everything must be for him. And now the quick return he obviously hoped for was delayed.

"That would be great. Have her call me on my cell. I don't want to miss her."

"Rest assured, I shall see she contacts you posthaste. Enjoy your meal." He retreated to the employees-only area past the bar.

Keenan hadn't touched his burger.

"Don't worry. She'll give me a call and I'm sure we'll get this all worked out in no time. Let's just eat and then we'll go find out what happened to your family, okay?"

He nodded and they made quick work of what was probably an excellent meal, though it might as well have been burned to a crisp for all the attention Reina paid it. Her stomach was so tied up in knots she barely ate a quarter of her food.

There were no good options. He couldn't stay. He couldn't go back to the time he thought of as his own. The only solution she saw was condemning him back to his portrait.

Essentially a death sentence.

Chapter Four

Keenan followed Reina into a small cottage on a quiet, tree-lined street. He didn't recall this part of town. He could have sworn they were in the area of Lawson's farm, but instead they were in the middle of an established neighborhood with flowering trees, neatly cut lawns, and bicycles in the front yards.

Her home bubbled over with color. A mismatched hodgepodge of purple, red, and silver cushions covered the sofa, a relatively tame, multi-hued area rug dominated the dark mahogany wood floors, and white curtains fluttered around a large bay window, letting in a good amount of natural light. The light-blue walls were surrounded with white trim. A glance down the bright-yellow hall showed a terra-cotta-painted kitchen. A three-wick candle fought for space on the fireplace mantel among an assortment of pictures of Reina and her daughter.

A comfortable space. He spied a four-season room out the back. A neat, well-cared-for garden could be glimpsed through the floor-to-ceiling windows. Flowers were just beginning to bloom in the spring air.

"Make yourself at home," she said with a sweeping gesture.

She was kind, this woman who seemed intent on bossing him around.

"Come on in." She tugged on his arm, leading him through the living room and into the kitchen. "Let me get you something to drink. Did you have enough to eat? Are you still hungry?"

He shook his head. "No. Thank you. I'd love some water, though."

She nodded and opened a door to a large white box covered with pictures and pieces of paper.

The bottle she handed him crinkled in his grasp, the material thin and pliant in his hands. The top twisted off and the water inside was cold and clear. Refreshing. He downed it in a few seconds, alleviating the scratchy dryness in his throat. "Thank you." He nodded toward the box. "Is that your ice box?"

She frowned. "Um, refrigerator."

"Do you mind?" He waved a hand toward the box. At her nod, opened the door. A wave of cool air hit him in the face. "Amazing."

"Why don't we go have a seat in the living room." She tugged him over to the sofa in the next room.

He let go reluctantly, not wanting to end the connection. The feeling that he knew her somehow persisted. But he'd remember a woman like Reina and he was certain they'd never met. "Are you sure we have not met before?"

"Is that a line, sugar?" She smiled flirtatiously, but the blush staining her cheeks contradicted the attitude. When he just raised his brows, she cleared her throat. "Sorry. No, we've never met. I've visited the museum often enough, though. Could you…um…see anything from the picture? I mean, right before you came through. Were you aware? What was it like?"

He settled in his seat, racking his brain. "It's hard to say. Not really. My memory is spotty."

"What *do* you remember?" She leaned forward.

He had to concentrate not to stare down her blouse. Her position afforded him a splendid view of her figure. And splendid she was. Her long black hair hung loose, tangling about her shoulders but doing little to hide her body from his view.

She'd asked him a question. He focused on what little he could recall. "A storm was brewing, as were my thoughts. Clouds partially obscured the moon. But the light along the docks was spectacular. I set up my camera…" He rubbed his temple, trying to ease the ache behind his eyes. "Glimpses are all I have after that. Still frames in my head. The waves. The light piercing the clouds. Rain approaching from out at sea."

"And Abigail Ashford?" Reina asked.

"What do you know of Miss Ashford?" The name tasted sour on his tongue. He was less than pleased to hear such a foul sound from this doll's lips.

"I've heard the story a thousand times. The docents at the museum love to tell of the star-crossed lovers."

His laugh sounded bitter. "Star-crossed? Lovers?" He shook his head. "As if that witch could ever truly love anyone other than herself."

Reina tensed. A moment ago, she had leaned toward him, an eager smile on her face. Now she sat straight, back stiff, expression stony. "They got it wrong then. Don't know if that's good or bad." She stood. "Mia should be home any minute. We have to figure out what to do with you before she gets here."

He rose along with her. *What to do with him?* As if he were some object she needed to store in her attic. "I beg your pardon. I have imposed on your hospitality for too long." He had taken too much of her time. No matter his sense that he knew her—she was, in fact, a stranger. "I'll leave. Do you know of a flophouse where I could stay?"

Some of the tension left her shoulders and she turned to face him. "I'm sorry. Please stay. I'm just a bundle of nerves. I didn't mean to be so rude."

Strange music suddenly played. He scanned the room, looking for a radio, but didn't spot one.

She gasped and pulled a rectangular object from her pocket. "Is it that late already? I totally forgot I have to work tonight." She tapped the object, then shoved it into the back pocket of her pants. "I'm fixin' to call in sick. Mia's going to be home soon and we need to figure out what happened to your family."

His family. Had they cared when he'd disappeared? Or maybe they were happy to get rid of a stain on the family name. Not that it mattered. He needed a chance to come to terms with his father. He should have made the attempt long ago, but upon his return from the war, he had been unable to face his father's ire.

With shaking hands and a tendency to drop to the ground at loud noises, he knew his father would see the truth. That Keenan was weak. A little boy having nightmares even though any threat was long past.

His father was a strong man. He wouldn't understand, or forgive, such weakness in his son. Or so Keenan had reasoned when he returned and stayed in Havenport rather than moving closer to where his father and younger brother had moved to in Ohio.

He regretted not even trying to make things right with his dad. And now, he might never have the chance.

♥ ♥ ♥

Reina faked a cold on the phone with her boss, Larry. "I'm sick. I can't make it in tonight."

He cursed on the other end of the line. "Get your ass in here. No one cares how you *feel*. Fake it."

"I look like shit, Larry." She kept her voice low, raspy, as if she'd been coughing all day. *Cough. Cough.* "Trust me. No one would pay to see me tonight. Look, when I'm better I'll pick up a couple of those extra shifts you've been bugging me about. I'll call you tomorrow." She hung up the phone before he could continue. *Asshole.* Heartbreakers had gone south since Larry had taken over management. Treated the women like crap, watered down the drinks. She'd been planning on leaving for a while, but she needed a new job first. She couldn't afford to be unemployed for too long. She'd always avoided the lunch shifts she'd just promised, but after missing tonight, she'd need to make up the money somehow. Her budget was tight. Teenagers came with lots of expense.

"Why would people pay to see you? Are you an actress or a singer?" Keenan's voice came from the doorway.

Her laugh sounded harsh. "No. Though I suppose you could say I do work in the entertainment industry." She did *not* want to pursue this line of questioning, so she changed the subject. "Anyway, I'm off for the night now, so let's see if we can't figure out what happened with your family. Let me grab my computer." She opened the credenza and grabbed her laptop.

She placed it on the coffee table and patted the seat beside her while it booted up. "Have a seat. I'll need your help on what to search for."

He stared at the screen, his mouth gaping.

"What?" she asked. She figured it out a second before he responded.

"What is this? How can you find my father on this…this…"

Of course he would have no idea. She had no idea when computers were invented, but she was damned sure they didn't have laptops in the 1920s. "It's really hard to explain. I don't entirely understand how it works myself." She shrugged. "This is a computer. It's connected to the Internet." She sighed. There was no way she was going to be able to explain. He had to see it in action. She connected and opened Google. "I can type in what I want to know and the search engine will pull up anything that might be connected. Give me your dad's name, address, everything, and we'll see what I can find." She held her hands over the keyboard, poised to type.

"Mom?" Mia burst through the front door. She screeched to a halt when she caught sight of Keenan.

"Mia, honey." Reina jumped up.

Keenan also stood. "Hello, miss."

A gentleman. Reina sure wasn't used to that.

"Holy crap," Mia whispered on an exhale, her eyes huge in her pale face. She'd refreshed her lipstick, the matte black making Reina want to take a washcloth to her face.

She didn't. Reina could remember a time when she'd rebelled against her mother. She hadn't reacted well, and Reina ended up pregnant and on her own at sixteen. If makeup was the worst of Mia's rebellious streak, she was welcome to it.

"What's going on?" she asked.

"We're still trying to figure that out," Reina responded. She didn't like Mia being here with him. Truth be told, she didn't know as much about Keenan as she originally thought. His comments about Abigail Ashford made it clear the whole *Lovers* legend was a load of bull.

"Did you go see Aunt Jane?"

"Tried. She wasn't around so I'm waiting for her call."

"Oh." Mia continued to stare at Keenan until he cleared his throat. She blushed a fiery red and dropped her gaze. She fiddled with the handle on her violin case.

She'd forgotten Mia had orchestra practice after school in preparation for the spring concert. "How was practice?" Despite the blue-streaked hair and the heavy metal T-shirt, Mia was an honor student, first violin, and had several activities outside school, such as dance and theater. Her heart swelled with pride.

She shrugged. "Fine. Can I sleep over at Sam's tonight? I don't have much homework this weekend and I can do it on Sunday. Please?"

Normally, she'd insist the homework get done before the fun, but in this case… "Sure. Go pack a bag."

Mia grinned happily, then suppressed it for a more teenaged look of apathy and a shrug. "Cool." And ran to her room.

"You let your daughter sleep at a boy's house?"

Reina narrowed her eyes and stared daggers at Keenan. "First off, none of your business if I did, so quit with the judgmental attitude. Second, Mia's a great kid and I'm a good mother. Don't act like you know what's better for her. You don't. And third, Sam is short for Samantha."

He put a hand over his heart and bowed his head. "I apologize. I didn't mean to deride your parenting skills. I spoke without thinking."

"Yeah, you did." She sighed and rubbed her temple. "Sorry. You hit a sore spot there. Being a single mother isn't easy. It doesn't help that I had Mia so young. I get judged a lot."

"Again, I apologize. I have no children, so who am I to judge?"

She rolled her eyes. "As if that ever stops anyone." She returned to the sofa and patted the spot beside her. "Come on. Let's see what we can find on your family."

♥ ♥ ♥

They spent the next few hours on Reina's computer. Keenan marveled at the amazing device. He wanted to know more about how it worked, but put the urge aside in favor of finding out what happened to his father and brother after he disappeared.

They didn't have much luck. After a while, Reina slammed the lid closed. "Ugh. I give up."

He slumped back into his chair. They'd moved to the kitchen table a while ago. The move had done much to clear his head. Sitting side by side with Reina had been distracting, to say the least.

Warmth spread across his leg. He opened his eyes and looked down to see her hand resting on his thigh. His breath hitched. If the situation weren't so balled up, he'd be pleased at the attention. Maybe move things along a little faster.

He shouldn't be having these thoughts about a woman who was only trying to help him. Her motion was one of comfort, not seduction.

"Don't worry, darlin'. We'll figure it out. We'll go to the library tomorrow and see if we can't get a little help. The Internet's great, but sometimes it doesn't have info on stuff that happened a long time ago. At least, not on specific, non-famous people."

He nodded, stifling a yawn. The day had been exhausting.

"It's getting late. Why don't we get to bed?" She stood and stretched. Her arms rose above her head, pulling her shirt tight across her breasts. She'd changed into a sweatshirt with a Havenport College logo. A thin line of her flat stomach was exposed above the waistband of her tight-fitting pants.

He turned his head, but the image remained in his mind. Much too tempting.

"You can stay in the guest room. It's a little tight in there, but the bed's comfy." She waved her hand toward the hall. "Come on. I'll show you."

He followed her up a set of stairs to a landing with four doors. Door number one led to a bathroom with black-and-white tiled floor, a huge mirror surrounded by an ornate, brushed-silver frame, and a shower curtain of bright purple with glittering beads along the bottom.

The second door had a warning sign below his eye level, but just about perfect for Reina. She pointed at it and said, "Mia's room. She's the only one who can navigate her way through. It's not a large room, but you could get lost in there among all the stuff she has on every available surface."

She indicated the third door. "That's my room." She opened up the final one. "Here you go."

She flipped on a light and waved him into a small room with a twin bed pushed up against the far wall. Blues and yellows dominated the room. The effect was cheery but restful. Candle sconces flanked a large double window, their meager light flickering. When had she lit the candles?

The double doors to a closet had been removed and a navy-blue curtain hung in their place. She pulled the curtain aside to reveal a desk littered with folders and books. "I do my work in here when I need a bit more privacy than the desk in the living room allows. I just finished my college degree. It took me longer than most, but…" She beamed, obviously proud of her achievement.

As well she should be. "You graduated from college? Impressive."

"What about you? Did you go to college?" She frowned. "Or did you go right into the Army after high school?"

He shook his head. No one from his family had ever studied past high school. His brother was supposed to have been the first. "My brother was supposed to have gone. I sent any money I could afford back to my father to help pay for Liam's education. He was brilliant, my brother." His smile resembled a grimace rather than a genuine expression of pleasure, but the memories were bittersweet. "Whether or not he completed his degree, I have no idea. Miss Ashford trapped me before he graduated. I hope he continued after my disappearance. He was to be the first O'Connell to attain such an achievement."

She cleared her throat. "I guess that's one more thing we need to find out." Her gentle smile warmed the room. "Tomorrow. Tonight, we both need to get some sleep."

He stepped further into the room, and she quickly dodged to the side. A blush stained her cheeks and her eyes darted around the room, anywhere but at him. "Okay, then. Great. Um, if you need anything, just give a holler." She sprinted out of the room, closing the door gently behind her.

A wise move. Not that he would take advantage of the situation, but he had to admit, the temptation she offered was difficult to resist.

The flickering of the candles caught his attention. He stepped closer and was surprised to find they lacked a flame. The flickering light came from within. Strange. He touched a tentative finger to its side. Cool to the touch. He picked it up and turned it over to inspect the odd light. He flicked a switch at the bottom, turning the light off and on. Interesting. He placed it back where it belonged, keeping it on as he'd found it.

With nothing to change into for bed, he stripped down to his sleeveless union suit, glad he had not been wearing the warmer long-sleeve version. He climbed in between the cool sheets and closed his eyes. He tried to think through his problems, but his wayward mind kept straying to the way Reina's pants hugged her rear as she'd climbed the stairs ahead of him. So close he could have bridged the gap with barely any exertion. Instead, he'd broken into a sweat with the effort to keep his hands off. He drifted off with images of Reina swirling through his head. His thoughts ungentlemanly, to say the least.

Chapter Five

At nine thirty the next morning, the doorbell jolted Reina from her sleep. She threw on a pair of jeans and her sweatshirt from the night before, then jogged downstairs.

She peeked through the side window. Adam stood on her porch.

"Adam," she exclaimed as she threw open the door. "What are you doing here?"

He held up a canvas bag. "Jane sent me. She wanted to come herself, but wasn't feeling well. We thought you could use a few things."

She frowned. "Oh, no. Is she okay?" Poor Jane. She had been looking tired the past few times Reina had seen her. "Does she have the flu? Damn, I thought we were past the season by now."

He shook his head. "No. She's not ill. Just a bit tired. She asks that you come to our house tomorrow evening. She's called the coven together to see what they can do to help with Mr. O'Connell's situation."

Hmm, too tired this morning but fine by tomorrow evening… Reina kept her suspicions to herself and took in Adam's overly happy demeanor. Was Jane pregnant? No.

She better not speculate. They'd tell her when they wanted her to know. Jane had been trying to conceive for some time. She'd miscarried a year ago and the couple had been devastated. They would understandably be cautious about spreading the good news until they were certain everything was fine.

"Thank you for your help."

Keenan came up behind her. The heat from his body warmed her back even though he kept a few steps away, careful not to crowd too close. She found she liked his consideration. On the one hand, she wanted him to get closer, but on the other, she appreciated he wasn't going to force her into a closeness she wasn't ready for. In her line of work, men tried to take that choice away from her more often than not.

"My pleasure," Adam responded. "I brought a few items you might find useful. Clothing, mostly. You are close in size to my brother-in-law, so he has offered you these few items."

"Oh, that's fantastic. I didn't even think. Come on in." She took the bag and waved Adam into the living room. She perched on the sofa arm and pawed through the items. Jeans, T-shirts, an unopened package of underwear…obviously not everything came out of Bastian's closet. "How much do I owe you guys?"

Keenan pulled a money clip out of his pocket. "I'm no forty-niner. I can pay for my own clothing, thank you. I've got a bit of lettuce." He pushed several bills toward Adam. "I don't know the value of these items, please…"

"Don't be silly. I brought you here. I can…"

Adam waved a hand and frowned at her, but spoke to Keenan. "These items are a gift, freely given from one time-traveler to another. However, the issue of money is sure to come up again."

Keep your mouth shut. She wanted to offer to pay for everything while Keenan was here, but she got the distinct impression that would not go over well. In fact, she vaguely remembered Jane mentioning something about having a problem with money when Adam first came to this century. Guess she should expect Keenan to have a few old-fashioned notions in his head.

"Is it possible you brought something of value with you? Or know where something could be found? That's how I made my money when I came here. I knew approximately where my ship was lost. Bastian helped me locate it. We were able to salvage a veritable treasure trove of lost valuables."

Keenan shook his head. "I had very little." He dug in his pocket, pulling out a few coins. "This is all I have. I was caught unprepared."

Reina sifted through the money he placed on her coffee table. "These are in great condition." She inspected the dates. "Old, too. Maybe they're worth something?"

"Perhaps," Adam said. "Do you mind...?" He gestured to the coins.

Keenan nodded. "Any advice you can give would be greatly appreciated."

Adam stood. "I'll take these to be appraised."

They walked him to the door. "Thanks, sugar," Reina said. "See you tomorrow?"

"Yes. It's not my place to interfere in coven business. However, I do believe Jeremy, Dean, and the rest will be accompanying their women. We will keep Keenan company as the coven discusses the magickal aspects of the issue."

He and Keenan shook hands. Adam left.

An awkward silence ensued. "Um, I better go take a shower. Then we'll head out to the library. My water pressure's pretty good if you want to shower downstairs."

She led him to the downstairs bath. "Here's a towel. Everything you need should be in there." They brushed past each other in the doorway.

Damn, she had to get it together. Anytime she got within view of him, her hormones went wild. He wasn't real. Getting close to him wasn't going to end well for anyone.

"Thank you, Reina."

She nodded and ran up the stairs. That was the first time he'd said her name. She liked the sound of it on his lips. What would it be like to have him whisper her name in the throes of passion?

Shoot. She rushed through her shower. She had to get this over with. Find out what she could about his family this afternoon, and tomorrow night find a way to get him back in the picture and out of her life.

♥ ♥ ♥

Keenan examined the stack of books on the table before him. History books mostly. Reina was trying to catch him up on everything that had happened in the world since the war.

On top of the stack was a book on World War II. He found it hard to believe that there had been another world war, let alone the atrocities that had occurred during it. Americans in internment camps, the Holocaust... He shuddered and reordered the stack.

He pulled out a small volume called *History of Havenport* and read a bit about the Havenport Hostilities. Reina had mentioned the town would be celebrating the anniversary of the events in the coming month. That much had remained the same. Planning for the event had been underway in his time as well.

She had left him on his own to go through these histories while she talked to the librarian in an attempt to dig up information on his father. From the frown on her face, it didn't look like she was making much headway.

His book fell shut while he watched her. Tied back in a high ponytail, her long black hair still fell below her shoulder blades. A pink camisole and cardigan replaced the oversize sweatshirt from last night. Instead of the tight blue broadcloth, she wore a pair of khaki pants that fell midcalf, and a pair of slip-on white shoes. Adorable. Though, he had to admit, he preferred the tight-fitting top and pants she'd worn the day before. They seemed more…her. Still, his hands itched to pull out a camera and snap a few shots. Light from the skylight above her filtered down to cast her in a warm glow he wished he could capture.

He shifted in his seat, trying to adjust the fit of his pants discreetly. The pants—she called them jeans—were rugged, yet comfortable. His borrowed shirt hugged his chest, but without his union suit underneath, was snug rather than confining. The boxers would take some getting used to, but overall he liked the clothing of this century.

Time passed slowly. Tomorrow night couldn't come soon enough. He needed answers, and this Jane person seemed to be the one who had them.

He only had to figure out what he would do if Reina and her friends wanted to force him back into that picture. He'd already lost one hundred years. He wasn't prepared to spend an eternity trapped with Miss Ashford, of all people. He needed to return to his own time and make things right with his father.

A sense of foreboding brought his head up. He scanned the area around Reina for a threat.

There. A man stared at Reina with a calculating look on his face. He stood a little over six feet with short blond hair and an air of arrogance that immediately pricked Keenan the wrong way.

The mug turned abruptly and dumped an overstuffed box of books on the circulation desk. A woman greeted him with a smile that dropped for a bare moment before she forced it back into place. He thrust the books toward her and strode away. She scowled behind his back, but then sighed and struggled to move the box out of the way of a customer who had been shoved aside when the goon cut in line.

Keenan rose, prepared to come to the woman's assistance, when he realized the man hadn't left as he'd first supposed, but instead maneuvered his way across the library to approach Reina from behind. Keenan changed direction to intercept.

The librarian nodded at Reina and disappeared through a door behind her desk.

The man arrived a split second before Keenan. "Reina. Shouldn't you be at home taking care of our daughter?"

Keenan pulled up short. Their daughter? This was Mia's father? He could have sworn Reina mentioned the father wanted nothing to do with her or Mia. From the way the man had made such a calculated approach, it didn't appear that way.

Reina stiffened. She closed her eyes for a mere second before opening them, straightening her spine, then turning to confront the man. "Hello, Harold. Mia's with a friend. Besides, she's fourteen. She doesn't need me at her side every second of the day. What are you doing here?"

"I brought a box of used books to donate to the library. You know I like to do what I can to help others."

She snorted. "Yeah, right, like you read." She rolled her eyes. "Your mom made you drop them off, I bet." She tossed the end of her ponytail off her shoulder.

Keenan held back a smirk, pleased to see her stand up to the bully.

Harold's face flamed red. He stepped forward to tower over her. "Bitch," he snarled.

Keenan fumed. What kind of man talked to a woman like that? Particularly a woman who had given birth to his child.

But Reina was having none of it. "Back off, Harold. Or does Wilma need to call the police?"

Harold scowled but took a step back.

Keenan met Reina's gaze, and she smiled.

Harold frowned, then twisted his head to the side until he peered at Keenan. "What do you want?" he sneered as he drew himself up to his full height, about an inch or so taller than Keenan.

The difference didn't bother him. He'd dealt with plenty of men taller than himself. Height didn't necessarily mean strength. Of body *or* character. This Harold appeared in good shape, but there was a look in his eyes that didn't measure up.

Keenan relaxed his stance. Acted as if he had no concern whatsoever, didn't notice the tension rolling off Reina's ex. He smiled.

♥ ♥ ♥

Reina stifled the glow that came with Keenan's presence. The feeling was too good.

Of course, Harold had to step in and ruin the moment. What had she ever seen in him? He still acted like the spoiled teenager she'd known back then.

Harold scowled. He didn't want her for himself, but he didn't want any competition, either. "This your new guy, Reina? What does our daughter think about him? He knows about her, right?"

She bristled. "None of your business."

"Mia is my business."

"Impressed you know her name." What in tarnation did he want from her? "Are you going to tell me what you want?"

His lip curled. "I want my life to go back to normal. But that's not going to happen, is it? You had to go get yourself pregnant fourteen years ago, and now I have to live with it."

She'd never asked for anything from him. This sudden insistence that she was making his life difficult made no sense. "What in the Sam Hill's wrong with you?"

His hand curled into a fist. She flinched. He'd never hit her, but the look on his face…

Keenan stepped between them. "Apologize."

"To her? I don't think so. Now get the hell out of my face." Harold shoved both hands against Keenan's chest.

She gasped. "Hey," she exclaimed, prepared to come to Keenan's defense, completely forgetting her fear in the face of her anger over Harold's brutish behavior.

But Keenan didn't flinch. He raised a brow and looked at Harold's still-raised hands.

Coward that he was, Harold dropped them to his side and shrugged. "Not worth it. I'd hate to upset Wilma." He tilted his head toward her and some of his bravado returned to his expression. "We'll be talking soon anyway. At least our lawyers will. See you around." He spun on his heels and left.

Reina felt as if he'd punched her in the gut. Lawyers?

Keenan wrapped his arm around her shoulder. "Are you all right?" He eased her into a chair, then knelt on the floor, his forehead creased in concern.

"I reckon I'm fine." No, she wasn't. "Harold just knows how to push my buttons." Understatement of the year. What did that crack about lawyers mean?

"Let me see you home. We can continue our research another day."

She breathed a sigh of relief. "Good idea. There's not much more we can do here anyway. Wilma said she'll dig around and see what she can discover. There wasn't anything in the library's files, but she knows some people who might be able to help. She's going to give me a call if she finds anything."

He nodded. "I shall have to thank her for her assistance."

She glanced at her phone for the time. "Okay. We'll come back for that later. We can do some more searching online and have some dinner."

"Lead the way."

They waved to Wilma on the way out. The old librarian gave her a sympathetic look that told Reina the confrontation with Harold had not gone unnoticed. She winced. Just what she needed. More people talking about her life.

At least Wilma seemed to be on her side. Not that long ago, Wilma had sneered at her whenever she came into the library. Apparently her son had been a frequent customer at Heartbreakers. Why he told his mother, Reina had no idea. Seemed like strange info to share with mom.

But ever since Reina had joined the Havenport coven and become good friends with people like Jane and Adam, Wilma had relented. First with fewer sniffs of disapproval and finally with downright warmth and smiles. Reina suspected some of her fellow witches had dropped a hint in the librarian's ear that Reina wasn't such a bad person. Or maybe Mia had softened Wilma's heart. Despite the cold shoulder, Reina brought Mia in often. Free books and activities were right up Reina's alley. Tips at Heartbreakers were good, but a kid and a well-kept home weren't cheap.

Her house was only a few blocks from the library, so they were home in no time. The blaring music gave away Mia's return from her sleepover. "Mia?" she called.

No answer. Not that she'd expected one. Keenan had a pained look on his face and covered his ears. "Sorry," she yelled over the din. "She's connected to the house's speakers through Wi-Fi. I'll get her to turn down the racket."

He gave her a confused look. That explanation must have gone right over his head. She hadn't explained Wi-Fi to him yet. She waved him toward the kitchen. "Make yourself at home. I'll be right back."

She sang along to Metallica's "Enter Sandman" as she jogged up the stairs and paused outside Mia's door. She knocked, then opened the door after a slight pause.

"Mom!" Mia glared at her and stomped over to where her phone was plugged into the wall. She tapped pause and the house went silent. "Can't you knock?"

She rolled her eyes. "I did. You're on the house speakers. You wouldn't have been able to hear me if I pounded on the door with a battering ram."

"Oh." Mia blushed. "I only meant to have it on in my room."

"No biggie." It happened all the time to both of them. Some days they had competing music on the intricate sound systems in the house. Courtesy of David, an electrician who'd wired her house one summer after they'd been dating for a year. Nice guy, but Reina had dumped him after realizing he spent every penny he ever made without any thought to the future. She sometimes felt like she was barely staying afloat, but she religiously saved for Mia's college and for her own future. Getting too involved with someone without those priorities was out of the question.

She wondered if Keenan was a saver or a spender.

Goodness gracious. What was she doing wondering about something like that? *Not an option. Get your head on straight.*

"Can I sleep over at Sam's again? She needs help learning her lines for the school play."

"Sure," Reina agreed with relief. Having Mia out of the house gave her more time to figure out a place for Keenan to stay until this whole mess was solved.

"Did you fix Keenan yet?"

"Fix? What?" She forced her attention back to her daughter, only to realize they were both on the same topic. "Oh…no. We're going to meet Jane tomorrow, see what she has to say. Want to come?"

"Nah. Sam wanted to go to the movies. Can I?"

The way she fiddled with her phone rather than look her in the eye made Reina cautious. "What are you going to see?"

"The new superhero movie, probably." She blushed but picked her head up to meet Reina's eyes. "Afnan is going to be there. Billy, too. We, uh, thought we might meet up with them. Head over to Mellie's after."

Ah, boys. She should have known. Not bad choices. She'd known them since Mia was in kindergarten. The benefits of being home during the days was she never missed any of the in-school PTA events. It was a great way of meeting all the kids her daughter knew. Afnan and Billy had been brats in the earlier years, but they'd actually become decent teenagers. Plus, she knew their parents. Billy's mom would definitely be skulking in the back of the theater.

"Okay." She picked her way through the mess on the floor to sit on the edge of the bed. "What do you think the rules are?" They'd had the "talk" years ago. Reina was pretty open about everything with Mia—unlike her own mom, who tried to keep Reina out of sex-ed for fear it would turn her into a slut.

Mia rolled her eyes, and Reina had to force back her grin. The gesture made her look so much like a little mini version of herself. It gave Reina a little thrill.

"No drugs, no alcohol, no sex..." Mia sunk onto the bed with her. "No fun." She laughed and pressed up against Reina for a hug.

Reina soaked up the moment. Her daughter put up a good front sometimes but would then fall back into little-girl mode so quickly it made Reina's head spin.

"Seriously, though. Make good choices, okay?"

"Yeah, Mom." Mia turned and gave her a wicked grin. "You, too."

Chapter Six

Keenan poked around in the kitchen until he found a kettle and tea. Amazing. The tea was individually wrapped. There was so much about this era to appreciate. And yet, much to be wary about as well.

He put the kettle on to boil and found cups for Reina and himself.

The incredible noise they had walked into had gone mercifully silent within moments of her disappearing upstairs, but she didn't immediately return.

Make himself at home. He was afraid he could do just that quite easily. But this wasn't his home. He lived in a one-room apartment down by the docks. The walls were bare and the smell of fish permeated the room, rather than the delicious scent of pie he associated with Reina. The whole house smelled like her. He took a deep breath.

The scent calmed him. And he desperately needed calm. Loud noises always set him off. He'd hoped to become hardened to the sensation. Working on the docks overloaded his senses, with all the yelling of the deck hands, the howling of the boats' horns, and the traffic on the nearby street. No such luck, apparently.

The constant cacophony didn't set him off as much as sudden noises. Walking into this house with the music blaring had hit him hard.

He didn't think Reina had noticed anything amiss. Luckily, her delay in returning gave him time to compose himself.

Meanwhile, he searched the refrigerator and her cupboards to find the necessary ingredients to create a meal for the three of them. The least he could do in return for his room and board was cook for the lovely ladies.

In moments, he had a pot of sauce simmering on the stove and meatballs browning in the pan. A simple dish of spaghetti and meatballs would do for this evening.

"Oh my. That smells wonderful."

He spun around to find Reina staring at him wide-eyed in the doorway. "A simple meal. Should be done in about two hours. Will Mia be joining us?"

"Mm-hmm." She hovered over the sauce, taking in a deep breath. "This doesn't smell like jarred sauce. And real meatballs? Not frozen? Be still my heart." She picked up the spoon and stirred the sauce, lifting it to her mouth for a taste. "Did you make this all from scratch?"

"Of course."

Her tongue peeked out to taste the sauce, and he found himself licking his own lips in response. He turned to the meatballs, flipping them over so they'd brown evenly. Almost ready to join the sauce. That didn't take nearly enough time, nor distract him sufficiently.

He cleared his throat. "Spaghetti and meatballs was always my favorite meal as a child. One of my father's best."

"Your father did the cooking? My mother never let my stepfather anywhere near the kitchen."

"I assure you it was out of necessity. My mother died when I was ten." And he missed her to this day. "My father did his best, but he never truly recovered."

She wrapped her arm around his waist, pressing against his side. Her head tilted and she gave him a sympathetic smile. "I'm so sorry. That must have been tough."

"Yes." He did his best to ignore the warmth of her body, the tantalizing feel of her curves pressed against him. "My mother was a wonderful woman. I miss her dearly. Dad did his best but raising two boys on his own wasn't easy."

"No. Being a single parent is tough. It must be worse when you know what you've lost." She gave him an extra squeeze before dropping her arm and stepping away. Her cheeks had taken on a rosy glow. "I was lucky. I never knew any different and I was so happy not to be saddled with Harold, being a single parent seemed like a blessing."

"That was Harold at the library, yes?"

She nodded. The smile fell from her face and a worried crease appeared between her eyes.

"What did he mean when he mentioned your lawyers would be talking?" Harold's parting shot had obviously upset her. He just didn't completely understand it. The man had been an absent father for all of Mia's fourteen years, he couldn't possibly intend to play a role in the young girl's life at this point.

"It's the first I've heard of it." She rubbed her temples. "And now I'm going to have to hire a lawyer. If he thinks he can take Mia…" She glanced down the hall, then sank into a chair at the table and leaned forward to rest her head on her forearms. "Shit."

"You believe he wants to take Mia away from you?" What kind of father would do such a thing to his child? Children needed their mothers. And Reina appeared to be an excellent one.

"I don't know what he wants. I can't imagine he wants to be a full-time dad. Maybe he just wants visitation rights? Parade Mia around in front of his parents to prove…I have no idea what. It's not like he hasn't known exactly where we've been all these years." She lifted her head but continued to stare down at the table, her palms flat against its surface. "I made sure he knew about her. I would never have kept her from him, but I can't say I wasn't pleased when he showed no interest. He's an asshole, and we've done fine without him."

"Why do you think he's made this sudden about-face?"

"His parents. Has to be."

"After all these years?" That made no sense. Why would the grandparents suddenly decide to take an interest?

"I'm guessing he never told them about her. His parents thought he could do no wrong, he made sure of it. Couldn't risk getting cut off from the Windspear family money tree, could he?" Her tone dripped disdain. "But I have no idea how they found out. When I told him I was pregnant, he made it perfectly clear I wasn't to tell them a thing. And I haven't."

"Did you know them well?"

"Never met them. All I know about them is that they're filthy rich and don't approve of people like me."

"Beautiful, graceful women with warm hearts? Yes, I can see why they'd hate you." He schooled his expression and nodded as if he'd just described someone terrible. He got the response he was looking for in her smile, and his spirit lightened.

"Thanks." She slapped her hands on the table, then stood. "Enough about this. Nothing we can do about it at the moment. Let's see if we can't find out any more info on your dad and brother. Wilma gave me a couple websites she thought might be useful. I'll go grab my laptop."

He returned to the stove to see to dinner. It felt good to be here with her. Real good. This wasn't his place. Not his house, not his kitchen, not his family. He needed to keep that in mind before he got attached.

If it wasn't already too late.

♥ ♥ ♥

The next day, Reina and Keenan dropped Mia at the movie theater, then drove to the edges of town where Jane and Adam lived.

Their house was enormous. Reina always felt like she should sneak in via a side door and slip into a maid's uniform or something. Luckily, that feeling immediately went away when she was met with Jane and Adam's genuine warmth and friendship. Jane said the house reminded her of her family's country house in England, without the acres of rolling hills and intricate gardens. This home had a *mere* five acres.

Reina snorted. Mere. Damn, but it was amazing how differently they'd grown up, yet were friends. Astonishing still that she was accepted into this coven of witches. She sometimes felt like the odd one of the bunch. After spending so many years as the girl from the wrong side of the tracks, she expected to be treated the same. But they weren't in high school anymore, and her friends were better than that.

Keenan stepped out of her Bug and stared up at the mansion. He whistled low.

"Yeah, I know," she said, stopping next to him. "Don't let it get to you. You've already met Adam. He's just like he seems. And Jane's amazing. You'll love her."

"I'm sure I will." But he didn't make a move to go inside. "She must be powerful, your friend Jane?"

"Yes, immensely." She bit her lip, hesitant about broaching a touchy subject. "Um, I know you're not exactly wild about witches, but Jane's a great person. So are my other friends. Not all witches are bad. In fact, the central facet of our way of life is 'an it harm none.'"

He faced her, leaning one hip against the car door. "I am coming to understand that. I suppose I can't judge all witches by the one who cursed me."

"Exactly." She released a sigh of relief. "Ready?" she asked, gesturing toward the door.

"Yes." He crooked out his elbow and tilted his head in her direction.

She placed her hand on his arm, suddenly shy, not used to the courtesy. She sure could get used to it, though. They approached the door arm in arm.

Before he could ring the bell, the door flung open. Daisy came bounding out with a happy bark, Christa following close behind. "Daisy, get back here."

Keenan stumbled backward. His face paled and his arm shook. He angled his body so he stood between her and the dog. She clutched his arm. "It's okay, darlin'. Daisy's a sweetheart." She squeezed his bicep and stepped forward to get a look at his face.

He was pasty white, his lips pressed tight together. A sheen of moisture dotted his upper lip. He closed his eyes for a fraction of a second, then seemed to pull himself together and forced a smile. "Daisy?" He held out his hand, palm down for the dog to sniff, and laughed when she bypassed his hand to rub against his legs and sniff him all over.

Reina barely had to bend over to pet the eighty-pound Gordon setter. Since Christa obviously hadn't meant for her to get out, she grabbed Daisy's collar and kept her still until Christa took over.

"Sorry. She heard you pull up and couldn't wait for you to come in. Silly dog," she said, a huge smile on her face as she leaned over and kissed the dog on the top of its head. "Come on in. It's such a gorgeous night. We're outside on the deck." She led the way, Daisy running ahead.

Reina whispered in Keenan's ear, "You okay? I should have warned you. Christa usually brings Daisy when we meet up here rather than at the tavern. The dog can be a handful."

"I'm fine," he replied, but his voice had a sharp edge to it.

She bit her lip and dropped the subject. Something bothered him, and it wasn't the dog. Daisy ran back and forth between them and where Christa had disappeared out back. Keenan smiled and reached for the dog every time she came near.

The dog had surprised them, though. She wondered if he suffered some sort of post-traumatic stress from the war. She'd suspected he did based on his photographs. His reaction seemed to reinforce the idea. Maybe she should reach out to someone who could help him work through the trauma.

Stop. What was she thinking? If they were successful tonight, he wouldn't need to work out anything. He'd be back to his portrait, hanging on a wall of the museum.

The idea filled her with a tight knot of sorrow in her gut. She'd miss him.

Her life with Mia was a good one, but there were times she wished for someone, an adult, she could share her troubles with. Keenan had done that for her. He'd made her laugh, cooked her dinner… It had been years since anyone cared enough to do such things for her. She liked the feeling.

Her stomach twisted even more. She didn't want him to leave.

♥ ♥ ♥

Keenan surreptitiously wiped his sweaty hands against his thighs. The dog didn't seem to mind, but the fact he had so little control irritated him greatly. It was one thing to be frightened of bullets and grenades, and another to be scared of a sweet-natured dog.

The dog wasn't the only thing that had him on edge. The women had gathered in a circle, their heads bowed together, with the occasional glance sent his way. Reina ran to her friends with a quick, "Be right back."

"They're always like this when they get together."

Adam appeared at his side. "Come with me. I'll introduce you to the lesser halves."

Keenan followed Adam back inside. A bunch of men hung around the kitchen island, each with a beer in hand. Adam went to the refrigerator and pulled out two bottles. He handed one to Keenan. "Thank you. It must be nice to dip the bill without having to worry about the coppers." He'd come home to liquor being illegal. Which likely saved his life. Unlike some of his friends who had returned before he had, he hadn't been able to succumb to the lure of oblivion the hooch provided.

"It is indeed. I must admit to being pleased to have missed that era," Adam replied. "Let me introduce you. Gentlemen, this is Keenan O'Connell. Keenan, this is my brother-in-law, Bastian." A man with dark hair and a stiff posture gave a slight bow. "Like myself, he was born in the late eighteenth century and traveled forward through time to be with his love. Winnie has no magickal power herself, but is an honorary coven member, while Bastian has been relegated to the outskirts with the rest of the men, despite his own abilities. Unlike the rest of the men you'll meet tonight, Bastian has magickal abilities of his own."

"My wife has dubbed the coven meetings as 'girls' nights' that I am not permitted to attend," Bastian said. "I am not entirely displeased. My sister has always embraced the craft more than I." He grinned.

"Next to him is Jeremy." Jeremy nodded a greeting. "And his brother Dean. Jeremy's wife, Christa, is quite a talented witch, rivaled only by my dear Jane. Dean's fiancée, Lila, is a former ghost with no magickal powers. She's another honorary member, though. With her history, she has a unique viewpoint that might prove useful in your case."

Witches and now ghosts? Keenan's mind boggled as he turned to the final member of the group.

"I'm Braeden. Nice to meet you. You'll meet my girlfriend tonight as well. She may try to balance your chakras, or something. We'll see. I know it's a lot to take in, but as you can see, you're in good company. Nothing too strange for us. We've seen it all."

"It's nice to meet you all." He took a long pull on his beer to give himself a moment to think. "What exactly are chakras?"

Everyone chuckled. "None of us really know, to be honest," Braeden replied. "But we always feel better after Jen balances them, so…" He shrugged.

"The ladies should join us in a few moments," Adam said. "Tell us a little about what happened? Reina mentioned you were trapped in a photograph?" Adam frowned. "Ever since coming to this century I have disliked the medium. With my suspicions confirmed so clearly, I shall resist Jane's attempts at taking my photograph in future."

Dean rolled his eyes. "Under normal circumstances, pictures don't capture a person's soul. There's something else going on here."

"Yeah. Christa said something about a witch trapping you?" Jeremy asked.

Keenan nodded. "Yes. As far as I can tell, Miss Ashford performed some kind of spell to trap us in the photograph together." He rubbed his forehead. "The memory's foggy."

"The first thing we must discover is whether you were trapped in the picture or if you are the result of little Mia's burgeoning powers," Bastian chimed in.

Keenan slammed his bottle on the countertop. "I've had enough of the suggestion that I'm not real. I remember my life. I remember my family. God knows there are times I wish I could forget…"

Adam clapped him on the back. "Forgive us. We are being unconscionably rude. Such was not our intent. We merely want to solve this matter to everyone's satisfaction."

"Great. Me, too." Keenan's only worry was that he might not agree on the definition of *to everyone's satisfaction*. The general feeling so far appeared to mean stuffing him back into the nonexistence he'd been in for the past one hundred years. Definitely not what he would consider a happy ending.

Chapter Seven

Reina felt the first moment of peace she'd experienced since Mia's power yanked Keenan out of the portrait. There was something about being around her fellow coven members that made her feel welcome and calm. They were a treasure, though not everyone was here tonight. Marcie was working late at Serendipity, while Lauren was out of town with her boyfriend, Cooper.

"I can't thank y'all enough for meeting tonight. I'm at a loss."

Her friends gathered around with murmured words of encouragement.

"Of course. We are always here to help one of our own." Jane held up a bottle of wine with a raised brow. "Red or white?"

"Red, please." Reina recognized the label as one of her favorite cabernets. Jane always made a point of having all of their favorites available whenever she hosted the coven meetings. The perfect hostess. She claimed the skill was drummed into her, having been raised as a socialite in Regency England.

They took a seat around a wrought-iron table with a bright-yellow umbrella strapped down tight in the center.

When opened, it provided just the right amount of shade on a sunny day. The floral cushions on the chairs were comfortable as well as stylish, and Reina sank into hers gratefully. She closed her eyes as she inhaled the fruity scent of the wine and took her first sip. *Ahh.* So good.

"I am confident we shall find a solution to your dilemma quite quickly," Jane said.

"I don't know how." Reina chewed her bottom lip and looked over her shoulder to make sure none of the men had come closer. "I'm not so sure it's as simple as I thought."

"What do you mean?" Christa asked. She leaned over to pet Daisy, who'd taken up residence propped against her owner's leg.

Heat rushed across her face. Her friends gave her searching looks. Christa quirked an eyebrow, while Lila tilted her head to the side, and Jen squinted. Jane tried to hide a smirk, but Reina caught the look of amusement.

She cleared her throat before she mumbled, "I'm not sure I want to get rid of him anymore."

Smiles broke out on everyone's faces. Jen leaned forward and strained her neck, obviously trying to get a look into the kitchen where the men hung out. "Really. Is he as good-looking as he appeared in the photo? It was kind of hard to tell in black and white."

"Even better," Christa said, then blushed. "Don't tell Jeremy I said that." She grinned and twisted her wedding ring around on her finger.

Christa was just stating fact, not expressing interest. Besides, she was used to good-looking men. Her husband was a fine sight. In fact, all the ladies of the coven were extremely fortunate in their lovers. They weren't necessarily to Reina's taste, but there was no denying they were all fine-looking men.

Reina preferred dark hair, light eyes, and a sexy close-shaven beard. Not to mention she liked a man tall enough she could wear her stilettos, but short enough she wouldn't need to strain her neck for a kiss. Having walked arm in arm with Keenan, he was the perfect height. Oh, man. She was so screwed. "I think I have some...*feelings* for Keenan."

The ladies clapped. Not what she expected. "Y'all, this is bad. I can't have feelings for a picture. He's not even a *real person*."

"Of course he is."

She turned to Lila. "What do you mean? He was pulled out of a photograph. Of course he's not real. How could he be? The real Keenan ran off with Miss Ashford in the twenties." She thought about his reaction to any mention of Miss Ashford. Was that wish fulfillment on her part?

Lila shook her head. "I may not be magickally inclined, but I can sense people. He's most definitely a person."

"Yeah, but not a real person. He's just whatever my daughter's magick conjured up. There's no way he could be real...is there?" Reina hadn't even considered that he might be *the* Keenan O'Connell. "How would that be possible?"

Lila shook her head. "I have no idea. But if he were less than a real human being—a ghost or some remnant—I would feel the difference." Having spent more than a century as a ghost, Reina supposed Lila ought to know.

Reina slumped in her seat, stunned.

Jen chimed in. "It's strong *jaadoo*, yes. I've never seen it done, but my mother once told me of a spell that could trap a soul. Perhaps that's what happened with Keenan."

Maybe Jen knew something she didn't. Different cultures had different ideas about magick. Jen called it *jaadoo*, but in the end it was similar, if not exactly the same.

"Was Miss Ashford a witch?" Christa asked.

Reina thought back on every reference Keenan had made about the woman. He called her a witch just about every time. Reina had been more worried about the implications that he despised magick rather than what it said about the woman everyone thought he loved. She nodded. "Yes, I suppose so. He's called her such on more than one occasion."

"No love lost there then, sounds like." Jen raised her glass and tipped it toward Reina. "Good to know," she said with a grin.

"Yes, it appears the stories of *The Lovers of Havenport* were greatly exaggerated." Jane tapped a finger against her chin. "I wonder—" She hopped up from her chair and jogged into the house. The rest stared after her in surprise before rushing to follow.

Reina's steps were a tad slower. Her head reeled with this new information.

♥ ♥ ♥

Jane rushed into the kitchen. The clack of her heels warned the men, and they all turned to watch her entrance. Her face flushed, eyes bright. Adam leaped to his feet and met her halfway. "Jane?"

Keenan's gut tightened. He searched the faces as all the women followed, looking for Reina. That she lagged behind worried him. He gave her a questioning look, but she just shrugged.

"Dean," Jane said. "Did you get the picture?"

Dean nodded. "Sure. Being on the board of the Historical Society has some perks." He hopped off his stool and strode across the room to a crate approximately the size of Keenan's portrait.

"Is that…?"

"Yeah. It's the *Lovers* portrait. I had one of the workmen box it up for me. I just got it today, so I haven't opened it. Do you have a screwdriver or something I can wedge it open with?"

Adam opened up a drawer and took out the tool, then handed it to Dean.

It didn't take long for Dean to crack off the top. He pulled the picture out, unwrapped the packaging protecting it, and everyone gasped.

"Where's Miss Ashford?" Keenan asked. The picture no longer contained an image of the spoiled woman screaming her rage as he'd last seen it. Instead, the photo was a simple ocean view with an empty dock. The sun reflected off the lonely ocean waves, the wooden boards weathered and sun-bleached.

Reina moaned. He swung toward her in concern. Her face was ashen, her mouth pulled down in a grimace. He rushed to her side and helped her onto the stool he'd only recently vacated. "Are you all right?"

Her beautiful blue eyes were wide with fear. "She escaped, too. I didn't think…"

Jane approached and patted Reina's hand where it lay fisted on the countertop. "Of course you didn't. Why would you?"

"I think I saw her."

"When?"

"Right after you came through." She reached toward him, so he took her shaking hand in his. "You went down to the dock, remember? I called your name and I was afraid someone might have heard me. When I looked around, there wasn't anyone near, but I saw a woman striding off in the distance. I blew it off figuring she was too far away to have heard your name. It didn't even occur to me that Miss Ashford might have come out of the picture, too. I thought I got Mia out of the room quick enough. I should have realized something was wrong. Her dress should have been a dead giveaway, but I brushed it off. There's lots of oddly dressed people walking around these days, what with the reenactment coming up. And I was just so worried about you."

Keenan gripped her shoulder, though he wished he could pull her into his arms to provide the comfort he suspected she needed. But that would be inappropriate for two people of such short acquaintance. He didn't wish to make her uncomfortable. "You did the best you could. There was no reason to believe Miss Ashford escaped along with me."

She rewarded him with a slight smile. "Thanks, darlin'. But I should have anticipated this. Or at least double-checked that you were the only one Mia's magick affected."

"Shoulda, coulda, woulda," Dean quipped. He tugged Lila to his side. She went gracefully, settling into his embrace like she was made to be there. "No point in going over what we all should have done. The past is the past. We need to figure out what we're going to do now."

"Precisely," Jane agreed. "Christa and I will scour *On Magick Most Powerful.*"

"What is that?" Keenan asked.

"It's a book of magick. You can find a spell for pretty much everything in there," Reina explained.

"Quite right." Jane tapped her chin with her forefinger. "We shall have to research multiple spells." She ticked off on her fingers. "A spell for finding the witch, one for trapping her, one for sending Keenan home…" At the mention of the last spell, her eyes darted toward Reina and quickly away.

Home. He wasn't sure how he felt about that. Was it even possible? He regretted leaving his father and brother to worry, but he had yet to settle into life after the war. The first peace he'd known was with Reina. Cooking dinner for her and Mia had felt right. He could picture many more nights spent in the same pursuit.

Which wasn't going to happen if he were sent back to nineteen twenty-three. Should he resign himself to going back to the hell he called home, or should he find a way to stay here? Could he forget about the past and look toward the future?

He kept his mouth shut, unsure what he wanted to do. At war with himself, just as he'd been since he returned from combat.

Reina grabbed his arm. "Don't worry. We'll set this right." Her earnest blue eyes gazed deeply into his.

He patted her hand and smiled. "I know."

♥ ♥ ♥

They left to pick up Mia from Mellie's Diner before they came up with a definite plan. *On Magick Most Powerful* wasn't an easy book to sift through, and nothing seemed quite right.

Reina wasn't worried. Jane and Christa would continue to pore over the book, while Jen promised to research if there might be an Indian *jaadoo* solution to their problem.

Meanwhile, everyone would keep an eye out for Miss Ashford. The consensus was that Adam would likely be the first to get word of a strange woman about town. Owning the most popular tavern in Havenport, he tended to cross paths with just about everyone at some time or another.

They dropped Mia off at Sam's to spend the night again. Luckily, it was a long weekend and school was closed. Reina was extremely grateful Sally didn't question why Reina wanted her daughter out of the house. At least she hadn't asked yet. Reina was well aware she'd be facing an inquisition as soon as they had a moment alone, so she was going to have to figure out an excuse before too long. Something that didn't involve having a time-traveler staying in the guest room.

While Reina's gut told her Keenan was a good guy, she wasn't comfortable having a stranger in the house with her daughter sleeping just a few doors away. Sam's was a great solution for a short while, but they were going to have to figure out another place for Keenan to stay soon.

"I've been wondering," Keenan said.

Reina jumped. She'd been so lost in her own thoughts while watching the roaring fire he'd built in her rarely used fireplace. "Oh. Sorry, darlin'. The fire had me mesmerized there for a second. Beautiful."

"Yes." His voice had a dreamy quality to it she hadn't heard before.

She glanced at him. His head immediately turned away toward the fire. Had he been looking at her?

"Firelight can be difficult to capture on film."

They lapsed into an uncomfortable silence. "Uh, you were wondering about something?" she asked.

"Yes." He shifted at his end of the sofa so that he was looking at her. Arm across the back of the couch, one knee bent so his leg rested on the sofa with the other on the floor. "Everyone seemed to have the idea that Miss Ashford and I were involved in an…intimate way. You even called us the lovers of Havenport, as if we were a story of some kind."

She nodded and tucked her legs under to get more comfortable. "Your story was quite the draw at the maritime museum. It's such a romantic tale. Star-crossed lovers who risk everything to be together…I've heard the story so many times, I still can't believe it's a bunch of malarkey."

"Lovers." He grimaced. "Nothing could be farther from the truth. Miss Ashford is a spoiled, manipulative little brat. When I made it clear I wasn't interested in a relationship, she tried to force my hand."

"Really, how?" Not as romantic a tale, but fascinating nonetheless. And truth be told, Reina was coming to realize she was very happy Keenan wasn't madly in love with some woman from the past.

"She claimed her fiancé was brutalizing her. That he'd raped her, gotten her pregnant, and now her father was forcing her to marry her rapist. She tried to tell me she loved me, but we barely knew each other. I think she wanted me to run off with her. But I knew her fiancé and didn't believe her story. He was a good man."

She slapped a hand over her mouth. "Holy cow. I can't believe they got it so completely wrong. And I devoured every word."

"She worked hard to make people believe it. I didn't realize it at the time, but Miss Ashford was spreading rumors of our 'love' to everyone in her acquaintance. I think she repeated the lie so often, she began to believe it herself. She was clearly unhinged when I rejected her at our last meeting."

"So tell me about the last thing you remember. You mentioned you were at the docks taking pictures. Do you remember her being there?"

He nodded. "The light was perfect. I'd been trying to catch that moment…ah, it's hard to explain."

"I have no artistic ability whatsoever." She picked up a twisted, deformed vase with a single yellow fake daisy in it from the coffee table. "I made this in a mother-daughter art class. Mia insists on using it no matter how many times I've tried to throw it away. That's the extent of my talent."

He took it from her, twisting it this way and that as he examined the vase. "It's a start. I have no talent with sculpture, either. But I love photography."

"I've seen your work. It's beautiful."

He tilted his head. "How? I've never shown my photographs to anyone."

She raised her brows in surprise. "There's a whole book of your art." She smacked herself on the forehead. "I'm such an idiot. I don't know why I didn't show it to you straight away." She stood and walked over to the bookshelf next to the fireplace. There was a matching case on the other side. Books competed for space with knickknacks and photographs. She ran her finger along the titles, looking for the right one.

"Here it is." She pulled a volume from the shelf. "*Glimpses of War* by Keenan O'Connell."

"What?" Surprise colored his voice.

He snatched the book from her hands and flipped through its pages. "I don't understand. These are mine, but I never showed them to anyone."

Tears stung her eyes as they flipped through picture after picture of men in combat. There was something so striking about his photos. They always brought out her emotions and empathy. She sniffed. "They're wonderful."

"But how did they end up in a book?"

"Go to the introduction at the front." Once he was at the right page, she put her hand over it. "Your father wrote the intro. It's very moving. If I remember correctly, your landlord contacted your father when you weren't around to pay your rent. The story goes that he found your camera and the photos you'd already developed and was so moved by your talent that he couldn't bear for them to never be seen."

"My father?" He shook his head. "That doesn't sound right. Your historians probably got that one wrong, too. My father didn't approve of my photography. Not man's work, he used to say." His voice was steady, with a hint of steel she'd yet to hear from him, even when he spoke of Miss Ashford and what she'd done to him.

She didn't believe it for a moment. The colder he sounded, the deeper the pain. She removed her hand and tapped the page. "Read it, darlin'. I think your papa may have had a change of heart."

♥ ♥ ♥

Keenan's throat tightened and his eyes burned. He rubbed his nose. Damn. The letter from his father wasn't particularly well written or eloquent, but they were definitely his father's words. And they meant more to him than any conversation he'd ever had with his old man.

"Looks like he was hit pretty hard by my disappearance."

Reina inched closer to him on the couch. "I'm so sorry." She placed her arm around his shoulders, squeezing tight. He felt her all up and down his side.

He closed his eyes. She was offering him comfort, but not of the kind he desperately wished. He twitched his shoulders, and she dropped her arm. The result was what he'd wanted, but he missed her warmth immediately. "Thanks, doll."

"I've just had an idea. The publisher might know something about your father and what happened to him. We can ask Winnie to check with some of her contacts in the publishing industry."

He tilted his head, trying to remember all the couples he'd met last night. "Which one was Winnie?"

"Bastian's wife. She was wearing that great flowered sundress with the navy cardigan."

He just lifted a brow. The description told him nothing.

She waved him off. "Never mind. Winnie's an author. A pretty popular one, too. I think if she asks her agent, they'll do their best to get an answer for her." She yawned, moving her hand in an attempt to hide the motion.

"It's late. You should get some rest."

"No, I'm fine. I'd like to enjoy the fire for a little while more."

They settled back in their separate corners. Before long, her eyes fell closed and her mouth opened with the lightest of snores. He unfolded an afghan from the back of a chair and laid it over her. He'd wake her in a moment so she could spend the night in her bed and not end up with a pain in her neck all day tomorrow.

He wanted a moment to look at her without worry she'd notice or make her uncomfortable with his stares.

She was beautiful. He'd always favored dark hair and light eyes. And so peaceful in her slumber, he could watch her for hours. But he wouldn't.

He sighed. He had no right to be here with her in this way. They weren't lovers, no matter how much he might like the idea. He was a virtual stranger to her, and she to him. A stranger she was eager to be rid of.

"Reina," he whispered, not wanting to jolt her out of her dreams.

She groaned something unintelligible and snuggled further under the throw.

He shook her shoulder gently, but she didn't wake. Leaving her here wasn't a good idea. He'd fallen asleep in many awkward positions. It was never restful, and usually involved aches and pains the next day.

Her bedroom was only one flight up. He'd carried heavier packs into battle than she looked to weigh.

He gathered her into his arms. She still didn't wake. Instead, she snuggled into him with a happy sigh. He breathed deep to savor her apple-pie scent. Ah, she made him hungry. Though not for pie.

He hitched her closer and carried her up to her room. The door was ajar, so he nudged it open with his shoulder. He shifted her weight to free a hand to lower her comforter, then lay her on the bed. Her arms clung to his neck. Untangling them was one of the harder things he'd done, since the move was completely against the instincts fighting for control

But she was asleep and had no idea what she was doing to him.

He finally got her settled, boots off, covers up, and snuck out of the room. The shower called to him. As cold as he could take.

The chilling spray shocked his body into submission. It didn't work as well on his mind, but with his body under control, he forced himself to not think of the beautiful woman sleeping in the next room.

That brought his thoughts back to his family. What if he couldn't go back? How would he feel knowing his family had no idea what happened to him? It would help to know whether they thought he left willingly or not. Although each option brought worries of their own. If they thought he'd been killed, he would be distressed at the worry he caused. If they thought he'd simply left of his own free will, but didn't bother to contact them ever again, then they would have been left thinking he was a horrible person.

He didn't know which was worse.

Chapter Eight

Reina walked into the kitchen to the delicious scent of bacon and eggs. Keenan stood at the stove, whistling a tune and scrambling the eggs. She peeked under a grease-soaked paper towel and snatched a piece of bacon.

"If you're going to keep on feeding me like this, I'm going to have to start going to the gym ten times a day."

Keenan turned with a smile, and her knees went weak. She sunk into one of the kitchen chairs to hide her reaction. He did crazy things to her insides with the merest glance.

"I went too many years with nothing but Army rations. It's a pleasure to make a decent meal for someone I…"

Reina sat stock-still, desperate for him to finish his sentence.

He cleared his throat. "For someone I like."

Okay. A bit tepid, but "like" was a good start. "Well, your efforts are greatly appreciated."

They ate in a companionable silence. While Reina did the dishes, she asked, "What do you think about heading into town today? We can stop by the bookstore. They have a few books on Havenport history. Maybe we can find something that will help."

"Sounds great."

Now to bring up a more delicate topic. "Mia's going to come home tonight. I, um…" Shit, she didn't know how to say something without sounding like she thought he was some type of child molester.

"Ah. Yes. I figured such would be the case and spoke with Adam the other night. We came to the agreement that I could stay in a room above the tavern while I do some work for him. He said I can move in tonight. Though not until after seven o'clock. I start work tomorrow."

She blinked, her eyes wide in astonishment. She'd been so worried about the issue and he'd taken care of it all on his own? "You know I don't think you'd do anything, right? I wouldn't have let you spend the weekend here if I did. It's just…I have to be extra careful with Mia. She's fourteen, impressionable…"

He smiled. "You're a good mom. I get it. Should we head on over to the bookstore?"

She nodded. "Sure. Give me a few minutes to get ready." She pushed away from the table and ran up to her room.

The day was supposed to be unseasonably warm for May in Havenport, so she threw on capri pants and a light sweater set. She could take off the outer sweater if she got too hot. A touch of makeup completed her look. Damn, she looked like a preppy TV soccer mom. Not her norm. She couldn't even picture where she'd gotten the sweater. It had been stuck in the back of her closet for at least a year. Why had she pulled it out now?

It came to her as she studied her reflection. She always did this. She was trying to make herself look like someone Keenan would like. She'd been doing it all weekend. Now she realized the bevy of strange looks her coven girls had given her last night. She'd worn one of her boring "going to parent-teacher conference" outfits. None of them had ever seen her in anything like it. She tended to like a little flash in her clothing.

She tore off the stupid sweater set and grabbed the tight-fitting, blinged-out Havenport tee she usually wore with these pants. A little more eyeliner, a darker shade of lipstick, and she was ready.

Keenan didn't comment as they left her house, but she was entirely familiar with the appreciative gleam in his eyes, and her confidence boosted. She'd shown her true colors, and he hadn't sneered or looked like he was ready to bolt.

She put the key in the lock and was surprised to find a note wedged under the doorknocker. "What's this?"

No address or name marked the outside of the envelope. Keenan stepped to her side. Something made her uneasy as her hands touched the paper. A shiver of foreboding swept over her arms and across her chest. "There's something about this paper. It's not good. Bitterness, sorrow, rage…" Her breath choked in her throat. The paper fell from her fingers and fluttered to the ground.

Keenan caught her before she fell. She clung to his shirt, steadying herself against his strong, warm form. "Get the letter. I can't…I can't touch it. The emotions are overwhelming."

He helped her to one of the wooden rocking chairs on her front porch. She sank onto the cushion and gestured toward the paper.

"He's mine. You can't have him."

He turned the paper over, inspected it from all sides. "That's it. She didn't sign it."

"Well, no secret what she wants." Her breathing slowly returned to normal, the frightening foreign emotions drifting out of her head. "Can you maybe tuck that into a pocket or something, darlin'? I think we should drop it off to Jane—no." If Jane was pregnant as she suspected, she didn't want to expose her to the nastiness she sensed in that letter. "Marcie. We'll bring it to Marcie and see if she can't use it to find out what's going on with Miss Ashford."

Letter tucked away, they got in her car and headed toward town.

♥ ♥ ♥

"Who's Marcie?" Keenan asked as Reina drove them into town. He didn't like the pallor of her skin, but she refused to see a doctor.

"Oh, she's another member of our coven. She wasn't at Jane's the other night, though."

"And she lives in town?"

"Actually, she works at Serendipity. It's a shop right next to the bookstore. We can kill two birds with one stone."

"Sounds like an excellent plan." He had to admire this woman. Nothing kept her down for long. She obviously wasn't feeling well, but ignored her own discomfort to continue on their search for his family. Her generosity humbled him.

"I wish I could do more."

"More than save me from eternal imprisonment?" He chuckled. "You know I'm real now, right?"

A fiery blush lit up her cheeks and she bit her lip. "Yeah. Sorry about that, darlin'. I was so convinced you and Miss Ashford had run off to live happily ever after, I never considered you could be anything other than a manifestation of Mia's out-of-control powers." She frowned and chewed on her lip some more.

The sexy look on her face almost distracted him from her obvious distress about that lack of control. "Tell me more about these powers. I've always thought of witchcraft as the devil's work, but nothing I've seen you or your coven do has reinforced that position. The opposite, in fact. Your friends all seem eager to help."

"They're a good group. I feel blessed they came into my life."

"How long have you been together?"

"Hmm. It's been a few years now. Shortly after that book you saw last night, *On Magick Most Powerful*, came to Jane's attention. She realized if the book was attracted to this town, it was because there must be several magickal beings in the area. Magick tends to attract more magick."

"And are they all as well intentioned as your coven?"

She shook her head. Her hands tightened on the steering wheel until her knuckles turned white. "We've had some issues."

Curiosity had him pushing into something that was none of his business. "Issues?"

She sighed. "The book is very powerful, and we're not the only witches aware of its existence. It came into some wicked hands not that long ago." She shook herself. "But that's been taken care of now. Nevertheless, we meet regularly and try to keep an eye on any magickal energies in town."

They turned onto Main Street and Reina pulled into a parking spot in front of a shop called Wags and Walks. A young couple occupied a wrought-iron bench out front. They sat inappropriately close, the man playing with a lock of the woman's hair as she laughed at something he said.

Keenan turned away, struck by the longing that stirred in his heart at seeing the obviously in love couple. He let a vehicle pass, then hurried to open Reina's door and assist her from the car. She seemed surprised each time he did this, but he couldn't resist the urge to take her hand, watch her unfold her shapely legs from the cramped quarters, and gaze into her face as she gave him a quizzical yet pleased smile.

"Thanks," she said. She blinked her huge eyes as she stared into his. Then, with a bashful smile, she turned and he let her hand drop. "Serendipity and A New Chapter are over there." She pointed to a pleasant brick building with two matching green signs, one after the other, hanging over the sidewalk.

They crossed the street and entered the first shop. The bookstore. The comforting scent of books and coffee greeted them. A bell jingled as the door swung shut. No one else appeared to be in the store, but noises from the back indicated someone must be there.

"Olivia? Lauren? You here, sugar?" Reina called out.

"Just a minute," a voice shouted from a distance.

"Sounds like Olivia." Reina smiled. "Lauren must not be working today. Olivia's a sweetie, but not a magickal bone in her body. You want to see if Marcie's around?" She pointed toward a door at the far end of the shop, which looked to lead into a different type of store. "Or shop for some research books first?"

"Books first." He had a feeling that their conversation about Miss Ashford's note might take its toll on Reina. She'd likely insist they stay and get the books they'd come for even if she would be better served heading straight home.

A young woman popped out from behind a stack of books. "Hey, Reina. What can I get for you?"

"Any books you'd recommend on Havenport's history?" Reina asked. "Something that's not at the library."

Olivia tapped her chin, her gaze trained on a shelf of books to the right of the cash register. "Hmm. Are you looking for something in particular? I have *The Women of Havenport*, or Trish Cahill's *A Personal History of a Havenport Madam*."

Keenan raised his brows at the last title. Really? People wrote about those types of activities in these days?

Reina blushed. "No, nothing like that. We're actually trying to find out something about Keenan's fa—um, his ancestors. He's a descendant of Keenan O'Connell."

Olivia's eyes widened. "Oooh. The lovers? Do you mean the stories about them escaping to live happily ever after are true? I always thought old man Horton got rid of them and we'd find their skeletons someday at the bottom of Hero's Chasm."

"Jeb Horton wasn't the villain history has portrayed him to be." Keenan kept his fisted hands behind his back. Jeb had been kind to him. It was outrageous how his memory lived on in the minds of a town he'd done so much to rebuild after the war decimated the lives of so many soldiers and their families.

Reina put a hand on his arm, bringing instant comfort. He gave a slight nod to show he understood he needed to keep a rein on his temper.

"Yup. Keenan knows quite a bit that's going to shock our little town. But what he doesn't know is what happened to his, I mean, the original Keenan's father and brother. Do you think any of that's covered in any of your books?"

It seemed a far-fetched hope, but he loved that she wasn't going to leave any stone unturned. Reina was quite a woman.

Bells over the door jingled as someone entered the shop.

"Be right with you," Olivia called without turning around. She and Reina studied the shelf, pulling out a book, then putting it back in its place.

He darted a glance over the girls' shoulders and tensed.

♥ ♥ ♥

"I can wait."

Reina groaned internally. Shit. Why was Harold here? Had he seen her enter A New Chapter? Or was he actually here to buy a book?

She snorted. He must have seen her. No way Harold frequented bookstores. Back in high school, he'd do just about anything to avoid reading. The few months they'd been a couple, he'd had her do all his summer reading and give him the CliffsNotes versions. He didn't give the impression he'd changed much.

Keenan glared at the door. His presence calmed the nerves that started skittering inside her stomach the second she heard that cold, heartless voice. She turned.

Harold smirked and waved an envelope at her. "Glad I spotted you. I was about to drop this at the post office, but might as well save the registered mail fee and deliver it in person."

Registered mail? That couldn't be good.

"What do you want now?" She folded her arms across her chest, then rolled her eyes when his immediately focused in on her breasts. Scumbag.

He stalked up to her and held out the papers. "Here. I'm suing for custody of Mia. After seeing you gallivanting around town with a stranger and finding out he was actually living in the same house with my daughter, I couldn't stand by and do nothing."

Her stomach dropped. Black spots popped at the edge of her vision. If not for Keenan's hand supporting her elbow, she might have fallen to the floor in a dead faint.

"What?" Her voice came out in a thin, reedy whisper. "Why…?"

"You've kept her from me all these years. My only consolation when I found out last week that Mia was my daughter was that I assumed you were a good mother. But I've been doing some digging…" He shook his head mournfully, like he regretted what he was saying, even though his eyes twinkled in amusement.

"Last week?" she interrupted. "Wait one cotton-pickin' minute. I told you about Mia the day I found out I was pregnant. You know, the day you dumped me because your parents wouldn't approve of you getting some little 'backwater white trash' pregnant." Now she was fit to be tied. How dare he? "And if you think I'm going to sit back and let you take my daughter away from me, you *ain't* right. What is this really about?" He didn't care about Mia. Why would he do this?

He frowned. "I wish you had told me, then I'd have gotten to know my daughter. You took so much away from me by keeping this secret." He shoved the papers at her, forcing her to grab them before they could slip to the ground. "I've hired Nate Gibson at Gibson and Burns from Providence. I'm sure you've heard of them. They're the best divorce and custody attorneys around. With your, uh, *interesting* employment and now with this guy…" He indicated Keenan. "Shacking up with you, I'll have no problem proving you're an unfit mother." He turned on his heel and sauntered out the door.

Reina staggered. Her heart pounded and panic soured her tongue. What was she going to do?

Keenan said a few words to Olivia, but she couldn't hear over the ringing in her ears. She let him lead her out to her car without protest.

"I don't think I can drive. I—" An orange-brown cat rubbed up against her legs, bringing her tripping to a halt. The cat hissed and ran off.

"I'll take care of it. Let me have your key."

She nodded and dug in her purse. She finally handed it over with a shaking hand. Even finding her huge key ring at the bottom of her purse was beyond her right now.

"You know what? It's a gorgeous day. I can smell the ocean. Hear the waves. Let's take a walk."

"Okay."

They strolled down Main Street as if it were any other day. But her heart ached, her head spun, and her breakfast threatened to spill with each step. She couldn't process what had just happened.

"Mia's father seems determined," Keenan said.

She flinched. "I have no idea why. He's known about Mia her entire life. He's never wanted anything to do with her. And I've never asked him for one penny."

"You're a good mother. No court would take a child away from its mother. Particularly to give to a father she doesn't even know."

"I might agree with you, except…" She didn't know if she could state her fears out loud.

"Except…?" he prompted.

She took a deep breath, then let it out slowly just as they reached the corner where Royce's Tavern stood. "Let's go around to the deck. No one will be there at this hour. Adam won't mind."

"All right."

They strolled around the building to the back and up onto the deck. It was normally one of Reina's favorite spots. The view was beautiful, and at night Royce's was lit up with twinkling lights that gave it a magickal feel.

They settled into a pair of chairs overlooking the water. Keenan sat patiently at her side.

"I'm afraid." She cleared her throat. What would he think when he learned what she did for a living? Would his opinion of her change? "I'm afraid Harold has a point. The courts won't look kindly on me."

"You've been taking excellent care of Mia for fourteen years. Why would they want to take her away now?"

"He's going to make up a story that he knew nothing about her. That he somehow just 'found out' about her and would have wanted to be part of her life."

"Is there no one who can corroborate your story?"

She snorted. "No. It's my word against his. I told him, he dumped me. Then he started spreading rumors about me, saying I slept with all his friends. They weren't going to tell the truth. The lie made them all feel like studs."

"These boys had very little honor. My dad would have tanned my hide if I treated a woman that way."

"Sounds like your dad was a good guy."

"Did no one believe you?"

"I gave up trying. My papa—stepdad, actually—believed me, but my mama, she threw me out of the house. Called me a slut for all the neighbors to hear. And since I was pregnant…"

♥ ♥ ♥

"Did your stepdad help?"

She shrugged. "He gave me some money, but Mama kept him on a pretty short leash. She must not have known about the money or I'd never have seen a dime. I like to think he would have done more. I mean, I know he loved me, but he was too weak to stand up to her." She rocked back and forth, leaned forward, and put her head in her hands. "I can't believe this. How am I supposed to fight Harold? He'll have the best lawyers money can buy. I can't begin to compete."

He squeezed her hand. Her courage amazed him. "You'll win because you're the better parent. Mia's not a baby. The courts will take her wishes into account, and I can't see her wanting to go live with a stranger."

"A stranger that can give her everything money can buy. He's got a huge house, flashy cars…"

"Material things." He nudged her shoulder until she looked up at him. "Your daughter won't be swayed by those things. She loves you."

"She's fourteen. She hates me right now. What he has to offer is more than I can ever…"

"You're wrong. He has nothing to offer her. Nothing important, anyway. I'll bet she understands that more than you think." He pulled her into his arms as he'd been longing to do since they'd met. She tensed slightly, but relaxed into him. "Besides, no one in their right mind would want to live with *Harold* when they could live with you."

She laughed. "Thanks." She looked up at him and stilled. Her gaze fluttered between his eyes and his lips.

Did she want him to kiss her? He leaned in slowly, giving her plenty of time to pull back, relieved when she leaned forward instead.

Their lips met and they sighed simultaneously. Her hand came up to cup his jaw and play with his beard. He cradled her head with his left hand and swiped a lock of her hair off her forehead with the other.

He held back so he wouldn't surprise or alarm her with his passion. But he couldn't help but think there was a room waiting for him on the third floor of this very building. He groaned.

She drew away with a quick little laugh and brushed her thumb across his bottom lip. He almost groaned again. "Well. That was…" Her thought trailed off, but he knew what she meant.

His heart pounded. Several deep breaths were needed to bring his breathing under control. He probably looked like a fool, but the grin on his face wasn't going away anytime soon.

Someone cleared their throat behind them, and they swung around.

Adam and Jane stood arm in arm at the French doors that led into the dining room. Jane had a knowing smirk on her face as she poked Adam in the ribs with her elbow. "Told you."

"I bow to your good judgment." He raised Jane's hand to his lips and kissed her knuckles.

Reina blushed bright red.

Keenan stood and held out a hand to help Reina up. Once she was standing, he retained hold of her hand when she made no move to let go. Propriety would say he should let her go, but he was beginning to realize this new time wasn't as formal as that he used to know. And he liked it.

"Perhaps now would be a good time to show you the apartment?" Adam asked.

It probably wasn't wise to go somewhere he could be alone with Reina, but he did need to see where he'd be staying for the time being. "That'd be great, thanks."

"I better head home. Mia will be home in a few hours and I need to make sure the laundry's done, get dinner ready…" She cleared her throat. "Um, I'll stop by later."

She gave Jane a quick hug on her way out and was gone.

He scratched the back of his neck. Without her by his side, he felt cast adrift. He'd come to rely on her in such a short time.

"Let me show you the apartment," Adam said.

"Oh, yes," Jane piped in. "I do hope you like it."

"I'm certain I shall," he replied.

The apartment was more than he'd expected. One room, maybe a small kitchen, and a shared bathroom were all he needed. What they showed him was way above any place he'd lived in the past decade since leaving his parents' home.

The door was directly at the top of the staircase and the only one on the landing. They entered into a good-size living room, complete with a sofa, two chairs, a comfortable throw rug, and a large television mounted to the wall. The decorations were tasteful, if a bit feminine for his tastes. He wondered what Reina would think of it. Probably too monochromatic for her. She loved bright colors, and this room was decorated in beige and soft green.

Crap. He shook his head. He had to stop thinking of everything in relation to Reina and what she might say.

Jane watched him with a hopeful look on her face. He smiled and nodded. "It's terrific. So large. I was expecting something smaller."

"Oh, you haven't seen anything yet. There's a darling little eat-in kitchen and a great master bedroom. I just loved decorating. I know it's a little on the plain side, but we figured any tenants we had would want to put their own style to the place. Maybe Reina could help you decorate it more to your liking."

Adam took her hand and tucked it into the crook of his elbow. "Enough matchmaking, my lady. Keenan, you're welcome to stay here as long as you need. Until you find a paying job somewhere more to your liking, I'll appreciate your help getting the wine cellar better situated like we discussed."

Jane elbowed Adam in the ribs and he looked down at her. She raised her eyebrows and said, "And…" When Adam knotted his brows and looked confused, she continued. "And…we were hoping you might take a few photographs for us?"

He furrowed his brow, confused. "Photographs? For what purpose?"

She pressed her hands together and held them to her chest. "Oh, I've always loved your photos. I thought it would be lovely to have photos of Havenport hung throughout the tavern. But modern pictures just don't have the right feel. I thought maybe you could do it the old-fashioned way."

The idea of getting his camera and taking photos again lifted his spirits. "I would love to, but I don't have my equipment anymore. I have no idea what happened to any of it."

She waved a hand. "Oh, we can take care of that. Sophia Segarra over at Time After Time Antiques has a display of old cameras I've often admired. We can see about refurbishing one of those. Will you do it?"

"Yes, I would be honored."

Chapter Nine

Reina rushed home to be there when Mia returned. She had no idea what she would tell her.

The truth, she supposed. But how much of it?

Cookies would help. Chocolate chip. Mia's favorite.

She got the ingredients from the cupboard and started mixing. She wanted her daughter to be greeted by the delicious scent of the cookies baking. Put her in a good mood before she tore out her heart.

Her timing was perfect. With five minutes to go until the cookies were done, Mia walked through the door.

"Mom, I'm home." She strolled through the kitchen door and slung her bag over a chair. "Mmm. Chocolate chip? What's the occasion? Do I have to wash the car or something?"

Reina laughed. "Don't worry. No manual labor required." She sobered. "But we do need to talk. Go have a seat in the living room. I'll get these out of the oven and bring them in."

"What happened?" Instead of doing what she'd asked, Mia sunk into a chair at the table.

"Don't you want to wait for cookies?" Reina pleaded. She needed another moment. She wasn't ready.

"No. Tell me. I'm freaking out over here."

She pulled up a chair next to Mia. "It's your father. He's back in town."

"Yeah. I know," she said, and slumped into her chair.

Reina blinked rapidly a few times and rubbed her ears. "What?" How could she know? She'd never told Mia her father's name, only that she had dated a boy in high school who'd wanted nothing to do with her once she became pregnant.

Mia scuffed her feet against each other.

The oven timer beeped. Reina ignored it, but Mia stood and pulled the cookies out. She used a spatula to serve two piping-hot cookies onto a plate and brought them to the table.

"What do you mean, you know?" Reina asked.

"I may have run into my grandparents the other day. They told me he was home."

"How do you know who your grandparents are?"

Mia picked at one of the cookies. Reina took the other. She broke off a piece and popped it into her mouth as a distraction. The gooey milk chocolate was sweet on her tongue, but not tasty enough to make her misunderstand what she was hearing. No matter how much she wished she could. It was not possible that Mia had known all this time.

"Don't be mad." Mia tore her cookie to crumbles without taking a bite. "I was curious. And it wasn't exactly hard to figure out. I mean, I know what Grammy thought. But I never believed it. I know you must have loved my father. And you're not exactly the kind of person who sleeps around, you know?"

She did, yeah. And she breathed a sigh of relief that Mia knew it as well. "But what does that have to do with your grandparents?"

"We saw them once through the window at Mellie's Diner when Gramps met us for lunch a few years ago. You had gone to the bathroom and they walked by."

"And he told you they were your other grandparents?" She tried to stuff down the hurt that her stepdad had gone behind her back that way.

Mia snorted. "Nah. He cursed. Tried to keep it under his breath, but I heard." She smirked. "I learned more curse words from Gramps than most of my friends have ever heard."

Reina rolled her eyes. He had been a cursing champion. "Yeah, me, too." They smiled at each other in silence for a moment, reminiscing. Reina's mother was a bitch and a half, but she'd somehow managed to marry a decent man. She missed him in the two years since he'd been gone.

"So he cursed…" Reina prompted.

"Yup, and when I gave him the stink eye, he explained that the people passing by weren't good people. That they hadn't taught their son how to be a proper gentleman." She shrugged. "I put two and two together."

"So what happened when you ran into them recently?"

She stood and sorted more cookies onto a plate, then brought them to the table. As she settled into her chair, she stuffed a cookie in her mouth.

Reina waited out the familiar delaying tactic. She could understand her daughter's need to collect her thoughts. Her own were whirling.

Mia cleared her throat. "I may have, like, mentioned to Sam that they were my grandparents." She took another bite of cookie and mumbled, "They, uh, may have overheard me?"

Reina slapped a hand to her head. "Oh. My. God." She stared at her daughter, who had the grace to blush. "Seriously?"

"Well, it's not like you were ever going to bother telling them about me." She crossed her arms over her chest and pouted.

Oh, man. She'd screwed up. "Oh, sweetie. I'm sorry. I was trying to protect you." She sighed, tears blurring her vision. "After Harold turned me away, I figured that was the end of it. He…he wasn't particularly nice about the way he handled things back then."

"He was a teenager. Did you expect him to handle it well?" Mia asked with an eye roll.

"Well, so was I," Reina responded with some asperity. "I grew up real fast."

"Sorry I was such a burden."

"Oh, sweetie." She reached out and grabbed Mia's hand. "You've never been a burden. The opposite. You are the greatest thing that ever happened to me." When Mia looked less than sure, she leaned forward. "You know what my mama was like. I didn't have the happiest childhood. That's probably why I fell for Harold so quickly. He seemed like a way out."

She'd never thought about it before. Hell, she'd avoided the subject as much as possible, but it struck her how right this line of reasoning felt.

"When he dumped me, I'll admit it hurt. I was scared, too. And once I told Mama, well, you know. The S.H.I.T. hit the fan. I didn't know what to do. But through it all, I had you. Even before you were born, I'd place my hand on you." She rubbed her now-flat stomach, remembering the feeling of having Mia growing inside her. "And I'd know we'd be okay as long as we were together. And, if I do say so myself, I am an awesome mother," she joked. But inside she cringed. With Mama as her only role model, she'd had to wing it on the parenting front. Mia was a good kid, but sometimes she wondered how much that had to do with her mothering skills versus the luck of the draw.

"You are a good mom," Mia whispered. "It's just…I've always wondered what it would be like to have a dad, too."

Reina hid her wince.

♥ ♥ ♥

The next day, Keenan searched through the cameras at Time After Time Antiques. Adam had introduced him as a descendant of…well, himself. Miss Segarra's eyes had practically popped out of her head, but she'd done a good job of tamping down that excitement and not asking him any questions. He needed to figure out a convincing cover story. People were entirely too interested in the "real" story of *The Lovers of Havenport*.

But Adam had bought him a little time to come up with something by telling Miss Segarra that she would learn everything once the book came out. Right. If he ended up staying here, now he had to come up with a tell-all exposé on his own life while pretending to be his own great-grandson.

The store was a haphazard display of items. No rhyme or reason to any of it. He'd already poked through dozens of items considered "antiques" that were common household items from his point of view.

He scanned a shelving unit toward the back that looked like it might have some potential. Finally! His gaze fell upon a camera similar to the one he used to own. He turned it over in his hands. A little worn, and the lens bed didn't want to lock in place, but nothing he couldn't fix.

"Miss? I'll take this, please." He felt a little uncomfortable with Adam's instructions to the owner to place it on his tab, but as he was planning on using it for their project for the tavern, he'd have to consider it a loan until the job was finished. These pictures were going to have to be something extra special to make up the price of the equipment. He'd already given Adam a list of items he needed for his darkroom, so that expense would have to be included as well. He was building up quite a debt with the couple.

He'd work it off. The wine cellar they wanted him to restore would be a lot of work, but he had some ideas that would create a nostalgic feel the couple might like. He could give it the authentic look of a gin joint, make it a place to attract more paying customers. Maybe they could use it for special events. He'd think of something to make it up to them for all they'd done for him since he'd emerged from his prison.

"Here you are." Miss Segarra wrapped the camera in several sheets of plain white paper, then slipped it into a plastic shopping bag. "Too bad you didn't come in yesterday. I had a 1918 Kodak Autographic Brownie camera in perfect shape stolen just last night. Such a shame. Called the police, but…" She shrugged.

"Is that all the thieves took?" The exact camera he used to own, stolen yesterday? What were the odds?

"Yes, that was it. So strange." She shook her head and held the bag out to him. He took hold of the handles, but she didn't let go immediately. "Sure you can't give a little preview of that book of yours? I'm dying to know what happened to your grandparents. I just *knew* they got away. I can't wait to tell my book club. My friend Darcy will be beside herself." She paused, and when he only smiled and shrugged, she let go of his bag. "Well, we've all read your great-grandfather's letters. Seems a shame your ancestor never let his father know he was okay."

Keenan stopped in the act of turning toward the door. "Letters?"

"You don't know about the letters?" Her eyes lit up and she leaned forward eagerly with her elbows on the counter next to the register.

He shook his head. "No. I don't know much about what happened after I, um, after my great-grandparents left. Part of the reason I'm in town is to find out more."

"Well. Call the *Havenport Herald* and ask for Darcy Prentice. She can tell you tons. She's crazy about history."

"What about the letters you mentioned?" *Come on, lady.* He balled his hands and the strap of his shopping bag dug into his palms.

"It didn't all make the papers. But the letters were beautiful." She held a hand to her heart. "So touching. He was so proud of his son. Darcy said people were quite angry at the time. Lowlife runs off with the boss's daughter…all that nonsense." She waved a hand dismissively. "But Keenan's father wrote letter after letter to the paper letting people know his son was a war hero. They only published a small portion. The newspaper archives have the rest. Darcy dug them up and let us read them." She sighed, her smile dreamy as she stared off into the distance.

More than a little creepy given she was talking about his father, not some unknown person from the distant past. "Do you know what happened to him? Or his other son?"

The dreamy look faded. She shook her head. "No. Sorry. But Darcy had dug up so much information we couldn't possibly go through it all. Ask her, though. She's likely to know all about it."

Excitement bubbled up inside him. He couldn't wait to tell Reina. Finally, a clue to finding out what happened to his family.

♥ ♥ ♥

Reina tried to rub the gritty feel out of her eyes without success. The mirror needed to be hidden for at least a day to give her red, swollen eyes time to recover. And she wasn't even done explaining everything to Mia.

Last night, they'd both decided a little time to calm down and get their thoughts in order was a good idea. She'd taken the coward's way out, for sure, but she had way too much going on at the moment. Mia was home from school now, but homework came first, and Mia always had a ton of it during the week.

Her phone alarm went off, and she cursed. She needed to either get ready for work or call Larry and say she was never coming in again. Decision time. Quit or not? She needed the money, but her job was a liability when it came to a custody battle. Maybe it was time to stow her pride and take the job Dean had offered at his foundation. She'd wanted to do it on her own, without a leg up from friends, but maybe that was stupid. With her hard-won degree, she was qualified for the position. And Publicity Director for a large charity would look much better to a custody judge than stripper.

She picked up her phone and dialed the club. "Hey, Gina. Larry there?"

"You calling out sick again? He's gonna be pissed," Gina sang.

"Nah, hon. I'm not calling out sick. It's quittin' time." Decision made, she said the words with relish. She should have done this long ago.

Gina squealed. "Oh, honey. That's great. Did you get that day job you were pining over?"

"Not exactly, but I'm working on it. Get Larry for me, okay? I want to get this over with." She paced the length of her kitchen, too nervous to sit still. "Oh, and Gina? While I'm on with Larry, go clean out my locker. You can have my stuff. I won't need any of that anymore." If Gina waited until Larry was off the phone, he'd be sure to steal what little she had left there. Better if Gina got it than that snake.

"Sure thing. And let us know when you land that job. We'll have a girls' night."

Reina laughed. "Not sure I can handle another girls' night."

"Yo, Larry," Gina shouted. "It's Reina."

"That bitch better get her ass in here. Tell her to cake on some makeup and shake her ass. She's fired if she misses another day."

Oh man, this would feel good. She'd been dreaming of this day for a while now. The money at Heartbreakers was good, but she was tired of the whole scene.

"Get your ass in here, Reina."

"Charming as always, Larry. This is just a courtesy call. I won't be—"

"Don't give me any shit about being sick. You—"

She yanked the phone away from her ear as he called her every name in his extensive dictionary. "Larry!" she shouted. "Larry. I quit."

Blessed silence.

"You can't quit."

Wow. She'd never heard him speak in such a quiet tone. Almost defeated. "I can. And I am," she said.

"But—"

"No buts. I've made up my mind." She hung up as he built up steam on a new round of curses. Her hands shook, but she felt like laughing at the same time.

"Did you just quit your job?" Mia asked.

Reina swung around to find Mia standing in the doorway, hands on her hips. "Yes. Yes, I did."

Mia broke into a grin. "How'd it feel? Did Larry throw a fit?"

"So good." Reina laughed. "And, of course. Gramps could have learned a thing or two from Larry about cursing."

Mia joined in the laughter. Still smiling, she asked, "So why now? Did you get a new job?"

Well, she would have to explain sooner or later. "No, not yet. But I'm thinking of finally taking Dean Pearce up on his offer to work on publicity for his charity." She took a deep breath. "Anyway, I quit because my job was a liability I can't afford anymore."

Mia's brow wrinkled in confusion. "Whaddya mean?"

"I was leading up to this yesterday… Okay, you know your dad's back in town. I talked to him yesterday and…he's suing me for custody."

"What?" Her mouth dropped open and she sunk into a chair.

Reina got out the papers she'd yet to read fully. "I need to read these for more detail, but it looks like he wants full custody. He's claiming I never told him about you and that…" She cleared her throat. This one hurt. "I'm an unfit mother. He is using my job as an example of being a bad influence, so…" She shrugged. Once Mia was old enough, she'd been honest about her job. She wasn't ashamed. It paid the bills, and she and other mothers at the club got together when their kids were little to share babysitting duty. She'd done the best she could with a child when she was still practically one herself.

"What a load of crap," Mia exclaimed. "You're a great mom. No way am I going to live with some stranger just because he couldn't figure out how to use a condom fourteen years ago."

"Mia!" She tried to act offended, but the knot in Reina's stomach loosened the tiniest bit. Teenagers were notoriously hard to read, and despite knowing her daughter loved her, she hadn't been sure how she would take the news.

"But—"

The doorbell rang, giving sound to Reina's now-shattered nerves. But? But what? She stared at Mia, waiting to hear the rest of the sentence.

But Mia had other ideas. "I'll get it." She jumped out of her seat and shot toward the door.

Reina raced after her.

"Hey, Mr. O'Connell."

Reina slid to a stop. Keenan stood in the doorway, a welcoming grin on his face. Great, if her heart raced any faster she'd have an aneurysm. "Keenan." She'd left him only about twenty-four hours ago, but seeing his handsome face made her realize she'd actually missed his calming presence at her side. She peeked around him to see who had brought him over, but there were no cars loitering outside. "How did you get here?"

"I walked." The smile slipped. "Is now a good time or should I come back later?"

Chapter Ten

Reina pulled her daughter out of the way and stepped back. "Sorry, darlin'. Come on in. Now's fine. Have a seat." She waved him into the living room.

He took a seat at one end of the couch, while Mia took an armchair. Reina hovered over them both. "Tea? I'll be right back." Her face was flushed, her hands shaky. Damn, he shouldn't have just run over like this. He'd been too excited at the prospect of learning more about his family, he hadn't given thought to whether or not Reina wanted to see him.

With Reina out of the room, he was left alone with Mia. He hadn't had much chance to talk to the young woman since he'd arrived. "Did I come at a bad time?" he asked.

She shrugged. "Maybe a little. But I'm glad you're here."

He raised a questioning brow.

Instead of continuing, she made designs on a pillow covered in multicolored sequins. When she rubbed a finger one way it turned silver, the other and it turned purple. He let the silence continue. His father used to use the trick on him and he always ended up spilling his guts.

Sure enough, after a few seconds, she looked up with a grimace. "Mom said you guys are trying to find out what happened to your dad? Do you miss him?"

Ah, Reina must have told her about meeting her ex yesterday. "I do. We'd had a falling-out not long ago. To think of him worrying, wondering what happened to me…" He shook his head. "I regret I didn't get a chance to make things right with him."

"I never knew my dad." She smoothed the pillow to a consistent purple. "I know he's an asshole. And I don't want to go live with him or anything, but…"

"But you're curious about what he's like."

She nodded.

"And I'm guessing you're worried how your mom's going to take it if you want to spend some time with him?"

"Yup."

"Tell your mom the truth," he urged. "I haven't known you both long, but I get the sense she's open with you?" At Mia's nod, he continued. "I wasn't with my dad, and I regret it. He was hard to talk to, but I should have made more of an effort."

"My mom's easy to talk to. But having me hasn't been easy. I don't want her to think I'm ungrateful. I give her a hard time sometimes 'cause…" She shrugged. "Whatever, I don't mean anything by it."

"She'll understand. She just wants you to be happy." He leaned forward, looked over his shoulder to make sure Reina hadn't returned, and whispered, "But if you want my advice, I'd mention what a wonderful mother she is, that kind of thing. A little flattery never hurts."

Mia grinned in response. "Sure. Thanks."

"Thanks for what?" Reina walked in carrying a tray with a pitcher and three glasses full of ice.

"Nothing." In the two seconds it took for her mother to put down the tray, Mia's expression went from a happy smile to a sullen frown. "Mom?"

Reina handed out full glasses, then settled onto the couch across from him. "Hmm?"

"I want to get to know my dad," Mia said in a rush, her words tumbling over one another.

Reina's face went chalk white. He was glad she was sitting or she might have fallen. "Oh?" she asked weakly.

"I mean, I don't want to live with him or anything. Yuck. But I've never had a father. My friends are always talking about hiking and camping with their dads. I want to see what it's like."

Keenan's impression of her father made him doubt she'd be doing any of those things with him.

"Well, sweetie, I get it. And if you want to try a visit or two, we can surely arrange that. But..." She glanced his way, a hopeless look on her face, then turned back toward Mia. "I don't want you to be too disappointed. I'm not sure how much time he really wants to spend with you."

"What's that supposed to mean?"

She rubbed her temples. "I think he's working an angle. Something to do with his parents."

Mia shot to her feet. "Oh, so he couldn't possibly want to get to know his daughter, right? There has to be some other reason. Who'd want to be my dad, right?"

This conversation was going completely off the rails. "That's not what your mom meant," he chimed in.

"I'm sorry, sweetie. If he knew you, he'd love you instantly. But he's a selfish bastard. Always has been. And he's known about you your whole life. So why this sudden desire—not just to meet you, but to uproot your whole life?"

"I don't know, but I have the right to find out. And you're not going to stop me."

"I don't want—" Reina fell silent as Mia stomped out of the room and up the stairs. She dropped her head into her hands, gripping her hair to the point he worried she'd rip the strands out.

He slid over until he sat right next to her and put an arm across her shoulders. "Hey. You okay?"

She sniffed and leaned against him, letting her hands drop from her head to rest on his arm that he'd wrapped around her waist when she leaned into him. "Sure. I really screwed that up, huh?"

"Nah. She's just dealing with a lot right now. She was just telling me what a good mom you are."

She snorted. "Bet she's changed her mind on that one."

He gently tugged on her chin so she'd face him. "Not a chance." He kissed her forehead in an effort to avoid kissing her on the lips, as he longed to do. As he backed up, she lifted her face and leaned forward, capturing him in a kiss that set his pulse skyrocketing. It took every ounce of his strength to keep the kiss light, to not sweep her into his arms and press her down beneath him, covering her body completely with his.

She pulled away with a shaky laugh. "Talk about poor timing." She wiped her mouth and sighed. "Um, I better go try to work this out. She needs a moment, but if I give her too much, she'll work herself up into a lather and it'll be days before I get her to talk."

Reluctantly, he let her out of his embrace and she headed for the stairs.

♥ ♥ ♥

Reina tromped up the stairs, her mood lightened. Wow, what a kiss. Sweet and hot all at once. But her timing seriously sucked. The knot in her stomach tightened as she raised a fist to knock on Mia's door. Her hand shook. She had to take several deep breaths before she let her knuckles touch the wood.

Knock. Knock. "Mia?"

Silence.

"Come on, sweetie. We need to talk. Can I please come in?" She pressed her ear to the door. Nothing. She knocked again. "Come on, Mia. You know I think you're awesome. Your dad would be crazy to not want you. It's him I'm worried about. He's an asshole. I don't want you to get your hopes up and be crushed if he doesn't come through the way you want."

Still nothing. Maybe calling her father an asshole wasn't the best parenting move of the year.

Enough of this. "Mia, I'm coming in. You can't give me the silent treatment. We need to discuss this."

She pushed open the door with ease. Only in the past year or so had Mia noticed the lack of a lock on her door. Before that, she'd never cared and left her door open more often than not. But Reina supposed teenagers liked their privacy. She was actually considering adding a lock but hadn't gotten around to it yet. Right now she was glad she'd pushed the chore off.

Clothes littered the floor, the comforter dragged half-on, half-off the bed.

The empty bed. "Mia?" Where was she? She backed into the hall. All the other doors were open. She did a quick search. No Mia.

She ran back into her daughter's room. The window was open. Shit. The window slid up without a squeak when she shoved it higher and leaned out. Why the hell hadn't she cut down that damn tree? She'd considered it, but it was so damn expensive she'd convinced herself she was being ridiculous.

Now she regretted that decision.

Clouds had rolled in and the sky was darker than it should be. Branches swayed in a strong breeze. The scent of rain was on the wind. A storm was coming.

And her daughter was out in it all alone.

She sunk onto the messy bed, grabbed Kit-Kat—the stuffed animal Mia had cherished since kindergarten—and curled up with the doll clutched to her stomach.

She didn't have time for this shit. She'd cry it out later when Mia was home safe.

Keenan appeared at the door. "Are you all right?" He scanned the room. "Where's Mia?"

"She's run away." She stood and pulled her cell from the back pocket of her jeans. "I'll call some of her friends, but my bet is she's gone to find her father."

"That's a phone?" He pointed at her cell and shook his head. "Nevermind. I'll check outside. Maybe she didn't go far." He jogged down the stairs.

As she made call after call, she marveled at how nice it was to have someone at her side. What a difference another adult made in a crisis.

After she'd exhausted Mia's friend list and left a dozen messages and texts for Mia, she ran down to see whether Keenan had fared any better.

She spotted him from the porch rounding the corner down the street. When he caught sight of her, he broke into a jog and reached the house moments later.

He opened his arms and she sank into his embrace, letting his warmth provide what little comfort she could accept at the moment. "She's not answering her phone and none of her friends have seen her."

"Has she ever run away before?"

"No. Never. That's what's got me so freaked. This is completely unlike her. I mean, we've had fights before. She usually needs a bit of space—goes to her room, listens to music—but she always, always comes back out and we talk it out." She shoved her hair away from her face. "I can't believe this is happening."

"Did you call Harold?"

"I left a message." She rubbed her chest where a tight sensation threatened to rise up and choke her. "I'm not exactly proving to him that I'm mother of the year."

"Yet you called anyway. You're putting Mia's welfare ahead of this fight with her father. I think that proves what a good mother you are." He squeezed her shoulders, then stepped back. "So what next? Should we head over to his house?"

"Yes." She left him to run inside and grab her keys. At the last minute she pulled out her phone and called Sally. "Can you come to my place and wait here in case Mia returns?"

"Of course. I'll be right over. Sam's trying to reach Mia, too, but she's not picking up. I'll call you the second we hear anything."

Crap. Mia wasn't even answering Sam's calls? *Please let her be okay.* "Thanks." Tears burned her eyes as she shoved her phone back in her jeans pocket. She'd always thought of herself as alone, but the outpouring of help from her friends was proof of the good life she'd built for herself and Mia. If only Mia thought so, too.

♥ ♥ ♥

Keenan waited on the porch for Reina to get ready.

A nagging sensation gnawed his gut. Something wasn't right about Mia's disappearance. He scanned the street trying to figure out what bothered him.

Kids ran away. He'd done it himself once upon a time. So why did it bother him so much that Mia, a moody young lady, had taken such a drastic step? The fight with her mother seemed dramatic enough to prompt such an act. She was certainly going through a tough time. Learning about her father was bound to cause upheaval in her life.

A woman appeared around the corner where he'd searched earlier. Her skirt danced around her knees, the sleeveless top out of place in the chilly air of early evening. Dark blonde hair was swept up with long strands loose and whipping about her head, obscuring her face. Something stuck up from the side of her head. A feathered headband.

Miss Ashford. Anger surged through him. She'd ripped him from his life. His family. All to fulfill her selfish desires when he refused to be manipulated.

He didn't bother to take the two steps off the porch but jumped and landed several steps away and ran toward the witch. He screeched to a stop before her.

She smirked, head up, chin tilted to give the effect of looking down on him though he towered over her by at least a foot. She wore the same dress he'd last seen her in, a dark-gray knee-length dress with beads sewn into the fabric to catch the light. He'd thought it charming before her true nature was exposed.

Dark, muddy brown stains splattered the dress along the hem and several beads appeared to have been ripped off, leaving jagged tears along the neckline. She was a mess of wrinkles, totally at odds with the crispness he usually associated with her attire. Dirt ringed her fingernails and a smudge across her cheek resembled a days-old bruise. Instead of an overwhelming scent of flowers, he detected the sour stench of old sweat.

Not having maids to tend to her every whim had taken its toll.

"What the hell are you doing here, Miss Ashford?"

"Abigail, please, Keenan. How many times do I have to tell you to call me by my first name? There's no need for such formality between us." She fluttered her eyelashes and smiled coyly.

The sight turned his stomach. "There is no *us*. There never has been. Why did you trap me in that photograph? What did you think to gain?"

The sweet smile disappeared. Her eyes flashed cold and she sneered. "Stop it. I didn't *trap you*. I secured *us* until such time as we could truly be together. You're mine. Why do you seek to vex me so? I grow tired of your games."

"Games? This isn't a *game*, you bitch." His hands shook with the force of his anger. Not good. He took a deep breath and released it to the count of ten. "What do you want, Miss Ashford?"

His continued use of her full name made her lip curl in

a snarl. That small satisfaction might be petty, but in this crazy situation he'd take it.

"I've come to see if you've finished your dalliance with that, that *woman*, and come to your senses."

"First off, 'woman' isn't a dirty word. Second, none of your business." He crossed his arms over his chest and stared her down.

"Oh, Keenan." Her sweet, innocent act returned. "I forgive you. You've had your little fling, but it's time to return to me. We've waited so long to be together. I don't wish to wait another moment." She reached out as if to embrace him.

He stepped out of her reach. What the hell was wrong with her? How could she be so delusional? "Miss Ashford, I've made it quite plain that we are not together. That we will *never* be together. So tell me, is there a way to reverse the damage you've done? Can you return us from whence we came?"

She pouted. "Damage? What damage? Why would you ever want to return to that dreadful time." She waved her hand dismissively. "I find I quite like this era. Without my father's interference, there's nothing stopping us from being together here." She grinned. "And the fashion is exciting, don't you think? When you've come to your senses, you must take me shopping."

"Not going to happen."

She pouted. "I see my spell ended too soon." She tapped a dirt-encrusted nail against her chin. "Or perhaps it's because of that woman who dragged you out before my spell ran its course."

"Ran its course? What else was supposed to happen?" He didn't like the sound of this.

"You were *supposed* to give up this ridiculous idea that we don't suit so we could live happily ever after."

She made no sense whatsoever. "How exactly was that supposed to happen when I wasn't aware of time passing? When I stepped out of that photograph it was as if waking from a dream. But I clearly remember the fact that I can't stand you."

A tear leaked from the corner of her eye, and he had a moment of remorse. Then he remembered what she had done to him and he hardened his heart. He wasn't going to fall for her crocodile tears. She'd turned them on when proclaiming Jeb Horton, a man he knew to be decent and caring, had raped and gotten her with child in an effort to force her hand. Her act had been so convincing he might have believed her had he not known for a fact Jeb had been somewhere else when she proclaimed he'd done the dastardly deed. Keenan didn't believe it then and he didn't believe it now.

She sniffed delicately, then must have realized the act was lost on him because the image of a sad, delicate young lady swept away to be replaced by a cold, calculating, spoiled brat used to getting what she wanted. "I was told the spell would bring us to true love."

"Told?" True love? His thoughts immediately turned to Reina. Maybe the spell had worked after all, just not in the way Miss Ashford had hoped. Perhaps someone did him a favor. "Who told you?"

She wrapped her arms around her waist and shivered. "It's getting chilly out here, *dahling*." The endearment made him wince. He much preferred Reina's sweet Southern drawl to this woman's pretentious, grating pretense of affection. Reina was genuine, where Miss Ashford was anything but.

"Come with me and I'll explain everything."

He shook his head. Much as he wanted to know exactly what had been done, he had more important things to deal with at the moment. Mia was still missing and he couldn't do anything until he knew she was safe. "Not now. I have something more important to do." He stared straight into her eyes so she wouldn't mistake his meaning. "But you will explain all this to me. Meet me at…"

"No. I don't think I will. I think you're going to come

with me and we're going to go back into that portrait until it works properly."

He laughed. "I don't think so." He turned his back on her and started back to the porch to wait for Reina.

"And I thought you might be interested in what happened to the girl."

Chapter Eleven

Reina rushed outside, but left the door unlocked behind her. Sally had a key, but there was no point in locking when her friends would be here any minute.

She skidded to a stop. *Where's Keenan?*

She scanned the street but didn't spot him. "Keenan!" she shouted.

No response.

"Shit. I don't have time for this." Had he found her daughter? Seen her in the distance and run after her?

Sally rounded the corner and jogged up. "Hey. You're still here? Did you find her?"

"No," she said, shaking her head. "And now Keenan's gone and I don't know what to do." *Get it together, girl. You've managed on your own a long time. This is what you're good at.*

"Why don't you go? I'll be here. If either of them come back, I'll call you right away."

Reina nodded. "Yes. I can't wait around. I have to find Mia. If he comes back, just…" She shoved a hand in her hair. She'd never had much help, but now she felt lost without it. "Just tell him I had to leave without him. I don't know where…"

"Hey. It's okay. I'll keep an eye out for him. And for Mia. Just calm down a bit." They hugged. Sally pulled back and held her at arm's length, keeping strong eye contact. "Mia's a great kid. It's a lot to take in. Ya know?"

"No kidding." She rolled her eyes. "Thanks." Another quick hug and she hopped in her Bug and took off toward Constitution Boulevard, the gateway to the Havenport mansion district.

It took her twenty minutes to make the drive. She'd only been there a few times back in high school. When Harold's parents were away, of course. What an idiot she'd been, falling for his bullshit. She'd believed all the crap he'd fed her. How his parents managed every moment of his life, dictated his friends, his girlfriends... How they'd beat him if they found out about her.

So she'd met him in secret, pretended she was okay with sneaking around because as soon as he "escaped" to college, he'd send for her. He'd take her away from her own abusive mother and they'd live the life they wanted, not the one demanded of them. Because he loved her.

The prick. The only one he loved was himself. He'd proved that the minute she was late with her monthly cycle. He hadn't even waited to see the results of the pregnancy test.

She pulled her car all the way up to the front door, ignoring the cutout area clearly meant for parking. Frankly, she didn't give a shit if she blocked someone from pulling their shiny Jaguar out of the garage. They'd have to wait until she found her daughter.

She threw the car into Park and marched up to the door. If he upset her daughter, she was going to rip his...

The door opened before she could knock. She expected a maid, or someone equally as willing to block her from the house upon orders. Mrs. Windspear held the door open with one hand, and with a quirked brow and kind smile, asked, "May I help you?"

She wasn't as intimidating as Reina had always supposed. Her golden blonde hair was liberally interspersed with gray and fell to the tops of her shoulders. She wore tan capris and a light-green sweater set Reina was fairly certain she'd seen in the window of Find Your Bliss Boutique. From the window only, since Reina knew there was no chance she could ever afford something from the posh clothier.

But the look on her face wasn't full of the hate or disdain she'd expected.

"Hello, Mrs. Windspear." She took a deep breath. "I'm looking for Mia. Have you seen her?"

"Mia?" She stumbled back a step. "Are you…are you Reina? Come in, come in. I'm so happy you finally decided to speak with us."

Reina's mouth dropped open. *What?* "Finally decided…what are you talking about?"

Mrs. Windspear waved her into a luxurious sitting room. White sofas with strategically scattered dark-blue pillows matched blue accents around the room. Every last knickknack was perfectly placed and completely the opposite of anything Reina would ever have in her home.

"Have a seat. Would you like some coffee? Tea?" She held up a little bell, poised to ring.

Reina shook her head. "No. I'm not here for a nice little sit-down and snacks. I want to know if you've seen Mia." She closed her eyes so she wouldn't have to see the scorn she knew was about to appear on her lightly weathered features. "She ran away."

Gasp. "Ran away? Oh, dear. But she's not here. We've begged Harold to let us meet our granddaughter properly, but he says you won't allow it."

Her eyelids popped open. "He said what? I've never said any such thing. Up until a week ago, I had no idea you had any interest in meeting her."

Mrs. Windspear twisted her fingers in a string of pearls around her neck. "We didn't know. Had you bothered to tell our son he was going to be a father fourteen years ago, maybe we would have had a chance to know our granddaughter." Her face flushed and she clamped her mouth tight.

Reina got the impression she wasn't used to letting her feelings loose like that. She actually seemed somewhat surprised at her own outburst.

"I did tell Harold. And he dumped me faster than a knife fight in a phone booth." She dropped onto the corner of a pristine white chair. "But none of this matters right now. Where's Harold? I have no idea where he's living. I assumed he'd be somewhere around here." But if she didn't know where he lived, how would Mia have known where to find him?

"I spoke with him just a short while ago and he didn't mention seeing her." Her heels clicked on the marble tile as she strode over to a small table in the entryway and grabbed a cell phone plugged into the wall. She wandered back into the room with the phone held to her ear. "Harold. Miss Mills is here. You have a lot of explaining to do." Pause. "Never mind that now. We'll discuss it later. Mia is missing. Have you seen her? Miss Mills thought she might seek you out." She listened for less than a second, then apparently cut him off. "Enough. As I said, we'll discuss this later. Your father and I will expect to see you at dinner tonight." She hung up and clutched the phone to her chest. "He hasn't seen her."

Reina's stomach dropped. Much as she hadn't wanted Mia to run to her father, she'd counted on finding her with him. She'd already exhausted all her friends.

Where the hell was Mia?

♥ ♥ ♥

Keenan cursed under his breath as he followed Miss Ashford to a house less than a mile from Reina's. Boards covered the windows, the out-of-control lawn was part weed and part dead grass, and the porch sagged to the point he worried it would give out beneath his weight.

He would have loved to photograph it.

"She's in there?"

Miss Ashford nodded. "Yes, *dahling*," she drawled. "Mind you, she's a bit tied up at the moment."

He balled his hands into fists, the urge to hit Miss Ashford nearly overwhelming. But he needed to keep his cool. "Is she alone?" Surely it wouldn't be this easy. Miss Ashford must know the minute he secured Mia's safety he would leave in a flash. Without Mia, Miss Ashford had no leverage to make him bow to her will.

She gestured toward the house with a smirk. "See for yourself."

The wicked smile sent unease coursing through his gut. Something wasn't right. What would he see when he stepped into that house?

With a deep breath, he carefully placed his weight on each stair, making sure the boards were steady before continuing.

The front door creaked open. Cobwebs filled the corners and weak light filtered in through cracks between rotten boards over the windows. A crash of thunder and streak of lighting announced the storm seconds before rain pelted loudly onto the roof. His steps set off a cloud of dust.

Miss Ashford sneezed. "Pardon me. Such a shame to let such a lovely little house go to waste." She shrugged. "Oh well. She's in the back. Follow me."

She led him down a nearly black hallway into a kitchen with dingy yellow tiles and rusty brown appliances. A camera—his camera?—lay on the Formica countertop next to the stove. An easel in the center of the room faced away from him so he couldn't see what was clipped to the large piece of cardboard propped on it.

Dread spread through him. Mia wasn't there. He focused on the easel. Or was she? "You didn't."

Miss Ashford's giggle was like a knife piercing his lungs. He couldn't breathe as he walked slowly around to the front of what his gut told him was a portrait of Mia.

"Please, no," he whispered.

His worst fears were confirmed as he finally got a good look at what was on the stand. He fell to his knees.

♥ ♥ ♥

A call to Sally confirmed her fears that neither Mia, nor Keenan, had returned. Reina let herself cry for a good two minutes before wiping her eyes and starting her car. Mrs. Windspear had promised to call if Mia eventually made her way out there. There was no point in staying. She had to do something.

She found a pack of tissues in her glove compartment and mopped up while she hit speed-dial for Jane. The Bluetooth kicked in and ringing came out over her car's sound system as she made her way along Franklin Avenue toward downtown.

"Did you find her?" Jane skipped the formalities, unusual given her generally strict adherence to the niceties.

"No. And now Keenan's missing. You don't think—" She stopped to take a deep breath. She did not want to acknowledge the fear that had begun growing the minute she realized Mia was not with her father. "You don't suppose this could have something to do with Miss Ashford, do you?"

Gasp. "To what end? Surely she can't think kidnapping your daughter would cause Keenan to fall in love with her?"

Reina forced her eyes to stay on the road when she wanted to hit something. "Why did she think trapping him in that photo was going to make him love her? She ain't right." *And now she has my daughter.* "Shit. I'm going crazy. I don't know what to do next."

"Calm down. We'll get her back. I'm headed over to Serendipity to gather the ingredients for a location spell. Christa's working on figuring out the exact nature of Miss Ashford's portrait and whether we can do anything for Keenan. We'll meet at your house in an hour. We will find Mia. And Keenan."

"You're working on a spell?" The knot tying up her stomach eased slightly. Jane had successfully completed a location spell at least once before, as far as Reina knew. If the coven was working on this, they wouldn't fail to find Mia. "Thank you."

"Hold on a second while I switch over to Bluetooth in the car."

The leather of the steering wheel creaked beneath her grip. She glanced at the speedometer. Shit. She eased off the gas. Killer Curve fast approached, and if she didn't slow down she'd end up just like Ronnie Pekkamen from her senior year. He'd taken the curve too fast and, well, it wasn't called Killer Curve for nothing. But people never learned. There was a three-car pileup just the other day caused by some idiot driving too fast.

"All right, I'm back. Perhaps you might like a distraction?"

"Yes, please." She'd done all she could, so being able to think of something else would be a huge relief. Even if only for a moment.

"Adam spoke with Darcy Prentice." Jane paused as if expecting a big reaction to this news.

Oh-kay... "Um, why?" she asked when Jane didn't continue.

"Oh, dear. I gather Keenan didn't mention his encounter at Time After Time Antiques? You know Miss Segarra, yes?"

"Sure. Love her store." She'd found more than a few treasures in that little antiques shop. Among the high-priced antiques, she sold a number of damaged items on the cheap. Reina loved searching for hidden treasures that just took a little bit of elbow grease to turn into something fantastic.

"Like so many Havenport residents, Miss Segarra is a fan of the Lovers legend. She knew a few tidbits not commonly known and told Keenan Darcy was her source. Darcy's a bit of an amateur historian and, it turns out, has a habit of digging through the *Havenport Herald*'s old files. She knows more than most about Keenan's disappearance, and what happened in Havenport after the scandal. She promised to gather what information she had and forward it to you."

"Oh, wow. That's great." But not good enough to get her mind off Mia's and Keenan's disappearance. "Keenan will be so excited. Once we find him." Thunder rumbled so close the car trembled. A shaft of lightning lit up the sky. Not a good omen. "I'm really starting to believe his disappearance isn't a coincidence. Do you think Miss Ashford somehow convinced him to go with her?" It wouldn't be a hard task for the evil bitch. If Miss Ashford threatened Mia, Keenan wouldn't hesitate to sacrifice himself. He was an amazing man: brave, smart, honorable.

Silence.

"Jane?"

"I just don't know. It makes no sense, and yet where else could he be? I do not believe him to be the type of man to desert you at such a time. Particularly since he is in love with you."

"What?" She couldn't have heard her correctly. "But we've only known each other a few days. He couldn't possibly be in love with me." And yet she was fairly certain she was in love with him.

♥ ♥ ♥

"Get her out of there. Now." Keenan's hands shook with rage and fear. He couldn't let this happen. *Damn, she looks so scared.* Wide eyes dominated her pale face. Blue-streaked hair flew out around her head, as if the camera had captured her in the midst of spinning to face the photographer. The large oak tree from Reina's yard loomed tall behind her, and she crouched slightly. She must have just leaped to the ground after escaping from her bedroom window. Reina probably hadn't been off the mark to think she'd been running off to find her father. Chances were she would have called her mother at some point to explain. He could see her cell phone sticking out of her pocket.

"Are you saying you would like to join me in our own portrait if I do?"

Hell, no. But what choice did he have? He nodded. The words wouldn't come.

"Excellent. Now all we need is a photographer."

"Who took the initial photograph?"

"The woman who bespelled your camera, of course. I couldn't very well take the photograph myself, now could I?"

She stepped toward his camera, but he snatched it up. There was no way he was letting it out of his hands. How had she gotten a hold of it back then? He generally didn't let it out of his sight. That camera had made it through the war with him. He thought back to that last day on the dock. He'd set the camera down to move a garbage can he didn't want in his shot, then Abigail approached. Fishermen had long since retired for the evening, so the dock was fairly deserted. He could remember his annoyance that Abigail's meddling might cause him to lose the light of the sunset he'd wanted to capture. For the life of him, he couldn't remember seeing anyone near his camera. He supposed it didn't matter. That person was probably long dead by now.

"Come now, *dahling.* That will do you no good. I'm the only one who knows how to work the spell, and the only one who knows how to *un*work it. So let's find someone to hit that little button there, and we can go on to find love ever after."

He was tempted to take Mia's photo and the camera and scram, but what if she was right? Reina's coven was filled with powerful witches, it was true. But they'd been at a loss as to how Miss Ashford had trapped him. What if they couldn't figure out how to free Mia? He couldn't take that chance.

"First, we bring Mia back to her mother. I'm not leaving her here."

She crossed her arms. "Fine. It makes no difference. I have no interest in keeping the brat." She tilted her head and studied the portrait. "Although, I must say, I do like her clothing. Don't you think I would look quite charming in that top?"

She fluttered her lashes. He fought back the urge to vomit. He stepped toward Mia, but Miss Ashford snatched her off the easel. He winced as the clips holding paper to cardboard flew in all directions. The corner of the portrait tore. "Careful," he yelled.

"On second thought, I'll hold on to this." She held it up with Mia facing his direction, one hand at each corner. "This paper is so delicate. It would be such a shame if it were to rip. I have no idea what would happen to the little one should that happen." Her coy smile hardened. "You're going to do exactly what I say if you want to save her."

He nodded curtly and followed her out the door.

What should he tell Reina? How would she react to knowing he had put her precious daughter in jeopardy? All because Miss Ashford couldn't take no for an answer. He trudged down the street, camera tucked into his jacket pocket. Miss Ashford pranced beside him, the portrait rolled and tucked under her arm.

They rounded the corner and approached Reina's house. Cars lined the street outside, including Reina's Bug, as she called the strange bright-yellow vehicle. The front door stood open, but all he could make out were several shadows milling about inside.

"I'll meet you at our spot on the docks. Bring the girl's mother. And *only* her if you want to get this portrait back in one piece." Miss Ashford snatched the camera from his grasp.

He let her have it. Mia's portrait was too important to risk in a struggle. Miss Ashford had him behind the eight ball. He nodded and headed into the house.

Chapter Twelve

"Keenan! There you are. Where have you been?"

Reina's startled gaze flew toward the door at Christa's exclamations. "Keenan?"

He didn't look well. Face pale, lips tightened to a thin line, hands clenched into fists at his sides.

"Are you okay, darlin'?"

He strode forward and took her into his arms. Her eyes widened in surprise at the unexpected gesture in front of the group. The entire coven and their significant others were crammed into her living room.

Her stomach dropped. "Mia?" she gasped. "Oh my God. What happened? Is she okay? Do you know where she is? She's not…she's not…" She couldn't say it.

"She's alive." He held her at arm's length to look deep into her eyes. "Miss Ashford has her."

Reina's brief flare of relief crashed and burned. "Where? How do you know?"

"Reina, why don't you sit down?" Jane gestured toward the couch. "You're about to collapse."

Keenan shook his head. "No. We don't have time. Mia's trapped." He closed his eyes briefly, then snapped them open to look at Reina. "She's in a portrait. Like I was."

They all gasped.

"Miss Ashford will release her if I agree to take her place."

"Nonsense," Adam said. "We shall find another way."

"I've already agreed. I have to meet her at the docks where the first picture was taken. I'm just here to get Reina."

"Me? Why?" Her mind buzzed in all directions. What in tarnation was she supposed to do? She had to save Mia, but she couldn't let Keenan sacrifice himself. Jane and Christa came up on either side of her, lending the support she desperately needed.

"What does she want with Reina?" Christa demanded.

"She needs someone to take the picture." He scratched at his beard. "On second thought, everyone take a seat. Let me explain."

Jane and Christa maneuvered her into an end chair while everyone else sat or perched on the furniture. She didn't have enough seating for this many people at once. Keenan remained standing. He paced as he described Miss Ashford's approach and how he discovered Mia's predicament.

Reina cringed. Her baby was trapped. Scared. Heat rose in her cheeks. A buzzing started in her ears. She'd never been a violent person, but she was going to tear that bitch's head off for doing this to her baby.

"Problem is, I'm not entirely sure Miss Ashford has the power to reverse the spell."

Reina's head picked up at that. "What? She can't get my baby out of there?"

"I don't know. We all assumed Miss Ashford was the one with the magick, but she's not. Someone else ensorcelled my camera. She may have paid for the spell, but she didn't cast it herself."

"Who did?" Christa asked.

"I have no idea. Whoever it was is most likely dead. They'd have to be over a hundred years old."

Jane gasped. "Mrs. Cunningham."

Reina frowned. "From that old TV show?" What was Jane thinking?

"No. Mrs. Cunningham is Havenport's oldest citizen. Remember, she turned one hundred last month. There was a big article in the paper and I had my students draw birthday cards for her."

"I'm not following," Keenan said.

"I met her when I delivered the cards. She's a witch."

"You can't possibly think…"

"I do. I know it sounds absurd, but magick is unpredictable. It brings forces together when needed. The spell has a purpose. Maybe having the witch who cast it be around when it comes to fruition is necessary to complete the spell."

"That's a stretch." This was not helping. She needed to get Mia back. Now. She leaned forward to rest her elbows on her knees and cradled her head in her palms.

"True. But one worth investigating," Adam said. "Jane and I will visit this witch. Even if she is not the one who cast the spell, she was alive when it was done. She may have known the original witch, and therefore might know how to undo its terrible price."

That was something. Reina perked up. "You're right. Havenport's a small town. The witches might have had a coven just like we do."

"And if they did, they might have shared their spells," Christa chimed in. "I'll go with Jane and Adam. If we figure out the original spell, I can help make a counter." She pulled out her phone and held it to her ear. "Mom's in town. She's great at this. I'll have her meet us there."

Jane, Adam, Christa, and Jeremy rushed out with brief messages of encouragement to Reina.

"The rest of us can go with you. Confront the witch." Dean stood.

"No." Keenan shook his head. "She insisted I bring Reina, that's it. We can't risk scaring her. She'll have a hold of the portrait. She could easily rip it."

Reina's heartbeat tripled. "He's right. We can't risk Mia. But we're not giving you over to her, either." She couldn't lose either of them. Especially now that she'd realized how much he meant to her.

Keenan dropped to his knees before her. "It's okay. This is all my fault. I don't belong here, anyway." He gave her a brave smile, the right side tilting higher than the left in that adorable way that could charm the dew off honeysuckle.

She fought the urge to punch him and swiped a tear off her cheek, then glared. "It's not your fault, actually. It's that bitch's. So here's what we're fixin' to do." She cleared her throat and searched for Jen. She sat on the opposite side of the room on a chair Braeden must have dragged in from the kitchen. "Jen, can you amp up the weather a bit?"

The soft pitter of rain falling on the roof intensified. Jen smiled. "Of course."

"Perfect. I want you guys there. Just…hide somewhere so she doesn't see you."

"I have keys to the maritime museum," Dean said. "We can go in through the loading dock. It's on the opposite side from where she wants to meet you. We can use Jen's storm to hide our approach."

"Once we're in, I'll lessen the intensity so we can see proper," Jen chimed in.

"Great. There's a ghost that haunts that edge of the dock. I'll ask him to alert you guys if we get into trouble. Lila, you can still sense your kind, right?"

"Yes. You're talking about Ralph, yes? He's a friendly sort. I'm sure he'd be willing to help."

"We should hurry. Miss Ashford is not one to wait for what she wants." Keenan stood and held out a hand to help her up.

After a deep breath, she took it. They stood toe to toe. The heat of his body warmed her. What if something went wrong? She pulled him in, wrapped her arms around his waist, and gave him a tight hug.

♥ ♥ ♥

"It's going to be okay, Reina. We'll get Mia back safe. Once Miss Ashford gets what she wants, she has no reason to hurt her." Keenan tucked a strand of her silky hair behind her ear. Damn, he was going to miss her.

They'd pulled over a block away from the museum to give the others a chance to get there first and settle in. Jen had come through with a torrential downpour. He could barely see a foot in front of him.

He swept his thumb across her cheek to catch the trail of tears. "Don't cry. I promise she'll be all right."

"And you?" She sniffed and shoved his hand away. "You seem fairly determined to give yourself up to her."

"I'm determined to save your daughter." Why was she mad?

"That's a given. What I don't understand is why you're making no effort to save yourself as well. Do you want to get away from here, from me, that badly?"

So that's what she thought? "Reina, I don't ever want to get away from you. I love you. If I could—"

Her lips cut off the rest of his sentence, which was fine since he couldn't seem to remember what he'd been about to say. All thoughts fled. He could only feel.

The softness of her mouth, the heat of her breath, the slickness of her tongue. He couldn't get enough.

Thunder boomed overhead. She tore her lips away, then rested her forehead against his. Their heavy breathing mingled, fogging the windshield. "I love you, too," she whispered.

Warmth filled him. For so long, he hadn't believed himself capable of any feeling other than sadness and fear. Reina had brought him back to the living in more ways than one. But reality settled in immediately. He wouldn't hesitate to do what needed to be done.

♥ ♥ ♥

"Promise me we'll be together. Mia, you, and me."

Keenan's silence scared Reina. She trusted him to save her daughter. She wasn't convinced he'd save himself in the process.

He finally nodded. "I'll do my best."

Normally she'd trust his best, but not at the moment. "I'm not losing either of you."

"But Mia is your priority." He smiled. "You're a wonderful mother, and a terrific dame. If anyone can do it all, it's you." His smile faded. "But—"

"Screw that. I don't want to hear any 'buts' from you."

"Fine. However…"

She rolled her eyes but let him continue.

"…just know that if it's a choice between Mia and me…I understand. I'm willing to give up my life for her." He put his finger against her lips to shush her. "As would any parent. So if I end up back in that portrait, I want you to know how much you've meant to me."

The sound of someone clearing his or her throat startled her so much she jumped. Keenan didn't seem to notice. She swung around to peer into the back seat. "Ralph," she exclaimed.

"Hey, girl. The others are in position. The flapper chick is taking shelter on the museum's deck. I don't think she noticed anyone. She's drenched and in a pissy mood. Expect a hissy fit when you get there."

"Does she have the portrait?" Panic gripped her.

"Sure does."

"Is that the ghost?" Keenan scanned the back seat, obviously not seeing a thing.

How far he'd come! Cursing witches when he first arrived, now a ghost was a mere curiosity.

"Who's the hunk?" Ralph asked. "He looks familiar."

"This is Keenan O'Connell."

"No. Not *the*…" Ralph's eyes went wide. He leaned forward to hover over the seats and scanned Keenan from top to bottom. "Wow. Tell him his photo didn't do him justice."

She chuckled.

"What?" Keenan asked.

"Ralph's an admirer." Her amusement didn't last, her thoughts never far from her daughter's welfare. "We better go. I don't want to keep her waiting too long. Ralph, let them know we're heading over."

"Sure thing." Ralph disappeared.

Reina drove the last block and pulled into the museum parking lot. She slammed the car into Park and faced Keenan.

"We have a lot to talk about," she said.

"I—"

"No. Not now. When we get back. Once Mia is safe. I *am* going to save you, too." They were going to have that conversation. Shit. He'd said he loved her. And she sure as shit loved him, too. She wasn't going to let that go.

♥ ♥ ♥

The rain tapered to a drizzle. Keenan followed Reina around the museum and out onto the small deck overlooking the water.

Miss Ashford hunched over, leaning against the railing looking like a drowned rat. The rabid look on her face didn't help the impression. Her ritzy dress peeked through what looked like a wool blanket she'd wrapped around herself like a cloak. A corner dropped down, covering one eye.

"I've been waiting forever." She sneered at Reina. "I guess you're not as fond of your daughter as I'd have thought."

Reina lunged forward, and he just barely got a hold of her arm to hold her back.

"You bitch. Give her back to me right now!" she screamed.

"Tsk. Temper, temper." Miss Ashford waved a finger in Reina's face.

She was lucky Reina didn't bite it off. Keenan had a hard time keeping the angry mother back. If the situation weren't so dire, he'd have let her go. He'd love to see his Reina give the uppity Miss Ashford the comeuppance she so richly deserved.

"Where's Mia?" he asked.

Miss Ashford's hands were empty. She shoved the blanket off her head, showing her hair hadn't escaped the nasty weather Reina's friend had enhanced for their arrival. Water dripped from the knotted strands that straggled over her eyes. She stepped aside and revealed the easel with Mia's portrait once again clipped to a square of plywood.

Reina gasped and took a step forward.

He once again held her back. Miss Ashford now had a hand on one corner. If she pulled…

"Mia." Reina's voice came out tortured, rough around the fresh tears spilling down her face.

The sound pierced his heart. He couldn't stand to hear her so upset.

"Let's get this over with. Let her go, and Reina will take our picture."

Miss Ashford snorted. "I think not. If I release the girl, you'll simply refuse to go through with your half of our bargain." She shook her head. "No. The instructions for ending the spell are on the back of her portrait. The mother will take our photograph first, then she's free to rescue her child while we go on to be together. Forever."

There had to be another catch. Had Miss Ashford really not thought this through? What was to keep them from simply releasing him from the spell once more the minute Mia was safe?

"I can see what you're thinking." Miss Ashford waved her finger in his direction this time. "I've thought of everything. The spell only has enough power for one more photograph. Once the spell's worn out, nothing's going to get us out of the portrait. Except true love." She blew him a kiss. "So when we finally do wake up, you'll be so madly in love with me, none of this"—she waved a hand in the air indicating Mia, then Reina—"will matter in the least."

His stomach sank. Damn. There was no way he'd ever come to love Miss Ashford. He supposed it would be like death. Eventually, the picture would rot away, and so would they.

Mia's frightened face stared out from the portrait. He turned to Reina, whose scared expression mirrored her daughter's. They were worth any sacrifice he had to make. "Fine."

He pulled Reina into his arms. "You'll be all right. I promise."

She sniffed and wiped at her tears. "No. I'll figure out a way to get you back."

"I grow bored." Miss Ashford yanked the edge of Mia's photo and pulled. A small tear appeared.

"No!" He jumped away from Reina. He didn't dare get too close to Abigail. One wrong move and she could destroy the picture for good, and he had no idea what that would do to Mia.

Abigail pointed to a spot behind her, where Reina couldn't help but capture them both in the camera lens. "Stand there. Not too close." She stepped away from Mia's portrait, but remained close enough she could grab it before he could get to her. "The camera's right there." She pointed to the railing where he hadn't noticed the camera lay open and ready.

Reina grabbed the camera, her posture rigid, eyes clear and shooting fire at Miss Ashford. Her evil glare gave him comfort. She'd be all right. He knew it.

She raised the camera toward her face, but paused, head tilted to one side. A slight twitch of her mouth caught his attention. What? He suddenly wished he had magickal powers of his own and could read her thoughts.

She winked. And with a flash of light, everything went blank.

♥ ♥ ♥

Reina watched in horror as a piece of photo paper fluttered to the ground where Keenan and Miss Ashford had just stood. She clutched the camera to her chest and slowly approached the paper that now rested half propped up against the deck railing.

Keenan stared out at her, eyes squinted, brows furrowed, head tilted slightly to his right. He must have seen her wink. She wished she could have explained rather than leaving him to wonder what was about to happen.

The back door to the museum burst open. Lila wrapped an arm around her shoulders while Braeden picked up the newly made portrait.

"Are you sure we can reverse this?" Reina asked.

"Definitely," Lila said. "Jane and Christa are already on their way. They know what to do."

Reina nodded. She approached Mia with trepidation. The portrait looked okay from a few steps away, but what if…?

They all gathered around and inspected every inch of the page. "There's a little tear in the corner, but it's nowhere near Mia. She should be fine," Jen said.

Reina unclipped it from the plywood so she could turn it over. Just as she thought, nothing on the back. "The bitch lied. She had no idea how to get Mia out."

"Not surprising. Good thing we didn't need to rely on her." Dean strolled over to the door and held it open. "Let's go inside where it's warmer. Jen did a great job with that storm, but it's left the night air a bit chilly for my tastes." His sleeves were rolled up, his collar unbuttoned. He didn't look the least bit cold. He pulled Lila to his side and ran a hand up and down her arm. She had noticeable goose bumps on her legs and her arms folded over her chest in an effort to warm herself. She smiled up at him in appreciation.

"Sounds good."

They filed in and milled about while waiting for the others to arrive. Reina wandered into the room where *The Lovers* portrait once hung. And there it stood. Exactly as it always had. "What the…"

"We faked it," Dean said.

"How?"

"It's beyond me. Witchy stuff." He shrugged. "All I know is that I had to have something here before they reopened after the renovations. My position with the Historical Society doesn't give me leave to keep paintings forever. So the ladies did some of their hocus-pocus and no one's the wiser."

They were interrupted by the door opening and excited voices raised in greeting. Reina ran back into the other room.

Jane and Christa rushed over to give her a big hug.

"You won't believe…" Christa began.

"Mia first. Then Keenan. You can get them out?" She bit her lip. They'd been trapped long enough. She couldn't stand the thought of them caught like that another moment.

"Of course," Jane said. "Bring me the portraits and the camera."

Reina propped Mia's portrait back up on the easel that someone had thought to bring in. Jane and Christa stood in front of it for a few minutes, each with one hand on the camera and the other on the painting. Reina paced while the rest looked on in silent support.

With a pop, Mia stood within the circle of their arms, next to the easel. Reina cried out and ran to her. Christa and Jane had the forethought to leap back, or Reina might have run them over. She pulled Mia into a bear hug, swaying back and forth. She breathed deep to inhale the sweet scent of the vanilla lotion her daughter loved so much. She couldn't smell vanilla without thinking of Mia.

"Mom, jeez. I can't breathe."

Reina laughed and held her at arm's length. She'd never been so happy to hear Mia's exasperated teenage angst voice. "Are you okay, sweetie?" She didn't let her answer before pulling her back in for another hug.

"What the eff? How did I get…"

"Hold that thought, sweetie." She turned toward Jane and Christa, who had Keenan's portrait pinned up where Mia's had just been. They leaned their heads together while they whispered to one another.

Reina's smile slipped. "What's wrong? Why haven't you brought him back?"

"Mom? What's wrong?" Mia whispered, her voice high and tight, as if she'd woken from a particularly scary nightmare. "What is that? Is that Keenan?"

Reina hugged her closer. "It's going to be okay, sweetie."

Jane turned and gestured her over. "We need you, Reina. This one's a bit trickier because we don't want to release Miss Ashford quite yet."

She turned Mia so she could look her in the eye. "It's going to be okay, sweetie. We're going to get Keenan back."

"He's a nice guy, Mama. He treats you right. You have to help him."

Mia hadn't called her mama since she was six.

"I will, sweetie." She squeezed Mia's hand, then let go and rushed over to stand with Jane and Christa. After a deep breath, she asked, "What do you need?"

"You love him, right?" Christa asked.

"I, uh, well…"

Jane laughed. "I do believe that counts as a yes."

"Good," Christa said. "Place your hand on the painting. Touching him if you can."

Reina did as requested, careful to avoid touching any part of Miss Ashford. "What's this going to do?"

"The spell is designed to bring the subjects to true love. So we need your love for Keenan to bring him out."

"Why didn't you need me to touch Mia?"

"We all love Mia," Christa explained. "But while Keenan seems like a great guy, we don't really know him. Add having the bitch in the picture, we need a little help to focus."

Reina nodded and settled in while Jane and Christa circled her and whispered under their breaths. *Why is it taking so long?*

And suddenly, Keenan stood before her. Just like with Mia, she pulled him into her arms and held him as tight as she could. Unlike Mia, he returned the hug twofold, lifting her up and swinging her in a circle until her feet flew out around her and the others dodged out of the way. Laughter filled the room. Reina threw her head back and laughed with the rest.

He finally set her back on her feet but kept her close. Everyone else faded from the room as she savored his kiss. "You saved me," he whispered when they finally drew back for air.

"Told you I would." She smirked, then reached up for another kiss.

"Mom," Mia hissed.

Reina giggled and settled for resting her head against Keenan's chest.

Epilogue

A few hours later, the entire coven and their significant others gathered at Royce's Tavern. Mia was spending the night with the Windspears. When Reina called to let them know Mia was okay, they'd had a long chat.

Mrs. Windspear had apologized for Harold's behavior. He'd fed them a pack of lies and they'd taken him to task over it. Reina gathered he was in some trouble financially and had been trying to use Mia as a bargaining chip to get more out of his parents. They were having none of it, so he dropped his suit for full custody.

But Mia wanted to get to know her grandparents, and they'd all agreed to work on getting together more often. Starting tonight. Reina was even letting Mia cut school the next day. She figured her daughter deserved a break after all she'd been through.

Reina wasn't likely to get any sleep, but it was what Mia wanted.

She and Keenan sat together in a booth, leaving the other side open for the rotating friends who stopped by, then flitted off again. Royce's was doing brisk business and they were all having a great time celebrating the success of the evening.

"Hey." Christa leaned a hip against their table. "I think Jane mentioned Darcy might have some info for you?"

Keenan straightened next to her. "Yes. She's the historian who might know something of my family?"

Christa nodded. "That's her. I cornered her and asked if she knew anything."

"And?" Reina asked with bated breath. It would mean so much to Keenan to find out what had happened.

"Turns out she knows a ton." She pulled a thumb drive from her pocket. "All your father's letters were scanned into the newspaper's archives about a year ago. She copied them onto this drive."

Keenan took the thumb drive gingerly. "My father's letters are on this stick?"

"You plug it into the computer and you'll be able to see everything he wrote."

His mouth hung open as he turned the drive over and inspected it from all sides. "Hard to believe."

"You'll get used to it." Reina bumped him with her shoulder.

"Did she say anything about what the letters contain? Miss Segarra indicated a few things, but..."

"She didn't say much. Just that your father was proud of you. He only stayed in Havenport for a little while, but your brother moved here permanently."

"What happened to him?"

"He lived a good life, from what I understand. Got married, had kids. He named his son Keenan."

A sheen of tears clouded his eyes. Reina squeezed his hand for support.

"What happened to the kids? Did they stay in town?" Was there a chance Keenan could have relatives here?

"Yes, they did. And I hope you don't mind, but I reached out to his grandkids. They'd love to meet you."

"Oh, wow. Christa, that's amazing." Reina beamed.

Keenan looked stunned. "Thank you."

"No problem." She straightened and grabbed a pitcher of beer from a passing waitress. "Here. I'm headed over to the bar. I'll talk to you later. Enjoy." She plopped the pitcher on the table between them and left.

"Are you happy?" Reina asked. "Did you still want us to try to send you back?" She bit her lip, waiting for his answer. She didn't want to ask, but felt she needed to raise the option. Just in case.

He pulled her in close for a kiss. "I couldn't be happier. And don't be silly. I've never been so dizzy over a dame before. I'm not about to ruin it."

Before she could ask about the odd expression, Jane slipped into the booth across from them. "How are you holding up?"

Reina smiled and leaned back to snuggle against Keenan. "I'm good."

He rubbed her arm and kissed the top of the head before asking Jane, "What happened with that woman you went looking for? I gather she was the witch who cursed my camera?"

"Indeed, she was." Jane took a sip of her wine.

A surge of anger swept through Reina. "Did she say why she did it?" She couldn't be sorry because she'd ended up with Keenan, but she was still upset on his behalf.

"Money."

Keenan snorted. "Shocking."

"And how did she justify breaking the witch's *rede*?" Reina poured herself another beer from the pitcher. Realizing Keenan probably had no idea what she was asking, she explained, "The witch's *rede* is 'an ye harm none, so mote it be.' We can't harm someone with our magick. And if we do, anything we visit upon someone else will come back to us threefold."

"She figured she was doing everyone a favor. No real harm."

Keenan choked on the sip of beer he'd just taken. "No real harm? Tell that to my father and brother."

Jane reached across the table and patted his hand. "In her mind, she tricked a dangerous beast into a trap. She realized Miss Ashford was somewhat deranged and if she didn't help, someone else would. She figured she was getting rid of a psychopath and guaranteeing her victim would find true love. That's why she chose the spell she did. She knew you'd come out of the portrait the minute the woman you were meant to be with passed by."

"Wait." Reina held up a hand to stop Jane from continuing. This was crazy. "I visited that portrait dozens of times. Nothing. If we were 'meant to be' why didn't he come out the first time? Or any of the other dozens of times I was there?"

"That must be why you've always felt so familiar to me," Keenan said with a warm smile in her direction, before turning back to Jane. "She makes a good point, though. Why now?"

"I'm not entirely sure. Maybe the timing wasn't right. Too many people in the area confused the spell, blocked it from working? Or perhaps Reina needed to be in love with you before the spell could take effect."

Heat spread across her face. She cleared her throat. "So it wasn't Mia's magick that pulled him out."

"Only partly. I do believe her power was the catalyst, but if you and Keenan hadn't been destined for each other, her magick wouldn't have had any effect on him."

"Whoa." Reina took that in. She believed in destiny, of course. A woman who could speak to ghosts tended to be a believer. But she'd never extended that belief to her own happiness.

"Jane?" Adam called from across the room.

Jane's head swiveled to find her husband, and she smiled before standing to leave. "I'll leave you to digest all this new information."

"Destined, huh?" Keenan kissed her cheek.

She shifted in the booth so she could face him. "Sounds like it, darlin'. Seems like you're stuck with me."

"Sounds like I'm a lucky man." He cradled her head in his hand and brought her forward for a passionate kiss.

When he pulled back, Reina groaned in protest.

"It's been a long day," Keenan whispered against her lips. "And it just so happens my new apartment is right upstairs. What do you say we retire for the evening?"

"I'd like nothing more."

About Emma Kaye

EMMA KAYE is married to her high school sweetheart and has two beautiful kids that she spends an insane amount of time driving around central New Jersey. Before musical theater and tap classes entered her life, she decided to write one of those romances she loved to read and discovered a new passion. She has been writing ever since. Add in a playful puppy and an extremely patient cat and she's living her own happily ever after while making her characters work hard to reach theirs.

♥ ♥ ♥

For more information on Emma, please visit her online at
www.Emma-Kaye.com
emmakayewrites@hotmail.com

Also by Emma Kaye

Love time travel? Try another Emma Kaye time travel romance.

Destined for Love
Can a twenty-first century doctor find love in Regency England with a widowed viscount?

Time for Love
A woman finds much more than she bargained for when she travels through time to Regency England.

Echoes of the Past
Can a time traveling witch find love in present day Lobster Cove, Maine, or will her curse get in the way?

For You
A time traveler and an earl's widow find love in Regency London—but time may not be on their side.

Timeless Tales – Short Stories
In Her Dreams featured in Timeless Escapes
Timing is Everything featuring Granting Her Wish, Losing Patience, & To Have and to Hold

♥ ♥ ♥

Havenport – Novellas
Baby, It's Cold Outside
featured in Christmas in Havenport
Under Her Spell
The Ghost of You
On Her Own

♥ ♥ ♥

The Duke's Christmas Wish featured in the Christmas Ever After Regency romance anthology.

In Days Past

by Lita Harris

♥ ♥ ♥

Liz Taggart lands a permanent job after decades of stringing together a living with everything from dog walking to serving burgers. Her quiet existence is fodder for rumors that are put to rest when a school buddy becomes a regular at the historic Royce's Tavern. A diary found in the basement of the building reveals connections unknown to her.

Newly divorced, Will Powell confides in Liz each time he orders a beer. Their friendship grows deeper with each conversation. He has loved her since they were teenagers and is careful not to scare her away, especially when his ex-wife shows up.

Liz and Will have their own baggage that needs to be put to rest so they can move on with their lives. But will they grow apart instead of finding a way to intertwine their pasts without judgment?

♥ ♥ ♥

Dedicated to ~

Past Lives ~ Future Loves

Chapter One

Adam Royce slid beer kegs off the handcart and spun each metal container on its rim to land with precision inside the under cabinet. "Here you go, Miss Elizabeth. We might as well take care of stocking the coolers while we are slow."

He was too young for Liz, and way too formal. No matter how many times she'd asked him to call her Liz, he wouldn't. Even though her mid-fifties put her out of the running for someone so young, she saw no harm in admiring his bulging biceps. Adam rarely broke a sweat, the daily workout he got hoisting cases of beer and boxes of steaks kept him in shape. When he asked her to take a full-time position as a day manager, she was ecstatic. Gone were the days of stringing together paychecks from unsteady odd jobs to pay her rent. She wasn't able turn him down.

She looked around the room. A lot had changed. At least based on the stories she'd heard, one being that her great-grandmother had been born there when the tavern operated as a brothel. She grabbed two dirty pilsner glasses and ran them up and down the twin bristle brushes in the soapy water. She relished the peace and quiet of the early morning. The lull allowed her time to catch up and get ready for the onslaught of fishermen who had been out in the Atlantic since sunrise.

Too early in the season for tourists, she would have to make do on the tip money from the locals. Which wasn't bad, but during tourist season she could easily clear a hundred a day. At times she missed her other jobs. Especially being a dog walker. But ever since she started dating Will, she wanted to have more time to have a life outside work.

She pulled her purse from next to the microwave underneath the bar and freshened up her lipstick. No mirror needed. She could apply the brightest, reddest shade while driving on the interstate and not miss her lips.

She wrinkled up her nose at the smell of hops and yeast, then fanned herself with a nearby drink menu. "Adam, it would be great to get some fresh air in here."

"You must be a mind reader."

She smiled and watched him walk across the room. *Ah, youth.* If she could go back a few years…nah, never mind. Sure, she could have done things differently. Maybe if she had been more proactive instead of letting life string her along, she would have gotten more out of her existence.

"Thank you, dear!" she shouted.

She did her best to be social, and fought against pulling inward. But the lighthearted, carefree Liz the townspeople knew wasn't her at all. Will knew her heart. He ignored the rumors she grew up with. Most people took her silence, lack of friends, easy friendships with men because she didn't trust women, and inability to hold down a job as signs of a loose woman. Will knew she preferred to keep to herself, and hated gossip. The fact she didn't divulge her personal business made her an easy target.

She'd built up an impenetrable shield, deflecting the side stares and curious looks. How many people could say their great-grandmother worked in a bordello? If the legend was even true. Over the years, Liz heard pieces of lore but nothing definite could be found to substantiate the claims.

She spritzed window cleaner on the mirrors behind the first-shelf liquor. For the first time, she realized what it felt like to be in charge. Responsibility and feeling important mattered, but most of all the newfound respect changed how people spoke to her.

Adam wouldn't tolerate any off-color remarks thrown her way, no matter how large a tab a customer rang up.

If her son had survived, she imagined him to be like Adam. Kind, caring, smart, and a hard worker. For that reason, she did the best job she could even when her arthritis flared up. The sea air could be hard on her joints, but she did her best to keep in shape. That's what led to so many jobs. Well, that wasn't the only reason. Working hard kept her mind busy and off the loss of her deceased husband, Walt, her only love. When he went out to sea and never came back, her heart lost hope and she struggled to move forward.

"Miss Elizabeth, look what I found in the basement. I thought it was a piece of wood wedged between the rafter and ceiling to shore it up. You might be interested. You enjoy local history."

Adam handed her a threadbare book, the spine barely holding the pages together. She lifted her glasses from the beaded chain hanging from her neck and examined the inside of the front cover.

"Hmm, Darcy would be interested in this, too. She's more of a history buff than I am." She thumbed through the weathered pages. "I can't make it out. It looks to be written in fountain pen and faded."

"I suppose the dampness from the stone basement damaged the papers. Take it with you. See if you can find something in it that might be interesting. Perhaps a story that we could use to lure people in here."

She closed the book, held the arm of her glasses, and peered over the lens. "You have plenty of customers."

He nodded. "True, but the winter months get slow and I would be more comfortable with a stronger cash flow."

"You should talk to Olivia then. That girl is a financial genius. So young and look what she's done with the old bookstore and the empty space next door. Good head for finances on that girl."

"Hmm, perhaps. Speaking of customers, we must prepare. The boats will be coming in. Downstairs to get more kegs."

"Don't worry. I got it." Liz's curiosity followed the book. Why would someone stick it in a damp cellar? She couldn't believe that the mice didn't chew it apart. The pages were brittle and threatened to crack under her touch. Best leave it until she could take it home and read it in peace. Probably some silly journal a sailor had hid from his girlfriend or wife. She knew a lot of those guys fooled around when they were at sea. A different girl in each port.

Her father was one of them from what she heard. The stories were plenty, but she ignored them. It had been bad enough that the people in town called her the bastard child. Rumors died off as the people who spread them passed away. And her skin grew thicker with age, her heart protected.

She would let people get but so far. Her outgoing nature gave the impression they knew her. But no one did. Not even Will.

♥ ♥ ♥

Will needed a beer—quick. He hated construction jobs down by the waterfront. Within an hour, his throat would be scratchy from breathing in the salt air. He considered moving out of Havenport many times. Got close once, but his wife at the time refused to go because she didn't want to leave her mother. But it was okay for her to move away when she left him for another guy. *Hypocrite.*

Once the divorce settled, he was too poor to even think about moving. He got to keep the house, in its dilapidated state, but at least he still had a roof over his head. A simple man didn't need much. He'd grown up along the docks, longing to see more of the world.

As a boy, he would sit on the jetty and stare out across the sea, wondering what existed on the other side.

One summer he met Roger, a kid from Vermont who'd never seen the ocean, and they got to talking. They planned to explore the world. They got as far as patching up a rotted rowboat that had sunk as soon as it hit water.

Roger's family ended their vacation and went back to the mountains, and Will never ventured from Havenport.

He walked into the tavern for a cold brew. "Hey, love. Sam Adams or whatever you got on tap."

"Finishing up early today." Liz tipped the pilsner glass just right so the head flowed perfectly.

"This job seems to be working for you." He downed the beer as smooth as water.

"It does, doesn't it? That Adam is a sweetheart. I got lucky." Liz rested her elbow on the bar and propped up her chin.

He slid his hand into hers and squeezed her fingers. "No time for a manicure?"

She pulled her hand away. He'd never known her to have chipped polish. He didn't mind and even reveled in the comfort that she had become more at ease with herself. Like when they were kids. He'd always had a thing for Liz, but the timing had never been right.

He watched her hide from people during her teenage years as classmates made up stories and harassed her. But he knew the heart behind the hurt. Even though her reluctance to confide in him and tell him of her years away from town, he knew the stories of her being married numerous times were false. But the townsfolk believed what they wanted to, especially homespun tales of a woman who was different and didn't buy in to gossip and hate.

Yes, Liz Taggart was as sweet as they came, and he finally had his chance to get to know her better.

"Haven't had the time. Adam's got a good business here. Keeps me hopping." She wiped glasses dry with the precision of a machine and stacked them just as quick.

"Dinner? Do you have time for that? And I don't mean here." He knew the restaurant would be her first choice. She was a creature of habit, and he wanted to introduce her to more than what the fish-smell air had to offer.

Liz glanced at her watch. "What do you have in mind?"

"In the mood for a steak house?"

"What's wrong with the steak here?" She lifted his arm and wiped the bar.

"Nothing. The food's great. But don't you get tired of always being in the same place? Being around the same people? Even the dogs in this town don't change."

Liz laughed. "That's not true. Lauren Bishop just got a new pup."

He reached over the bar and clasped her hands in his. "Lovey. Please, at least the next town over. I feel that every breath I've ever taken in life has been in this town."

"Don't you like it here?" Her hands cupped his.

"Yeah, but I'm not getting any younger, and I want to do different things."

"Like skydiving?" Liz laughed.

"Not on my list, but I don't think going to a different restaurant is asking too much." He released her hands and sat back. "If we stay here, you'll be waiting tables and running shots."

"Harwood seems like a nice town. I hear they have some nice places there."

"Exactly. It's not too far and it's something different. I'll pick you up at six?" He got up from his chair.

"That sounds fine."

"Good." He leaned over the counter and kissed her. "See you later."

He left the bar and jumped into his faded and beat-up pickup truck.

The truck rolled down Main Street, releasing puffs of smoke from the tailpipe.

Finally. A real date.

He'd never formally asked Liz out. One night, while she closed up the bar and before she took the full-time gig, they got to talking. He had been taken by her sincere gaze. No woman ever paid him that kind of attention. Not even his former wife of thirty years.

Funny, he felt like he hadn't even been married. More like he and his ex-wife had been roommates. He wasn't going to live out what little time he had left by getting into another relationship like that.

So many years wasted.

He pulled into his driveway, running over a metal garbage can lid. He got out of the truck and looked up at the roof.

"Damn squirrels nesting and destroying what's left of the shingles."

Maybe he'd been the problem. All work and no play. He spent his life taking care of other people's homes but not his.

He picked up the smashed lid and shoved it onto the matching steel can. A rusty rake perched against the house caught his attention.

With a swift brush through the brittle leaves from last fall, he hacked away at the pile. Metal prongs scraped against concrete. Each scoop of leaves made his shoulders feel lighter. He gathered the mess and tossed it into the can.

The house would have to go.

♥ ♥ ♥

"Adam, do you mind if I cut out early—like, five?" Liz refilled empty napkin holders along the bar.

"No. You've more than put in your time. I am the one who got lucky with this arrangement." Adam pulled a bucket of lemons from the refrigerator under the bar and sliced them into thin wedges.

She flipped through the tattered book he had given her. "Have you looked through this at all?"

"No. I expect it is nothing more than a teenage girl's thoughts or some fisherman's tall tale. You look through it."

The lone customer left the bar. She used the lull of midafternoon to prepare for the evening rush.

Her curiosity of what waited to be read in the leather-bound journal excited her more than the latest rag magazine she wasted five dollars on at Corky's.

Adam went to the back room to check on the daily fish haul. Predictable. She found that comforting. Her turbulent life welcomed stability. Her mother brought crazy into their lives. Never a steady paycheck. Utilities turned off for nonpayment. Because of that, she always paid her bills as soon as they landed in her mailbox. And she worked so much to keep her mind busy and dull the pain.

Every time she looked at the sea, she thought of the day Walt's body washed up on the jetty three days after he went missing. His boat washed ashore in the next town a week later. The coroner believed Walt had fallen overboard, or at least that's what the circumstances led him to believe. Only Walt's fishing cap provided proof he had been on the boat. She kept the hat in her closet, surprised it survived.

The book weighed heavy in her hands so she opened it to find out what story it held. She flipped through the pages where words were legible.

It started that night I heard the wagon wheels clanking against the dusty dirt road. I prepared myself for the dance—at least that's what we called it. It wasn't proper for a lady to have gentleman friends, but a girl has to earn a living. Anyway, Barney played the piano. I could hear him plinking the keys downstairs.

Liz placed the book facedown on the bar and poured herself a ginger ale and grabbed a bag of pretzels. She picked up the book and leaned against the cash register.

Intriguing.

He was a talented gent. A little portly for my taste, but very nice to us working girls. He'd write songs for us and it made us feel special. Havenport, a sleepy sea town at that time. Men working on fishing boats. Every once in a while a new man would pull into town thinking he would make his next fortune from the locals. Like we were too ignorant to see through his con game. The girls might play along to milk him for his money, and then who was the ignorant one?

"So it's true!" She spun around looking for Adam, only to find the bar empty. She shoved a pretzel into her mouth and kept reading.

Well, never mind that. Back to what happened that night on the docks. There were less people in the town back then. All I wanted to do was earn enough money to get out of here. I'd grown up with a father who had little time for me. My mother died in childbirth. Never knew my grandparents. I guess they knew Havenport held no future for them around these weathered pilings in the eastern seaboard. I can't blame them. Though it would have been nice if they took me with them.

Pain seared through Liz's heart. This young girl sounded like her. Wait. This young girl must have lived in the building. Why else would a diary be stuck in the rafters? Hidden away so no one would find it.

"Ahem."

Liz dropped the book. "Lord, you startled me."

Adam bent down to pick it up. "My apologies. You must have been deep into that book. I've been standing here for a few minutes and you didn't notice."

She took it from his hands. "Did you know this place used to be a brothel?"

Adam narrowed his eyes. "What?"

"A whorehouse. A bordello." She clenched the book.

He blushed. "I know what that is. But why do you say so?"

"I heard stories but never thought they were true. There's so many legends around here. I figured, how can a fishing town have a whore...I mean brothel? I thought that only existed in the Wild West. Can I take this home to finish reading it?"

"Of course you can. Keep it if you wish. You seem to get much pleasure from its contents."

She slid the book into her purse. "I find stuff like this fascinating. Didn't you ever walk around town and wonder who walked the streets before you?"

Adam shook his head. "Not really. Too distracted, I guess. I leave things in the past. I much prefer the present."

"I always have. Even as a little girl, I'd stare out the school windows and..."

"Continue."

"Oh, never mind." The veins in her neck tightened. The less she said, the less he would know her.

She cleared her throat. *Will!* She had to finish up or she'd be late. And one thing she prided herself on was her punctuality.

"Do you have anything that's pressing that I need to do before I leave for the day?" She filled the straw holders next to the cut-up fruit.

"No. It has been rather quiet this afternoon. I can manage. Mark and Megan will be in soon. Enjoy your evening."

"I will. Thank you." She grabbed her purse and held it under her arm, protecting the book like it was her most valuable possession. Something written within its pages was meant for her.

She could feel it.

Chapter Two

It had been five years since his wife left him. Will heard from her once when she checked to make sure her check was in the mail to her new address in Phoenix, Arizona. For a person who didn't want to leave her beloved town of Havenport, Dolores had no problem packing up her belongings and moving across country once her mother died.

He picked up a pile of newspapers from the coffee table and dumped them into a wooden crate on the front porch. Recycling would be his new obsession. He wanted his ex's stuff out of the house. He didn't have a reason to hold on to anything. If she wanted it, she should have taken it.

He embraced his new life. He cooked what he wanted—no more pork chops. He hated them and didn't realize how much until he found a package in the basement chest freezer.

It took him forever to clean out the useless piles of her stuff. Collections, Dolores called them. Bull. She was a hoarder looking to fill the hole in her heart with stuff.

He tossed a Venetian glass clown into the trash. The wasted years he spent holding on to things kept him imprisoned in his home. No more.

He didn't understand the power of connecting to another person until he hung out with Liz and had that first conversation. His ex-wife never engaged him like that. What a fool he'd been.

He rummaged through the piles of papers in the corner of the living room.

"Ah, there you are." He thumbed through the yellow pages of a local phone book from 2009. Not sure if the information would be any good, but he gave it a try.

"Hello, Meyers Junk. Can I help you?" a young woman answered.

He cleared his throat. "Ah, yes. I need a dumpster or two to get rid of household items. Can you do that for me?"

"Yes, sir. Is this an estate clean out?"

"Does the death of a marriage count?"

He could hear the young girl catch her breath. "It could be if you want it to be."

He started laughing. "No need to be so cautious. I need people to come and empty the place like it's being sold."

"So you need someone to come inside?"

"Yes."

"Okay, Mr....?"

"Powell. Will, since you're so nice."

"Mr. Powell, I'll have a representative come to your home and go over the disposal plan so we can give you a price. Does that suit you?"

"As soon as you can."

"I can have someone there tomorrow."

"After two in the afternoon?"

"Yes."

"Works for me. Thank you, and your name?"

"Carrie."

"Thank you, Carrie. You have a nice day."

He hung up the phone and closed the book. His shoulders stood tall and chest lighter. "Hmm, and she always said to throw these old phonebooks away. She can deal with it. They will be with the rest of her stuff."

Will danced up the steps, his life finally under his control. Though it took time to rid himself of the chains and guilt of divorce, he'd still taken the step to get on track with what he wanted.

First thing on his agenda—his date with Liz. He shuffled through never-worn clothes in his walk-in closet. Dolores tried to dress him like a *GQ* model, but he was a jeans and T-shirt guy, though he knew enough to put on a tie for a date.

Could he even call it that?

What if Liz didn't think of him in that way?

Whatever it turned out to be, he would get a steak dinner and good conversation out of the evening.

Liz was smart. Throughout school she held back and he never understood why. She would never raise her hand to answer a question yet she aced all her exams. On the rare moment a teacher did call on her, Liz always had the correct response.

Maybe that's what intrigued him. That coy, intelligence-behind-the-eyes look.

Havenport was too small for her, yet she never left. Unlike him. He would leave in a heartbeat. Something kept her on the sandy soil she'd grown up on.

He settled on a charcoal-gray pin-striped suit. Tags hung from the sleeve. Another item he never wore. Dolores tried her best to turn him into something he wasn't. He slipped his arm through the jacket, then the other. Slowly he guided the jacket up his back.

"Holy moly. It fits." He strutted around the bedroom, doing his best impersonation of a proud peacock. He didn't care that the suit was out of style.

He rattled the hangers some more in search of a shirt and tie. "White shirt, black tie. Even I can pull that together."

If the jacket fit, the pants had to fit. If not—well, the jacket could conceal a wardrobe miss. So could the dim lighting in the restaurant. However, that would not diminish his five o'clock shadow. He jumped in the shower, shaving while the water ran down his body. Efficiency impressed him.

With a quick towel swished down his back and a quick *whoosh, whoosh, whoosh* of his hair, he was ready. He sucked in his stomach muscles in an attempt to look fit.

"Nah, she ain't gonna buy it." He found a pair of sharp-toed oxfords. He blew the dust off them and used a towel from the shower to shine the leather. "These threads may be old but they're new to me."

He glanced around the bedroom. "All of this—gone."

Will pulled the front door behind him and turned to lock the dead bolt with the key. It wouldn't turn.

"What is this some kind of freakin' curse you put on me, Dolores?"

He looked above as if expecting an answer to fall from the sky. Instead a raindrop landed on the tip of his nose. He jiggled the key until the cylinders fell into position and allowed the key to turn.

What did they say about the shoemakers? The shoemaker always has holes in his shoes. The carpenter's house is always the last to be fixed.

He walked to the car. No pickup truck for this dinner date. The car was not as impressive, but easier for a lady to get into. He grabbed a sweatshirt from the back seat and dusted off the dashboard and front seats.

On his way to enjoy the night with Liz. His dream girl.

♥ ♥ ♥

Liz paced back and forth in front of her living room window. Her hands beaded with sweat. It wasn't like her to be nervous. It's not like they were going on a date. Was it?

Confidence wasn't her strong suit. Sure, her facade made people believe her to be strong and fearless. Her stonewall manner helped her get through school when classmates would make up stories about her. Calling her a bastard child. Well that part turned out to be true. Though she heard the stories, she didn't have a clue who her father was, and her mother never provided any information.

It was difficult growing up in a town where families went back generations and everyone knew your business. She hated that and withdrew even more as she got older, but she loved the town, the ocean, and how much her mother enjoyed living there.

Yet with Will she opened up a bit. Maybe the liquor made it easier to confide in him. Or could be she simply trusted him because he was easy to talk to. He never chimed in with the rest of the kids that made fun of her, yet they had never connected before.

Well, things were different in the sixties. Havenport represented itself as a tourist destination as the fishing industry began to wane. It grew into a town caught between old and new money.

Her mother never explained to her why they moved from Connecticut to the sleepy seaside town. Liz heard rumors of her mother, Amanda, being cut off from her family. The only history she knew of her lineage was that her mother was named after her paternal grandmother, Liz's great-grandmother.

Apparently, Mom embarrassed the family and their old money wasn't to be tainted by her illicit behavior. Liz blamed her illegitimate birth as the reason they were shunned.

Whatever the cause, she created her own life and grew content. She removed the diary from her purse and sat in the faded armchair in front of the window as she waited for Will to arrive.

My father was gone most of the time, so he left me to live above the saloon with Tilly. I loved that lady. You'd never know that she was a madam. It didn't matter to me. She treated me like a daughter, and that's all I cared about. I'd sit in the window wondering what my mother would have been like, had she lived.

She laughed to herself. "Damn, I could have written this. Hear that, Amanda. This girl was just like me. Sitting by the window waiting for her, except her mother was dead. You might as well have been."

If only she'd had a better relationship with her mother. But she'd raised herself, made mistakes, recovered, and moved on.

The day she lost Walt brought the challenge of her life. *You didn't need him. What could he ever do for you?*

What mother says that to her recently widowed daughter? Amanda wallowed in misery and took it out on Liz, who never would have been that kind of mother to her son.

Those words of hate seared through her heart decades later. The day she'd lost her son she'd walked away from Amanda. She never told her mother she was pregnant. The judgment and opinions sure to be thrown at her like daggers were best not given an audience.

Amanda learned of the baby when Liz started hemorrhaging during a visit of obligation. At least her mother called an ambulance and showed up hours later. *The world doesn't need another bastard child.*

She never saw her mother again. Liz was a widow, her deceased son far from a bastard child. And none of it was anybody's business.

With her shoulders snapped back, she shook her arms, purging tension from every fiber of her being.

She placed the book on an end table in the living room. A walk would do her good. She went into the kitchen and poured a glass of ice water with lemon from the fridge. The cool liquid soothed her nerves as it ran through her body.

Struggling to keep her feelings of her mother at rest, she couldn't help when something triggered a memory she thought she had come to terms with. *Enough.*

An enjoyable evening would be welcome. Will's insistence to drive out to Harwood could be the break she needed to spread her wings.

Even if it was only to a steak house the next town over.

She checked her makeup in the reflection of the toaster. A little less foundation and eye shadow didn't show the wrinkles as much. Plus, she didn't give the impression she hid from something.

Her stomach growled. She made sure not to eat too much, saving her appetite for a juicy, medium-rare steak dinner.

Hmm, five fifty.

She went back to the living room and glanced out the window. No Will. He hadn't changed much since they were kids so she expected him to show up at six o'clock on the dot. He did what society expected of him. Didn't take risks, which was why she thought he married the witch that left him. Liz never thought that Will really loved his wife. Just got married because that's what you were supposed to do back then.

She pulled out the book again and sat down to read a few lines while she waited.

Pardon me, you didn't come here to listen to me ramble on about my miserable childhood. No, you want to know about the murder.

Ring. The doorbell startled her.

♥ ♥ ♥

Will waited with his hands in his pockets for Liz to come to the door. He made mental notes of what needed to be fixed on the house. New stairs. Front door cracked.

"Well, hello. Right on time like I thought you'd be." Liz smiled and stepped onto the porch.

She looked lovely. He admired her in black dress pants and a red lightweight sweater, something besides the jeans or khakis she wore at work. Good thing he'd showered and shaved so he wouldn't look grungy next to her. He didn't dress to go to a four-star restaurant, but he could pass the dress code in his only suit.

"I hope you're hungry." He held her elbow and helped her down the worn stairs.

"Famished."

"Good, because I heard the chef makes the best steak on the eastern seaboard." Sweat beaded on his palms. At fifty-five, he didn't know how to act on a date. He didn't have a lot of experience. He married right out of high school and didn't have much of a social life. His ex ordered him around, and he listened.

He didn't want to make any mistakes. He reached into his coat pocket, wiping the sweat on the lining, and pulled out his keys.

"Oh, no pickup truck?"

"No. I figured this is the better option." He smiled.

"Nice and fancy."

"I could go get the truck…"

Liz laughed. "No, Will, this is fine. I've never seen you in a car. I thought the truck was all you had."

If Dolores had it her way, all he would have been left with was the run-down pickup. He wasn't much of a fighter, that he knew, and that's why he relied on his attorney, who turned out to be no better than a first-year law student. Mistake made. Lesson learned.

Whatever it took, he would enjoy the rest of his life and put Dolores in the past. That started with this dinner with Liz. He looked forward to a sit-down dinner without her having to leave the conversation to switch out a beer keg. Adam told her repeatedly not to do it, but she waited for no one.

To be honest, Liz worried him a bit. She was sweet, but that attitude of not needing anyone left him feeling out in the cold. Hopefully he would find a way into her world. Maybe he would start by offering to fix her front stairs. But he didn't want to offend her, either.

Damn, dating was tough. Maybe he should forget the whole thing and toss a TV dinner in the oven. *Don't be a fool. You'll be fine.*

He opened the car door for Liz and closed it gently after she settled into the passenger seat. He took a deep breath and cleared his lungs. Out with the old, in with the new. Fresh air to invigorate his senses and get him back on track.

Why worry?

They'd been friends since childhood. The dinner should have no more expectation on it than that. Maybe she didn't even consider the evening a date. He wasn't good at figuring out a woman's expectations or emotional signals. Dolores had reminded him their entire marriage.

He slowly pulled away from the front of Liz's house. "Do you need to stop anywhere along the way?"

She looked straight ahead, her purse in her lap held by both arms cuddling the leather. "Nope. I'm fine. But thanks for asking."

He watched her from the corner of his eye as he maneuvered the car through the small-town streets. Stop signs stood at nearly every corner. A flashing streetlight was on the busiest of roads.

"Will?"

"Yes?"

"How long have we known each other?"

Was that a trick question? He wasn't very good with dates and didn't want to say something that made her appear old to him. "Um, since second grade?"

Safe answer. She couldn't argue that. He remembered the day she walked into the classroom. Long, wavy, brownish-red hair hung in braids. Her shoes were worn and seemed too small for her feet. She had on a yellow cotton dress that had seen too many washes. But there was something special about her. When she smiled at him that day he knew they would be in each other's lives for a long time.

Until Dolores put her hooks into him and made his life hell. It wasn't all her fault. He allowed it and never had the courage to stop her from steamrolling over him. That's why he liked Liz. She let everyone be who they were. No judgment, even though she'd grown up with plenty thrown at her.

"That's right. Just around Easter time." She nodded.

"Yep." He turned onto Junction Road that connected Harwood and Havenport. The restaurant was only a few streets away.

"So we've known each other a long time."

"Uh-huh." Confusion and uncertainty settled in.

"Then tell me something. Are we on frigging date?"

His hands gripped the wheel. If he answered incorrectly, it could ruin the night. But if he told her the truth and it wasn't what she wanted, then…well…it would ruin the night.

Courage doesn't manifest itself. If you want it, go for it.

He pulled into the lot of Albee's Steakhouse and parked the car. He cut off the ignition and turned to Liz.

"Are we on a frigging date? No. We are on a date." He slid his hand to her nape and pulled her into him. His insides trembled, yet he felt confident. Something he'd never experienced with his ex. His lips landed expertly on her mouth.

And he lingered, taking in the passion he longed for.

Chapter Three

Two days had passed since Liz's date with Will. She never thought at her age she would get involved with someone. Especially with a former classmate. She hadn't stopped smiling since he'd unexpectedly kissed her in the restaurant parking lot.

She barely remembered the dinner. Her mind kept returning to his kiss during every course of the meal. She came home that night trying to figure what she needed to do. Would they jeopardize their friendship if they got into a relationship and it didn't work? Could a new level of intimacy change the way they dealt with each other?

Intimacy.

She wasn't ready for that. Conversation, sure. But she hadn't been intimate with anyone since she'd lost her husband. The thought of being with another man frightened her. What if she froze? All the years she had been a faithful widow in spite of what some people in town thought. Had she challenged the gossip, it wouldn't have changed anything. She simply ignored it and let it die away.

Her life wasn't anyone's business, then or now. *Will. Okay, he might need to know something.*

She decided she would play it as she always had. Quiet and keep to herself. At this point, she didn't owe him anything. Well, maybe the dinner she prepared.

Pot roast simmered on the stove. Potatoes boiled in preparation to be mashed. And broccoli. She hoped he liked broccoli. *Who doesn't?* Oh, well, if he didn't, there would be plenty of pot roast. She cleaned up spilled flour on the counter as homemade biscuits baked in the oven.

She had never made a sit-down dinner for anyone. Walt ate in the boat and grabbed sandwiches when he came home for a short time in between trips. She learned how to cook by watching food shows on television. Her mother never made a meal. She could remember one time when her grandmother had cooked a ham, but other than that she had been on her own for most of her life.

Many nights she would stare at the stars and wonder if she had wasted away her existence. Not that she could change any of the past, but she could go in a different direction and bring new experiences into her life—even at her age.

The first place she would start would be to get rid of the house. It needed so much work, and she couldn't afford the major repairs. The two-story structure required too much time to maintain.

She would check with Cooper, the restoration specialist, and see if he wanted to buy it. What little historical value the building had might be enough for him to be interested in restoring it for someone else.

Plus, it was just a house. Wood, glass, and nails. The thought of living on one floor excited her. *Damn.* That meant she'd have to go through stuff and get rid of things.

Ring.

She tossed the tattered dish towel on the counter and left the kitchen to answer the front door, pausing for a second to straighten the hem of her shirt at her hips.

Will's shadow filled the frosted glass.

"Hi." She smiled and motioned him into the vestibule.

He walked in and handed her a bouquet of sunflowers. "They remind me of you. Always cheerful, sunny, and pleasant."

That was sweet of him, but there were plenty of times when she didn't feel like a nice person. She tried her best to keep a positive demeanor, but it was difficult when she felt that everything she did—even getting up for work—took the effort of lifting an elephant off her chest.

"Thank you. They're lovely. And I have the perfect container for them," she fibbed. She never received flowers before and wasn't the type of person to buy them for herself.

She walked into the kitchen. Will stayed behind.

"What can I use?" she whispered to herself. "Hmm. Will, can you come here please?" She couldn't reach the cabinet over the stove.

"Boy, it smells good in here."

"Can you reach up here for me? There's an old glass milk bottle that would be a perfect vase for these."

Will guided her to the side and reached above, opening the cabinet with ease. "Which is it?"

"The clear narrow-neck bottle behind the square bottle." She blushed from embarrassment. He must be wondering why she held on to such useless items.

He pulled the bottle down and filled it with water. "I think this matches. It reminds me of my grandmother's farm. She used to pick wildflowers along the dirt road and fancy up the dinner table with the day's bouquet in a milk bottle."

She felt a little bit better. She'd gone her entire life not caring what people thought of her, and suddenly she had a smidgeon of concern where Will mattered. The dating thing was awkward.

Will placed the floral arrangement in the middle of the kitchen table. She didn't have the heart to tell him that she needed that space to finish preparing their meal. Such a small room to work in and every inch of space was premium.

"Thank you again. Dinner's almost ready. Why don't you go into the living room and put on the television while I finish up in here?"

"You sure? Can I help with anything?"

"Yes, and no. I have everything under control. Dinner will be ready in ten minutes. Look, the dining table is already set. That's how close we are to sitting down."

"Okay."

He strolled into the living room, taking in every bit of information he could. Like it would be the last time he saw her house.

It could be, depending on how the evening went. Her penchant for solitude might kick in and she'd be more comfortable at work. At least there she could be busy and not have to entertain anyone. Just fill the chilled glasses with beer and pass them down the bar.

♥ ♥ ♥

Will's eye caught the plaster walls of Liz's living room. Slight bulges interfered with an almost-perfect finish. The old sea houses couldn't help but get beat up, even inside, from the sea air and winter storms. Even though her house sat away from the water like his, the salt in the air wreaked havoc on the most expensive of building materials.

Some of the transplants from the cities began to use tile and marble as a way to combat the warped wood that the New Englanders embraced. However, tile and marble were a recipe for disaster. Many kids and adults ended up in the emergency rooms with busted ankles and wrists.

No, give him the old weathered wood no matter how warped it got. Something that aged along with a person. It told a story and had character.

"You sure you don't need any help?" he yelled into the kitchen.

As soon as he called out, Liz appeared with the pot roast carved and ready to serve.

"That looks and smells delicious." He got up to help her place the platter on the table.

"I hope you like it. I've never made it before. Not sure why not—it's so easy to cook."

He knew why. It didn't make sense to cook for one person. He learned real fast it was much easier for him to stop at one of the food places in town. Mellie's had the best burgers and Royce's the best steaks.

"Well, I know I'll enjoy it. You can't ruin a pot roast." *What an ass.* He couldn't believe he said that. He meant it as a compliment but it sounded nothing like one.

Just get through dinner.

He discreetly wiped his sweaty palms on his pants. Dinner, that's what they would focus on. Surely at their age they had plenty to discuss.

"So what did you do today?" *That sounded stupid.* "You know what, Liz? I don't know what's going on. I mean, we get along so well, but ever since dinner the other night, it seems like things have changed between us. Or is it just me?"

Liz motioned for him to take a seat. He spread a linen napkin across his lap. She stabbed a piece of roast, put it on his plate, and sighed.

"Of course it's not only you. We've known each other for a lifetime and things are changing between us. We're faced with the 'what if this doesn't work and it kills our friendship?'"

He nodded. That's what worried him, but he couldn't put the words together. He enjoyed how easy he felt around her, except today. As if he had to be on his best behavior because he didn't want to screw up anything.

"I'm so glad you feel the same way. It's an entirely different attitude being a couple. We are a couple, aren't we?"

Liz sat and placed her hand on his. "Let's get through dinner and take on the world's problems instead of figuring out our own right now? Hmm?"

He laughed. "Agreed. Hand me some of those mashed potatoes and the gravy boat. I'm hungry and I'm not going to be shy."

"Good. I'm glad, because I also have apple pie." She ladled gravy over his meat and potatoes.

"Homemade?" His stomach rumbled with excitement. He hadn't had fresh apple pie in years. The last time was when his ex-wife's sister had made it for Thanksgiving.

"Please, with my limited kitchen ability? You're lucky if this pot roast doesn't do you in. I picked it up from Led Zeppoli. I couldn't bake one for what they charge, and they're *soooooo* good."

He nodded. A nice homemade dinner. He'd deal with the bakery pie. At least it wasn't one of those boxed ones from the grocery store.

"Do you mind if I light these?" Liz pointed to two taper candles in the middle of the table. "I enjoy burning candles, especially when I eat or read."

"I don't mind at all." Even if he did, would it matter? It was her house. He just hoped they weren't those fruity or floral smells that made him gag.

She reached across him and lit the wicks. *No fruity smell.* He sighed with relief. This wasn't the time to get nitpicky, but sometimes he blurted out stuff without thinking first. That used to annoy his ex-wife, and he didn't want to start off on bad terms with Liz.

They ate quietly while he strained to think of what to talk about. *No politics. No religion.* Even on his best days, he made a point to stay away from those topics.

He swallowed a bite of potatoes and cleared his throat. "So how do you like working for Adam?"

Liz laid her fork on the edge of her plate. "He's a sweetheart to work for. Very considerate and caring. He's a hard worker himself, so you don't mind doing extra."

"He seems to treat you well." He bit a piece of pot roast. The perfect balance of garlic, salt, and black pepper burst in his mouth.

"Yes, very. I wish I had agreed to work for him sooner. I was afraid to put all my eggs in one basket."

"What do you mean?"

"Oh, you know. With juggling my other jobs. If one ended, I had the others to carry me through. Working for one place... Well, what happens if he closes the place or decides that he no longer wants or needs me to work there?"

"Point made, but isn't it easier to worry about one job instead of many?"

"*Touché*." Liz laughed.

Her smile warmed his heart. For too many years he'd watched her carry a look of concern on her face.

He wanted to make sure she would be happy.

♥ ♥ ♥

Liz cleared the table as Will wiped a spittle of gravy from the corner of his mouth. He seemed to enjoy the meal.

He stood up from the table and gently took her wrist as she reached for his empty dinner plate. "I'm not letting you clean up by yourself. I can imagine the work you put into this meal, especially after working at the tavern all day."

"I won't argue. Are you washing or drying?"

"Washing." He carried two handfuls of dirty dinnerware to the kitchen sink. "I don't know where anything goes. I can't do any harm washing the dishes."

"And pots." She pointed to a gravy-soaked pan on the stove.

He hung his head. "Of course. And pots."

"You never tell me about your workday." Liz stacked the dishes on the counter to the side of the sink.

Will turned the water on until steam scorched the tip of his nose, then scrubbed the dishes with detergent and a sponge. She could never wash a dish with water that hot.

He must not have any feeling in his hands. She wondered how that would translate into him touching her. *Hmm.*

She shook her head to clear the thought. Why did she even think that way? She couldn't go there. It had been so long, she wasn't even sure what to expect or how to act in a relationship. She put too much pressure on herself. And him.

Friends. That's how they were going to start. It would be better if they got to know each other as adults. They weren't those same kids who'd met in grade school.

But what could they do to move them along?

"There's not much to say. Something breaks and I fix it. End of story."

"There has to be more in your life." She wanted to smack herself. Those words sounded like a therapist helping Will find his passion.

He shook his head. "Um, nope. You know Dolores packed up and left. No kids. No pets. Just my work, then me going home to an empty house. One that needs a lot of fixing, but I'm not in the mood to work on it once I get home."

Boy did she understand. If she hadn't decided to buy her house, she wouldn't even have that worry. For the longest time she'd put off becoming a homeowner, but a dip in the housing market changed her mind.

Though cheap and in need of repairs, she quickly came to appreciate that no one could ever tell her to move. It belonged to her. She paid it off in ten years and the taxes were hardly anything since it needed so much work. Some of the repairs, like the roof, couldn't be put off any longer and would need to be taken care of soon. She hated to deplete her savings, but didn't have a choice.

"Will?" She lowered her head, unsure how to ask him to do something for her. She wiped the last dish dry and put it in the cupboard.

"Yeah?" He turned on the water and sprinkled cleanser into the porcelain sink.

She watched him scrub the yellowed sink with cleanser. She had never seen it sparkle so much. He even scrubbed the silver drain and basket. He might be worth keeping around, just for his cleaning skills.

She stifled a laugh. "I need some work done on the house. And…"

"You want me to do it." He smiled.

"No. I mean, maybe. Not necessarily. Over the years, I've had a few people give me quotes but I never knew if they were taking advantage of me. So I guess what I'm asking is, can you look around? Tell me what I absolutely have to have done. Nothing that *should be* but doesn't *have to be*, at least not right now. Only what…"

"I get it. The big stuff that matters—roof, basement, stairs. Stuff that could end up getting someone hurt if it's ignored any longer."

She smiled. "Yes. I'm kind of embarrassed to even ask this but I know I've been neglecting the place."

He took her hand. "Listen, tonight we are on a non-date, but that doesn't mean that we have to talk about stuff that can be discussed anywhere."

She followed him into the living room and sat on the couch next to him. "Thank you."

"Tonight let's see where the conversation takes us. I'll come look the place over this Sunday. Does that work for you?"

"Sure. It's not like I'll be in church."

"Yeah, me, either. So I'll be over around noon. In the meantime, let's find something else to discuss or we could watch TV if you want. No pressure."

That's what it was.

She hadn't been able to put her finger on it until now. The pressure of her own expectations weighed on her. Not by him.

The more time she spent with him, the more her reserve weakened. Not because she didn't want to be with him, but it made her vulnerable and she didn't like that.

Maybe a game of cards. The clock read seven thirty. She didn't want to send him home so early, but nothing physical was going to happen between them.

Was this how older people dated? Would she be comfortable getting to know someone on an intimate level at her age? It's not that she thought of herself as old, just not curious like a teenager would be.

"Oh, I want to show you something." She reached into the end table drawer and removed the tattered journal. "Look at this."

Will leaned closer. The heat of his cheek reached hers. "Yours?"

"No, but somehow I feel connected. I think that's why I'm curious, yet reluctant, to read it. Adam found this shoved in the basement rafters. I haven't read much and can barely make out some of the writing. The ink is faded. Looks like fountain pen."

Will gently pulled the book a little closer to him.

"I imagine so. Wagon wheels on a dusty road. I don't think ballpoint pens existed back then."

She moved away to put some distance between them. The intimacy level ratcheted up and made her uncomfortable. "Iced tea. Would you like some?"

"Sure."

She closed the journal and placed it on the end table. "I hope you don't mind homemade."

"Not at all."

Chapter Four

Will watched her leave, then opened the book to where Liz had inserted a scrap of paper for a bookmark.

Anyway, I fixed my hair before heading downstairs. It had been a dry summer and the townsmen would scatter seashells on the road to hold down the dusty dirt and keep it from swirling around into the buildings. We kept our windows open back then. No cooled air for us. That would come later.

The carriage wheels crushed the shells spread on the makeshift road in front of the saloon. The noise ricocheted in the night air.

I couldn't help but peek out the window. A knot in my stomach yanked tighter as each shell gave way. I was used to boots pounding the weathered floorboards of the front porch, but each step pounded heavier than the last. My gut told me to stay upstairs, but my hunger to know tugged me away from my safe zone.

"Ah, you couldn't stay away from it." Liz laughed as she handed him a tall glass of iced tea with a lemon wedge on the rim.

He thought he may have invaded her privacy, but it's not like the words were hers. Still, he realized she might consider it differently.

"Sorry. I didn't mean to intrude. I enjoy history. It's not often you come across something of a personal history, especially in this town."

Liz waved her hand. "No problem. I didn't know you liked stuff like this."

She joined him on the couch, seeming more relaxed. He followed her cue.

"Yes, I used to write a little. I'd…oh, you'd think it was silly."

Liz sat back and placed her hand on his knee. "Tell me."

"When I would work in some of the old houses around here, I would imagine stories within their walls and sometimes write what I imagined to have happened."

"Will, I never would have thought such a thing."

"See, I told you it was silly." He sipped his drink.

"No, it's not. It shows you have an imagination."

"That I do. I've wanted to get out of this town for years. Not so much to move and leave permanently, but to see how life is in other places. Dolores…"

"You don't have to avoid her. I know she was a part of your life for a long time."

He dropped his head and muttered, "Too long. We never should have been together. I mean, she's not a horrible person, but we wanted different things."

Liz stared into his eyes as he spoke. She got him, and that's what always attracted him to her. He held his breath for a second. *It's now or never.*

He put his drink on the coffee table. Liz quickly placed a coaster underneath the glass. "Sorry. Habit."

"I have to be honest with you." He turned to her and brought her hands to his chest.

Liz's eyes followed his.

"I—I know this has been awkward, but there is a reason and I'm not sure how to explain it." His chest tightened enough to cause him to halt his breathing for a second. What if he royally screwed up their friendship?

"Just get on with it. What are you dying or something?" She laughed.

He cleared his throat. "Not that I know of, but you might have a role in accomplishing that."

"Stop joking. What's up?"

"Me and Dolores, we were married a long time. Didn't always get along, but we were married."

"Yeah, so."

"I think part of the reason I could never surrender my heart to her is because it belonged elsewhere and I was too stupid to do anything about it."

Liz squirmed in her seat but didn't pull away.

"Will you just spit it out? You've never had a problem saying anything."

Her hands tightened in his. A deep breath soothed his chest and helped him to focus. "Okay, here goes. How long have we known each other?"

Liz squinted her eyes and tilted her head. "Hmm. Let me see…a very long time. Months, years, decades. Your point?"

"Fifty-four, to be exact. Remember we had that split class? You were in second and I was in third? The two grades shared a classroom because there weren't enough kids of one grade to fill a room?"

"Yes." Her eyes narrowed, as if she were trying to solve a complicated puzzle.

"Well." He rubbed her hands and gently squeezed them. "Since you walked into class that day, I knew you were going to be special. What I didn't know at that time, until years later, is that I would fall in love with you."

He dropped his shoulders, feeling like a thousand-pound weight had rolled off his back.

Liz sat back, pulling her hands away. "What? You were married, for cripe's sake. How do I factor into the picture?"

He stood and paced the floor in between the television and coffee table. "I knew I should have kept my mouth shut. It was stupid to say anything."

Liz folded her arms across her chest. "Slow down. I wouldn't say it was stupid. Unexpected? Yes. Are you sure?"

He nodded. "Since sixth grade. And again in eighth grade. And in high…"

"Stop." She held her hand out, palm facing his chest like she wanted to stop a runaway train. "How could you go all these years and never say anything to me? I mean, we've spent hours talking."

"I was married."

"After your divorce. How could I not pick up on something?" She shook her head.

"Maybe you didn't want to."

She looked him straight in the eyes. "No, it wasn't that. I never knew you felt about me in that way. I thought you only considered me a friend. Plus, you were dating Dolores right out of junior high."

"True, but we were too young to marry. You know how guys are."

♥ ♥ ♥

Liz yanked her hands from his grip and stepped back. "Oh really? Go ahead. Tell me how guys are.'"

Will heaved a heavy sigh and scratched his head. She hoped he didn't mean anything by what he'd said. Will had a way of saying the right thing the wrong way. It had gotten him in trouble all the time with the ex. Liz thought he'd gotten better since Dolores left and he wasn't on edge.

He reached for her.

"Explain yourself first."

"Guys are stupid. We wait too long to figure things out. We think things just happen. We don't need to work on relationships."

"Stop. I get your point. You sound like a self-help book. I think you can stop reading it."

He took her hand. "I'm trying to tell you it has always been you, only I didn't act on my feelings when I should have. Plus, you took off for two years. No explanation. Nothing. By that time, I'd married Dolores and figured that would be my life until one of us croaked."

Her stomach sank. It's not like she could have said she had the same feelings for Will for as long as he, but she enjoyed spending time with him now. Maybe it was time to tell him about those missing years.

She walked him to the kitchen table and sat across from him. "About that time."

Will lowered his head and looked up into her eyes. "Go on."

"I met Walt when I worked at Corky's after school in my senior year."

"I never heard you talk about a Walt."

"You're correct. You know me. I keep my business to myself, even though it's backfired because people like to make up their own stories."

"I think it's because you are so secretive in a town where everyone's business is fair game. Mainly because someone else's life is more interesting than their own."

"All the more reason to keep quiet. That trait comes from my mother. The less you say, the less people are involved. Anyway, Walt worked on one of the lobster boats as a first mate. Our relationship played out in between me serving coffee and him returning with lobster traps for the market."

"You fell in love with him?"

"I did. Crazy in love. Walt had an opportunity to buy into his own boat up in Gloucester, so he told me and I agreed to go with him, but only if we were married first."

Will's eyes never wavered as she spoke. Her hands softened in his as she soaked into the comfort he gave her.

"And you did?"

"Yes, but not in Havenport. I didn't even tell my mother, not that she would have celebrated or anything.

Well, you know what our relationship was like. Cordial at best."

Will nodded. "Yes, I remember once when your mother dropped you off at school. I had never seen you so upset. You didn't talk to me for days. I thought I had done something wrong."

"Well, you didn't. Anyway, we married in Provincetown on the way up to Cape Ann. Walt was a good man. Treated me well. Always there for me. Funny." She smiled and remembered back to their wedding day. Walt had picked a bunch of clovers for her bouquet. *If this doesn't bring you luck in this marriage, then nothing will.*

"So we found a little apartment over a store on the main street. I can't even remember the name. A one-bedroom, galley kitchen, and living room. Old but clean, and across the street from the ocean.

"How come you never told me any of this?" Will gently stroked the back of her hand.

"What's to tell until now? It's in the past and it didn't matter."

Will took her chin into his hand. "Are you sure you want to tell me now?"

She pursed her lips. "I guess. I mean, if we're going to do this relationship thing, you should probably know. I'm aware of your baggage."

"Because in this town it's hard not to." He laughed.

"Well, he spent the spring working on the boat that needed much more work than he expected, but he was committed and tackled the job. He paid for it and had no choice but to make his plan work. I waited tables at the local diner. And we did it. The boat was seaworthy in time for lobster season, and Walt figured he would also pull in whatever else he could catch. Then I got pregnant."

Will's face dropped. She watched his expression. His eyes grew even more serious.

"You okay?" She squeezed his fingers.

He nodded. "Continue."

"Walt started working even more hours. Barely sleeping. He wanted to make sure we'd have enough money to care for the baby and so I didn't have to work. He wanted at least one parent to be home with the kid. He wanted a big family. I'd never seen him so happy as when he found out he would be a dad."

Tears welled in her eyes. She fought back the onslaught of pain shooting through her chest. She hadn't thought of that time of her life in decades. Shutting it out made it easy to live with the memory.

Will leaned across the table and hugged her. Her shoulders melted into his body. She felt safe, and he was being genuine. How vulnerable could she allow herself to be?

"So what happened?" he whispered into her ear.

"One day Walt kissed me goodbye. I was only two months along and getting ready for work. I went on with my day slinging dishes and waiting for Walt to come home, but he never did."

"He left you?" Will sat upright, almost angry that Walt would leave her.

"Walt's body washed ashore three days later. His boat a week after. No one ever figured out what happened. No storm. The boat had been fixed so there wasn't anything wrong with it. But he made a mistake and went alone. He got into trouble, and no one knew what happened on that boat."

"And the child?"

"Stillborn at five months." She wiped a tear and turned from him.

♥ ♥ ♥

It had been two days since Liz told Will what happened to Walt. He couldn't push her for more information. His chest ached every time he thought of her recanting the loss of her husband. He should never have let her keep on talking, dredging up a painful past. Liz never brought up the loss of her baby, and he knew enough not to pry. She would tell him if she wanted him to know.

He planned to surprise her for lunch. Liz worked a split shift so she would have plenty of time for a break. He finished up early, which he liked to do on Fridays so he could have a longer weekend. Plus, he had an extra-special present for Liz and he wanted to give it to her at Royce's. This way she wouldn't make a scene if she turned it down.

Liz sat with her back turned to him in a booth across from the end of the bar. Her favorite place to hide when she wasn't on the clock. He walked up behind her, brushed her hair aside, and kissed her on the back of her neck. She spun around.

"You scared me."

"Do many men kiss you like that?" He slid into the booth to sit across the table from her.

"No, and that's a dangerous way to approach someone, especially in a bar."

"Restaurant," he corrected.

"Whatever. We serve liquor, it's a bar."

"That serves the best steaks in town. I'm hungry."

"You're in luck. Word has it that I'm available for lunch. Wings for me."

He appreciated a woman who wasn't afraid to eat. No salads unless she wanted one and not because she wanted to appear delicate. Liz was the strongest woman he knew.

"Your usual?"

He nodded.

"Cathy, medium-rare steak, mashed potatoes, mushroom gravy, green beans for him. I'll have diablo wings, coleslaw, and corn on the cob. Thanks, dear."

"No meal?" He slid off his windbreaker.

"That is my meal. I pick when I'm here. Plus, I'll eat later tonight."

He sat back and wondered what happened to her baby. He tried not to dwell on it, but when he looked at her he imagined a child alongside her. She would tell him if she wanted him to know.

"Hey, I have a surprise for you." He reached in his jacket pocket. "I know you're not going to fight me on this so I will warn you up front, there is no negotiation." He slid an envelope from Havenport Travel Agency across the table.

"What?" Liz opened the packet.

"You deserve it. You need a vacation. No strings attached. You have your own room, so no pressure. I thought that both of us needed a break from this place, and since we're friends first, what harm would it be to go away together?"

She stared at two plane tickets to Bermuda. "Will, I can't accept this."

"Accept nothing. I want to travel. I don't want to go alone and I thought you could use a change of scenery."

Liz closed the envelope. "Does this have anything to do with what I told you the other day?"

"No, not at all. Thanks, Cathy." Will took a steaming pumpernickel roll from the basket on the table.

"You sure?"

He buttered the roll and handed it to Liz, taking another for him. "I'm sure. Look, I've been here my whole life. Never went anywhere because Dolores didn't want to. Well, I want to see something besides old houses, broken-down docks, and the same Main Street every day."

He gulped down his water.

Liz sat back, her fingers tapping on the table. He stared into her eyes, watching her consider the offer.

"Me, too. The only time I left here was to go to Gloucester, which looks the same as Havenport." Liz clasped her hands together. "No strings attached?"

"Nope, none. I just want a travel partner. It wouldn't be any fun on my own. Who would I have to talk to? Don't you want to try one of those piña coladas?"

That brought a smile to her face. She seemed to lighten up and sit higher in her chair. He studied her face for disagreement or objection.

"Here you go." Cathy placed their meals on the table. "Enjoy."

"I think you have yourself a travel buddy. I have to talk to Adam." Liz picked up a hot wing and offered him a bite.

"Already done. I spoke to him before I bought the tickets."

"That's mighty bold of you. What if I would have said no?"

"Then I would have asked Adam to go. He seemed keen on the idea."

She blushed.

He played it well. Seeing a smile on her face made him happy, and that was all he needed. The trip would give them a chance to get to know each other in a different environment.

"What if I didn't want to go to Bermuda?" She wiped her hot-sauced-stained hands on a wet towel.

"Then we would choose someplace else. We're not fixed into the place. You want to go somewhere else? We'll go. Just tell me what you want to do."

She sat back and crossed her arms. "There is a place I've always wanted to go, but I don't think I'm ready for a trip like that."

"Where?"

"England. I've always wanted to see a castle in person. To walk the halls like our ancestors did. Speaking of which, want to see where Adam found that journal I showed you the other night?"

"Sure, after we finish our lunch?"

"Well, hurry up."

"Did you finish reading it?"

"No. I want to take a night when I have nothing else to do. Make a cup of hot chocolate and immerse myself in the mystery of her life. So far I've learned that this place really had been a brothel."

"That's the legend." He scooped up the last bite of mashed potatoes.

"Her journal mentions that on the first page. So there's proof. Isn't that an interesting history to have in this town?"

"I would think brothels were a commonplace business back then. Men moving around all the time. Needing attention, that kind of thing."

"Will! I'm surprised to hear you talk like that."

"What? It's not that I think it should be like that. I'm just saying given the period of time, I doubt women found this place too exciting. Hundreds of years later, neither me or you find it very thrilling."

"Maybe it's not an exciting city, but I love this town. That's why I came back here after the ba…"

He lifted his head from his plate. "What?"

"I didn't finish telling you the other day, but after Walt washed up, I lost the baby. That's why I came back to Havenport. I needed to be in a place that embraced me. This has been my home. My safe harbor."

Chapter Five

Liz thought it best to take a break from Will for a few days. It wasn't that she didn't want to see him, but she needed to come to terms with her confession.

And if they were going to be together on a trip, she wanted to take advantage of all the alone time she could.

The sun burned strong for a May morning. She took her tea on the back porch along with the journal and set them on a side table.

Witch hazel grew against the railing and lilacs released a subtle scent. She stretched out on the wicker lounge that had seen better days. She'd wanted to replace the outdoor furniture many times, but couldn't justify spending the money. She planned to live the rest of her life on her own and not answer to anyone. Life certainly threw her a curveball when Will got involved.

Was she so set in her ways there wasn't room for anyone else? *Possible.*

She would have to be more trusting if her relationship was going to work. She'd become so conditioned to shut out people, she felt like she had cut herself open with a knife when she revealed her marriage and miscarriage to

Will. She didn't know how to handle being so vulnerable. Her insides trembled when she relived the moment.

Enough of that.

She sunk into the pillow seat that remembered every curve of her body and closed her eyes, book resting on her chest. The sun stayed out of her eyes thanks to the porch roof. She thought of slinging a hammock at the other end of the porch but never got around to it, afraid she would get stuck. She couldn't remember the last time she took a midday nap, and relaxation won over her desire to read.

For just a few…

Her eyes were too heavy to open so she gave in to the demands of her body. She imagined herself floating on the clouds above. Birds singing as they flew by. Each wisp of air bringing her higher, away from the boredom of her life.

A day to herself, no one to ask anything of her. It was an unusual transition. Keeping busy for so long and now settling into a stable schedule would take time to accept.

The book weighed heavy on her chest, and she opened her eyes in an attempt to read it. The sun had shifted and challenged her ability to see. She closed her eyes and waited for a cloud to block the rays.

She hovered between sleep and wakefulness. *A young boy reached his hand out to her. He said nothing. She couldn't see his face clearly, but he felt familiar. She squeezed her eyes tighter, hoping to clear the fog that kept him hidden. She tried to walk toward him but he stepped back with each advance. She struggled to wake.*

It wasn't the first time she had that dream. She woke with sweat on her chest. Sometimes her dream involved Walt standing on the sea, waving goodbye, then sinking into the ocean. She shook her head to clear the images that had haunted her for decades. She knew she should have done more to move on with her life, but each step sucked her in like quicksand.

Maybe Will knew what she needed when he offered the trip. He would be good company. She would have her own room to retire to whenever she felt she needed to be alone. Even the brochure had said the balcony off her room would be separate from his.

She would have to kick in money for her portion of the trip. Under no circumstances could she could accept his generosity. No, if she paid her way, then she owed nobody anything and she could enjoy the trip on her terms. That's the only way for it to work for her.

Good. She'd found a way to be comfortable with the situation. The sun glare lessened and she sat up and opened the book. She held it tightly and focused on getting to know who'd written the words. To see if she could feel a presence. She had that gift at times. Call it intuition, but she considered herself a person who could get to the meaning beneath the obvious.

I pulled stray strands of hair from my silver-plated hairbrush and tucked it in my vanity drawer. They were the only belongings I had from my mother. I had already lived longer than she did, and I couldn't imagine her to be anything more than a ghost in my past. I guess that's what happens when only you survive childbirth.

Pow. Pow. Pow.

I ran to my bedroom door, but an unseen force held me back. I don't know if it was fear or a sense of danger that made me stop. Or something that I couldn't see. Whatever it was wouldn't allow me to leave the room.

I pressed my ear against the crack where the warped door met the jamb. A draft filled the space between the side of my face and the cracked wood of the doorframe.

The piano music stopped and glasses shattered.

"I told you to stay off my property."

I recognized Murphy Walsh's baritone voice. His whisper could reverberate throughout the sawmill. The knot in my stomach twisted tighter. The hair on my neck stood up.

Pow.

A chill ran down Liz's spine. The style of the girl's handwriting was captivating. Crisp, clean lines, each letter slanted perfectly, but her words brought fear. How horrible to be so young and live a life like that. To grow up in a whorehouse fearing lawlessness.

She continued to read.

Screaming filled the downstairs and carried up to my room. The pit of my stomach sank like a cannonball.

"Damn you, Walsh. What's the matter with you? You shoot a man in cold blood in front of a saloon full of witnesses?" Sheriff Hankle yelled. He would have no choice but to lock up Old Man Murphy. Any resident of Havenport knew not to step foot on Walsh soil. Whoever had was foolish and likely dead after the gun went off.

With no reason to get involved, I pulled the pin from my bun and crawled into bed. Someday I would get out of this town. I wouldn't sell my body like the other women did, but I would find some way to leave this place and find a home.

As good as Miss Tilly is to me, this life is not what I yearn for. The big lights. A bustling city. Not some place where my hair smells like fish on a good day.

♥ ♥ ♥

Will showed up at Liz's house like he'd promised. Her parked car sat in the driveway, but he would take inventory of repairs outside first. No sense in bothering her until he knew what had to be done. He wanted to focus on the safety concerns and keep her costs down. No one ever got rich working and living in Havenport, so he didn't want to come up with costs that would outprice the house.

He bounced on each stair as he walked up the front steps. The boards were thin in areas and split where attached to the stringers. The railings rocked as he tested them. The entire front stairs would have to be replaced. An easy fix. Only four steps. He should have enough spare wood in his workshop. The materials had already been paid for and left over from other jobs so he wouldn't pass the cost on to Liz.

Dolores used to complain he made their place look like a junkyard, but he knew what he had, and everything was organized for easy access.

He saved his customers money when he could. All he needed was enough to live on, make his bills, and have a little extra. Maybe Dolores believed that he wasn't driven enough, but his method worked for him.

With the steps assessed, he moved on to the front porch. No soft spots on the planks and the railings were sturdy. The porch roof helped protect the wood from the elements.

Overall, good old craftsmanship. He missed that in new buildings, though Cooper Smith brought that back with his rehabilitation business. He liked working with Cooper when the opportunity arose. Good man.

Will examined the doorway. Nice hand-carved molding, a simple fluted design that would be easy to patch with wood filler and then restain. The cedar shingles were weathered—he'd expected them to be, given the location—but they seemed strong, so a stain or paint job would help spruce up the look of the house.

Estimating the work to be done on Liz's place made him think of what waited for him at his house. He thought it would be easier to burn it down and start over. Maybe once he purged the contents to a manageable level it wouldn't seem so bad. He wouldn't allow Liz into his place until he cleaned it up.

He rang the doorbell and waited.

Nothing.

He peeked into the living room window and didn't see her. She had to be home, unless she'd gone for a walk.

Will walked around the foundation to look for deficiencies. These old bricks were notorious for the mortar flaking away and leaving them loose enough to let critters find a way into a warm house. He kept on top of this with his house. He hated mice and made sure they wouldn't have an easy way into his home.

He walked around the left side of the house and stumbled over a wooden cellar door, built on a forty-five-degree angle, attached to the house. The type where the doors opened outward so one could climb down cement stairs to get underground. Those freaked him out. They were creepy, especially when looking at them from the basement. His grandmother had them, and it frightened him anytime she'd asked him to go into the basement at night. Moonlight would seep through the brittle doors, and he swore he'd see things move. Could have been his childhood imagination running wild, but he never got over that.

Liz's doors would be the first thing to go. He could make a nice root cellar or cold storage out of that space and give her a regular door that wouldn't trip someone.

From his vantage point on the ground, it seemed the roof shingles had some life left in them, so he could save her money on those, at least for the time being.

He walked deeper into the yard and over iron brush that scraped his knees through his jeans. *Damn wild rose.* He made a note to rip them out. It didn't matter how pretty the flowers looked when in bloom. They were a hazard to walk through.

"Yeow!" His toe stubbed hard on the weeds. "What the hell?"

He put on his worn leather work gloves and pulled away one thick stalk of bramble out of the ground. He cautiously poked his toe through the mess in front of him.

Beneath his foot lay a flat stone. He pulled a tangled mass of dead roots and intertwined branches apart. His hand followed the edge of stone along the ground up approximately two and a half feet, then two feet across the top. A headstone.

But whose?

Sgt. Frederick McCallister
Died for his country this day
April 12th, 1865

McCallister? McCallister?

A familiar name, but he couldn't place it. There were so many families playing around in people's yards that he wouldn't be surprised if his house stood on a few bones.

"What are you doing back here?" Liz stood at her back door with her hands on her hips, as if scolding him for sneaking onto her property.

"I told you the other day I would stop by on Sunday to take inventory of home repairs. You've got quite a list here. Starting with this dead guy." He pointed to the tombstone.

Liz walked down the stairs. "What do you mean?"

He waved his hand to bring her closer to the plot and pulled back the brush so she could get a better look. "This. You didn't know it was here?"

"Nope. Nothing was ever mentioned about it when I bought the house."

"Didn't you have an inspection?" He narrowed his eyes.

"Yeah, they said the house should be burned down and rebuilt." Liz laughed. "But I bought it anyway. I could afford the house."

"Still, this should have been marked on the survey."

"I didn't get one—well, not a new one. I think the one I have is as old as the house itself. I cut expenses where I could. It's not like much has changed since this town settled. Well, except for the waterfront. Those damn rich people tearing down the waterfront warehouses and putting up those buildings that block everyone's view of the sea. That always annoyed me."

"This must be on the survey. Do you have it?" He let go of the weeds and rubbed his palms together to get rid of the brittle wood flakes.

"Somewhere. It's one of those I-need-to-do-this-one-day projects."

He knew that well. His house kept piling up with stuff long past its life expectancy: papers, mail, plastic bags. He never seemed to find the time to sort through his chaos and get his house in order.

Will watched Liz tap her fingers on arms folded across her chest. "Are you bothered by something?"

♥ ♥ ♥

Liz didn't have the heart to tell him she wanted to be alone. She planned to be by herself today and think through her relationship with him. Too much had happened in a short period of time. The relationship with Will put pressure on her. She kept reliving the losses of her husband and baby in her mind, and needed time to decompress and let the stimulation settle down. After Will reminded her that he'd promised to be there on Sunday, she remembered the "date." She softened her stance. Maybe she should ask him in for coffee. After all, he did come out as he said he would.

"Do you have time to stop in?" She smiled.

"You have coffee ready?" He shoved his pencil and pad into his back pocket.

"Always. I couldn't get through a day without it, but you know that." She smiled and walked up the back steps. He followed her and opened the door to let her go through first. "Always a gentleman."

"I try to be."

For the first time, she noticed his eyes were blue and had tiny wrinkles at the corners. He looked younger than fifty-five. She credited his new healthy glow to being rid of Dolores. That woman could bring anyone down and drown them in misery. He'd been saddled with a woman who didn't respect him. She'd never figure how he'd tolerated his ex.

"Have a seat." She motioned to the kitchen chair next to the back window. Her favorite place in the house, especially when the sun's rays streamed through in the early morning. She would sit at the table, coffee mug in hand, and watch the hummingbirds gather at the two feeders. Once in a while she would see a bold squirrel standing on the porch rail trying to reach the cracked corn in the feeders meant for the blue jays.

It would be nice to have someone sitting at the table with her who loved nature as she did. Could that person be Will? She wasn't sure, but he seemed to be in the running.

Guilt swelled through her as she'd just wanted him to leave her alone so she could be with her thoughts. Maybe he knew better and they needed to be around each other to sort it out.

Will got up from the table and grabbed cream from the refrigerator. She poured a cup of coffee in a mug with a surface crack down its side and joined him at the table.

"Does the name McCallister mean anything to you?" She peered over her steaming cup.

Will shook his head. "Nope, not immediately. For a minute it sounded familiar but I couldn't place it."

She squirmed in her chair. "Do you think there's a real body in there?"

"As opposed to a fake body?" Will laughed.

"Don't be sarcastic. You know what I mean. Maybe it's just a memorial stone. No body fertilizing my weeds. People do that all the time when a person is presumed dead and the remains aren't recovered."

"Hmm. Could be. I think it's worth checking out."

"Where would we even start?" He didn't slurp his coffee. She liked that.

"My guess would be the library. Wilma still works there and is pretty good at keeping records of old things in this town."

"You're right. I say we go now." She stood up, eager to get started. The dead guy in her yard creeped her out the more she pictured him buried a few feet from her kitchen door. Chills ran up her back. She was spooked more than she'd expected at having an unknown corpse in her backyard. The sooner she could find out who it belonged to, the quicker she could get it off her property.

"It's Sunday."

"So? We'll go to Martha's house instead. She would love the company. She's been bored out of her mind ever since she retired from the library."

Will finished his coffee and took their cups and washed them. She wasn't used to having someone do little things like that. Walt wasn't the most considerate person. Oh, he was good to her, but he wasn't one for details. She enjoyed having Will around. Why did she ever think to put some distance between them?

Relax. She would have to work on letting him get closer.

"Ready?" Will extended his hand.

"Up for a walk? Martha's not too far from here. We'll see what she knows, and if we have to go to the library at a later time, we can."

They headed out the back door. She took a picture of the headstone with her phone. She'd been living there for decades and had no idea. She lacked the skills of a gardener, but couldn't believe she hadn't come upon the stone.

And the one time a neighborhood kid had cut the grass in the backyard, he'd never said a word. Maybe that's why he never came back.

She slipped her hand into Will's as they headed down her street. He squeezed her fingers ever so slightly.

"You had no idea you had a dead body in your backyard?"

"My answer hasn't changed. No." She laughed. "Why would I keep that a secret?"

"Devalued property?" He squeezed her hand tighter.

She appreciated his attempt at humor and conversation. She knew her awkwardness got in the way of their relationship moving forward. Would she ever trust someone enough to surrender her heart with abandon?

Probably not. Though she wanted to open up to Will. A life of hurt and rejection made it difficult.

But she pushed through. It was a start, and it seemed like Will was willing to take it slow and let her move at her own pace. He was a great guy, eager to please. She'd sensed that back when they were kids, but she was busy taking care of her mother and never had a chance to enjoy being a kid.

The one regret she had in life was she never put herself first, which was ironic since she had been alone most of her life. Even at work she did what the customers or her boss wanted. She didn't like conflict—she'd had enough of that with her mother.

Chapter Six

"It's beautiful today. I haven't taken a walk through town in a long time." Will closed his eyes and took a moment to bask in the May sun and let it warm his face.

"I like this time of year. Wildflowers in bloom. Look at Martha's yard." Liz pointed over the white picket fence lining the property. "Her house looks like a New England postcard. I always thought Martha had the cutest house in town."

"Have you ever been inside?"

"No. Never a reason to. I see her around town mostly."

"I was in there once to do some repair work on a kitchen window. It's just like you would imagine."

Liz stopped at the gate and faced him. "And how would I imagine that?"

"Um, wainscot on the walls. Simple but functional decor. A bowl of lemons on the kitchen table for two."

"Seriously?"

"Let's see." He opened the gate and held Liz's hand until they'd walked up the front steps. A white rocking chair sat at the far end of the porch. A calico cat lay on guard in the windowsill. "You sure she won't mind us stopping over without calling first? She can be kind of strange."

"I'm sure it's fine." Liz knocked on the front door.

The cat didn't move an inch. A low purr escaped its lips as it ignored them and continued sleeping. He preferred dogs but wasn't home enough to care for one. Never had a liking for cats.

They waited for Martha to answer the door. He heard a meow on the other side. "Cat lady?"

Liz laughed. "What makes someone a cat lady?"

"A person who has more than one cat."

"Not a cat person?"

"Nope."

He hoped he didn't across as too mean toward cats. It's not that he hated them, he just couldn't connect with them like he did with dogs. They were loyal, helpful, a solid companion. Cats, well…they were good for keeping windowsills free of dust.

"Hmm, no answer. I know she's home. Her car's in the driveway." Liz leaned over the porch railing. "Martha!"

He jumped at the timbre of her voice, having never heard Liz yell like that. Will walked down the steps to the stone walk leading to the backyard. He could make out a rake and wheelbarrow where the stone met the grass.

"Come on. I think she's in the back."

Liz joined him and walked up the pavers. Sure enough, they found Martha hunched over a pile of fallen branches and weeds she must have ripped out of the ground.

"Martha," Liz called out in a much softer tone.

Will didn't wait for Martha to open the gate. He swung it open and let Liz walk through first. Martha stood and shielded her eyes from the sun.

"Hi. What brings you here this gorgeous May afternoon?"

Liz cupped Martha's elbow to help her cross over foot-high edging separating her garden from the lawn.

"I need to pick your brain about something that might be of interest to the history of Havenport," said Liz.

"Iced tea? Lemonade?" Martha rubbed her dirty hands on her denim shirt.

He smiled. Typical. When he worked for her, Martha never let him go thirsty. "Lemonade for me."

"Iced tea." Liz nodded.

"Be right back. Got to clean up my hands first. Have a seat in the gazebo." Martha ran up the back stairs that led into her kitchen.

"I've never been back here. It's beautiful," Liz said.

"Yeah, she keeps it nice. Too much work for me. If it were up to me, I would blacktop every blade of grass on my property." He escorted Liz to sit.

"Why?" She sat on the gazebo bench.

"Don't get me wrong. I like the yard, but its upkeep is way down on my priority list." He had grown resentful of having to care for it when Dolores still lived with him. She would buy hundreds of dollars' worth of plants, but would expect him to clear the yard, keep it weed free, and maintain the plants. They were her plants—she should care for them. He never minded keeping the grass cut but didn't appreciate the extra work put on him.

"I can understand that. I work so many hours that I'd forget I had a backyard, as you discovered today. Maybe I need to look further into what might be there. Maybe there's an entire cemetery with who-knows-what buried in the dirt." Liz shuddered.

"Don't get yourself crazy thinking of things that might not even be." He remembered that about her. When she was a teenager she would worry about what *could* happen instead of focusing on that moment. He knew she didn't have it easy growing up and assumed she was being proactive by thinking ahead to ward off an unnecessary or avoidable crisis.

"You're right. I keep telling myself it's a memorial stone. Nothing to worry about." Liz leaned into his chest.

He pulled her closer. A soft scent of lilac came from her hair. He buried his nose in the loose waves. "Don't worry. I'm sure it's nothing."

Martha walked toward them carrying a wooden tray with a clear glass pitcher of lemonade complete with fresh lemon slices floating in the drink. He assumed the other plastic container held iced tea.

"Here we go." Martha set the tray down on a small wooden octagon snack table. "There, all cleaned up and ready for a conversation."

Martha poured the respective glasses of refreshments.

"So how can I help you?" Martha sipped her share of iced tea.

"Well…" he started.

Liz jumped into the conversation. "Will found something in my backyard and I don't know what to do with him."

"Him?" Martha asked.

"Ah, yes," Will interjected.

"A dead person," Liz whispered. "At least I think it's a dead person. There's a tombstone with the name Sergeant Frederick McCallister."

Martha slammed her glass on the table. "Well, I'll be. They did it. The family buried him right in plain sight."

Martha leaned back with her hand clasped over her mouth, her eyes fixed as if she was mulling over whether to reveal a secret.

♥ ♥ ♥

Liz leaned forward and put her hands on Martha's knees. "You know something."

Martha tapped the tip of her nose with her index finger and narrowed one eye. "What?"

"Listen, if this is going to put you in some type of compromising situation, don't tell us. Or if you're not sure and want to refer—"

"Not necessary. Just thinking if any of them are still alive or around here." Martha winked. "I'm thinking not."

"We know at least one is dead." Liz smirked.

"Or do we?" Martha winked again, but this time with a wicked smile.

"So?" Will leaned forward with anticipation.

Martha refilled their glasses. "Well, from what I know, the McCallisters were regular Yankees and their family landed somewhere in Boston in the early 1800s. A few of them came down this way and settled into Providence, then Havenport. They were a big family. Lots of boys. But there was one who went against everything his parents set out to do. You know the type of kid. A pain in the ass no matter how good the parents are to him. And in the McCallister clan, that would be—"

"Frederick," Will said.

"Bingo." Martha touched the tip of her nose with one finger and pointed to Will with another.

"So what happened?" Liz leaned closer. She wanted to hear everything Martha knew.

"Frederick ran off and joined the Confederate army. The family, appalled as they were, loved him. He was blood."

"Was he killed in battle?" Liz hung on to every word.

"Not sure. I guess you can dig him up and see what you find. From what I know, the family didn't speak much after Frederick enlisted with the opposition. But I don't know a mother alive who would turn her back on her child, so it makes sense that he would be close to her in death."

"You mean there might be more dead bodies in my yard?" Liz gasped.

Martha laughed. "No, the rest of the family is in the town cemetery. At least the parents and some of the siblings. I'm not sure if there are any descendants floating around. Probably. But I don't know of them."

Liz leaned back and crossed her arms. Will wrapped his arm around her shoulders and hugged her.

"Maybe your first instinct is correct. It might be a monument. I doubt the family would risk burying a son who fought on the other side on their property."

Martha stood and smoothed her jeans. "You never know. People are always finding stuff in the ground and buildings around this town."

True. Liz thought of the journal she meant to finish reading. What were the odds of Adam finding something that old in his basement?

She looked at Will. Yes, what were the odds of finding someone to share her life with at this stage of her existence?

It wasn't time to question things, even if that included the uncertainty of a dead guy in her yard.

"Martha? What would you do?" Liz shifted. Shivers ran down her spine as she thought of Dead Fred as weed fertilizer, but on the other hand, it seemed dishonorable to exhume his body. She didn't even know if she had the right to do that. There must be some type of legal process she'd have to go through.

It might be best if she planted rosebushes around it to hide it better. Wait, that would mean she'd have to clean out the yard first. It's not like she could even hire someone to do it. What if the townspeople got upset finding a traitor amongst their homes?

Ugh! She hated complications. All these years she lived there—clueless. She never should have agreed to let Will walk around her place looking for things to fix.

She looked over at him intensely watching Martha, waiting for her to tell them more.

"I'd like to see it." Martha gathered empty glasses and placed them on the tray. The lemonade and iced tea were almost gone.

Liz hadn't realized she drank so much while they were talking.

Will squeezed her hand, reassuring her it would be okay to let Martha see the grave site. She tightened her grip knowing he was right.

"Would you come over in a bit? I'll make some sandwiches and we can have a late lunch?" Liz offered.

Martha picked up the tray and headed toward her house. "I'd like that. I'll be interested to find out what's there. Got a hoe and pick?"

Liz's eyes grew wide. "Not that I know of, but then again I've never been in the shed. The previous owners may have something in there. See you at four?"

Martha nodded and disappeared into the house.

Will pulled Liz's hand. "How can you own a place and not know what you own?"

"Sometimes it's best not to know things. All my life I moved forward. No sense in going back on what could have or should have been."

Will pulled her toward him so she faced him, her face inches from his chest. "You know what I know?"

She stepped back to see his face better. His eyes were bluer than she'd remembered. He had a serious look on his face, one that she'd never seen. Mouth tight, teeth clenched, his shoulders straight and strong.

Oh no. He's leaving. She finally mustered the courage to go all-in with the relationship, and he was going to dump her. Not that she had much practice, but who would want to take on a relationship with someone who had skeletons hanging around? Literally in her case.

She raised her hand to his chest. "Listen, if this is—"

"Sssshh. Let me gather my thoughts." He shuffled from one foot to the other.

She started to sweat, her nervousness increasing with every second of silence that passed.

♥ ♥ ♥

Will cleared his throat. "Listen, there's no better time to say this than now. I mean, it's not often one finds themselves under a gazebo on a beautiful May afternoon. Liz, we've known each other a long time, *a long time*. The more I think about us being a couple, the more I ask myself why."

Liz began to slide her hand from his grip. "I understand. It's crazy."

"You're right. It is. Why I didn't figure this out sooner and be done with it?"

He watched tears well in her eyes. She took a step back and dropped her hands to her side. "I think we should—"

"Get married, right?" He sighed in relief.

"What? You're not breaking up with me?" Liz swiped a tear from her cheek.

"What? No. I want to marry you and hope you want to marry me."

"Will Powell, you're an ass." Liz stamped down the gazebo steps, leaving him behind.

"What did I do wrong? I'm romancing you." He chased after her. She jogged down the stone path and ran ahead.

He wheezed as he ran to catch up, his chest tighter with each step. "Liz. Stop. I can't—"

The impromptu jog wasn't his style. He slapped his hands on his knees and stood with his feet apart, trying to catch his breath, staring at her leaving him in the dust. "What the hell did I say?"

He lowered his head and took a few deep breaths to clear his head and will away the pain in his stiff thighs. He realized he needed to be in better shape. Then again, he relied on construction work to keep him fit. His fitness plan wasn't working as well as he'd hoped.

He lost sight of Liz. She must have gone back to her house. He switched to a leisurely stroll instead of challenging his heart. He glanced at his watch. Martha would be at Liz's house soon so he'd better hurry up.

His attention turned to honeysuckle and lilac peeking through white picket fences. He had never noticed them before. Then again, he wasn't the type to walk anywhere. He relied on his truck to get him around, as he always tried to cram as many jobs into a day as he could.

Each step presented something new. Ants digging holes in sidewalk cracks. Which neighbor had greener grass. Salt air seeped a bit into this part of town, though they were at least twenty blocks from the ocean.

He stopped and picked a rogue daisy at the bottom of a school crossing sign. He missed so much right under his nose. How did the saying go? We grow too soon old and too late smart, or something like that. He realized how much time he'd spent existing and not living. He would do his best to straighten out the mess he'd made with Liz. Once he figured out what he'd done wrong. He wasn't very good with words, but his heart would help him get there.

The hairs on the back of his neck rose as a slight breeze caught him. A slap on the rear nearly sent him to the ground.

"Yes." Liz jogged past him.

"Yes, what?" he called out to her.

Liz turned around in a slow jog, faced him, and cupped her hands to her mouth. "Yes, I will marry you."

He stopped. His cheeks hurt from smiling. *She said yes.* He watched her turn around and head straight ahead. He hadn't noticed she had run around the block. Maybe jogging would be something they could do together. He smiled as he picked up the pace to get to Liz's house.

A few feet ahead, he stopped dead in his tracks. He didn't even have a ring to give her. He hadn't planned on proposing to Liz without being prepared. But he knew he wanted her—always had. Some things you have to work at, and she was one of those things in his life.

Had they gotten into a relationship when they were younger, it may not have worked. Her reputation scared him away at first, so he left her alone and remained a friend. He wasn't confident enough to trust his own beliefs.

Peer pressure weighed heavily throughout junior high and high school.

He learned too late that other people's opinions didn't matter. He let her go once and he wasn't going to let that happen again.

He gathered up wild daisies and a purple spiky flower he hoped wasn't a weed or some poisonous plant. Plots of land filled with broken shells and random flowers dotted Havenport. He figured the seagulls dropped seeds as they flew over the empty real estate.

The flowers smelled nice. No immediate itching, so they should be safe to give to Liz. He also planned to help her clear out her backyard so she could pretty up the place. Liz, the one woman he wouldn't mind mowing the grass or planting flowers for.

In the short time they've been a couple, Liz had shown him more consideration and affection than Dolores ever had. *Witch!*

With enough wildflowers in hand, he picked up speed as he walked to Liz's house. A last-minute thought brought him down his street to see if he had something nice to wrap around the flowers, or at least a jar to put them in.

He walked up the steps, whistling as each step lightened his heart. Every breath brought him to a happier place.

She said yes.

As he dug for his keys his smile quickly faded. The hairs on his neck stood up like razors pushing through his skin.

What the he—

"Good afternoon, Will. Make me a cup of coffee?"

Dolores sat on the rocking chair, gently swaying as her patent-leather high-heel hung from the tip of her toes.

Chapter Seven

Liz skirted around her kitchen making turkey sandwiches with lettuce on wheat bread cut into triangles. It was one of the few things her mother used to do that Liz held on to. When she was a kid she thought it was the coolest thing. Like her mother had some kind of magic to make a sandwich that way.

She waited for Will to show up. Martha would be over within fifteen minutes. Fortunately, Liz had done her food shopping for the week. With Will spending more time at her place, she needed to keep the pantry stocked.

I said yes.

She grinned recalling Will's awkward but adorable proposal. What did she expect at her age? Him on his arthritic knee and bad back while balancing his body with his slightly better knee? She laughed at the visual. She wasn't a kid and didn't expect him to approach her like one. But she wasn't expecting a proposal, either.

Her heart was lighter when they were together. She was looking forward to seeing him. He made her laugh. There was no reason not to marry him. She did love him the best she could and wouldn't mind living with him.

Living together!

Could she commit to sharing a house with someone? She was used to being on her own. It would be nice if someone found her on the floor and called the ambulance. That was as good a reason as any to get married at her age. Practical and loving—what more could a woman ask for?

Where the hell was Will? He hadn't been that far behind. Maybe he got cold feet and changed his mind. That, she could deal with. She had mastered the art of rejection and was well equipped to deal with a disappointing situation. It was the positive and spontaneous skill that she lacked, and was cautiously apprehensive. But she had been working hard to crack that emotional wall since she'd decided to allow Will into her personal life.

Maybe he got sidetracked. Home repair emergency or something. It could happen, and she would have to get used to him running out if called.

"Hello? Liz?"

She looked out the kitchen door. Martha walked around the backyard.

She wiped her hands and tossed the dish towel on the counter. "Looking for Dead Fred?" She chuckled.

Martha turned to her. "Yep."

Liz walked toward the pile of knotted vines and pulled them back. "There he is."

Martha ran her fingers over the worn lettering, then kicked her way through the weeds. "Yep, he's in there."

A chill ran up Liz's spine. "How can you be sure?"

Martha leaned down and pointed to a round, smooth stone. "You see these?"

"Barely." Liz laughed. "I know this garden is a disgrace compared to yours."

"So gardening isn't your thing. Follow the trail of these stones. It starts at the side of the headstone, down the side in front. Across, then back up to the stone on the opposite side."

"So?"

"That's the outline of the grave. Common to do decades ago. Especially if the body was interred on family property."

"For what reason?" The hairs on her arms raised. Not sure why a dead body would upset her, but it did. She wrung her wrists together in an attempt to reel in her nervousness, unsure what to do. *Will? Where are you?*

"I could check with Anthony at the funeral home to see what your options are."

She wasn't sure she would be comfortable digging up Fred. It wasn't like he could hurt her. Maybe there were other people buried on her property. She shuddered. Just thinking of the possibility of more corpses underfoot creeped her out—too much for her to digest. "Sure. I guess it wouldn't hurt to look into exhuming him. Maybe search for someone in his family who might want him."

"I'll check to see what can or needs to be done. Another option is you can remove the stone and plant a garden over him. Daisies or daffodils would look nice."

She liked the idea. It would be cheaper, and with the marker gone she might forget he was there. What would Will suggest? *Where the hell is he?*

"Thanks for coming over."

"Do you take care of your yard yourself?" Martha asked.

A kind way of being asked why the grounds were so unkept. "Yes, I ignore it all on my own."

"I could always help out if you're too busy. I know you work a lot. And I can only do so much at my place."

She considered Martha's offer. As much as she wanted to throw her arms around her and scream a resounding yes, she couldn't take advantage of her time. Though it was hard to pass up Martha's talent for tending to a beautiful landscape.

"I don't have much money to spare." Liz held Martha's hand.

"Did I ask for any? Money, I've got. Time, I have. Untapped canvas? That I don't have, and you do."

"But I would feel funny not paying you to work on this."

"How does this sound to you? Whatever I can spare from or split off from my garden, we can use. If there is something special you want, you pay for it."

Liz nodded. She could show her appreciation with a home-cooked meal. She enjoyed making dinner for Will, and maybe Martha would enjoy a night out.

"How does this arrangement sound? I will make Sunday dinners. It's the one day I get off from Royce's." Yes, she liked that idea.

"That sounds like a good deal. It does get lonely eating alone since Al died."

"Good, that's settled. You can start whenever you want to. No rush. It's not like it couldn't wait another day."

Martha turned to leave. "Oh, that's where you're wrong. At one time, most of this land belonged to Murphy Walsh. One of the most beautiful coastal seaports that ever existed. Then the land was broken up and different people moved in and did their own thing."

"Murphy Walsh? Wait right here." Liz ran into the house and grabbed the tattered journal and hurried back outside. "Adam found this in his basement. Murphy Walsh is mentioned in here."

Martha took the book and opened it to reveal a faded entry. Her hand flew to her mouth. "Do you know what you have here?"

Liz shook her head. "Not a clue. It reads like some young girl's diary."

"Exactly. You see this?" Martha pointed to a faded signature.

"It looks like an *L*."

"Exactly, Lucille Buckley. She is your great-grandmother."

Liz stepped back. "Impossible. My mother never mentioned a Lucille. And what is the likelihood of Adam finding her journal and giving it to me?"

"You don't know anything about your family history?"

"Not really. My mother never said much."

"Make me some tea and I'll inform you of your lineage."

♥ ♥ ♥

Will's stomach sank when he saw Dolores making herself at home on his favorite chair. She respected that it belonged to him and never sat in it while she lived there. As much as he wanted her to leave, he couldn't be mean to her—that would only put her on the offensive and make his day a living hell. He needed to get back to Liz's house. She must be wondering what had him tied up.

"Why are you here?" He stuck his key in the lock and twisted it so hard he nearly snapped it in place.

"Aw, come on, Will. Don't be upset with me. I stopped by to visit."

He held his anger and swallowed hard. "Visit what? You've taken everything that you wanted except the house. It's mine. Divorce and property settlement say so."

"Coffee?" Dolores tilted her head and pouted.

The last thing he wanted to do was bring her into his home. He'd spent months purging her tasteless stench of perfume and removing anything that she insisted be a part of the house that he didn't like. As soon as the junk guys cleaned out the rest of her stuff, any evidence of her having lived there would be gone. Okay, so he might be a tad bitter. Wasn't he allowed to be? He'd wasted decades with someone who didn't appreciate him and tossed him away like he didn't matter.

He would never do that to Liz. Dolores had to go.

"Not even a grain. Listen, I don't want to be rude but I have someplace to be."

Dolores uncrossed her legs and rose from the chair, slowly walking toward him. "Come on, Will. Where's the love we had for each other?"

He stepped into the house and turned to her. "Seriously? Love? You wouldn't know the first thing about love. You made sure of that when you left and took every cent from our bank account. Don't talk to me about love."

He slammed the door behind him.

"Will. I'm sorry. I made a mistake," Dolores yelled through the door.

"I am asking you nicely to leave. You don't have any ownership here. Don't think for a minute that you do. Go away and let your boyfriend love you."

"Will!" Dolores kicked the door.

He flung it open. "I'm telling you one more time. Leave quietly or I will have you removed. You gave up your rights the day you walked out."

Dolores pursed her lips and wiped away a tear. "I was wrong."

"Too bad. So you were wrong. You know what, darling? So was I. I was wrong staying in a marriage I knew had no connection. No consideration or appreciation. All you saw in me was a handyman to take care of your house and hand over a paycheck. Now leave."

Dolores shoved her foot in the door. "So you're happier with the town whore?"

Blood coursed through the veins in his neck, his face flush with anger. He pushed her foot from the door and stepped out onto the porch. The flowers he'd gathered for Liz were beginning to wither in his fist. Dolores had an ugly side that he'd spent too many years ignoring because she was his wife.

No more.

He pointed his finger in her face. "I am telling you this once. Don't you *ever* say anything bad about Liz. You have no idea what you are talking about. Just because your dalliance didn't turn out like you'd planned, don't think you can waltz back in here like you were on vacation. You are dead to me. Gone."

Dolores stepped back as he stepped closer.

"I don't want to see you, hear you, know anything about you. Go and ruin someone else's life. The best thing you did for me was leave."

"That can't be true." Dolores crossed her arms and shook her shoulders, trying to appear strong.

"Oh, it's true, sweetheart. Leave. I don't ever want to see you again. Don't think that we're going to have a friendly divorce and the occasional dinner and reminisce about old times. Ain't gonna happen."

He unclenched his fists and took a deep breath. His shoulders slumped from the tension release. He had never spoken to her like that, but he was angry that she thought she could weasel her way back into his life. He loved Liz and that would be his new direction in life.

"I'm sorry." Dolores wept.

"Too late. Don't matter. Leave." He went back into the house and slammed the door behind him. *The gall.* He briskly ran his fingers through his hair. *Why did I let her get to me?* He wasn't prepared to deal with her, that's why. Once Dolores left, he never planned to see her again. She had chosen whatever-his-name over him. No consideration for his feelings.

His mistake was being too good to her. He didn't like that she dredged up his anger. He considered it a useless emotion.

He placed the flowers in a glass milk bottle, filled it with water, and picked out a few delicate pieces of Queen Anne's lace that didn't survive his tight-fisted rant. He leaned over the sink and splashed his face with cool water to help him calm down. He waited for the droplets to evaporate instead of wiping them dry.

Four o'clock. Liz had to be wondering what had held him up. He would be honest and dialed her number.

"Hello?" Liz answered.

"Hi. Sorry, I'm running late. Nothing like proposing, then disappearing." He chuckled.

"I wondered about that," Liz said cheerfully.

He could tell by the lilt in her voice she was concerned but relieved. He loved her calm demeanor. No drama. She'd confided in him that she found drama to be exhausting, and for that reason she didn't have female friends.

He couldn't take drama, either, and had spent a lifetime of it living with Dolores. Speaking of which…

"I got home to find Dolores on my front porch." There. He said it. No lying. Straight to the point.

Silence on the other end of the call.

"Hmm." Liz grunted.

"I didn't ask her to come here. She just showed up." He wanted Liz to know Dolores meant nothing to him.

"I get it. Just curious why she's showing up now."

"I didn't even ask. I figure her boyfriend got tired of her and she needs a place to live. Is Martha still there?"

"No. She left a few minutes ago. I'll bring you up to date when I see you."

"Be there in a few. I hope you saved some sandwiches for me."

"Yep, we didn't even eat. There's plenty. See you soon."

He hung up and grabbed the flowers. He decided to take the car instead of walking because it would probably be dark by the time he got home. As he backed out of the driveway, he saw a lavender envelope sticking out of his mailbox on the house.

Later.

♥ ♥ ♥

Liz searched through her freezer to find something better for dinner than turkey sandwiches. She would have to pick up more food and a bigger variety on her next shopping trip. Having a fiancé meant Will would be spending more time at her place and eating over. Neither could afford to keep eating out—too expensive. Plus, she liked having him over. They could talk without people listening, like when they were at the bar. No interruptions. Except now, Dolores had inserted herself in Will's life and Liz didn't trust her.

What a day. Dead guy, great-grandmother, ex-wife. For someone who liked being alone, she sure had an influx of company, be it dead or alive.

Prepared chicken wings found deep in the bowels of the freezer would make a good dinner. Having people for dinner would help her rotate her food supply quicker. Hot wings with baked beans and corn on the cob. Perfect.

She wasn't shy about eating in front of people and enjoyed a good meal. That's how she and Will reignited their relationship. He came into the tavern one night after Dolores left and Liz gave him a plate of the hottest wings they served. He ate them without balking so she knew he was worth talking to.

Her small kitchen needed some sprucing up so she grabbed a pile of unread local newspapers and tossed them in a recycling bin on the back porch. Time to change things. The universe reached out to her. Forcing her to be aware of things she needed in her life. Maybe that had been happening all along and she finally paid attention.

She turned the oven on to 425 to preheat, then filled a Dutch oven with water and a cup of sugar to sweeten the corn. She clamped the can opener onto the rim of the baked beans and tossed the contents into a pan.

Even Dead Fred was growing on her. She had lived with him in her yard for years. It was foolish to be afraid. As long as she wasn't going to put an in-ground pool in the yard, he could stay.

Martha would come up with a pretty way to hide the grave. Then again, it was a part of local history, and maybe Liz was meant to embrace that.

Change surged through her being. She felt both lighter and vulnerable. It would have to be that way if she accepted other people into her life. A difficult balance. How do you open your heart without making yourself subject to rejection and hurt? Nearly impossible. You had to give in more.

That was the chance she would take. It was nice having people around. Even her talk with Martha was fun. She noticed how different conversation was outside the bar. More in-depth, detailed. She felt a connection that never happened with the small talk she'd had through her life.

And she discovered she enjoyed cooking, as limited as her skills were. She trimmed crust from two slices of rye bread from Led Zeppoli, cut them into triangles, and garnished them with pepper jack cheese, a slice of green olive, and arranged them neatly on a plate. Not a fancy appetizer, but it would tide her and Will over until dinner.

No sooner did she finish washing her hands did a knock rap on the back door. She turned to Will walking into the room with a milk jar full of wildflowers.

"For you."

She took the makeshift vase and placed it in the center of her kitchen table. "Beautiful. Thank you."

Will grabbed a sandwich and consumed it in two bites. "Sorry. I'm starving."

"I figured you would be hungry. There's more for dinner so don't be shy. Eat up." She pulled her chair out from the table. Seeing him and knowing that Dolores had resurfaced gave her pause. "Sit. I need to ask you something."

She patted the table, encouraging him to take a seat next to her.

"I swear—I didn't…" Will's words poured out before she had a chance to collect her thoughts. She placed her hand on his and squeezed it gently, a signal to slow down.

"You didn't know she would show up?" She slowly ran her hand over his wrist.

"No. I didn't. I stopped at my house to pick this up." Will pointed to the milk bottle. "And she was sitting on the rocker on the front porch."

She looked at the floor and sighed. "Listen. I don't know why she's here. It could be nothing, but…and maybe it's my nerves because things have been happening fast between us…but are you sure you want to marry me? I mean, have you thought about it, or was it an impulse?"

Will took both of her hands. "I have always wanted to marry you. I was young. I was stupid and too immature to ask you to be my girlfriend. Then you took off, and I didn't know where you went. Dolores started hanging around and we sort of just dated. I don't even remember asking her."

"But you married her."

"I did. But come to think of it, you're the first woman I asked to marry me." Will smiled, trying to be cute.

"You never asked Dolores?"

"No. She said we were getting married since we'd been dating. Apparently two years is the cutoff for women. She said if I didn't marry her, we were done."

"Did you love her?"

"I guess in a certain way I did. It was comfortable. There were a few good times."

She shook her head. "How can you marry someone you're not in love with?"

Will looked down at the floor, then straight into her eyes. "When you think the love of your life is gone, what's in front of you seems like the only option."

"That's—"

"I didn't mean it to sound like that. You know me. Sometimes I get the words wrong. It was an okay relationship, but I don't think we were each other's first choice."

She thought of Walt and knew from the start he was her true love. But she spent a lifetime of being lonely because she didn't want to betray him by loving someone else. She did love Will, but not in that crazy can't-live-without-him love. Maybe her age and the love she had for him was mature, different from what a twenty-year-old would feel.

Things may not have worked out with Walt, considering statistics and his penchant for drinking. What she liked as a kid may not suit her as an adult.

"Okay, so you're sure?"

"Honey, as sure as I'll ever be."

Will stood and lifted her hand to join him. He slid his arms around her and pulled her in tight, giving her the most passionate kiss she'd had in her life.

Chapter Eight

A week had gone by with no word from Dolores. The unopened lavender envelope rested on his rolltop desk. He wanted Liz to be sure of his intentions. The last thing he needed was his ex-wife mudding the waters of his newfound happiness.

It was his night to cook dinner, but he planned to surprise Liz and meet her at her job, then take her to dinner. Both of them had spent the past week working extra hours. Each took turns at cooking a quick meal, but today he wanted a hearty meal.

He had his mind set on a new restaurant he'd heard of in Kingston. It wasn't too far. The tavern was busy all week with tourists coming in for the Havenport Hostilities events, and he had received five last-minute calls for plumbing issues. One thing that you could count on in an old town: plumbing would keep you in business. That was his main line of work, but over the years he had taken on small carpentry and masonry jobs to bolster his business income.

He picked up the envelope and turned it over in his hand. *Just get it out of the way.* No sense in spending more time ignoring whatever Dolores had to say. He was surprised she hadn't called or shown up again.

He took a butter knife from the dish drain and slid the blade under the flap. The scent of her cheap perfume wafted up, and he shuddered. He couldn't stand the smell of it. She put it on everything and it reeked of rotten oranges, lilac, gardenia, and evergreen. He opened the window above the kitchen sink and waved away the stench.

He removed the matching stationery. Her handwriting had gotten even sharper with its high-pointed letters. He unfolded the note.

I need your help. I know I've been a bitch to you, and you didn't deserve it. You are the last person I should be reaching out to, but I don't know where else to turn. I have cancer, lung to be exact, and I need a place to stay. I was hoping you would find it in your heart to let me finish out my time at the house. I know no amount of "I'm sorry" will make up for what I did to you, but you were always a much better person than me.

He read the letter again, still the same cell phone number. His mouth dropped open. What did she expect him to do? He was in love with Liz and had made sure Dolores knew it. His heart belonged to her and Dolores meant nothing to him, but how could he turn his back on his ex when she cried out for help?

For a man who wanted to live a simple life, his was fast becoming complicated.

He had to tell Liz.

No, he had to show Liz the letter. He hadn't mentioned it to her, fearing she would withdraw thinking that his ex was still involved in his life. Would Liz not want to marry someone with baggage?

It had to be his own insecurity. Liz wasn't giving him any reason to doubt her, so he had to stop putting ideas into his head. He knew he had to allow himself to trust again. One thing he had learned from his divorce was relationships don't take care of themselves. Just because he thought everything was okay, didn't mean there weren't issues.

He was hell-bent on making his relationship with Liz work. It wasn't often someone got a second chance at something so important in his life. He'd be damned if he screwed things up.

But how did one turn his back on someone who had been a part of his life for so long? *Easy, if you were Dolores.* A chill ran down his spine. *Could she be lying?* He didn't know. After she'd left him, he couldn't trust her anymore. But then again, he hoped she wouldn't stoop that low and concoct a story just to get back in the house.

He leaned over the sink and splashed cold water on his face. As he turned off the faucet, he caught his reflection in the window. He hadn't aged twenty years, but he sure felt like he had. With a comb quickly run through his hair, he left the house and into his car.

Ah, Gus. It came in handy having friends who owed him favors. Gus detailed the old clunker for nothing and made it look almost new. He had to start spending some of his savings. After all, what was he going to do with the money? Take it to the grave? As long as he had enough to live on when he retired, he would be fine. His IRA was the one account his ex left alone. Dolores could have been mean and taken half of it, but he convinced her it was his sweat that had built that nest egg. For whatever reason, she backed off from that demand.

He didn't mean to avoid showing Liz the letter. A nice dinner could be ruined if he unloaded the news of Dolores. But he also knew that she would want to know and deal with it immediately. Liz's no-nonsense approach to problems was what attracted him to her when they were kids. She seemed older and wiser than the rest of his schoolmates. *Drama free.* A breath of fresh air.

The foul-smelling perfume filled the car. *Crap!* He hadn't thought that through. He would have to tell Liz. She was sure to think that Dolores had been in the car. The stench worked its way into the upholstery and would linger for days. Maybe Gus had a way of clearing out rotten odors.

He rolled down his windows to clear the air, then put his right arm over the back of the passenger seat and backed out of the driveway.

Crash!

♥ ♥ ♥

Liz needed to take a break. She couldn't believe how busy the bar was. Two people called out, but fortunately Adam over-hired. Smart decision. At least he had the foresight to plan ahead. The new girls were nice and unafraid to talk to the customers. They carried trays of drinks and steak dinners through the crowds with ease. Experience was always a plus, and Darcy was on duty.

The Historical Society had put a lot of marketing effort behind the reenactment and surrounding events, and it paid off. The tips were good. She made more in two days than she had in two weeks.

She missed Will, though. With the both of them so busy and only spending enough time to scoff down a small dinner, they hadn't had time to plan a wedding. They hadn't even had time to pick up her ring. That she did want. A simple band, an unbroken token of their love.

She didn't want a big wedding. A small, intimate affair suited her, something in the park at the gazebo. The expense of a wedding couldn't guarantee a successful marriage. She was too practical to throw away money on an event for the appearance of others. The money would be better spent on fixing up their houses.

Will had decided to sell his, but she hadn't decided what to do with hers. How easy would it be to sell with a grave in the backyard? She would have to disclose it. No matter how well Martha fixed it up, at some point someone would find Dead Fred in the ground.

No word yet on her legal position with disposal options, if she chose to go that route. She didn't want to be a pain and bother Martha, who was sweet to even help sort out the matter.

Sirens screamed as an ambulance sped past the tavern.

"Liz, can I get a Sam on tap?" a late lunch regular called from the end of the bar.

"One minute, Gus. Just cleaning up a bit. Getting off early today. I've had enough of these familiar mugs today." She smiled as she filled a pilsner.

Gus gave her a salute and waited patiently. She cared for her customers and took pride in that.

Another siren screamed past.

"What the heck?" Gus accepted the tall beer. He reached for his cell. "Hmm, my phone is going crazy."

"It must be something bad. I've never seen so much activity. Didn't even know we had a second ambulance." Of course she knew. She meant to say the town never needed to use the second rig.

She turned back to the bar and grabbed a small bag of jalapeño chips. So much for watching her diet. She figured she must have burned a pound or two running around. Even though they hadn't set an exact wedding date, Will asked if she wanted to get married in October since they both loved the fall. That gave her five months to plan. They would take advantage of autumn colors that filled the town square that time of year.

"You sure? Is he okay?" Gus snapped his fingers at Liz.

She wrung her hands tight in the dish towel she used to wipe the bar. A pit formed in her stomach.

"All right. We'll be there." Gus hung up the call.

She knew *we* meant her and Gus.

"What is it? It's Will, isn't it?" She dropped the towel.

"Yes. Martha was walking in the neighborhood when she saw the accident. He backed out of his driveway and got hit."

She felt like she'd been gutted. The universe couldn't do this to her. She'd waited so long to welcome someone into her life, and she'd be damned if he was taken away like Walt and her baby.

She steadied herself and grabbed her purse. "Gail, would you please take over? Tell Adam I had an emergency to tend to."

"Sure. No problem. Is it serious?" Gail asked.

"Not sure, but I will let you know once I know. Gus, can you drive please?"

"Of course, if you don't mind the stench of lobster cages."

She'd dealt with worse in her life. She followed him to his truck and climbed in, pushing aside sweatshirts and overalls to the middle of the front seat. *This can't be happening.* "Did Martha say how bad it was?"

"No, just that the ambulance was on its way." Gus turned the ignition.

"That must be the sirens we heard." She held her purse on her lap and clasped her hands, wringing her fingers as they got closer to the hospital. The few traffic lights were in their favor, and they arrived within ten minutes.

Liz slid down from the truck cab and raced into the emergency room up to the triage window. "Is Will Powell here?"

"Please have a seat, ma'am," the receptionist directed.

She refused to listen to the stranger. *Ma'am. No one calls me that.* "My fiancé is being brought in. He was in a car accident."

Fiancé. The word sounded so foreign to her, like she was too old to have a fiancé.

An EMT rushed a stretcher into the ER. She spun around for a closer look. Not Will.

"Will you please answer me?" Her grip tightened on her purse handles slung over her shoulder. She leaned over the counter. "Your name is Christine?"

"I asked you to please take a seat."

Another team of EMTs rushed in through the doors and into the examination rooms behind the next set of doors secured by a security guard.

"That's him." She ran to the door but the guard held out his hand, stopping her midstep. "I need to be in there with him."

Blood ran down the side of his face. She couldn't tell if he was awake.

"Ma'am, I have been nice and asked you to have a seat." The receptionist pointed to the hard-molded plastic chairs attached to the opposite wall.

"He needs me." Liz yanked her arm from the emergency room employee.

"Have a seat. I'm not asking you again. I can't contact his next of kin if I'm dealing with you."

"But *I'm* his fiancée."

♥ ♥ ♥

"Sir, do you know where you are?"

Will woke to a light shining in his eyes. Blood made his vision blurry. "What the hell happened?"

"You were in a car accident. I'm Dr. Smith. What is your name?"

"Will Powell. Is this the hospital?"

"Yes. Havenport Medical."

"Good. At least I didn't travel far from home." He laughed, and his hip hurt worse than when his arthritis flared up. "I don't remember driving."

"You were backing out of your driveway and got T-boned. We're going to take some x-rays to see if anything is broken. Are you up to that?"

He attempted to nod, but pain made it difficult to move. "As long as I don't have to walk there."

The curtain slid back. "Excuse me, Doctor. There's woman in the lobby being extremely difficult. She's demanded to be allowed in here. I normally would not interrupt but I'm afraid she's going to barge in."

Will forced a smile and noticed the woman's name tag. "Is she medium height, honey-colored hair?"

"Yes." Christine sighed.

"Please send her back. She's my fiancée."

"That's what she keeps saying, but our first concern is our patients' safety."

"It's fine, Christine. Send her in." The doctor patted Will's face with a saline-soaked pad. "Do you have pain? If so, where?"

"My left hip and my head." He winced as he tried to move his left leg.

"Stay still. We'll get you into x-ray soon. In the meantime, hold this over your eyes. It might help with the light. Someone will be in to get you when they're ready."

"Thanks, Doc." He held the saline pad over his closed eyes. The coolness numbed the pain somewhat. He tried to remember what happened, but nothing came to him.

"Will? You asleep?" Liz whispered.

He smiled. At least he was alive. He could live with a broken bone or two. But he—the letter!

The last thing he remembered was slipping the letter from Dolores in his back pocket on his way to Liz's house for dinner. He swallowed hard. *This could be the perfect moment to let her know. I'm already in the hospital.*

"Not sleeping, but not moving, either. Waiting for x-rays."

The squeal of chair legs scraped the floor. Liz sat next to him and laid her hand on his wrist.

"What happened?"

"Don't know. They said I got hit pulling out of the driveway."

"Yes, I know. Martha called Gus. She saw the accident." Liz gently rubbed his fingers. "How bad does it hurt?"

It felt like he struggled to lift a hundred-pound weight from his chest with every word. He didn't have the heart to tell her that he just wanted her to be next to him and save the conversation for later.

He sighed. "I've been better. How is the other person?"

"I wouldn't know. They would barely give me information about you."

"I get it. Like my fancy gown?" He let out a staggered breath. Why couldn't they shoot him up with a painkiller? He hurt more as his body began to relax. Pain seared through his rib cage and down his left leg. Drops of dried blood littered the sheet. He felt gross.

"So much for my plans to take you out to dinner."

"Don't you dare even think about that. Do you really think I care about missing a dinner?"

Another thing he loved about her, the level of concern and compassion she had for others. Even strangers. The first to help out someone new in town. Not that much needed to be done, but Liz went out of her way to make newcomers feel welcome.

"I'm starving."

"Well that's a good sign. Once we get you bandaged up and out of here, we can grab something on the way home."

"Sounds good." He went to speak more but changed his mind. *Do I?* He wanted to get Dolores out of the way. Knowing her, she would show up again once she found out what happened.

No secrets.

"Sweetie, would you hand me my pants? They shoved them in a plastic bag somewhere in this room."

She reached down and pulled out a bag stuffed under the stretcher. "This?"

He nodded. "There's a letter in the back pocket. Please don't get upset. Read it."

Liz removed the lavender envelope. "God, this smells."

"Yep. More so in the contents." He watched her eyes dart across the paper as she absorbed each word. She turned it over but the page was empty.

"Do you think she's telling the truth?" Liz narrowed her eyes and raised the corner of her mouth.

He took a slow, full breath. "Not sure, but that's a horrible lie if it's not the truth."

"I see." Liz folded the letter and slipped it back into its envelope. "Have you spoken to her?"

"No. I was on my way to talk to you. No secrets."

Liz agreed.

"Well, it seems you are in a pickle, Will Powell. Ex-wife, fiancée. What to do. What to do."

He removed the pad from his forehead and wiped what felt like dried blood from his face. "Liz? What are you thinking?"

"Oh nothing. Just assessing the situation. You possibly being bedridden. Dolores moving back into your house. It could be a cozy arrangement for you."

"Liz Taggart. Do I detect jealousy?" He attempted to sit up, but would rather have had his eyes bored out with a hot branding rod.

She sat back with her arms folded across her chest.

He couldn't figure out what was worse, not knowing if he damaged his body beyond repair or screwing up his relationship with Liz.

"I love you. You know that, right?"

Liz nodded.

"Then why the silence?"

"I'm thinking."

"About?"

"We agreed to get married in October, right?"

"Um, yes."

"I say we get married now. You know I don't want anything special anyway. So we get married, live in my house, and Dolores can live in your house until she figures something out."

He smiled. "I like that idea. At our age, every day counts."

"It does. And being angry about an ex isn't good for anyone."

The curtain flew back along the ceiling track. "Mr. Powell, we're ready to take you to x-ray."

Liz kissed him on the cheek, and they wheeled him away.

He'd found a good one and he wasn't letting her go.

Chapter Nine

"Hi, Adam. Fortunately, Will only suffered a broken rib and a hairline fracture to his thigh bone. I'll be back in tomorrow after I get him set up in the house," Liz said, leaving a voice mail.

Will had been kept in the hospital overnight as a precaution and to keep him off his feet for at least a day.

She was grateful she had an understanding boss. The patient advocate helped her locate an aide who would care for Will while she worked.

Everything was falling into place. Gus had offered to pick Will up at the hospital and bring him home—his new home. They hadn't even shared a bed yet and Will was moving in with her. Her insides shook at the thought of him seeing her naked. It wasn't sex that brought them together, and she figured they would get to it eventually but wasn't sure how.

The truth was, she'd had no desire to be with another man since Walt died. Despite her celibacy, rumors of her being a tramp continued. Just because she found it easier to be friends with men didn't mean there was anything more to their relationship.

She never had a close female friend. That she learned from her mother. A woman will turn on you faster than you can count to ten. Subconsciously, she must have believed that.

She was glad they had taken it slow with their relationship. They had to get to know each other in a different way. Fear of losing Will as a friend scared her.

Fortunately, in time she'd thrown caution to the wind and had gotten over that fear. Will made her feel secure. Solid. Like the earth stopped moving from under her feet. Instead of waiting for a sinkhole to open and swallow her up.

She took a shot of blackberry brandy to steady her nerves. It would work out. The intimacy would come naturally. First, Will had to recover.

With the medical care in place and Gus calling in other local contractors to help spread out the workload for Will's business, all that was left was dealing with Dolores. No one had called her to tell her about Will's accident. Not that she was owed an explanation, but Liz thought it only right. She hadn't informed Will that she'd invited Dolores for dinner.

Not the ideal situation, but Liz figured it would be easier to hash everything out over a home-cooked meal and at one time. This way there could be no misinterpretation.

Brakes squealed in her driveway, and she peeked out the kitchen sink window. Gus pulled a wheelchair from the back of the vehicle and brought it around to the sliding van door.

She ran out to help. "Thank you so much. He never would have fit in my car."

"No problem, Liz. He would have done the same for me. Hey, did they catch the person responsible for this?" Gus snapped open the wheelchair. Will would have it for six weeks.

She nodded and closed the van door. "I don't want Will to hear, at least not yet. It's not good. The other driver didn't make it. Teenager on the phone. Sad."

"Yeah, I had a feeling when I saw the car brought into the junkyard. Drinking?"

"No."

"That's good. I could never figure out why some people think driving and being on the phone is a good mix."

Liz thought of her unborn child. She would have been the kind of mother to take the phone away if her kid abused it. She may have been open to many things as a mother, but stupidity was on her short list of what not to do.

They walked around to the passenger side. Will lay against the window, sound asleep, mouth hanging open.

Gus pointed to his friend. "You think that's sexy? That's what you want to marry?"

She laughed. "There's a lot more to marriage than sleeping with your mouth closed."

"I guess. But I sure wouldn't want that unshaven mug snoring next to my ear."

Why do people assume just because you're a couple that—
Never mind.

"I'll wake him up. I don't want you rolling him onto the sidewalk because it will toughen him up." She grinned at Gus, who meant well, but he was a guy's guy, and soft and caring did not come to him easily.

"Will?" she whispered into his ear. "Come on, wake up so we can get you in the house."

He stirred and rubbed sunlight from his eyes. "I think the pills kicked in hard today."

"Come on. I'm sure you're hungry. I have some burgers and chili dogs ready for you two."

"Can I move in, too? Karen doesn't cook much for me anymore. Since the kids are out of the house, she said there's no reason to dirty a kitchen for two people." Gus helped Will slide down along the seat and into the wheelchair.

"Maybe the real reason is you spend too much time at the bar and she gets tired of waiting for you to come home." She threw him a snide look.

"Could be. But Royce's has really good food."

"Then why don't you bring Karen in for dinner one night? A real dinner—steak, chops, fish. Not the bar food crap you eat."

"What? Fried mushrooms and hot wings are healthy."

"Okay, you keep telling yourself and your cardiologist that."

"Hey, all this food talk is making me hungry." Will righted himself in the chair. "Can we get inside? I think the meds don't agree with the sun."

"Does he always get this cranky when he's hungry?" Gus pushed the chair up the temporary ramp he'd built.

"You do nice work. You're not charging Liz for this, are you?"

"Of course not. Hot dogs will be payment enough. Well, and a cold beer."

"I got you covered. It will just take me a minute to get the food on the table. Oh, Will, by the way, I invited Dolores for dinner tonight."

♥ ♥ ♥

Will's head cleared from its medicine-induced fog at the mention of his ex, never mind having a meal with her and Liz. He trusted Liz. Dolores was the wild card in his life.

"Why?" He rolled himself to the table.

"It's motorized. You don't have to do that. You're going to put undue pressure on your ribs." She fixed him two hot dogs with mustard, raw onions, and chili sauce.

"You sound like a wife already." Will laughed. "Thanks, sweetie."

"Yeah, maybe you're right, Liz," Gus said. "I should pay more attention to Karen. It's just with the kids out of the house, it's like we have nothing in common."

"Then this would be the best time to find out. Ketchup on your burger, right?"

"Yep. Buddy, you got a good one here."

He put his hand on Liz's waist. "I know."

That's why he didn't want Dolores to screw things up. Most times, he found it difficult to explain his feelings. The best he could do was comfort and love. Liz didn't put any demands on him. No expectations. Nice.

"Are you going to answer my question?" She wasn't getting out of this, no matter how much he loved her.

"I thought it would be comfortable here. Everyone can relax. You are going to be here so we don't have to worry about jockeying you around. I'm sure Dolores will be cordial."

Gus snorted beer through his nose and wiped it with his sleeve. "You don't know her very well, do you?"

Liz shook her head. "She's not someone I would have spent much, if any, time with. But I have to respect she is Will's ex-wife."

"Okay, you keep thinking that." Gus grabbed another bottle of beer and chugged it like it would be his last one. "Well, thank you for the hospitality, Liz. You are a wonderful hostess."

"Thank you for bringing him here. It made things so much easier." She handed Gus an unopened bottle of beer. "This is for when you get home. And do something special for Karen. I'm sure she will appreciate it."

Gus nodded. "See ya, buddy. Heal quick. We can only take on so much work. Oh, by the way, some of your clients weren't in a hurry, so they opted to wait for the work to be done once you're up and can get around on your own."

"Thanks, pal. I know you and John will take care of things for me. I owe you." He saluted his friend.

"Yes, you do. But for now, I'll take the lunch and beer. Later."

Will waited until Gus pulled out of the driveway. "We have to watch him like a hawk."

"What?" Liz laughed. "You just said how honest he is."

"Oh, honest he is. Punctual is another thing. His idea of timeliness differs from mine. My customers are used to my schedule."

"I'm sure he will be fine. He knows your reputation is on the line and he's your best friend."

"Let's hope it stays that way." He fixed a hamburger with lettuce, tomato, and raw onion, topped with ketchup. He had slept so much and ate so little he was starving. The two hot dogs didn't cut it, and he would be hungry for dinner, unless Dolores made him lose his appetite.

He appreciated Liz being such a sport with the ex-factor, but he knew how his former wife could be, and the last thing he wanted to do was lose his cool in front of Liz. It wasn't beneath Dolores to pitch a screaming match in public, never mind in a private home. But she was the one who needed help, and Liz might be on to something.

They had the upper hand.

"I've arranged for a caretaker while I'm not here. You okay with that?"

"Sure. I know you have to go back to work."

"I do. I mean, Adam said he would pay me for the day and a half I missed, but you know I make most of my money from tips."

He nodded.

A knock on the back door startled them. *It can't be her. It's too early.*

"Liz? It's Martha. I have some news for you."

"Come in. The door's open." Liz cleared the table except for a pitcher of iced tea.

"What a beautiful day. Will, you should be in the yard soaking up the sun. There is nothing better than nature to heal you." Martha sat at the kitchen table, the battered journal in her hand.

"Today's his first day home so I thought I'd get him settled in before he starts complaining because he can't move around. Then I'll gladly push him outside to complain to the weeds."

"Well, Dead Fred is there. He's not going to complain if I talk too much."

Martha laughed. "Oh, you're funny. Speaking of Sergeant McCallister, I found a distant relative. Her name is Olive. She lives in Connecticut. Heard rumors of a rebel in the family but never dreamed he would become her problem. From my conversation with her, she is curious, but at the same time doesn't feel obligated to incur any cost or have any desire to uproot him. She wouldn't even know where to transplant him."

"I see how that could be a problem." Liz sighed. "I anticipated Fred living here for eternity, so I'm prepared for that. She doesn't have any interest?"

Martha shook her head. "Not much, but she may change her mind. You never know. I gave her your number in case she wants to talk to you directly."

"Well, it's what you were expecting. I mean, if you're really freaked out by having him there, we can look into having him exhumed."

"I guess." Liz sighed.

"So that's your first bit of news. Ready for the second?" Martha clenched the journal with glee.

Liz poured three glasses of iced tea and sat next to Will. "Do I need to add a shot of rum to this?"

♥ ♥ ♥

"I doubt it, but I found it very interesting." Martha opened the journal to a page with faded fountain pen ink. "Do you see this name at the bottom?"

Liz peered at the faded script, straining her eyes. She reached for the reading glasses she kept hanging by the wall phone.

"Nope. The first letter looks like an *L*."

"It is. Keep reading. Just focus on the one word."

Frustrated, she took the book from Martha and carried it over to the kitchen window where the natural light helped to brighten the page. "It looks like Lu."

"Keep going." Martha egged her on.

"This better be worth it. I'm getting a headache." She moved the book around to catch the best light. "Not getting it."

"L-u-c-i-l-l-e. Lucille." Martha clasped her hands like she had just delivered the most exciting news to the world.

She closed the book and removed her glasses. "Sorry, Martha, but it means nothing."

"How far did you read this book?"

"Until the ink disappeared. The last passage was about her hair smelling like fish."

"You know that Royce's Tavern used to be a brothel long ago?"

"I heard that. Her story sounds like that of a girl who worked there. I mean, the shooting was a bit much, but that's what it was like back then. Law enforcement was different than it is today."

"Give me that." Martha reached for the journal. "Then you never read this."

Liz took the book and focused on the passage Martha's finger rested on.

"'To my future life. I'm standing in the port of New York harbor. It differs from Havenport, which I will miss immensely. But with my father gone and Tilly ailing, I cannot stay at the house because I will not make my living there. I need to be near the water and that is why I have not strayed from the shoreline. I wait for my husband to join me once his duty is complete. I will keep you safe, my baby Madeline, while you nest, and when you are born into this city that will become our home.'"

Liz looked up from the page. "How would Lucille even know she was having a girl?"

"Old wives'-tale beliefs. It wasn't uncommon to hold a pendulum over a pregnant women's belly. And some women just knew. Intuition. But besides that stuff, do any of those names mean anything to you?" Martha's eyes bulged like they would pop out of her head.

"No, I'm sorry." She handed the book back to Martha.

"What about the name Amanda?"

Liz sat back. She hadn't heard the name in relation to her since—

"My mother?"

Martha jumped up and hugged Liz. "Yes. This journal belonged to Lucille Buckley, married name Gibson, and she gave birth to Madeline, who gave birth to…"

"My mother." Liz sunk in the chair. *A descendant of a whorehouse.* It didn't surprise her.

"Do you know what this means?" Martha practically jumped out of the chair. Liz didn't see the wonder in it that her neighbor did.

"It means I was born of a brothel." Liz looked to Will, and he held her hand. As children, he ignored the rumors. Would he still?

"No, no. Well, yes, there's a story there. But I researched this and Lucille's mother, Pearl, died in childbirth. Her husband, your great-great-grandfather, was the town doctor, and Tilly Watson let him and Lucille live at the brothel in exchange for medical care for her girls. Tilly was a surrogate mom to Lucille and shielded her the best she could from the reality of the house. Lucille, your great-grandmother, met a man in the Navy and moved to New York so she could have better medical care available to her while her husband was at sea. She had a daughter just like she claimed she would."

Liz's stomach began to churn. The similarity was close to home. "What happened to the husband?"

"Oh, he came home in time for the baby to be born. But it was after that where Lucille's life got exciting."

Liz released an exaggerated sigh of relief. At least she hadn't relived history. "What was that?"

Martha smiled and rubbed her hands together. "Lucille began to write, but no publisher would buy her work, so she submitted work under the name Lucas Wallingsworth and wrote *To Have and Hold*. Are you familiar with that book?"

"Of course." Everyone had read that book in high school. It was a classic. Once she'd read it, she had forgotten about it. She accepted the author was a man and had no questions. The story did have a feminine touch, but she considered it great writing.

"So you, my dear, are the descendant of a pioneer. Lucille was the first woman to bamboozle a publishing house, and the book did so well she opened her own company and gave new authors an opportunity reserved for someone who was connected."

"Wow. Wait. Wallingsworth Press?"

Martha nodded.

Liz was filled with joy. Finally something pleasant in her background. Her cheeks tingled from smiling. "Proof that it doesn't matter what your beginnings were, it's what you do with it."

"Yes." Martha rubbed Liz's hand. "I think it's a fascinating story."

"Thank you for researching that. Do you know of any other books she has written?"

"You can find them under the name Lucy Wallingsworth. After her book became famous, she vowed to never hide her identity again."

"That's a wonderful thing you did for Liz." Will smiled.

"It's what I do. And with the Internet now, I don't even have to leave my house most of the time. But I'm sure the library has some information. Check with Wilma. I know she'll be happy to help you find any information you are looking for. If she doesn't have it, she knows who does."

"I can't thank you enough." A weight lifted from her shoulders as she stood up and walked Martha to the back door. Dolores would be arriving soon, and Liz needed time to absorb all she had learned about her ancestors.

"Make sure you hold on to that book. Who knows what else might be in there. And I haven't forgotten about Fred. I was waiting for you to decide what to do."

"Leave him. He's been there for centuries. A few more days or months won't matter."

Chapter Ten

"Well, that was something, huh?" Will rolled to the sink, doing his best to help Liz get dinner going. "I hoped you planned on something easy."

"Yep. Pizza. I'll call when Dolores gets here."

"Pizza? Are you serious?"

"Yes, why?"

"Nothing. I don't think Dolores has ever eaten a slice of pizza." He smiled. *Should be fun.*

"There's a first for everything. Look at us. Friends to marriage. Who would have thought? By the way, have you told her we're getting married?"

He shook his head. "I wanted to tell you about her letter first. I figured you have right of first refusal with anything that concerns me, and that includes conversations with the ex."

Liz smiled. "Listen, I'm not a teenager. I know things are going to come up and I can't stop you from having contact with her. But I do appreciate you taking my feelings into consideration. And as far as the pizza, I figured why spend the afternoon standing over a hot stove for a conversation that might last less time than it takes to turn on a burner. Me and you like pizza, so her preference wasn't even considered."

He wheeled himself over to her, taking care not to whack his leg into a piece of furniture. "That's one of the many things I love about you. Considerate but practical."

"Yep, that's me. The practical one." She tried to make a joke, but it wasn't. Liz, without a choice, expected to be the levelheaded one in the family. The child raising the parent. Her life had been upside down since birth.

But now that she had some familial knowledge of more than just her mother, he could see her curiosity percolated. Why wasn't she ever told about her great-grandmother, Lucille, and her grandmother, Madeline? Those would be the questions she would want answers to.

Especially Lucille. Her mother, Amanda, had to see the freakin' book lying around the house when they were reading it in high school.

How could a mother live a lifetime and not include her daughter in family history that would have an impact on her? Knowing the good things her great-grandmother did could have helped her take control of her low self-esteem years ago. Maybe that had been Amanda's intent. She was too jealous to watch her daughter have a better life than she had. Jealousy amongst parent and child. A sad situation.

"How about we take a trip and see Wilma when I'm able to get around better?"

Liz nodded. "I'd like that. I know it seems silly all these years later with people I don't even know. But when you do find out some amazing connection like Lucille, I don't know, it changes things a bit. I'm from that success. Yes, I would like to know more. I'm sure we can do some research here. That'll give you something to do while I'm at work."

He wouldn't mind at all. She was beginning to trust that he would care for her. Her guard lessened a bit more as time went by, and that endeared her even more to him.

Sometimes he would look at her and still see the sixteen-year-old girl with the brash mouth and long, silky honey-colored hair. He knew gray hairs poked out here and there, but none of that mattered. Liz was the whole package.

Knock. Knock.

"Doesn't anyone use the doorbell around here?" He spun around toward the kitchen archway.

"It's broken. Add it to your to-do list. And you'll never make it down the hallway on your own."

Liz left the kitchen to answer the front door.

"Who is it?" he yelled.

"Why, who do you think, my ex-love?" Dolores waltzed into the kitchen and swung her short faux-collared song jacket on the back of the kitchen chair.

"Hello, Dolores."

"Aw, no Dee?"

"Dolores is fine. I let Liz read the letter." Will held Liz's hand to send a message to his ex.

"Why would you do that? My request only concerns me and you."

"Not really. See, Liz and I are getting married. You remember how that goes. Being married makes you an interested party in your spouse's life. Except when it comes to adultery. And then you made sure I didn't know what was going on. It's a good thing for bank statements. At least I found out before you took my last dollar. I was able to buy lunch that day. Thank you for your consideration."

"Will," Liz whispered into his ear. "You're in no position to get upset. You have to rest."

"Oh, honey, he's as cool as a cucumber. He could never get mad at me." Dolores sprayed her perfume in the air.

"Listen, Dolores. You want to discuss your medical issue? Fine, Let's talk. But Liz is a part of this discussion. So come out with it. We came up with a plan that you can stay at my house…"

"Our house?"

"My house. I have the court papers to prove it. You stay there because I have moved in here. This way we both have what we want."

Dolores lowered her head. Her shoulders heaved slightly, as if she was sobbing. He wasn't buying in to her antics. It was bad enough he'd agreed to put up with her as long as she needed a place to stay. But he wouldn't fall into her manipulative web. It had taken him years to climb out of it once—not again.

"Dolores, I know Will is still aching, and it's difficult for him to talk. It literally hurts when he breathes so I'm trying to keep him calm. You're welcome to stay for pizza and go to the house. The stuff he needs has been removed, but you have everything you need there. You can call anytime."

Dolores stood and slid on her jacket.

"I guess no pizza?" Will smirked.

"No, thank you. Keys, please."

He handed her a spare set of house keys. "The guest bedroom has been set up for you and you should be very comfortable."

Dolores let her palm relax and stared at the keys. She slowly slipped them into her purse. "When are you getting married?"

"Tomorrow." Will smiled. That was the best news he had given to his ex since the financial settlement that let him keep the house.

♥ ♥ ♥

"What?" Liz shrieked as Dolores left the house. "Tomorrow? I don't even have a ring."

"I thought you didn't want one."

"I said I didn't have to have an engagement ring. I'd rather spend that money on the house or a trip instead of wasting it on a diamond that sits on my finger. But I'll have you know, Will Powell, a wedding ring will sit on this finger."

She held up her left hand, palm facing him, while she stabbed at her ring finger. "No woman gets married without a band on that baby. No woman."

"You're kind of scary right now. I didn't think it would matter. Seriously. We'll run and get you one tomorrow."

She threw her hands up in the air. "And why tomorrow?"

He reached out for her. "Give me your hand. I'm at a disadvantage with this broken leg."

Liz obliged Will reluctantly.

"I know we planned on October, and you were the one who suggested we do it sooner. I've had time to think, and you're right. Why wait at all? It's not like we have to get to know each other."

"Hmm."

"What's that hmm for?"

"Nothing. Just figuring out what I want to wear." Besides jeans, sweaters, and the occasional sparkly top for New Year's Eve, she had a limited wardrobe.

"I thought you didn't care about appearance?" Will poured her iced tea.

She shook her head. "I don't, but I don't want to look like I'm on my way to work."

"I get it. Maybe we're rushing things. Are you having doubts about marrying me?"

She kneeled beside him and held his hands in hers. "Not for a minute. I just never saw me in this situation, so it's not like I have appropriate attire at the ready."

"Do you want to take some time?" Will stared into her eyes. She knew he was looking for doubt. She had none.

"Maybe a day. Do you feel like getting out of the house?"

"Yes." Will nearly jumped out of the chair. "Call Gus, have him drop off one of the vans."

She reconsidered her suggestion. "Maybe it's not a good idea to take you out. I'd rather some time go by to let you heal."

Will pursed his lips. "Okay. You make sense. Why don't you take the rest of the day and go find what you need to make this happen? I'll take a nap so you won't have to worry that I'm wandering around."

"You sure?"

"Yes. I'll tell Gus to be on standby if I need something. You can always ask Martha to check in on me."

She smiled. "I don't like to leave you alone like this."

"I'll be fine." He smiled with reassurance.

"Okay. I have my phone with me. Do you need a painkiller before I leave? I wouldn't want you getting up and stumbling around while I'm gone."

"Good idea. Then I'm sure to sleep."

She helped Will into bed and handed him a painkiller with a glass of water, the TV remote, and a true crime magazine from 1970. There were a few more scattered around the house. Once Will was up and around, they could make a mad rush through the house and purge the clutter taking up valuable space.

"You all set? Need anything else?" She brushed hair from his forehead. He was slightly warm to the touch, but it could be from the stifling air in the house. She hated this time of year. Too warm for heat but too cold to throw open the windows. With not much rain in April and the unusual cold spells, the May flowers had a late start. Heads of yellow daffodils peeked through the weeds. She couldn't wait for Martha to ravage the yard and set a landscaping plan.

"I'm fine. Enjoy."

She grabbed a light windbreaker from the hall closet. Glancing at her watch, she calculated how to make the most efficient time of her day off. She backed out of her driveway slowly. Hard to believe so much damage could happen in a low-speed car accident. But she had proof sleeping in the rented hospital bed in her living room. The dining room would have been better, but Will had an outside view of the neighborhood and the TV sat in the same room.

She turned onto Main Street and passed the bridal store, thinking it wouldn't have anything she would want to wear. She parked the car in front of Wags and Walks. There must have been a rescue event recently because a medium, smooth-haired dog sat in the window.

The pup looked at her with soulful eyes, begging for attention. She looked away and felt his eyes on her back. She turned. He scratched the window, climbing, doing his best to convince her to at least consider taking him home.

I can't.

She turned away and walked toward the bridal shop. *Why not? They might have something not too bridey.* She pushed open the door, and a bell rang overhead. This was one store she had never been inside in all her years living in Havenport.

"Can I help you, Liz?"

"Leslie, hi. Umm, I need something for a special occasion." She walked past poufy white gowns. Even if she was younger and a first-time bride, none of them would be her choice of dress. She knew Leslie from high school. They were cordial but not the type who would have been friends.

"What type of occasion?"

Outside of Gus and Dolores, no one knew she was getting married. A smile spread across her face that was difficult to hide.

"My wedding." She stood straight with pride and didn't care who knew. She'd spent so many years keeping to herself that it was difficult to willingly offer up personal information. But the minute she and Will applied for the marriage license, the entire town would know thanks to the gossip hens at the town clerk's office.

"I see." Leslie let loose a genuine smile. "I didn't even know you were seeing anyone."

"Not much to say. It sort of just happened." She walked to the back of the store where dresses of various colors stood out against the white glare of the gowns that made the store the most money.

♥ ♥ ♥

"Thank God that freakin' cast is off. This has been the worst six weeks of my life." Will straightened his gray tie.

"But today that all changes for you, right, buddy?" Gus pinned a white carnation on Will's lapel. "Man, we've never looked so rich."

"If you mean as in clean and not dressed like two guys from the docks, I agree." He looked out the living room window of his old house. He was relieved that Dolores hadn't moved in like she wanted to. It turned out that what she thought was cancer was nothing more than an artifact on the image. It was typical of her to stir up a tornado when a gentle breeze would do. She moved in with her sister, and he hoped that would be the last he heard from her.

"I see the For Sale sign is on the front lawn." Gus opened the door for them to leave.

"Yep. Time to let it go. It needs too much work."

"Just like you, huh?" Gus laughed. "Seriously, though, what made you decide to retire? I mean, thanks for the customer list, but what if you change your mind?"

He stopped short of the doorway and plugged his hands into his pants pockets. "Who knows. Could happen, but Liz and I want to do some traveling. Neither one of us has and we thought it would be a nice honeymoon."

"Any particular plans?" Gus walked to the car and motioned for Will to get in.

"Liz found a place called Star Island. Somewhere in the Virgin Islands." He locked the front door and got into the car.

"I have to tell you, watching you and Liz at this relationship thing has helped me get along better with Karen. I never realized what a terrific woman I married." Gus drove, heading for the town square gazebo.

"I've learned a lot from her. I guess we have it figured out. I simply followed along and was happy with the way things were going for us. We're getting rid of her house, too."

Gus stopped at the red light. "What? Why?"

He rolled the window down enough to catch the fresh air. "Her house needs a lot of work, so when the Historical Society approached her about buying it as is, she said yes."

"Even with the dead guy in the yard?" Gus continued to the wedding site.

"Because of the dead guy. Even though he fought on the wrong side—according to the town history—his story belongs to Havenport. You know how those history types are. Plus, it will be another tourist trap to help with the local economy."

Gus pulled over and parked the car across the street from the gazebo adorned with tulle and pink tea roses, just like Liz wanted. Sparse, but elegant nevertheless.

People gathered on the lawn chairs set out on each side of the steps. Once Leslie helped pick out the dress, she promised Liz she would do what she could to help throw together a low-key wedding. Leslie did good.

He walked up the stairs with his best man, Gus, following. Liz had decided on Martha as her witness since they had developed a friendship deeper than Liz had ever had with anyone else.

The mayor waved his hands to instruct people to take their seats.

Violins played from the side of the stage. Clear weather promised a comfortable outdoor reception. Liz had few wants, but an outside wedding topped the list, and she got her wish. He recognized the locals in attendance and knew Liz would be surprised by how many people showed. She was more loved than she was aware.

Why not? He'd loved her for decades.

The music grew louder and his heart skipped a beat. Before him stood his gorgeous bride. Her hair casually framed her face, the back held loosely with soft pink tea roses. Her dress reached to her calves. A vision of love personified, draped in a color between a blush of pink and mauve.

She walked toward him. With each step, his smile grew wider. Adam held her hand and helped her up the stairs.

"Good afternoon, Mr. Powell. Nothing better to do on this day?" Liz squeezed his hand. A flash of light from her one-quarter-carat diamond engagement ring caught his eye. He had insisted on some type of prewedding ring, and she agreed if he didn't go into hock to buy one.

"I don't know. I might have to unplug a sink after we get this wedding stuff out of the way." He kissed her hand. "What's that?"

"Martha did this for me. It's my something old. I mean, besides me and you, but everyone can see that. She took Lucille's journal and bound it with twine and weaved in some flowers from my garden that she's been rehabilitating." She leaned into him and whispered, "There may even be some roots from Dead Fred wrapped up in here."

He laughed and turned to the mayor. "Let's get on with this. We have a reception to get to."

"Dearly beloved, we stand here in unison to witness the marriage of Elizabeth Emily Taggart to William James Powell. Love comes to us in many ways. Through an unintended meeting. A schoolmate. A church attendee. An old friend. You, Elizabeth and William, have known each other through a few chances in life and have discovered that it is with each other you belong. Both of you are upstanding members in this small-town community, as you can see from the people in attendance. Having known both of you for as long as I have been mayor, I am sure your life will be a wonderful marriage of the minds, interests, and love. Do you have anything to add?"

Liz quietly cleared her throat. "Will, you have always been a stand-up guy. You made me realize that I was living in a cave and you brought me light. I will always be grateful for your steadfast and loving soul. I promise to be the best wife and life partner I can be…which I think I've already proved by taking care of you while you were injured." She laughed. "I love you with all my heart and I can't wait to be your wife." Liz slipped a white-gold wedding band on his finger.

The mayor motioned to Will.

"Liz, if you had only known how long I have been in love with you. I know that sounds inappropriate considering I threw a marriage into my life along the way, but you have always been the one. The day you tossed a hamburger on the bar for me at Royce's and listened to me complain about the brutal workday I had, I knew I had to try and convince you that we were meant to be together. I love you and I'm glad you stopped to notice me. I will take care of you forever. I owe you." He laughed and slowly slid a matching band on her finger.

The mayor cleared his throat. "By the power vested in me by the state of Rhode Island, I now pronounce you husband and wife."

"Let's party!" Gus yelled while Will and Liz walked out into the crowd, greeted by rose petals and hugs.

About Lita Harris

LITA HARRIS spends her time between New Jersey and the Endless Mountains region of Pennsylvania, where she writes most of her books. She also lived in Alaska for a short time just for fun. An avid crafter, unused supplies clutter her basement and attempts at making pottery, jewelry, and stained glass are proudly displayed in her house, usually behind a picture or holding a door open. She also makes candles and homemade soap. With enough books to stock a small library she may need to construct a building to store her literary obsessions. She writes in multiple genres, including women's fiction, contemporary romance, paranormal, and cozy mysteries.

♥ ♥ ♥

For more information about Lita, please visit her online at
www.LitaHarris.com

Also by Lita Harris

Timeless Tales – Short Stories

Christmas Spirits featured in Timeless Keepsakes
Chasing Fireflies featured in Timeless Escapes
Trusting Kindness featured in Timeless Treasures
Till Death Do Us Part featured in Timeless Vows

♥ ♥ ♥

Havenport – Novellas

Winter Wonderland featured in Christmas in Havenport
New Beginnings featured in Welcome to Havenport
Kindred Spirits
Wishful Thinking

♥ ♥ ♥

Make Me Stay

by Nicole S. Patrick

♥ ♥ ♥

Luke Christianson has a duty that's more important than any other during his tenure in the Marine Corps. To fulfill it, he heads to Havenport, Rhode Island, to grant his late mother's last wishes. In a town he never knew existed he finds a place that helps ease his grief and discovers his artist mother was somewhat of a local legend. Luke also uncovers a lot about himself from a chance meeting with Darcy Prentice. The saucy and gorgeous journalist makes it easy to open up about his feelings and share his past. She's an unexpected source of pleasure, and Luke finds he's rethinking his next move. Can his newfound connections to the people in Havenport be a reason to stay? Luke might be willing to find out with Darcy by his side.

Dedicated to ~

Jen, Lita, Ruth and Desi, you are all so special to me. Our run continues....better and more creative with each installment.

Chapter One

Sweat ran down the side of Luke Christianson's temple, and the sounds of his unit's impromptu flag football game echoed from outside the barracks. Their banter mingled with the swish of the floor fan in the corner of the room, which did absolutely nothing to help cool down the inside of the plywood and aluminum building. He wiped his forehead on his sleeve and concentrated on the task of cleaning his weapon. The raunchy ribbing, and friendly f-bombs thrown in every two seconds were constant during the games.

This particular deployment had lasted longer than the others in this godforsaken sauna part of the country. Particles of dirt were permanently embedded in his nostrils. Dirt that was different than the domestic stuff—finer, which clung to every surface of his gear and equipment. He'd never rid his pores of sand, the stench of sweat-stained armpits, and let's not forget the melt-your-eyeballs fragrance of the latrine.

It didn't matter much, for he was counting down the days to disengage from this life and start a new one. Georgia seemed to be a good option. After all, Atlanta *was* a booming city—as good as the next, he supposed. Besides, his buddy had an "in" with the local carpenters' union in Buford. They offered a carpenter's apprentice program that catered to vets.

A plan.

He missed doing carpentry work and itched to feel the smooth handle of his tools in his palms again. The exact balance of a tool made working with them utter pleasure. He'd stashed his prized set at his buddy's house on his last leave. No more than a month or two of crashing on Jason's couch and he should have enough saved up for a decent apartment. He'd stay in Atlanta, for a while.

Would he miss serving? The question begged for an answer. Could he have made the corps a career? Did he want that life? The myriad of reasons for enlisting in the first place had made sense way back when he'd barely finished high school.

But a restless energy settled into his gut. It was time. He had no regrets about defending his beloved country despite the locals in the region not quite viewing the Marines—or specifically, his recon unit stationed here for the past six months—as comrades. They barely tolerated the troops, in fact.

"Mail call!"

Lieutenant Grant strode into the room with his booming baritone. Luke looked up from cleaning his weapon when his superior plopped a bundle at his feet.

"Christianson, here's a bunch for you."

"Thanks." He commandeered the bundle, along with his newly cleaned weapon, and sat on his cot. *Strange.* The postmark on the top letter, an eight-by-ten envelope, was dated more than three months ago. He ripped it and found another smaller one inside. It was worn and creased and had his name written in a familiar scrawl. His gut clenched and a sharp sting hit behind his eyes.

Mom's writing. He scanned the contents, then read its accompaniment from his mom's best friend.

"Hey, man." Drew Monroe, his bunkmate and the best marksman in the unit, strode in, interrupting Luke's digestion of the contents of both letters. He'd read enough, though—enough to know that Georgia would have to wait.

Drew groaned and sloughed off his boots. "You must be busting to get outta here in how many days?" Drew squinted over at the *Sports Illustrated* calendar tacked to the wall. "Two. I am not gonna miss your snoring, but I will miss you, man."

Aww, hell. Way to get choked up.

"Not that you'll miss this place," Drew continued. "I'm going to assume your plans include throwing back a few cold ones and finding yourself someone warm and willing?"

Not exactly, but he wasn't about to explain it to Drew.

"Yeah, besides you?" Luke kidded, mostly to hide his true feelings. He possessed a PhD in that particular skill. "And snoring? Look who's talking, eh?"

The words came out playful, but Luke barely felt the giddy tone behind them—the fake tone. Hell, he'd had zilch plans to hook up with anyone—besides committing to the carpenter gig thing—but that was before this task dropped in his lap. Whatever. He'd make do by himself. He always had.

"So where *are* you heading? Where was it? Atlanta?" Drew asked before pulling out a shirt and skivvies from his duffel bag.

"Rhode Island," Luke answered, but didn't elaborate. He stuffed the letters under his pillow.

♥ ♥ ♥

Two weeks later

Small Town, USA—cue the *Andy Griffith Show* theme—Mayberry here we come. Either that or he'd been plopped into the middle of one of those chick movies on that channel he never watched. Quaint street signs, narrow roads, birds chirping, people smiling at one another, holding hands, laughing, and clean, crisp air. The polar opposite of the den of crap he'd escaped. What a difference a few weeks made.

Obeying the snail's-pace MPH, he rolled past the Havenport sign and maneuvered his Ford F-150 toward the intersection. Just as the light turned red, he stopped and noticed a group of blue-haired old ladies, one more ancient than the other, crossing at the corner. One of the five moved at a slow trot versus a tortoise, and led the group. She turned around, making sure her ducklings still followed, turned her head to his truck, and stared dead-on. She stopped midway and winked. Luke couldn't contain his grin and tipped his head. He swore she blew him a kiss, but the gesture disappeared in a split second.

Yeah, Havenport certainly seemed interesting at the outset. He looked around while waiting for the light to turn. The architectural style of the buildings drew his attention. Facades, mostly, but he suspected they were authentically old. Partial cobblestones and cement slabs lined the walkways in front of the shops. A bookstore situated next to some kind of trinket shop, a bakery—all-American central.

With his phone GPS app voicing the next turn, he hung a left toward the *Havenport Herald. Leave it to Mom to write her own obituary.* God knew she'd had the most creative mind on the planet, something he never felt he'd inherited. Well, that wasn't entirely true. He loved working with his hands. Feeling the wood grain under his fingertips, the smell of sawdust, and the smoke of the miter saw never got old. Seeing how the swirls and patterns and textures of different types worked best for a project made him content.

Unbidden memories of Ben, the only man he'd ever thought to call Dad, surfaced, but with them came a cut of pain to his gut. Ben, no doubt, would've been able to identify the time period each building's facade had been based upon, as well as how to replicate it. Ben had been a master carpenter, and Luke would have been well on the way, too, until…

"I know what you'd say, Ma. Move on and move up." He spoke the words to the multicolored urn resting on the floor of the front passenger seat and shook his head. "Yeah, and for me to stop being batshit crazy speaking to a bunch of ashes."

Maneuvering the truck to a vacant spot behind a bright purple Volkswagen Bug, he parked, killed the engine, and stared down at the steering wheel. His stomach clenched—partially from hunger, since the black coffee and protein bar he'd bought back in that dump of a rest stop in Connecticut had worn off an hour ago, and partially from nerves. Hell, he'd faced the enemy with less stress. He sucked in a breath and expanded his abs, then let it out slowly. The dense aftertaste of burned dark roast didn't help the twinges invading his gut the moment he'd located the *Havenport Herald* offices.

It wasn't as if Mom died yesterday. The acute ache in his skull had stopped a while ago. The timing of being shipped out to Afghanistan soon after she'd passed away was the salve for his grief—at the time. The old saying—time helped ease pain—did, in fact, help. A bit.

However, Mom's last instructions had come out of nowhere. And with them all kinds of grief and feelings he'd gotten over were dredged up. Or had he gotten over them?

Why now? Why had Mom waited until he was just about to restart his life to dump these tasks in his lap? Luke replayed the conversation with Mom's best friend, Barb, in his mind. She'd written that freaking course-changing letter and sent his homeward-bound plan into a tailspin and him into this fool's errand.

"Luke," Barb had said, "Mary wanted her ashes scattered in the small town of Havenport, Rhode Island.

And she told me to send the instructions to you when you were leaving the Marines."

"Where the hell's that?" he'd wondered once he'd touched down in the States and dropped the scarce belongings he owned in his buddy's pad and fetched his vehicle. What should have been nights in Atlanta, throwing back a few with said buddy and maybe making a bit of money, hadn't materialized. Nope. First order of business pointed to a pit stop in this small, quaint, rich, touristy town. Had to be if the lady walking her dog against the crosswalk sign in stilettos and holding an umbrella over her poodle was any indication. And those yachts he'd spied along the waterfront weren't just for show.

"Not far from Providence, I understand," Barb had relayed. He'd also wanted to know if Barb knew about this at the time of Mom's death, but she hadn't. It was something apparently left out by that stupid-ass attorney who'd settled on Mom's last will and testament. The ashes were given to Barb, because frankly what the fuck was he supposed to do with them—bring them overseas on his next tour?

Pushing aside that conversation, because it did no good rehashing, he was resigned to the task at hand.

"Might as well get this part over."

He grabbed the envelope off the front seat, opened the door, and hopped out of the truck. Time to get this done. Alone.

Chapter Two

The old Murphy's Law adage couldn't have happened on a better day.

Darcy Prentice glared down at her left foot and what used to be a working heel on her pumps, the ones that cost her over seven hundred dollars. Yes, crazy to say the least, but the impulse buy had been her reward. A breakup present financed by an extra bit of cash she'd stashed for her portion of rent.

Oh yes, indeed. She'd used said money on herself with no remorse. No regrets. No more going halfway for rent with he-who-will-remain-nameless-for-all-eternity, and abracadabra, a new pair of pumps with the signature red bottoms. Only now, they were destroyed. *Stupid, stupid.* The lousy crack in the sidewalk in front of Mellie's Diner rendered her prized possession toast.

"So much for making an impression." The meeting with her boss in half an hour would either need to be rescheduled, since there wasn't enough time to head home to change then head back, or she'd settle for the alternative—the shoes stashed under her desk...a cross between the Wicked Witch of the West and a pilgrim.

She'd planned to be professional and put together, to pitch a new column to the paper. That was after the Havenport Historicals series ran for the next few weeks. Darcy had her deadline on those first and couldn't put more on her plate.

Oh, to have her very own column in the paper would be terrific. History, journalism, things to do—the combo fit her like the shoes: perfect, smooth, and comfortable. From the minute she'd concocted the idea in the shower, Darcy had a feeling it was her ticket to success.

What tourist wouldn't want to read about the history or six degrees of separation of Havenport's people, the legends who had shaped the town, while they were vacationing? The ritzy tourists, and the regular folk who made it their vacation destination basically year-round, would love it.

Hey, Candy Apples had her gossip column—which was terrific, by the way—so why couldn't she? A column for things such as tidbits on connections, historical associations, legendary people who may have visited, or better yet, similar to an ancestry column. Not just a series, but an ongoing column. Her fixation on that well-known ancestry website might just come in handy. It was her guilty pleasure, but also quite informative.

"Darcy's Deductions," she muttered to herself, loving the way the name flowed over her tongue.

In her mind the concept was brilliant. Hopefully the broken heel wasn't fate, or a sign, and not a good one.

Maybe this column would catapult her to a successful blog. And maybe management would be willing to pay her an extra hourly rate for the extra hours she'd need to put in. It would help to pay the bills. Not that she complained. She made ends meet and wasn't above taking a shift or two at Royce's once in a while when the need arose. Her folks could use the money she gave them every month, as well. She'd come back to Havenport for a few reasons, so she might as well make the best of it. Right?

Face it, you had to come back. What would her folks do without her support? Not that they appreciated it. That was a thought for another time.

Armed with renewed purpose, Darcy approached the front door to the *Havenport Herald*. Built at the end of the Revolutionary War, the building's facade had been restored by a local mason as part of the town council's plan to spruce up the town. That hunky town councilman Evan Washburn had done a stellar job making Havenport a priority and den for small businesses and entrepreneurs.

Once inside the building, she smiled at the security guard manning the reception desk and wobbled toward the employee entrance. Pulling her badge out of her coat pocket, she waved it in front of the red light and heard the reassuring click before pushing on the oak door.

As she pushed, the door flew open and she propelled forward and teetered. Didn't help that operating with one good heel furthered her compromised center of gravity. That cute investigative reporter barreled into her, causing her purse to slip off her shoulder and thump onto the floor.

"Oh. Hey, Darce. Sorry," Ronnie said, red-faced, and retrieved her handbag before handing it off.

Ronnie was an exceptionally good-looking, tall, buffed guy—and twelve and a half. He sidestepped her and held open the door so she could scoot past him. His button-down blue dress shirt stretched over an impressive chest. Darcy held back a grimace and pasted a smile on her face, but what she wanted to do was cover her nose and mouth.

He reeked of that awful expensive cologne she'd gotten as a sample in the sale paper this past weekend, a cross between fruit and musk, and together quite horrendous. Ronnie obviously bathed in the scent.

"I'm headed to Led Zeppoli. You want something?" He smiled, seeming embarrassed by almost laying her flat. A small dimple appeared on the left side of his baby face, and his brown eyes crinkled at the corners. His dark hair was cut in the latest style, longer in the front and cut tight in the back. She sighed. Yes, he was a baby.

"I'm good, thanks. Trying to limit the caffeine." She cleared her throat. She really needed to squash her cougar tendencies. Hey, twenty-eight wasn't old, but compared to Ronnie, who had apparently recently become legal drinking age, she was ancient.

"Good luck with that." He nodded and flew out the door.

Besides having no interest in robbing the cradle, Darcy was over dating anyone at work. Ever. Again. Been there, done that, didn't need another train wreck to blow her career into smithereens. He-who-shall-remain-nameless was the last coworker to see her naked.

Who needed sex anyway? She had her romance-novel boyfriends, all those delicious dukes, generals, cowboys, and brawny Scottish men. All good enough to keep her warm at night and not dirty her clean bathroom.

Keep telling yourself that. Pathetic.

Finding her way to her desk, she plopped onto the computer chair and glared at her shoes, pulling off the mangled one, then the other. She'd YouTube how to repair shoes later. Fifteen minutes until the meeting with or without her favorite pumps. The manila envelope in the top desk drawer held her pitch idea, the logo for Darcy's Deductions, and the tagline, easily put together in Photoshop. Having pitched this to herself and her cat a gazillion times, she was ready.

Upon opening her email, her shoulders slumped. Crap. The meeting had been canceled. Not rescheduled. Well, that stunk. She shot a quick and professionally polite email to the chief editor's executive assistant and asked that the meeting be rescheduled.

Why hadn't she taken Ronnie up on his offer of coffee? It was going to be a long day. She rummaged in her side desk drawer looking for a tea bag. There must be a green tea or an oolong bag or two stuck in between the paperclips.

"Darcy, you're on obits today." Anne, her coworker, threw the instruction over her shoulder then walked down the carpeted corridor.

Great. No meeting and obits for the day. With one last glance at the outline of her future success, Darcy closed the folder and shoved it back into the top drawer, then fired up her computer and word-processing program. The last document she'd saved was the Havenport Historicals series, which ran every week. And the next and last installment deadline loomed.

She needed a subject. With the war reenactment coming up this weekend, maybe something along the lines of a lesser-known historical figure? Time for some research. A good way to pass the time on obit day.

♥ ♥ ♥

Luke shifted his long frame on the hardest, most uncomfortable chair on Earth. His foot had fallen asleep ten minutes ago and he'd been waiting more than thirty minutes for someone from the obituary department. This was getting ridiculous. Small towns moved at a dead man's pace.

Would've been nice to be given an ETA on someone coming out to assist him, but the receptionist disappeared five minutes after instructing him to wait. And that girl with the pierced lips, who'd blatantly ogled his crotch, relayed she'd tell someone he waited. But nothing. No one.

Okay, patience wasn't one of his strong suits. Of course, he'd learned the hard way in the corps that patience and obedience went hand in hand, or else suffer the consequences. But he wasn't in the corps anymore, so screw patience, and cue action. He'd give it five more minutes before trudging through those closed set of doors down the hallway and demand to know if anyone actually worked at this backward paper. Once he ticked off this item, the next duty on Mom's last to-do list would take shape.

The envelope in his hand practically pulsated, and he itched to read the words just one more time before it was submitted for print. He may as well, for there was nothing else to do but wait.

Mary Christianson, née Sullivan, will at last be laid to rest, and her ashes scattered under the huge oak tree in Havenport Park on what would have been her fiftieth birthday. Provided the oak tree is still there and that irritating real estate mogul Mr. W hasn't chopped it down to make high-rise apartment buildings.

Leave it to Mom to make some kind of political statement. Plus, who was Mr. W?

Mary was a creative and free-willed spirit. She spent her childhood years at the same house on Main Street. Those at Havenport High School can attest that she never did things in the "normal way." At least, not normal as her family expected, but c'est la vie.

He continued to read, the words committed to memory at this point, for he'd read the page twenty times. But for some reason reading the cadence, the ebbs and flows of Mom's words brought her closer somehow. Luke pictured her hunched over her workplace, canvases and designs scattered in what she used to call organized chaos, wearing a paint-stained smock or a T-shirt of Ben's and writing her farewell onto paper longhand. No computer age for Mom. She hated anything that wasn't what she'd deemed "organic." Computers took away brain cells and killed your synapses, she'd rail.

Colors colored her life—every inch, hill, valley, and possession. School uniforms weren't safe, either. Utmost apologies to Principal Langston for the tie-dyed and fringe-wrought pants, which met with much derision among the student body. Mary hoped that lovely woman and amazing mentor might very well be alive.

Mary yearned for a life of a freelance artist when she kicked Havenport in the keister and left for parts unknown. Some folks in town she'd missed terribly. Others? Not so much. Especially Mrs. Franklin, who hadn't appreciated Mary painting that mural on her fence, no matter that said fence should have been condemned twenty years beforehand. The psychedelic magical mystery bus had been a definite improvement.

Luke chuckled silently at the image. It was something he'd have wanted to see.

Nonetheless, Mary spent many hours sitting under that favorite tree with a sketchpad in hand and a dream in her heart. She may have left her home to pursue an eccentric life, one filled with color and texture and creation, but her best creation of all will always be her son, Luke.

Aw hell, of its own volition his jaw clenched. He needed to pull it together or be embarrassed.

Luke will undoubtedly come to Havenport, meet those who are still alive who had known Mary if he chooses to seek them out, or simply leave in solitude, but I hope he does not. It's my wish that Luke stick around to see what a good place Havenport used to be, and hopefully remains. Mary's ancestors shaped this place, yet sadly Luke wasn't made aware of them, and for that Mary is ever remorseful. Mary closed that door after her father, William Sullivan, closed his when Mary and Luke left Havenport.

Yeah, Mom always relayed his grandparents were awful people, especially her father.

Oh, shit. Could the sperm donor who'd knocked up Mom still be here in Havenport? Christ, he hoped not. He had no family left, and frankly, he'd learned to get used to that idea. His Marine Corps buddies were all he needed. Nothing too deep and no obligatory connections, either. Sure, he was friendly with Jason and his wife back in Atlanta, but they'd just had a baby so he felt like an intruder most times.

"Bah…no use thinking of it."

Mary now resides in the art studio in the sky with her beloved husband, Ben, and their old dog, Picasso, who she suspects still pisses on the floor at least once a day. Best wishes to the friends Mary left behind so many years ago. May they embrace Luke, and may he seek

and find answers where they lay covered. Luke would benefit greatly
by knowing his heritage at last.

Answers? Heritage? *Really, Mom?* He had zero
questions. As far as he was concerned, his responsibilities
ended with scattering her ashes, putting her obit in the
paper, then heading back to Atlanta. There was no time for
mysteries, nor did he give a rat's ass about his ancestors.
Time to move forward, not backward. The past held no
relevance in his life or his future.

Mary died as she lived—on her own terms.

"And I'll live on my own terms," he mumbled to the
paper as he folded it and shoved it back into the envelope.

♥ ♥ ♥

"Darce, you've got a customer."

The comment made her jump, but luckily it was after
she'd hit Save. Again. Cripes. Losing another hour's worth
of work would suck. The last set of obituary notices she'd
readied for input in tomorrow's edition and all her edits
and tweaks had suddenly gone poof. God forbid IT answer
a support ticket anytime in this millennium to fix the glitch
in her word-processing program.

"There." She exhaled in a huff at the sight of the file in
her documents folder before minimizing the screen. The
Classifieds salesperson who Darcy couldn't remember
leaned on the wall of her prefab cubicle.

"And he's something." She fanned her face with
yesterday's edition.

Darcy blinked. Oh no, not another wacko wanting to
place an epitaph about his pet lizard. "Something, what?"

"Hot. *Smoking* hot," she whispered.

"Ahh." The girl was barely nineteen, and no offense to
the Goth community, but her dark hair with the purple
streaks didn't quite gel with what Darcy presumed was their

similar taste in men. Not to mention that yesterday, the girl had been sucking face in the parking lot with a guy who had more piercings than visible skin on his ears.

Hot and *smoking* hot were two totally different things.

The girl cleared her throat. She wanted an answer? "Um. Thank you. I'll be right out."

"Oh. No problem. Take your time. He complained he's been waiting a while but I'll keep him company." She smirked, and the metal rod sticking out of her top lip shifted.

Eww.

Ten minutes later, after a quick bathroom stop, Darcy pushed open the double doors to the reception area on their floor. The area outside Classifieds, Obits, and Special Features was decorated in pretty blues and grays, thanks to Sue, the receptionist, who as it turned out wasn't at the desk. No shocker there. Rumors circulated that Sue was pregnant—unmarried and pregnant. Not that anyone should give a hoot nowadays. Maybe the Havenport residents of the past had fed gossip into scandals, but who cared in this day and age? Her expanding waistline was all Sue's business. However, apparently being "preggo" meant Sue spent more time in the bathroom tossing up her breakfast than actually sitting at the desk, answering the phone, and fielding the many drop-in customers of the *Herald.*

Darcy sailed past the empty desk and stopped short. Goth Girl wasn't kidding.

"Can I help you?" she asked. Her voice sounded winded to her ears, or completely dumbstruck by the specimen who'd risen from the chair and approached in a swagger.

Jeez Louise, he had to be six-three, at least. She'd become an expert at height. Yeah, for he-who-should-remain-nameless was six-two and a half. He'd also made it a daily occurrence to point out that exact figure and how, compared to his vertical prowess, and her measly five-four, they didn't fit. He'd complained their mismatched heights made it difficult to kiss properly, or do other things.

Sorry, but no one she knew had control over their predetermined height genes. And, in her opinion, once two people engaged in the horizontal mambo, height was irrelevant. Insert part A into slot B and there you had it.

However, it never ceased to bother her when he'd criticized, "Can't you wear heels when we go out?" or "Have you been eating carbs? You know a person of your height can't hide the pounds." Darcy's eyes narrowed at the memory. Well, he could take the skinny Amazon bitch he'd shacked up with and stick her heels where the sun didn't...

"Um, hello?" A low, syrupy grumble in the question made her abs twitch.

Cripes. He'd stopped not a foot in front of her and probably imagined she'd gone crazy, or lapsed into a coma. Darcy couldn't help fixating on his left eyebrow, which was raised in inquiry. Bet he didn't have to wax those perfectly shaped sandy arches. And they matched his hair quite nicely. Wonder where else he might be blond...

Snap. Out. Of. It.

"Hi," she answered, trying to sound a half an ounce like a professional versus a nitwit. "Are you here to submit an obituary?" *Yes. Good. Get to the point of his visit.*

He nodded curtly, and she supposed it was because of her idiocy. "I am. Are you the person to speak to about that sort of thing?"

"I am," she responded, imitating a parrot. She really needed to concentrate on using her mouth to form coherent words and sentences related to the task at hand.

Hand. One of his clenched an envelope and the other a key ring circling his index finger. Hanging from it was a bulldog with the Marine Corps insignia.

"There's a form you'll have to fill out, and then I'll take down the pertinent information," she volunteered. That is, if she could actually concentrate on taking his information without staring into his icy-blue eyes. Why did men have to be blessed with long eyelashes when women went to so much trouble gluing and sticking and clumping enhancements to them? Totally not fair.

He nodded tightly again. Okay, apparently not the talkative type. "What I have to input is already done."

She blinked. "Oh, you mean you've already written the obituary?"

He flushed. Just a hint that if she hadn't been studying his features as if he were a nude model and she the artist—*no nudity thoughts needed right now*—she might have missed it. A hint of pink hit the tip of his nose, and traveled along the chiseled cheekbones before he swallowed and sucked in a breath.

"I didn't."

"You didn't?" Cue the parrot act again.

He frowned. "I didn't write it."

Darcy nodded. "Ah. No matter. I'll take a look at it and see if it needs tweaking."

He stilled. "It needs to stay as is…verbatim."

"Um, okay. I'll have to review the text anyway in case the word count is incredibly over, or there's curse words…stuff like that."

"There's actually a limit to obituary word count?" he asked, the inflection of his voice signaling the concept a criminal act, which in her opinion it kind of was. How could someone limit their loved one's tribute to an eighth of a page? But the *Havenport Herald* had rules and, well, she had to follow them.

"Generally," she explained, "obits are anywhere from two hundred to four hundred fifty words. Well, it's not a static count, per se, but suggested. And it depends on when you want it to run and how many…" She shook her head, since his eyes seemed to be glazing over at her rambling.

"Never mind. May I see?" she asked, and held out a hand, head tilted to the envelope, hoping he'd hand it over from the death grip.

His bunched shoulders relaxed a bit. "Sure."

The moment their fingers touched something sizzled between them. Darcy sucked in a breath. Tingles ran up her arm. He flinched.

Shit. Static electricity brought on by the clodhopper shoes she'd been forced to don since her Ls were a broken mess under her desk. A visible spark ignited between them. It couldn't possibly have anything to do with attraction, or desire, the kind found in those romance novels she devoured.

Nope. Her soles had generated more charge than Ben Franklin and his stupid key. Last time she'd worn them and picked up Oedipus, he'd hissed so much his hair stood on end. Poor kitty.

"I'm sorry, the carpet generated a spark."

"The carpet, or those shoes?" he asked while looking down at the culprits in horror. Darcy wanted to die. No matter that her sleek linen skirt, in her favorite shade of purple, fit just right. And her sweater set, a steal online at the overstock website, hugged her barely B cups in a nice way. The shoes were butt ugly. Plus, they were caked with mud from the last reenactment in the rain. But really, what kind of gentleman made a comment on a lady's footwear, good or bad?

"The heel of my Ls broke and these were the only things I had to wear," she grumbled, more than a little annoyed. Why was she explaining herself? This entire episode was bizarre.

"I'm sorry I shocked you." The tone of her words held no remorse, but Darcy didn't care. Gorgeous or not, the guy didn't have to be rude.

He blinked, taking in her explanation before mulling it over and dismissing it. "Can you just have this put into the paper tomorrow?"

"Tomorrow?" Technically, the last edits hadn't gone into editorial, but she glanced at her watch. The noon deadline might be possible. "I'm not sure. I'll try," she answered honestly.

His lips tightened. They were outstanding, dammit. Plump enough to balance with the rest of his face—from his strong jawline to his nose, which had a slight bump on it, as if broken. His lips weren't thin or weak like he-who-should-remain-nameless. And the hint of stubble above his upper lip put the *s* in sexy.

However, it was not her problem he might actually miss the submission deadline.

"The deadline for tomorrow's edition is noon," she explained. "And I still have to proof this before it can be submitted. Sorry." *Again with the apologies?* She needed to stop.

He crossed his arms so that the sleeves of his button-down denim stretched across his impressive biceps. Could his arms be any bigger?

"Believe me, it's fine, and it needs to stay as is."

Oh was it? "Excuse me, Mr.…." She trailed off, waiting for him to volunteer his name.

"Luke Christianson."

"Yes, well, Mr. Christianson."

"Call me Luke."

"Luke, I'm Darcy Prentice."

"Nice to meet you, Darcy." Could his voice be any smoother? And why did the sound of her name on his lips cause her heart to skip?

She cleared her throat and tried to recover. "I'll do my best to make tomorrow's edition, but I can't make any promises. Is there a wake or memorial service that you need to make people aware of? If so, we can always post it to the website first."

"No." She couldn't read his expression. Why the rush?

"Then why the rush?" she blurted without thinking. Jeez, this day was turning epically unprofessional.

Luke fell silent for a moment. Maybe considering his answer, or maybe she'd royally pissed him off by all her inappropriate questions. Honestly, taking an obituary announcement had never been this interesting or frustrating or downright annoying in the past. Most people filled out the form, thanked her, and left—the normal ones.

Finally he took a deep breath and licked his lips.

Do not stare.

"Listen, ma'am," he said, and she almost cringed. She wasn't *that* old. "I'm asking you to do me a favor, although you don't know me."

Yeah, but she wanted to… *Stop it.*

"I have a duty to get this obituary in the *Havenport Herald* on this particular date." He uttered the words with a quiet conviction.

The way he'd said *duty* made Darcy pause. Duty and a Marine went hand in hand. Her heart suddenly ached. He certainly could pass for a Marine with his standard-issue flat-top haircut—a bit bushier than regulation allowed, though. She knew because her friend in the reenactment group, Lucas, who called himself an old salty dog, went for a haircut nearly every day.

And, of course, because of her brother David.

"I realize this is short notice, but I couldn't get to Havenport any sooner than this morning." He chewed on his bottom lip and shook his head, like he berated himself for the shortcoming.

She had to ask. "Are you active duty?"

His gaze shot up to her face. "How did you know?" His body tensed and his expression grew guarded.

Darcy motioned to his key chain. "The Marine Corps insignia, and that." She pointed to his head.

His right sandy eyebrow shot up. "Excuse me?"

Heat catapulted to her face. "Your hair…err…the cut. My brother was a Marine, so I notice these things."

"Was?"

A lump formed in her esophagus. "He died."

He flinched and sympathy crept into his extraordinary peepers. "I'm truly sorry for your loss."

Darcy let out a shaky breath. "Thank you. As I am for yours."

"Mine?" he asked, and Darcy held up the envelope and the obituary, figuring it had to be someone he'd known and had lost.

"Yeah, thanks. And, no, I'm not active, just got out two weeks ago."

She nodded, letting him continue, and also because the low timbre of his voice made her insides quiver.

"You see, my mother died last year and she apparently grew up in Havenport and wanted her obituary to run in this paper on this date. Not sure why, or what the significance of the date, but I have to honor her wishes."

"The anniversary of the Havenport Hostilities is happening now. That might be why," she blurted. He just shrugged, and she thought she heard him mumble, "Beats me."

Tomorrow was also the first day of a few historical reenactments which would take place in town. Now she was curious.

"May I?" she asked, and started to open the folder.

"Suit yourself, as long as it gets in tomorrow's edition. Is there a fee?" He shifted his weight between his work boots and shoved his hands in his front pants pockets. His jeans were loose-fit carpenter type.

And fit him perfectly, of course. "No fee."

"So I can just leave it with you and go?" He ran a hand over his trimmed head and turned on one heel of his work boots toward the exit.

"Who wrote this?" Darcy asked, not wanting him to go. Not only was this obituary interesting, but it had been so long since the sheer presence of a man made her feel warm all over. He pivoted back to face her.

"My mother."

Without looking up from the page and trying to divert her attention from the cut of his pants, Darcy let out a chuckle. The eulogy was quite entertaining.

"Your mother wrote this?" she prodded, suddenly desperate to know the story behind the words, and somehow unable to ignore her brewing curiosity. Tingles made the hairs on the back of her neck twitch, a feeling she got when anything interesting happened.

She finally looked up, and a slow grin came over his face.

"I imagine not many people write their own obituary. Since there's no fee, I really do have to go."

"Wait." She'd just gotten to the part about Principal Langston and let out a hoot. "This stuff is great. And Principal Langston is still alive, by the way, although she's pushing ninety." This had to be the best obit she'd ever read.

Luke stared down at his boots. Darcy noticed his shoulders tightening, and there went the flattened lips again.

Uh-oh. Stupid, stupid. "I apologize. I didn't mean to offend you or your mother's memories."

It was his turn to laugh, and the sound eased some of the tension in the room. It also lit up his face. "Believe me, Mom wouldn't be offended. She was a bit, well…eccentric. And an artist."

Darcy matched his smile, and when she got a glimpse of his white teeth, her stomach jumped. "Yeah, I gathered that. I think I've actually seen that fence with the psychedelic colors. I can show you where it's located," she offered. Could she sound more desperate for him not to leave? But curiosity for his story, and his mother's story, had blossomed in her mind and she could not ignore it.

His face fell.

"Or if you have somewhere else to be, I didn't mean to assume…"

He shrugged. "I actually do have other stuff to do, so this is one of the things to check off the list before I skip town. But thanks."

Jeez, he probably had a girlfriend or wife somewhere, although there was no ring on his left hand. Not that it meant much. He-who-should-remain-nameless hadn't even been divorced when they'd started sleeping together—a fact quite unknown to her. What a sleazeball.

"Um, sure. No problem."

Cue the awkward silence. He cleared his throat. "Great. I'll just be going now. Thank you, Darcy."

"Wait," she blurted, and he turned back to her, eyebrow raised. "You'll need to fill out the form." Jeez, she'd almost forgotten.

He glanced at his watch, a large round piece with a thousand buttons. "If that's what's required."

"It's a formality, but I'll need contact numbers," she explained, and had the feeling as soon as he walked out the door she'd never lay eyes on Luke Christianson again. For a reason she didn't try to understand that wouldn't be right.

His brow furrowed. "Why would you contact me?" he asked, his face creased with suspicion.

A rush of heat flooded her cheeks. "Oh, I probably won't. But we'd still need to have some kind of way, you know…if needed." How lame.

Luke shrugged. "Um, sure." She could tell by the way he glanced at his watch and the door that he'd wanted to be gone ten minutes ago.

"It'll just take a minute," she assured him. "If you'll follow me." She didn't wait for his reply, merely tucked the envelope under her arm and pointed to the double doors leading to the back offices.

He let out a long sigh and nodded, shifting between his boots. "Okay, lead the way."

"The conference rooms are occupied, but we can use my desk," she said, glancing at him sideways. At least he still followed, although silent.

He also ignored the heads popping up from their cubicles. For the love of God, had none of the females—and one guy—ever witnessed a gorgeous man before? Didn't help that he towered over their cubicles, and with his sun-streaked hair and tanned face, put surfers to shame.

Darcy gestured to the chair at the end of her desk.

He folded his long frame into the plastic and metal chair and rested his hands in his lap. He had nice hands, strong fingers with square nails. Not buffed or manicured, like the sleazeball had insisted on every Tuesday. Nope. Luke's were work-worn, a little calloused and sexy.

OMG. She scoped his fingernails? What was wrong with her? Darcy yanked open the file cabinet under her desk.

"Son of a bitch," he exclaimed between clenched teeth.

At that moment if the floor opened and dropped her into the newsroom below she'd die happy. "Omigod. I'm so sorry…are you okay?" *I'm so fucking stupid.*

He barked out a laugh between wincing and rubbing his kneecap. "No, you're not. It's okay."

Oh. Lord. She'd actually said it out loud. Darcy placed her index fingers against her closed lids and massaged. A bowling-ball-size headache crept into her frontal lobe. This day needed a do-over. Big-time. First the shoe disaster, then she'd crushed the man's kneecap. "Jesus," she said in a puff, and tried to find the words to apologize. "You don't know me, but I swear I'm not usually this much of a calamity. Here's the form," she stated. "Fill out the highlighted parts when you can and leave it at the front desk. Go. While you have all your limbs."

Darcy slid the form over to him without looking up and resumed rubbing her eyelids. She'd head over to Led Zeppoli and get a triple espresso. Maybe he'd be smart, take the form, leave, and she'd never have to see him again. Yeah, that sentiment didn't sit right in her gut, but Luke Christianson and his "duty" were probably better off.

She heard rustling in her penholder and when she opened her eyes, Luke was still there bent over and filling out the form.

"Nice pen." He scribbled his signature, slid the form to her, and placed her favorite pen back in its holder, and again she was mortified. Of course he'd picked her happy poop emoji pen.

"My happy chocolate Kiss pen? Glad you enjoy it."

His mouth quirked and his shoulders shook in silent mirth. "If you say so. Thanks for your help, Darcy Prentice. And thanks for the chuckle. It's been a while since that's happened."

Her breath caught at his words as she watched him rise, wink, and saunter down the hallway.

Holy moly, what just happened? Her instant message on the email dinged. *Who was that?* from Sharon two cubicles over.

Great, now the whole office would have questions.

"Hey."

Darcy jumped at the sound of Luke once again at the side of her desk, with an expression of curiosity and embarrassment.

"Oh…hey," she stammered. "Did you forget something?"

He seemed to be contemplating a response and fidgeted with the key chain.

"Would you mind helping me out with something else?"

Darcy's jaw slacked open. *If you mean ripping off that tight T-shirt under your button-down…sure.* "If I can," she answered instead.

"May I?" He tilted his head toward her chair.

"Please."

He sat and rubbed the back of his neck before expelling a long breath. At that moment, Goth Girl popped her head over the cubicle. Jeez, was she standing on her chair? Darcy glared at her.

"Oops…sorry," Goth Girl said, all syrupy voice, but clearly didn't mean it by the way she leered at Luke and batted her eyelashes. Darcy resisted the urge to roll her eyes.

"I'll send you an email, Darce." Goth Girl took her sweet time sitting back down. She probably had her ear pressed against the fabric separating their workspace. An email? She'd never even conversed with the girl before this morning.

Luke bit his bottom lip. The word *duty* came back to haunt Darcy. He clearly needed assistance, and from what she could ascertain from their short interaction, he didn't know much about Havenport. A thought struck.

"You know, I could use a serious cup of coffee. The stuff here stinks." She grimaced at her cup of tepid tea. "There's a place not far called Led Zeppoli. We can talk there, you know…with more privacy," she said in a stage whisper, and pointed to the side of the room.

Affirmation dawned on his face. "How good is the coffee, because the sludge I had on the interstate feels like a dud grenade in my stomach."

"The best in Havenport," Darcy answered with a smile, hoping he'd accept. She shot a quick email to her boss that she had an errand, then grabbed her purse.

"Let's go," he said.

♥ ♥ ♥

For a midmorning in early May, the temperatures weren't exactly warm. Luke pulled up the collar of his button-down shirt and walked beside his first acquaintance in Havenport, Darcy Prentice. Besides the ugly-ass shoes, she was pretty hot. And the breeze didn't seem to bother her at all. She wore a light sweater in a shade of purple that lit up her eyes of a similar shade. They were one of the first things he'd noticed. He'd never met anyone with violet eyes before. Shorter than him by a little less than a foot, the top of her head barely came up to his shoulder, but he didn't care. He'd always been partial to shorter girls, ever since growing into his six-three, lanky frame back in high school. He tried to keep his stride short so Darcy could keep up. He was glad she'd suggested they get coffee. One, the shit back at the truck stop had sucked. His stomach had been doing flips ever since. And two, because he didn't know how to ask Darcy for help without the whole damned paper and gossips in their office knowing his business. Luke supposed they'd know his business soon enough when the obituary ran. *Wonderful. Way to stay inconspicuous.* He guessed that feat was impossible for such a small town.

They reached the Led Zeppoli place, a five-minute hike, and he held open the door. Her breath hitched and she smiled, seeming surprised he was a gentleman. If Mom and Ben had taught him anything—and they'd taught him a lot— they'd drilled into him to never shirk responsibilities or forget to do the right thing. Be a gentleman, Ben would say, even if no one knew about it or cared. God, Luke missed him.

Darcy scooted past him just as some moron walked out of the shop, and the jackass didn't bother to let her go first. No harm, though, for she was forced to brush up against him, and he caught a whiff of her hair. It was dark brown and wavy, falling to her waist. Most women he knew didn't keep their hair that long, and opted for the highlighted, processed new styles.

Oranges. Her hair smelled of oranges. She walked ahead of him, and he forced his eyes forward and not fixated on her behind. Her straight skirt hugged her curves just right.

Oh boy, it'd been a while since he'd slept with anyone, and hooking up with someone on this errand would be an epically bad decision. There would be plenty of time and ladies in Atlanta. Professional city girls who probably didn't work for a local paper, wear muddy hiking shoes, or smell like oranges. He'd settle for the impersonal and occasional hookup with someone out for pleasure.

Darcy wasn't that kind of woman. He knew it. Could sense it a mile away. *Then why accompany her for coffee?* Hell if he knew. Sure, he could use a contact in Havenport— someone who he might ask about scattering Mom's ashes at the park, maybe even recommend a place to stay that was reasonably priced.

That was the only reason.

She didn't wear any rings, but that didn't mean much. He'd spied two photos on her desk, one of a Marine— must be her brother—and the other a framed photo of a midnight cat wearing a Santa hat. The cat seemed miserable. No couple photos. It was in his nature to scope out places, something ingrained since the first deployment. He continuously took stock of his surroundings—exits, faces in a crowd, potential threats. Being in a recon unit, he ran a daily checklist in his mind for every scenario. Would be a hard thing to shake in civilian life.

"Thank you," Darcy said after they entered the shop and approached the line in front of the counter. The shop smelled of freshly baked bread and strong coffee. The aroma was so good his stomach growled. Loud. Loud enough to be heard over the din of the coffee orders being thrown around the place. He noticed Darcy's mouth quirk but she said nothing and waited behind a mother holding an infant. So he leaned in close to her ear and she jumped a bit.

"I know you heard that."

She gave him a sideways glance and licked her lips. They were shiny and also smelled of oranges. Must be her favorite fruit.

"Heard what?" she asked, doe-eyed, but her shoulders shook and she bit her bottom lip.

"Uh-huh," he countered, and straightened, easily peeking over her head at the chalkboard filled with a myriad of choices, various breakfast bakery items, and coffee flavors galore. "Wow. So many choices."

"The dark roast is amazing," she stated. "And the chocolate croissants…but…you probably don't want any."

Her eyes nailed him head to toe, and it was damned exciting. But wait… "Why not? Are they horrible?"

Her face lit up. "On the contrary. They are the best pastry on the planet."

Luke scratched the top of his brow and regarded her. "What am I missing? Why wouldn't I want one?"

She made a *pfft* sound. "Pulease. You have zero body fat. Do you even eat carbs?" She clamped a hand over her mouth, closed her eyes, and groaned, then turned an adorable shade of crimson.

Oh, yeah. Darcy Prentice had already made his trip to Havenport more tolerable.

Darcy pivoted and gave him her back. A slow grin crept onto his face as he waited his turn. Once at the counter, she stepped to the side but still hadn't looked at him again. After ordering a double espresso she handed the cashier her money, but he placed his hand over her wrist. It was delicate under his palm, and if he squeezed, he feared it would break. She wasn't petite in the usual sense. On the contrary, she had nice—really nice—curves.

"My treat," he told the young girl behind the counter. "I'll take a medium dark roast, black with one sugar, and two chocolate croissants."

She shouted the order to the barista and worker manning the bakery and coffee stations.

Darcy finally faced him. "Two? You must really be hungry. And that wasn't necessary. But thanks."

Luke grabbed his order and followed Darcy to a vacant table toward the back of the bakery. He sat facing the door, which was his normal MO. He was always prepared for anything. He pulled two napkins out of the metal dispenser, opened the paper bag, and placed a croissant in front of her.

He couldn't wait, especially given her recommendation, and dove into his. The melt-in-your-mouth chocolate hit his tongue and he almost moaned. "I will not embarrass myself, but holy crap, this is outstanding." After a gulp of even better java, Luke licked a bit of chocolate off his lip and noticed she was staring at his mouth.

He gestured to the napkin and her uneaten confection. Her mouth dropped open. "Oh no, I can't."

"Why not?"

Darcy blinked. "I don't actually eat carbs. I dream about them, but they don't like my hips or waist. Well, maybe they do like my hips." She laughed at herself then sipped her espresso.

"Hold on. First, you give me hell about not eating carbs, which I obviously do," he said, and held up what was left of the pastry, "and will never give up, but you admit you don't? That's the pot calling the kettle…something."

"Black," she finished for him.

"Yeah, black. Do *not* tell me you are one of those women who diet." Her body was near to perfect in his estimation.

She smirked. "First, what woman doesn't? And second, believe me, I watch. I try to stay…you know…fit." She took a shallow sip then placed her cup on the table before tugging the edge of her sweater down over her waist. Luke got a feeling she thought she was anything but fit and camouflaged her body. Did she not have a mirror?

He finished the croissant in three bites and shook his head. "You're fit. Believe me, I noticed."

Her eyes widened. "Well," she sputtered, then took another gulp of coffee. "What did you need my help about?" She tried to divert the conversation, and he had to give her credit. He hadn't meant to make her uncomfortable, but she was damned adorable when she blushed and stammered. Guileless. And it'd been a long time since he'd interacted with any woman who wasn't wearing cammies and wanting to get off, down and dirty and quick. Mindless sex, to relieve the tension of battle. The women overseas—the Marine women—were tough chicks.

Most didn't give a shit about carbohydrates.

"I'm sorry I made you feel uncomfortable." At her confused look, he continued, "Assuming you'd want to eat," he clarified. "It's just that…" Instead of finishing his half-assed excuse for an apology, he downed the rest of his dark roast. Shit, he apparently needed some lessons in civilian interaction.

"You didn't offend me." She glanced down at the napkin, flattened her lips, and her shoulders rose and fell in a long sigh. "Oh, what the hell." She bit into the croissant with such gusto he could only stare in wonder.

"Omigod, I forgot how amazing this tastes." She shut her eyes and swallowed. He gripped his cup.

He was in trouble.

Time to steer the conversation back to help, back to getting out of Havenport in one piece instead of watching the pure bliss on her face.

"I need to find out how to scatter ashes in Havenport Park, or actually find Havenport Park," he mused.

Darcy stopped midchew. "You plan to scatter your mother there?"

Luke swallowed hard and nodded, suddenly unable to continue. Her passing wasn't the acute pain he'd experienced right after she'd passed away, but doing this errand, laying her to rest, had permanence to it. He thought he was ready to face the task, but perhaps not.

"Yeah," he answered, suddenly hoarse and wishing he'd gotten the large coffee.

"When we scattered David's ashes, my folks did it under a tree in their backyard, so it was private." She bit her lip, thinking. "Hmm...in Havenport Park, I'm not so sure. You may need a permit or something. I can ask around at the *Herald* for info if you want?"

Wow. He felt honored she'd do that for him. "I'd appreciate that. David was your brother, the Marine?"

Darcy let out a long breath before nodding. "Yes. He died almost two years ago."

"KIA?"

She wiped her mouth and leaned back in her chair. "Actually, no. He'd left the Marines and was just about to adopt his dog. He was EOD. David was killed by a drunk driver."

His stomach sank. EOD Marines had dangerous jobs, and the dog handlers went out in situations he sure as shit wouldn't want to.

"That's tragic. EOD jobs in the corps are seriously dangerous, for sure. Many explosives guys and their dogs saved my life, and my unit's lives, more than once."

Her eyes filled with sadness. "David was the best."

They continued to converse with ease. Luke couldn't believe in the short time since they'd met how much he'd opened up and shared about his history in the corps. Not everything, but enough to feel good about unloading and proud to be able to explain his accomplishments.

Darcy laughed and threw back her head. He sucked in a breath. The column of her neck was sexy and she had a small mole right under her chin.

She wiped the corners of her eyes. "That stuff is hysterical. David used to say some of the guys in his unit were real ball-busters. So, what do you do? I mean, when you're not being a Marine?"

"I'm a carpenter with some training. I hope to eventually become a journeyman carpenter after an apprenticeship in Atlanta. Fingers crossed. But nothing's guaranteed." *Way to look unsure in front of a pretty lady.* He'd never felt this comfortable with anyone, at least not a female. And not for a long, long time. His corps buddies didn't count. Many were surface communicators. With the exception of when Mom died and his brothers rallied around him to make sure his head was screwed on straight, the guys kept things all business: mission details, military slang, and shooting the shit for laughs.

Darcy caused this warm, comfortable feeling to invade his insides, and damned if he didn't want the sensation to go away.

And talk about animated. Between nibbles of croissant, she waved a hand, fanned her face when she laughed, and constantly tossed her long hair back over her shoulder when she explained a point or pointed out a few of the locals who walked into the shop. When she laughed at his recollections of driving into town, her eyes twinkled.

"Oh, jeez. Those ladies were probably the Garden Club." She winked. "Collectively they are two thousand years old and all of them are terrible flirts."

Luke relayed stuff about his mother and told Darcy of the mission to spread the ashes in one week, on her birthday. She asked about his plans after Havenport and he explained about the apprenticeship set up by his buddy in Atlanta. Darcy seemed genuinely interested in that. She asked about his mom's artwork, too, and mentioned that crazy fence mural still being around.

Before he knew it, an entire hour had passed. His Swiss Army watch dinged every hour. "All I've done is talk about me."

"Sorry. It's the journalist in me."

He nodded. "Speaking of, aren't you supposed to be at work?"

She looked down at her watch and squeaked. "Wow. It's that late? No biggie. I've got time before the deadline for tomorrow's edition. I'll do my best to get your mom's notice included, Luke."

A weight was gone from his sternum.

They walked out of Led Zeppoli and she turned to face him. He didn't want their time together to end, but he had stuff to get done and a week to kill before the day.

"I have your number, so I'll let you know what I find out…" She held out her hand, which surprised him. "It was wonderful to meet and talk with you, Luke."

Their palms met, and he thought she sucked in a breath, but she recovered with a quick smile.

"One more question, before you go?" He couldn't let her hand go. It just felt right.

"Sure." She licked her lips. He wanted to lean down and taste them, but that would be totally inappropriate.

"Where's a good place to stay in town? I've got a few days here, so I might as well make the best of it. Sightsee or sleep." Yeah, sleep—without waking up in a sweat or hearing rounds fired in the distance would be a pleasure.

"The Havenport Inn is really nice."

He ducked his head. "It's not super-expensive, is it? I mean, those yachts I saw in the harbor were no joke."

She laughed and shook her head, then reached inside her purse and pulled out her wallet. She held out a business card. "Here's the number. One of my old high school friends runs the front desk. Tell him Darcy sent you and I'm sure he'll take care of you."

Wow, his luck on the favors just kept piling up today.

Luke took the card, and when their fingers touched a subtle blush hit the bridge of her cute nose. "I appreciate it…I mean, really, everything you've done for me so far today has been great." Hell, he felt like a blubbering idiot.

She tilted her head to the side and her long hair shifted. He suspected the waves were soft and silky, but he sure as shit wasn't going to run his hands along them, as much as he yearned to, and certainly not in the middle of this town. Nope. He had a duty, a mission as it were, and it would be better to stay in control and away from her fresh, sweet, open-and-honest type. With her sexy eyes, killer curves, and infectious laugh, staying in control and on task would not be easy.

"It's been my pleasure. Have a good day."

Throwing caution to the wind, he blurted, "I hope to see you around. Maybe, I don't know, tomorrow? That is, if you find out anything about the park?" He shifted between his work boots and prayed he didn't sound desperate.

"I'll call you as soon as I have the answer, okay?" Her eyebrows rose and she waited.

"That would be great."

Chapter Three

Okay, so Darcy couldn't stop smiling. So much so that Sharon commented on it during their daily lunch in the *Herald* cafeteria that afternoon. She barely ate her salad because, let's face it, that croissant at Led Zeppoli blew her daily points allotment out of the ballpark.

But she didn't dare disclose her meeting with Luke, or why she couldn't stop grinning like a fool. When Sharon asked, she made up a white lie about being excited for her pitch meeting. A little lie never hurt anyone. Yeah, a good excuse. Better than admitting the other…

Luke Christianson.

What the freak had happened to her? One hunky Marine, doing an amazing favor for his dead mother, and suddenly her ovaries kicked into overdrive? So what if his body put every single man's in Havenport to shame? So what if his smile and laugh was infectious? So what if he'd held the door open? And so what if she'd stopped herself from rubbing her nose into the middle of his chest and inhaling his scent before she embarrassed herself?

It was all in the name of a good deed. Right? *Keep telling yourself that, Darce.*

The flutters and heat hadn't left her insides since they'd said goodbye, which by the way, was the last thing she'd wanted to do.

He'd been exceptionally easy to talk to. Since the "cheater" debacle, male companionship simply hadn't existed. And belly laughs had been nonexistent for a very long time. Between the tragic loss of David and having to constantly soothe her parents, there wasn't anything to laugh about lately. Luke's recollections made it simple, natural. No pretenses, just good old-fashioned conversation.

Too bad he's only here for a short time. She frowned at her wilted cucumber and picked at the salad. He certainly had a nice set of plans for his future out of the Marine Corps, and who could blame him? David had always relayed that deployments took a portion of your soul every single time.

"You're awfully quiet now," Sharon commented while nibbling on her sandwich.

Darcy looked up at her friend and shrugged. "Just busy, and I need an idea for the next Historicals."

Sharon regarded her. "So who was that hunky guy?"

"Hunky guy?" Darcy feigned ignorance, but Sharon narrowed her eyes.

"The tall one, with the sick muscles who came in this morning? Phew." She fanned herself with a napkin. "If I wasn't married…"

"Oh, him? He submitted an obit." Darcy crossed her fingers in her lap. Sharon was worse than any gossip in town, including the Garden Club cronies.

"That's too bad. You need a man."

Darcy rolled her eyes. "I do *not* need a man."

Sharon threw her a sideways glance. "Yes, you do. And being in that reenactment group with the old men does not help. Tell me the last time you went on a real date." Sharon knew about the cheater and how he'd destroyed a lot of things in her life.

"I'm too busy with my jobs and my parents. Plus, I have zero interest in anyone." *Except Luke.*

Sharon tsked. "I call bullshit. Women have *needs*," she stated loudly, then popped a chip into her mouth. "Glenn takes care of mine, but he's my hubby, thank Jesus. What about you? The battery-operated thing does not count."

"Would you shut up?" Darcy peered over her shoulder at the table of reporters in rolled-up sleeves, eating off their trays. "God, how embarrassing," she mumbled.

Sharon had been her best friend since grammar school and her rock when David had died.

"You need to lighten up," Sharon lectured for what had to be the hundredth time since Darcy had moved back to Havenport. "And don't get me started on your parents. You do not have to cater to them all the time. It's seriously selfish on their part."

Sharon was right to a degree. Mom hadn't gotten over David's death. After all, he had been her baby and joined the Marine Corps after high school. Just when he'd planned to come home, the tragedy struck. It'd been a horrific shame having survived multiple deployments to die on native soil. Sometimes Darcy felt an obligation to take the place of both a son and a daughter. They'd kept his room like a shrine, and refused to move on. Even when David's military dog had been adopted, ironically by the Havenport town vet, her parents still yearned to live in the past.

Well, as much as she loved learning about the past, and was an ancestry junkie, she couldn't live there always wondering "what if." She took the stance of honoring history and the past, but not trying to relive it.

David would not have wanted that. If her brother taught her anything in his short life it was that life was for the living. She hoped she had courage to keep adhering to his mantra.

Darcy wiped her mouth, threw her garbage in one pile on her tray, and stood. "Been a great lunch, as usual, but I have to get back." Great. Diversion always worked with Sharon.

"Uh-huh," she said knowingly, and pursed her lips. "Run away. Don't forget you and Glenn have that reenactment meeting tomorrow. He's got a softball game with Evan Washburn after that, so he's super busy. I never see him. But he's so sexy in those skimpy period uniforms I can't complain too much."

Darcy laughed. "You're too much. Tell him I'll see him at the library in the morning."

Darcy headed back to her cubicle and plopped into her chair. The Havenport Historicals series needed another installment, and damned if she didn't have one single idea.

Luke's manila envelope lay on top her desk, his mother's obituary proofed—not that the prose needed editing. She'd submitted the piece onto the alphabetized listing of obituaries set to run in tomorrow's edition.

Mary Sullivan.

Firing up the computer, Darcy went to her favorite place, Ancestry.com, and did a search on Sullivans in Havenport. What popped up made her eyes widen. Well, now, Mary Sullivan did live here and was born in 1968. Wow, she had a bunch of connections, too. William and Valerie Sullivan, who were also born in Havenport.

Darcy felt guilty prying into Luke's mom's life, but her interest in Luke and his mother had been more than piqued today.

Darcy clicked through some of the leaves on the trees and drilled down her search. The Sullivans seemed to date back to the…*holy shit*…the Revolutionary War and General John Sullivan.

Darcy leaned back in her chair and grinned at the screen. Well, that was a bit of all right.

Chapter Four

The following morning, Darcy walked to the library with a large espresso in hand. So much for giving up caffeine. She needed it this morning. Sleep had been fleeting at best last night. A certain gorgeous sandy-haired man invaded her dreams, and that had been the end of her slumber. Even poor Oedipus complained at all her tossing and turning.

She waved at the librarian and found her way to the usual room the reenactment group used for their meetings. The glass conference rooms were often booked on weekend mornings, but their group had a long-standing reservation. The average age of the group was probably sixty, but she didn't mind. Their enthusiasm for the period made up for their lack of stamina.

"Hello, Darce." Lucas Cameron sat alone at the wood and metal table with the group's financial reports in hand. Their group was mostly funded by the Havenport Historical Society. However, Lucas made sure any donations specifically for the Rhode Island Revelers—as their group had named themselves—whether monetary or in materials, were kept in a record book. This season's reenactments would coincide with the Havenport

Hostilities and were set to run for a few weekends in May. The tourists loved seeing Havenport's history, and Darcy loved explaining it to the little ones.

"Hi, Lucas. You're hard at work already? Let me guess, you ran a few miles before I even got out of bed?"

His eyes crinkled at the corners. Rumor had it he was barely fifty, not that Darcy had the gumption to ask, but Lucas was a handsome man. In amazing shape, he was a fixture running most mornings along the waterfront, which explained his runner's body. Most of the women in Havenport, especially female patrons of Royce's, had the serious hots for Lucas. He had served his country in the Marines and beamed with pride about his days in the service. He'd never married, but he'd kept closemouthed about his personal life.

"Not this morning, sadly. And someone has to keep up with the finances. You want the job?"

Darcy nearly choked on her coffee. "You know me and math are arch enemies. I'm a writer, my friend."

"Yes, and a damned good one. That last Historicals piece was fascinating stuff."

"Why thank you," she said, and sat next to him.

Lucas kept his hair in a flat-top style, and although laced with salt and pepper, there were blond streaks mixed in. He took off his reading glasses and smiled at her. Wow, she'd never noticed the color of his eyes, icy blue.

"We have a dilemma," he said with a frown. "Glenn and the rest can't make the meeting so it's just us this a.m. Gerald got hurt on the fire truck last night."

"Oh, no. I hope he's okay." Gerald was a few years older than her, and she knew he was the sole provider for his wife and two kids at home.

Lucas ran a hand along his head and shrugged. "He broke his leg fighting a fire by the docks. According to his wife he'll be out of work for a while, but that's not the worst part. He was going to build our new setup for this reenactment series."

"That's right. Can't we just set up tents?" They'd made do before.

He nodded. "We could, but the *New Englander* wants pictures and an authentic feel for the magazine article we'll be featured in," Lucas said. "Complete with a wagon and a shelter. See, here's the plans Gerald had drafted." Lucas spread two preliminary renderings on the table.

There was a shelter with a spit for roasting and hanging period clay pots. "Isn't there anyone else in town to do it?"

"None who will work for what Gerald's charging us, I'm afraid. And I'm sadly not handy enough to do it. We will think of something for next weekend. So what's shaking at the *Herald*?"

Darcy took a sip of coffee and debated speaking to Lucas about Luke. In the absence of her own father being accessible and open to conversation, she cherished having Lucas to talk to about her job. He seemed genuinely interested in Havenport and had also grown up here.

"It's interesting that you ask, because the strangest and sweetest thing happened yesterday when I was on obits."

His eyebrows arched, reminding her so much of someone else that she blinked a few times. Must be that Luke invaded her brain every two minutes. She told Lucas about Luke and his mother's obituary, as well as his plans to scatter her ashes in Havenport Park. "I found out he does *not* need a permit per se, just approval, so I guess he's good to go. It's such an entertaining piece of writing. Not to be creepy, but you should read her obituary."

Lucas's face paled and he gripped his pencil.

"Are you okay?" If she didn't know any better, Lucas appeared to have seen a ghost. Darcy glanced out the glass walls into the main room of the library, but there were few people milling.

He swallowed hard and closed the ledger with a thud. Darcy swore his hand shook.

"Can I get you something? Sometimes I get weak if I don't eat breakfast," she suggested, worried. Beads of sweat formed on his forehead, making it shiny, and Lucas still hadn't uttered a word. What if he was having chest pains or something?

"I'll run and get you some water." She stood, but he placed a hand on her forearm.

"Don't. I just recalled I forgot to check on something at my house." He stood, shoved his arms in his jacket, folded the ledger book under his arm, and headed for the door.

Once Lucas left, Darcy stood stunned and watched him make a beeline to the library exit.

"Strange," she mumbled, and reached for her coffee. Lucas forgot the renderings as well. Darcy sat, sipped her coffee, and wondered what the hell had happened to make him so upset. She'd bet it had nothing to do with his house. But why lie? And what were they going to do about getting a carpenter on such short notice? The Havenport Historical Society was hoping the magazine spread would help boost donations.

Wait. She grinned at the papers. There was a new carpenter in town—for the next week, at least.

♥ ♥ ♥

Luke stepped off the curb in front of the Havenport Inn and tilted his head to the sky. It was certainly a glorious and sunny day in Rhode Island and a perfect time for a run. He'd awoken to guests of the Inn walking outside his door—one particular child whined about pancakes all the way. The demands faded down the hall, but the planted seed hurdled his stomach into hunger mode.

The Havenport Inn turned out to be a good place to hang his hat. Darcy's friend had hooked him up with a reasonably priced room—nothing fancy, but serviceable and more comfortable than any bed he'd slept in for months. It sure beat waking up on a cot in the desert.

After a quick shower, he found the dining room and was waited on by a super-nice waitress, then devoured a stack of fluffy pancakes. Too bad Darcy wasn't here to indulge in his carbfest. He couldn't help smiling over their conversation yesterday at the bakery.

As soon as his head hit the pillow his mind shot to Darcy. Her face, her amazing-smelling hair, and those to-die-for curves. Not to mention his fantasy of her being snuggled up beside him, warm curves against his body. He couldn't recall the last time a woman had affected him from minute one. Ever.

Mom's urn sat on top of the ornate dresser in his room, and he'd almost spoken to it to tell her about Darcy this morning. But that would be creepy and crazy. So instead he decided to go for a run after breakfast, maybe even to Havenport Park and plot what he wanted to do about scattering her ashes. Mom loved colors, so maybe he'd get flowers to add under that tree, which he hoped to God was still standing.

He started in a slow jog to get his muscles warm, and then trotted down Water Street. Might as well take in the sights. A few yachts were moored in Havenport Marina. They must cost a pretty penny. No one was out and about yet, although it was after nine. Saturday morning probably meant sleeping in. Something he just couldn't seem to accomplish. Early rising had been ingrained in him for years with the corps. Hell, no sleep was more apt. Missions in the dead of night had fucked up his internal clock. But now, in a civilian capacity, he had to get used to a normal schedule, whatever that turned out to be.

His trainers hit the boards along the waterfront in a steady tattoo, and he transported himself into his zone. Running helped to shed thoughts, stress, and shift him into a place where his mind was at rest. Picking up the pace, he stabilized his breathing and let his legs fly over the pavement. He turned right on Franklin Avenue and headed toward Havenport Park at the end of the road past Constitution Boulevard. It took a good fifteen minutes to get to the park. Once he spotted the entrance sign, he jogged past and saw baseball diamonds on his left and a large soccer field toward the back corner of the lot. The areas were lined by a wooden fence, resembling an old horse corral. A ginormous oak tree appeared, and he knew.

It must be the one.

Jeez, it looked almost prehistoric. Branches the size of limbs on the Jolly Green Giant jutted out of the trunk, which had to be six feet in diameter. Next to it sat a bench of worn wood, bleached from use. The tree cast a shadow on the bench and there was no way even the bright sun shining in the sky today could penetrate the massive amount of leaves on the branches. Luke ceased his gait, but walked around the base of the tree to slow his heartbeat. He bent at the waist and gulped a few fortifying breaths. The adrenaline rush of exercise was something he relished. It made him feel alive, and here in this town, amidst fresh air and nature, no gunfire or insurgents or fear, he felt liberated.

No wonder Mom wanted her ashes spread here. Birds chirped from the multiple nests stationed above on the mammoth branches. This slice of Havenport Park could only be described as peace personified. So quiet it was eerie.

He'd bet once the ball fields in the distance became inhabited by children and spectators, the silence would be penetrated, but not this early, for now the only audible sounds were the birds and the wind whistling through the branches above his head.

A perfect spot for Mom.

He had to admit the town seemed lovely. But what the hell did he know about lovely or peaceful? This fucking war against terror was going on longer than his twelve years in the corps, but he'd felt the need to escape his own war when he'd enlisted.

The war he'd waged against himself and his shortcomings and sins existed and would exist until he met his maker. He sat down on a grassy patch next to the base of the tree and stretched his legs. Maybe Mom was trying to tell him something? Damned if he could figure it out.

Why hadn't she come back here? Or better yet, why was it so important for him to be here now?

The tourist magazines and flyers in his room at the Inn made for easy reading last night. Havenport certainly had a lot to offer in terms of fun, dining, a tavern, shops, and more. A nice little getaway, if one was so inclined. But he had to remember he wasn't here for any kind of vacation, and as soon as the week flew by, he'd be on his way to Atlanta.

However, a part of him grew curious about how Havenport had shaped Mom.

Were any of her old friends still living here? One time he'd found Mom crying and asked why, since she'd never, ever cried. She'd found out her parents had died in some kind of accident. But nothing further was ever discussed, nor had he ever met his grandparents. That was at the beginning of adolescence. Oh yeah, good ole puberty and hormones. Thankfully, Ben had entered their lives and changed everything.

Bah…he had no use for melancholy. Time to move forward.

Luke pushed off the ground and wiped away the grass from his nylon running shorts. Hopefully Darcy had found out about that permit to scatter the ashes. Whether he needed one or not, Mom's ashes would be spread here on her birthday.

"I promise." He tipped his head to the treetop then headed back to the Inn.

♥ ♥ ♥

Should she just show up at the Havenport Inn? What if Luke wasn't even there? What if he'd stayed somewhere else?

"Don't be an idiot. He asked for your help, and you need *him* now," she muttered, before parking her purple Bug along the side curb of the lot.

Given the Hostilities festivities going on the next week, the Inn seemed booked. Maybe he couldn't get a room?

"Hey, Darce," a voice came from behind. She turned to Brett stacking brochures on the table beside the reception desk.

"Hi!"

"What's up, Buttercup?" he asked, flashing his perfect smile. "You doing any reenactments this weekend because there sure are a bunch of groups here." He noted a crowd gathering outside the dining room in period costume.

"Not the Revelers. We're on for next weekend," she answered. He nodded and continued his task. She bit her lip. "Did someone come in for a room yesterday and use my name?"

Brett's eyes flared, and she recognized that mischievous expression. It was a well-known fact that Brett was totally head over heels for his husband, but they'd all shared quite a few shenanigans in their friendships, especially with Sharon riding shotgun.

"Hmm…well I do recall a delicious specimen who *seemed* to know you, but that couldn't be true, for Darcy Prentice is allergic to men, right?"

Cripes. "Have you been talking to Sharon?"

He crossed his arms and regarded her. "We speak daily, why?"

"Don't you start on me, too." Did every one of her friends think she needed another relationship? She'd recently begun to feel confident on her own. A new apartment, a few good jobs. Who needed a man, anyway?

"You should start living again." He shook his head and continued to stack the pamphlets and arrange the other ones in the rack adjacent to the front entrance. "I had a cancelation and your recommendation checked in yesterday afternoon. Why, you planning on getting to know Luke, a.k.a. tight buns and abs?" The last few words were barely a whisper.

She narrowed her eyes. "You have no filter."

He grinned. "Thank you for noticing."

"It's not…like that." *Wasn't it?* "I have a job for him, that's all."

Brett stilled. "Clothing optional?"

"Stop." She groaned. He was as bad as Sharon. Luckily, the people who worked at the Havenport Inn were quite aware of his twisted sense of humor.

Darcy let out a long sigh. "We need a carpenter to build the reenactment set, and Luke told me he does that kind of work." She followed Brett back to the desk where he hauled a box from a shelf and unpacked more brochures.

"And you couldn't have called him?" he asked knowingly.

Busted. "I could have, but I just thought it would be nicer to see if he was interested in person, and you know…show him the location. Besides, he knows no one in Havenport." Yeah, it sounded long-winded and a bit lame, but it was better than admitting the truth.

Brett's lips pursed. "Hmm, nothing at all to do with the fact he's gorgeous, huh?"

"Is he?" she muttered, and grabbed a stack, hoping he'd stop the interrogation.

He looked left and right, giving his million-watt smile to a couple who waved before leaving the Inn.

"Do *not* tell me you didn't notice. Phew. If I didn't love my husband, and your man gave me an ounce of interest…" Brett used a brochure to fan his face. "Come on, Darce, we've always commented on men before."

And they had in great detail. But for some reason discussing Luke seemed wrong. As a betrayal somehow. After one day—well, technically one portion of a day— what the heck did she think she was doing or feeling about him? He was practically a stranger. This attraction to him could only be a reaction to a gorgeous guy. Brett was right.

She needed to keep things professional. Especially now that she'd uncovered Mary Sullivan's ancestor connection to Havenport. Maybe Luke might be interested in her idea to highlight Mary and her connection to General Sullivan in the next Havenport Historicals installment.

"He's not my anything."

Brett bit the side of his cheek. "Mmm-hmm. By the way, is he military? Sure has the bod for it. You know how I have a thing for men in uniform." His husband was a volunteer firefighter.

"Marine Corps, and yes, I noticed. I'd have to be dead not to."

"That's my girl," he said with a wink. "So Mr. Butt and Abs was super polite, and I, of course, gave him a wee discount due to his relationship with you."

Darcy shook her head. "There *is* no relationship. Jeez, we met yesterday and spent an hour in Led Zeppoli."

Brett smirked. "Oh, so you *did* have a date. Cue the hallelujah chorus, send in the bagpipes."

Darcy's shoulders shook. Once he started with his warped comments, her belly hurt from laughing. Yeah, she was blessed to have such a close friend. In addition to Sharon, Brett had seen her through dark days after David passed away when she'd barely been able to lift her head off the pillow or take a shower.

"We had a conversation and he bought me a croissant. That was the extent of things."

"Sounds like a date to me." Brett seemed mighty proud of his observation.

"I have to admit, it felt nice to talk with a man for once—not that you aren't a *real* man. You know what I mean."

Brett winked. "Someone you can picture naked?"

Heat invaded her face. Yes, indeed she'd visualized Luke sans clothing last night and it made for lots of tossing and turning. "It's just been a long time since I could actually have a conversation with someone who is intelligent and not a creep and…"

"Hot."

She rolled her eyes. "Yeah, he's hot, but it's more than that." Darcy wasn't about to tell Brett about the obit and Luke's plans. The debacle with Lucas still weighed on her mind. His reaction had to have been due to her flapping at the gums. Now that she thought about it, some people didn't handle death well. She sure hadn't, at least not since David had died.

"Well, he's leaving soon anyway." She frowned at her feet. This was an epically bad idea. Luke probably didn't want a job, for crying out loud. He'd mentioned relaxing for the week. "Besides, he's probably got a girlfriend, or fiancé. Or who knows if he's anything like he-who-should-remain-dead-to-me…"

Brett's face turned ashen and he scratched his pathetic attempt at a goatee. "Um, Darce, I don't think you should…"

"You know what, I'll just call him, or text him. This was a bad idea. He's probably a player anyway. Someone who looks as delicious as he does must have a string of women in each town or country."

Jeez, he resembled a bass on a hook.

"What's wrong with you?"

Brett pointed behind her.

Darcy closed her eyes and once again hoped the floor would swallow her whole. *Stupid, stupid.*

"Wow, every country? How do I ever get any sleep, huh?"

Oh yes, the silky-smooth timbre in his voice made her knees weak. Brett let out a hoot, pivoted on his spotless Louis Vuitton loafers, and sashayed into the back room. The coward.

Darcy slowly turned, squared her shoulders, and met Luke's stare. It was more of an amused grin, and it made her feel better. He ducked his head and rubbed his hair. The sheen of sweat on his arms and legs told her he'd been running. That and the skimpy nylon shorts, which hid nothing. She gulped. His Marine Corps T-shirt had a dark line running down the front of his abs and disappeared into his waistband where sweat must also have formed.

Darcy tried to keep her eyes on Luke's face, but it was damned hard. Plus, half the ladies in the lobby ogled him, and she wanted to punch their face-lifted mugs. Rich tourists with their expensive luggage in tow didn't hide their interest, yet Luke seemed oblivious and kept his eyes on her.

He crossed his arms high on his chest, making his biceps pop. "Were you looking for me?"

Good, he didn't make any mention of her idiotic comment, but she was no coward, either. "Yes. I'm sorry about the comment. It was terribly inappropriate. Brett and I trade them all the time."

"Men?" he asked with a sparkle in his eye.

Her face had to be a flaming mess, but she tried to pull off the cool and collected vibe.

She snorted. "He wishes, or used to. His husband might take exception to that now, I'm afraid."

Luke nodded his understanding and regarded her in silence. Yeah, it was time to explain the real reason for her visit, she supposed.

"So I was wondering if you're interested in a job."

His expression betrayed surprise and curiosity. "What kind of job?"

A group of guests filed past, causing Luke to have to step in closer. Heat from his amazing body radiated her airspace. He should be a potent, tangy, sweaty mess. Most men would. But he wasn't. *Of course not.* His scent was a combination of musky male goodness, some kind of spicy cologne—not like the putrid stuff she hated—and freshly cut grass. In fact, there were grass stains on his shorts, and a few blades were stuck to the laces on his trainers.

"Can you hold that thought?" he asked. "I'm probably not fit for company, especially not pretty company."

He thought she was pretty? Well…

Luke's nose wrinkled and he reached into his sock for his key card. "Can you give me ten minutes to grab a quick shower? I cannot in good conscience let you near my stench a moment longer. Unless you have somewhere else to be?"

An image of Luke standing in the shower, water cascading over his trimmed hair and slicing down his shoulders and lower, made her throat close.

"Sure," she croaked out. "I mean, I don't have anything else going on. Sure," she stammered again. "I'll wait."

He chuckled. "Awesome. Be back in ten or less." He pivoted and took the stairs two at a time, muscles flexing with every movement. She was transfixed. Oh boy, she was in serious trouble. The twinges and stirrings of full-fledged longing for the hot Marine had begun and left her breathless.

"You are so in trouble." Brett's voice next to her ear made her jump.

Cripes.

Darcy expelled a long breath and shrugged. "I know."

♥ ♥ ♥

Less than ten minutes later, after the fastest shower in history, Luke found Darcy waiting in the bar at the Inn. A mug sat on the bar in front of her.

He leaned forward to peer into her cup. "Tea?"

A blush invaded her face and she nodded. "I'm cutting down on the java today, or trying to," she mumbled.

She was dressed in a pair of jeans with strategically placed rips in the knees. She'd removed her army-green jacket and underneath wore a tee with some kind of writing across the front. He frowned down at the shirt.

"Is something wrong?"

His eyes shot to her face. Oh shit, she probably thought he was checking out her breasts, which were outstanding, but he certainly didn't want to appear a lecher.

"I'm trying to read your shirt."

Her shoulders relaxed. "It's says 'And though she be but little, she is fierce.'"

He nodded. "Shakespeare."

From the way her mouth dropped open she appeared surprise.

"Us Marines *are* educated, you know."

She turned crimson, and he found he enjoyed when she became embarrassed. She crossed her arms high on her chest, blocking the quote. "I didn't think you weren't. Which play?"

He arched an eyebrow. "*A Midsummer Night's Dream.* Helena says this of Hermia."

Darcy dropped her arms to her sides, leaned back in the bar stool, and tilted her head. "I'm impressed."

He flagged the bartender, took a seat next to her, and ordered a seltzer with lime. "My mother wasn't just an artist, she loved all things artistic—music, sculpture, and theater. I've read quite a few of old Willie's stuff."

Darcy laughed and it lit her violet eyes something fierce. He sucked in a breath and grabbed his drink before he made an ass of himself.

"Old Willie?" She shook her head and bit at her bottom lip. "Nice name."

"Does it mean something to you?" He motioned to her shirt.

She paused and took a sip from her mug. "I thought I was here to tell you about the job."

"But first, as I would call it, fair play?"

She groaned. "No more quotes, I beg you."

"Oh, I can go on for days," he teased. "Seriously, what makes Darcy Prentice tick? You interrogated me yesterday." Hell, he couldn't stop thinking about her today. And here she was in the flesh. *Hot damn*. It was another lucky day in Havenport.

"Interrogated? Oh, is that so?"

"It is. You'd give counterintelligence a run for their money." He reached over, grabbed a napkin out of the square dispenser which just happened to be near her, and their shoulders brushed. *Yup, oranges*. He knew it.

She'd braided her hair over one shoulder. It was so long that it hit her waist when she sat. Her face was also scrubbed free of makeup, but she certainly didn't need any. He adored the smattering of freckles running over her nose. She reached for her own napkin, turning her wrist, which had ink on the inside. Angel wings with a *D* in the middle.

By its own volition, his hand gently grabbed hold of her arm.

"This is outstanding." He couldn't help running his index finger along the edge of the design. It was in gray scale and beautifully shaded.

She stilled, looked him directly in the eyes, and blinked. "Thank you."

If a bomb went off in the lobby there was no way he would move.

"David used to say that to me. The saying on my shirt," she clarified. "I was a geek in school, then an English literature major in college. He thought it was ironic since I was so much shorter than him and I'd stick up for him in the hallway at school." She shrugged and tugged her wrist away, seeming embarrassed by the admission.

"How did you go from a literature major to a journalist?" he asked.

Her face changed in an instant; she shut down and became guarded. He felt as though a wall had been erected between them.

She cleared her throat and crunched the napkin on the bar. "Oh, you know, life and things change. Plus, the *Herald* is a good job."

He had a feeling she'd omitted some serious stuff, but he had no right to pry.

"So, about that job." He changed the subject, since it was obviously her intention from the way she'd shut down their personal sharing convo.

"Our reenactment group is actually called the Rhode Island Revelers."

"Reenactment? Civil War stuff?" he asked.

She shifted in her chair and her T-shirt molded more to her small but curvy frame. "Well, no. It's more Revolutionary times, to be exact. In any case, we are scheduled to do a demonstration this coming weekend, and our carpenter got hurt. He was supposed to build a set. With a hut, wagon—real authentic stuff."

"Okay," he answered, not really understanding where this was headed, but it sounded interesting.

She fidgeted with the tie on her braid. "So I hoped, well, since you mentioned you were a carpenter, that maybe you'd be interested in taking the job? Gerald can't do the work. He'll be laid up with a broken leg for weeks. The plans are already drawn up, not that you'd have to follow them."

"When does it have to be completed?" His plan had been to get out of Havenport directly after scattering Mom's ashes. The apprenticeship program started in ten days.

"Before next Friday," she stated. "That's when the *New Englander* magazine is scheduled to do a photo shoot."

Luke digested all the information, and his head churned. The timing worked. It might be a good way to make a few bucks. But he wasn't sure about the design plans Darcy had mentioned. What if he couldn't duplicate them? What if his skills were so dormant after all this time he sucked?

God, he wished Ben could help, but that was impossible.

"We can pay you, and most of the hut is already built. But I'll be honest, it's not a fortune." Darcy's words shook him out of his reverie.

If Luke were a betting man—which at his rank's salary he couldn't afford to be—he'd bet Darcy had no idea what the job paid. He could read her uncertainty as sure as he knew his own name.

"I'm not looking for a fortune, but I'd be interested in who'll buy the materials up front. If we're being honest here, my credit isn't stellar. Hell, I don't have a credit card. I canceled them last tour." Why he felt the need to admit that was anyone's guess. "I want to be up front."

She shook her head and shrugged. "Don't worry. The Historical Society is footing the bill for the materials. They have an account at the hardware store. The Revelers are paying for the labor…well…at least Gerald's fee. I'll get you an exact amount. I promise." She smiled and regarded him with a questioning look.

He wasn't about to let an opportunity that fell into his lap disappear. Plus, it was a way to spend more time with Darcy. That thought he'd have to decipher more, though.

"I'll do it."

The tension left Darcy's shoulders and she beamed at him then grabbed *his* wrist. "You have no idea what a lifesaver this is. I can't wait to tell Lucas. He's one of the founding members of the group and can give you all the details. You're welcomed to tweak the plans. I'm sure Lucas won't mind as long as we get the set done in time for the magazine."

Her enthusiasm was infectious, and he couldn't stifle his laugh. He'd laughed more in the past day than in the past year. The money would be nice, but the main reason to be in Havenport still stood—Mom.

"By the way, did you find out anything about Havenport Park and the permit? I'd hoped you'd have news. And, I'm sorry, I've Googled the laws, but I can't seem to understand Rhode Island. This needs to be done legit."

Her face once again turned crimson. "Oh, jeez. It totally slipped my mind. Well, it's kinda a gray area." She winced.

"What do you mean?"

"Well, some people I spoke with said don't ask, don't tell."

He chuckled. "That sounds a lot like a military thing."

She rolled her eyes. "I'm sure. On private property, as we did with David's remains, it would be fine. However, in a state-run park, it's advised you get permission from the park ranger first."

"I guess I can do that." Didn't seem too difficult.

"However, a 'guideline.'" She made air quotes. "Is to scatter the ashes at least one hundred yards away from a trail or traffic area."

Luke mulled over that fact. It sounded doable. "The oak tree is massive and off the main walkway. I ran to the park this morning. I *can* scatter her ashes around the base, then cover them with leaves. I'm sure no one would give me a hard time?"

Darcy agreed.

"It'd be my luck to get arrested trying to make Mom's final resting wishes happen."

"Look," she said, holding his right hand between hers. Her hands were soft and warm and he loved touching her. "I'm not going to tell anyone," she said with a sheepish grin. "And I'm sure the park police or anyone else won't bother you."

"I hope not, but Mom's obituary had the details in the wording," he reminded her. "This cannot turn into a dog-and-pony show—Mom wouldn't have wanted that." He rubbed the back of his neck, and this extra added detail settled on his shoulders. "I just cannot for the life of me figure out why she was so specific. Why the exact date of her birthday? And why would she need that specific date for her obituary to be put in the paper? She wasn't the sharing type. To be frank, I had zero knowledge Havenport existed until two weeks ago."

Darcy shrugged. "It said in the obit it was her fiftieth birthday, right?" At his nod, she continued. "It's a milestone, and to be honest, it's tragic she passed so young. Can I ask what from? I mean...I didn't want to pry yesterday. Never mind; I shouldn't."

"It's fine," he said, and moved his other hand to cover hers. The bolt of electricity had settled into a warm feeling in his gut, which was surprising. "Mom had MS. She developed it after I turned ten. It sucked because there were days she couldn't walk, let alone create her artwork."

"Oh. Thank you for telling me. You didn't have to."

He lightly stroked her knuckles with the pad of his thumb. "I seem to be able to tell you more than most."

She cleared her throat. "So that might be it. With your mom's date. She's finally come home, so to speak. By the way, what you're doing for her, for her last wishes, is extraordinary. And so are you."

"I'm far from that, believe me." No one had ever thought of him in that light before, and it was a bit embarrassing.

"Well, I think so, so there!" She gave him a raspberry, and he laughed.

The bartender came back and asked if they were interested in the brunch buffet being set up in the dining area.

"You hungry?"

She waved a hand and downed the rest of her tea before pulling back her sleeve. "I'm not, but I do have a few errands to run for my folks, and it's getting late. My Saturday schedule is a bear, and I'm sure you've got stuff to do. I'll let you know what Lucas says about the pay and the supplies."

"I don't have anything else to do today. You want some company?"

She shrugged into her jacket. "You'd *want* to go with me to my parents'? I barely do."

"They can't be that bad."

"Let me warn you, they're…" She scratched her chin in thought. "How do I put this without sounding rude? Needy and annoying?" Underneath the nonchalant and flippant words was a tone of resentment and a little desperation.

"You've never commanded a bunch of wet-behind-the-ears Marines, I bet."

She looked horrified. "Not on your life, although I'd bet my folks could give them a run for their money."

Chapter Five

After hitting the grocery store, Darcy told him the way to her parents' house. It was a nondescript place with a huge American flag waving on a long pole in their front yard. He'd insisted they take his truck, for when he'd taken a look at her purple Volkswagen parked outside the Inn…yeah, that wasn't going to happen. He'd never fit, at least not without eating his knees.

She leaned back into the upholstered seats and crossed her legs. He glanced over and noticed her eyes were closed.

"Earth to Darcy. You awake?"

She sighed and tilted her head when he heard the *crack*.

"Ooh, that had to hurt."

Her eyes were slits as she regarded him. "On the contrary, that felt amazing."

He winced and pulled his truck next to the mailbox on the curb. "Or the road to traction or a neck brace."

"I didn't sleep well, so yes, I am tired."

He mulled over that one, for he'd tossed and turned, but it was because of indecent fantasizing about her. He doubted that was the case with her lack of slumber.

"The thing is," she started to say, then turned to fully face him. He cut the engine and pocketed his keys. "I have to find a new topic for a series of...I guess you'd call the series a cross between human interest and history of Havenport. Events that surround the town, and I was up trying to figure it out."

"Sounds interesting, but sorry I'm no help. My knowledge of Havenport consists of Main Street, the Inn, the *Herald*, and DP.

"DP?"

"Darcy Prentice," he teased.

"Very funny." She chuckled. "Come on, can't keep the folks waiting for their food."

"It's ten thirty."

"Exactly. You'll see," she warned, and hopped out of his truck. He heard the back gate of the pickup bed open before he jumped out to help.

♥ ♥ ♥

"Do your folks have a bunch of people living with them?" Luke asked while juggling a six-pack of paper towels underneath one arm and a case of water hoisted on his left shoulder.

Darcy had her own set of stuff, more food than he'd shopped for in a year. She'd insisted on carrying most of the grocery bags, emphatically stating she did this every week. The woman clearly had issues accepting help.

"No, why?" she asked, and blew away a piece of hair that had became stuck in that orange-scented lip gloss.

He chuckled and shifted his grip on the water while following her up to the door of a split-level white house. "Um, well, you bought more food than I have in probably forever." He motioned his head to the six bags she clutched in each hand.

Darcy continued up the stone walkway and gave him a quick backward glance. "Let me guess, your fridge consists of stereotypical single-guy fare: ketchup, mustard, and a six-pack?"

He scoffed. "I'm feeling mighty offended here. I *can* cook. And my fridge, when I had my own place, was fully stocked."

She shot him a teasing wink, which he was beginning to really enjoy. "Uh-huh. What's your specialty?"

"I can grill, because all men can." He laughed with her. "My homemade barbecue sauce has been called orgasmic."

She stumbled a bit on the steps, but recovered.

"Modest, too, I see," she commented before stepping onto the porch and ringing the doorbell. Luke thought it odd, given this was her folks' house.

The door swung open to reveal an older woman. Luke pegged her at sixty to sixty-five years old. She wore an apron with little flying pigs on it, and she didn't seem happy.

♥ ♥ ♥

"Your father is waiting for his oatmeal. Did you get lost?"

Before she had an appropriate comeback, Mom fixed her gaze on Luke with a start.

"Oh, Darcy, really? You shouldn't have hired the delivery person. I hate to spend the extra money when you're perfectly capable."

Darcy wanted to slam the bags on the porch and hightail it. Yep, bringing Luke along had been an epically bad idea.

His face took on a crimson hue, but he handled it like a champ, merely smiled at her mother's rudeness, to which Mom seemed flustered.

What could she have expected, though? It was her own fault for thinking—no, hoping—her mother would be normal for a change. Of course Mom had to voice that idiotic comment.

Darcy pulled in a long breath and shifted the fifteen bags of nonsensical shit and food she purchased each and every week. Sharon's long-standing joke was that her folks were planning for the apocalypse. Why would anyone require this many cans of fruit cocktail and olives?

"Mom," she huffed out and avoided glancing over at Luke, "this is Luke, who is *not* a delivery person from the grocery store. Please say hello and be nice."

She pushed her way into the house because, dammit, the bags were heavier than a small elephant. Mom backed up, then slammed Luke with the stink eye when he crossed the threshold. Oh, joy.

Darcy heard him quietly mutter a "Hello" to Mom, but there was no response.

Cripes, this is going to be interesting.

He was strapping and long-limbed, and the house so cluttered with *knickknacks*, it was a miracle anyone managed to walk around without breaking their neck. The Prentices weren't quite ready for buried alive TV, but they reveled in collecting things. Shelves and curio cabinets were chock-full with porcelain statues of birds, bells, frogs, little cherubs, teacups, and saucers—whatever was Mom's fancy item of the week. One craze had been coat stands, all because David had made one in woodworking class back in high school. The multitude of stands had reproduced like rabbits on crack. Various sizes and designs and heights cluttered every inch of the entranceway. The life-size mermaid stand was kind of creepy.

No one owned this many coats to fill the racks, but Mom persevered in her foraging. And poor Pops had zero say in the matter.

All this clutter had the opposite effect on her personality. If she were to complete a psychoanalysis on herself, like he-who-should-be-gelded used to, she'd proclaim to be a minimalist. No clutter entangled her life.

Her apartment, car, closets, etc., were all organized with military precision.

Less was more.

Darcy sauntered past her mother to head to the kitchen and, Luke—educated, hunky Shakespeare-loving Marine—followed her in silence. *Smart man.* The less conversation he partook in with the folks, the better for him and for everyone, in her opinion. Pops sat in his usual chair at the kitchen table, directly in front of a large picture window overlooking the back yard, doing the *New York Times* crossword puzzle in pen.

"Hiya, Pops." She plopped the bags on the table and floor, then leaned over to kiss his weathered cheek.

He pushed his reading glasses up on his nose and smiled. It wasn't the vacant smile she normally received, which meant it had started out as a good day.

"Hi, baby girl." She sighed. Yes, he remembered her today. "Who's the strapping young man carrying all that water? We should have enough to fill our pool by now, you think?"

When Dad was on point, he realized how ridiculous Mom's grocery hoarding tendencies were each week and teased her mercilessly.

"So true. This is Luke. Luke, my father, Robert."

Luke gently placed the paper goods and water on the tile floor, then extended his hand to her father. "It's a pleasure to meet you, Mr. Prentice."

Pops dropped his pen and paper and they shook hands. "Do you work at the grocery store?"

"No, sir." Luke stood with legs apart, hands behind his back.

Pop's gaze faltered for a moment while he studied Luke. "You in the military, son?"

Luke shook his head and chuckled. "Recently discharged, sir, and apparently transparent." Over her father's head Luke winked at her, and she felt her face flame. When he turned on the charm, it was hard to resist.

"My son was a Marine. Did Darcy tell you?" Pop asked with a wistful tone.

She held her breath, hoping Dad wouldn't get too nostalgic. And of course Mom, who had followed them into the kitchen and silently lined cans of stuff on the island, frowned down at a can of peas. *Here comes the shit show.* "She told me, sir," Luke answered. "You must have been over-the-moon proud of him. Darcy explained he was in an explosives unit. We recon Marines had the utmost respect for those EOD guys."

Pops stared at the floor. "Yes, David knew his explosives. He was given commendations, posthumously," he added in a whisper before looking up. "Do you want to see his room and medals?"

Pop pushed away from the table, and Luke—bless him—stayed put with no reaction. However, she saw his sideways flicker with a signal for aid. She shook her head ever so slightly, and he seemed to understand.

"You know, sir, perhaps another time. I have an errand and Darcy said she'd help out."

"Oh, and what's that?" Pops asked her.

"Luke's building our reenactment set and I'm going to show him the lumber yard, hardware store, you know, around town a bit. So we really have to get going."

Pops cleared his throat and nodded while taking in her words, yet not fully understanding.

"If you need something, call me. I think I got everything on your list." She fished out the receipt from her back pocket and put it with the others in the bin on the side countertop. They sometimes remembered to reimburse her, but she'd eventually settle up.

"Not quite, Darcy," Mom added just as Darcy motioned to Luke to leave.

Pops scowled. "She does enough, Marian, so let her and her nice man go and do their errands."

Mom clamped her lips shut but agreed with a tight nod. "I'll call if I find I can't function without the stuff you forgot."

Once outside, she trudged to Luke's truck, not knowing what to say or the right words to explain the shit show that was her parents. How could she defend the debacle inside, and how in the hell would he want to continue to spend time with her after today?

It was the story of her life.

He-who-should-be-burned-at-the-stake   hated   her folks. Said they weren't normal, or sane.

There was truth in that. But you can't pick your family like your friends or your asshole ex-boyfriends. That fact was too bad, tragically.

Darcy dropped into the passenger seat and clicked on the seat belt while Luke slammed his door shut after sliding behind the wheel. Rubbing her eyelids in the hopes of cutting off the monumental headache that'd formed the moment she'd rang the doorbell, she knew she had to say something.

"Before you make any comments, can we drive away, please? I'm sure Mom is peeking through the curtains."

The truck's engine roared to life, and she heard him shift into Drive.

"Yep. She is."

Darcy thought Luke chuckled, but it had to be her imagination. No one could find humor in her sad, sad life.

She opened her eyes and studied his profile while he drove down the street in silence. He punched on the radio to a country station, but kept the volume low.

"Does your father normally forego wearing pants?"

For some reason, his nonchalant question tickled her into letting out a laugh, then another, and before she knew it her eyes were leaking.

"They teach you diplomatic skills in the corps?" she asked when she recovered. Guess the stress had finally made her snap. A wonder he hadn't dumped her on the side of the road.

"Yes, ma'am, among other things," he replied, and she caught the twinkle in his eye. For some reason the situation didn't seem so dire.

They fell into a companionable silence on the drive back to her car at the Inn.

"You're lucky he wasn't his usual commando."

"Yes, I believe I am." He swiveled his head and flashed his perfect white teeth before concentrating on the road again.

"Pops sits in that chair almost all day."

"Looked comfy." He turned left at the light.

"You remember I told you we'd scattered David's ashes in the backyard?"

"Yes."

"Well the backyard, as well as David's room, is a shrine. Never changed or updated. The dilapidated tree house David built when he was twelve is rotted and there's maybe five boards left precariously balanced among the branches. A swift wind and someone's going to be knocked out or worse."

Luke didn't comment, so she decided to continue.

"Pops's chair in the kitchen gives him a clear view of that tree. When we were kids he used to keep an eye on us in case we tumbled out."

"I see," Luke said in a faint voice, and Darcy glanced over at the crease between his brows.

She puffed out a breath. "I don't know why I'm dumping this on you…it's strange," she whispered the last word, wondering. But the soothing, almost cathartic feeling came over her insides whenever she was in Luke's company.

"Go ahead. Unload on me. It's nice to have someone to talk with about stuff and not surface shit."

Seemed he was a mind reader as well. "Yeah," she whispered, and flutters started low in her belly.

"Go on."

She swallowed hard and licked her lips. *What the hell, might as well unload it all.* "Pops has dementia. He was diagnosed right after David was killed. So he keeps vigil same as he did years ago. Every day. It's part of the disease regression. We all know David is never coming back."

A wave of despair set in as they rolled passed families walking along the edge of Havenport Park. Happy kids, couples holding hands. Yearning crept up into her head, and it sucked out her ability to breathe.

"They long for him. They deny his dying by keeping their shrines. And...they...wish it had been me, instead. Maybe I do, too, for he was their pride and joy."

Holy shit. Had she just said that out loud?

Luke probably thought she was a fucking lunatic. Debbie Downer for sure, and in serious need of antidepressants. Exhaustion set upon her like a heavy cloak. Darcy closed her eyes and leaned her temple against her side-door window.

She felt the truck jerk to a stop and opened her eyes. He'd pulled over but was still a ways from the Inn.

"Are you lost?"

Luke levered the gearshift into Park with a click. He twisted his torso in the seat, undid the seat belt, and slid toward her.

"Don't *ever* say that." His words were pleading.

She swallowed hard and was startled by the intensity of his expression. Icy-blue eyes darkened and he grabbed her hand.

"Hey, I'm sorry. I'm not certifiable, I swear." She tried to play off that whopper of a statement with whimsy.

He shook his head and gripped her hand. "Christ," he groaned, and stared at her, then reached his other hand to caress the outline of her hair. She sighed. No man had ever touched her with such gentleness, and damned if she didn't feel delicate and not ostracized for a few rolls of flab on her abdomen. Luke seemed to care about her, which was *crazy*. She'd always prided herself as being independent, but at this moment she could use a good, strong shoulder to lean on.

"You're so sweet and kind and patient with your folks," he continued. "And I know you carry the world on those sexy shoulders."

"Sometimes," she admitted, amazed that he'd figured all this out about her in a millisecond.

"Darcy, listen to me," he said, and his hand rose to cup the back of her head. The possessive way he did it thrilled her to the core.

"Life is a gift. But when it's gone, it's gone. No regrets. Bask in the fact you're alive and we met. I'm fucking blown away by you."

Then he leaned over and kissed her.

♥ ♥ ♥

Her lips tasted as sweet as honey. No, scratch that—orange honey. The ten minutes he'd spent in the Prentices' company explained everything. Her heart-wrenching confession hit his gut like a swallowed a grenade. He'd seen guys ten times bigger than Darcy and more bad-assed give in to the stress and off themselves.

Darcy Prentice was not going to be one of those people.

Her fingers dug into his shoulders and she settled into the kiss, accepting him, her arms wound around his neck. Oh yeah, the element of surprise was in his corner, but it was more than just wanting to taste her lips. He wanted to make her happier. Her folks were succubi lying in wait for their unsuspecting daughter to deliver their food. That made him livid. Mom and Ben never treated him or each other that way.

Luke couldn't blame her father's actions. The debilitating disease wasn't his fault. Her mother deserved entirely different scrutiny.

Mom would've told that nasty woman where to go and how fast to get there. Mom swallowed zero shit from anyone as a strong, independent woman.

She would've loved Darcy.

Dumb-ass. It was not the time to be thinking about her parents. All he wanted to do was feel, so he shut out all thoughts but this sexy, smart woman in his arms.

Their tongues meshed, and she moaned into his open mouth. He slid his hands under her jacket and gripped her waist. Her curves were soft and warm, and the unexpected attraction to her hadn't ever been this intense with anyone. Fiery pulses of desire shot to below his belt, but he had to keep control. He had to continue the slow savor of her mouth and relish whatever this volcanic reaction had sparked between them.

Darcy deserved his reverence. He suspected she hadn't had a man offer her it in a long time, if ever.

And, *holy shit*, if giving in to his baser impulse hadn't just become a major game changer.

They broke away in conjunction. His heartbeat thumped, and her breath sawed in and out.

She gripped the lapels of his button-down and gave him a hundred-watt smile. "Where the hell have you been all my life?"

He threw back his head and let out a hoot. "I don't know, but I know where I am now."

"Why did you do that?" She'd suddenly turned shy and glanced down at her hands, but he wasn't having it.

He placed two fingers under her chin and forced her to meet his gaze. "Besides the fact that you're gorgeous and you looked as if you needed it?"

Her eyes widened. "I needed to be kissed senseless?"

He pecked the top of her pert nose. "Oh, you'll know when I kiss you senseless."

Her mouth opened and closed a few times. He chuckled and slid across the seat to station himself behind the wheel. "Now show me where that hardware store is so I can build your set. Is there a workshop I can use?"

She swallowed hard and got herself under control, smoothing the tendrils of hair that came loose from his hands.

"Um…yes, the Historical Society's building has a yard. I'll call their proprietor, Ina, to get us access. Lucas is going to be so excited." Darcy clapped her hands and reached for her phone. "I'll tell him we'll begin today."

"We?"

"Uh-huh."

Chapter Six

Two days' worth of intense work assisting Luke cart two-by-fours and boxes of nails was not going to help her back survive a shift at Royce's, but oh well. She wouldn't have traded anything for the time spent with Luke the entire weekend. Plus, trying to concentrate on her work at the *Herald* had been a challenge. Despite her best efforts, Darcy anticipated the end of the workday when Luke reported his progress. Before long, he'd seemed to have the cronies at the Historical Society eating out of his hot Marine hand. They'd even bought him lunch.

She'd decided Mary Christianson or her ancestors would somehow make an interesting topic for the next Havenport Historicals. A prelim idea had been sent to her editor yesterday morning. What she hadn't been prepared for was Mary's or her ancestor's contributions to Havenport. Once the editor's interest was piqued she'd vaguely remembered Mary from high school. Darcy spoke to some of the Garden Club cronies, too. Many couldn't recall, but one lady actually remembered that psychedelic fence with mirth.

As she hammered and sanded pieces of wood in the

workshop with Luke, she'd broached the subject, nervous as to how he'd react.

"Would you mind if I used your mother or her ancestors in my next installment?" she'd asked him.

He'd been mildly curious about General Sullivan being part of George Washington's army and involved in the Battle of Rhode Island. Luke teased that if he remembered his history correctly, that battle was inconsequential since the Revolutionary troops failed to take Newport. His knowledge of history continually amazed her.

He'd paused to wipe sweat from his brow with a soft towel then clutched his chest. "You wound me. Us Marines know our country's history, even when it comes to the *Army*," he'd kidded, and continued with his precise measurements and cuts to the wood framing of the shelter.

Luckily, Gerry's miter saw had been left in the Historical Society's workroom. A quick phone call to Ina for access to the building, and the reenactment set was on its way to gorgeous *and* functional.

Lucas, it seemed, had gone MIA and hadn't returned her numerous calls. She so wanted to introduce them.

She realized Luke wasn't going to make Havenport part of his long-term plans, and frankly she didn't know how to feel about that deduction.

Of course, he had a life to get on with. Havenport was supposed to be a blip in his journey. But still, she couldn't—no, she *wouldn't*—ignore the feelings he'd ignited in their short time together.

The kiss, and the memory of his hands under her hair, occupied all of her thoughts. *Phew*, as Sharon would say. It had been toe-curling, gut-clenching delicious.

But it also hadn't happened again. His kiss was probably just a spur-of-the-moment thing.

She frowned down at her coffee.

What made matters worse was as he'd labored on the set, the muscles on his forearms and shoulders flexed and strained, making every thought catapult to his promise.

You'll know when I kiss you senseless.

Once he'd shed the button-down shirt—*good God she needed to put one of one of those portable handheld fans in her handbag next time*—she'd practically drooled. Hence, it'd been a long night of fantasizing and little to no sleep.

Hot body aside, Luke patiently explained his creative process. He possessed a true talent in carpentry. Darcy wondered where he'd learned the craft, but she didn't have the nerve to ask, nor had Luke volunteered. Perhaps he, like Mary, was a natural artist.

Speaking of which, the day to scatter her ashes in Havenport Park fast approached, after which he'd move on from Havenport.

"That stinks," she muttered, hating the empty black void in the pit of her stomach. Ironically, she'd discovered for all her blind dates, second dates, and relationships, which weren't all that many, actually *liking and admiring* a guy proved foreign territory.

Laughing over stupid stuff or making fun of herself. It was refreshing.

Most of her ex-relationships had been English major geeks in college, or the odd actor in grad school. Once she'd become an adjunct professor in another life, the men of academia were the only men in her circle: boring, safe, self-absorbed, and ultimately, heartbreaking idiots.

But they'd all been lacking. Maybe Sharon was right and she did indeed need a man. *Luke, perhaps?*

Sure, the myriad of letters after their names—PhD, JD, MBA—had been enticing. In hindsight, they possessed zero *substance*.

Nor courage.

Nor honor.

The benchmarks to which David had adhered. The core values with which he'd lived and died.

Luke did, too. He'd fought for his country, apparently *adored* his mother, and planned to honor her last wishes. Talk about the whole freaking package of yummy, amazing man.

She poured kibble in Oedipus's bowl and filled his automatic water fountain. Luke didn't seem to mind her inquiry, although he confessed he knew nothing about Mary's family history, other than she'd grown up in town and left shortly after high school to pursue her dream of being an artist. She must have been fairly young to have married and given birth.

Time to squelch her tendencies for digging up long-hidden answers. Luke's personal life or his mother's business was his until he decided to share. She'd have to be satisfied with what she uncovered thus far. Besides, it helped feed her love of history and how it'd shaped Havenport.

Plus, the Revelers would be ready for their first ever photo shoot.

The wagon fully functioned. She'd even learned to assemble the axle mechanism. He'd also completed the framing for the shelter. Luke worked fast, efficiently, and with such grace her stomach fluttered remembering how his hands caressed the slats on the side of the wagon after he'd sanded them to a smooth gloss.

DNA didn't lie, and if Mary Christianson had been as creative an artist as Luke preened about, then he'd certainly inherited that gene.

Too bad Lucas couldn't be there when she'd ridden in the wagon. His phone went straight to voice mail. Again. Lucas had an elderly mother residing in a fancy nursing home in Danbury, Connecticut, so maybe he'd gone to visit for the weekend? She'd try him again after her shift.

Darcy threw on her uniform for Royce's, a T-shirt with the Royce logo and a pair of black cargos and sneakers, and gave Oedipus a pat on his furry head. He administered his customary ass rub on her pants.

"Stop that. Now I'll need to roll my pants again." Her scold got her a high-pitched *meow*. Who was she kidding? Her cat ruled the apartment. The grumpy kitty sauntered toward his full bowl, quite effectively dismissing her.

The doorbell rang and she tossed the industrial-size sticky roller on the counter.

Lucas stood outside her door with his hands stuffed in his pockets. His usual impeccable jacket was wrinkled and he sported a shadow of a beard.

"Hi, Lucas!"

He nodded tightly. "May I come in?"

"It's good to see you." She held open the door and turned sideways, giving him space to slip inside her apartment. He'd remained silent as he walked past, and she detected a stale smell of alcohol. Not beer, more old gin or whiskey, and her nose wrinkled.

She recognized it by her experience waitressing at Royce's and a variety of college town bars after losing her job at Conn U after he-who-should-be-gelded fucked up her career.

Given their last interaction, and how Lucas had run off in a state, Darcy knew something was wrong. Her heart panged. By his rumpled form and the way he'd winced at her enthusiastic greeting, he must have a serious hangover. It wasn't his style at all. That, in and of itself, added fuel to her worry.

In the past six months since she'd joined the Revelers, Lucas had become her confidant and support system once Dad's dementia intensified. Not unlike Sharon and Brett, Lucas held little respect for the way Mom became more burden than parent. Always the gentleman, though, he'd never cast his opinions or ill feelings at Darcy the way Sharon made the situation with her parents out to be self-inflicted.

Nope. He used a more subtle approach and tried to help her manage her parents' expectations, even going so far as to find an aide and companion for them. Fat lot of good that had done, to be honest. Mom called or texted at least fifteen times a day, and God forbid she ever left a voice mail message. She'd dismissed the home health aide in two days, accusing her of stealing one of her bullshit collectibles. Darcy stuffed the memory away and concentrated on Lucas.

He'd walked ahead of her to the kitchen in silence and stopped at her two-seat oak table, but hadn't turned to face her. He gripped the back of the chair and stared at the wall.

"Please, sit down," she instructed, and swung around to face him. Her kitchen wasn't large by any means, and Lucas, a tall man, took up most of the space. Although, given his distressed demeanor he appeared smaller. Maybe it was the way his shoulders slumped forward in tension or worry. Her words seemed to snap him out of whatever misery he grappled with.

"Coffee?" She didn't wait for his answer but grabbed a mug from the drain board and shoved a pod into the coffee maker. While the slurp and roar of the brewing process echoed into the kitchen, she turned to him.

"You look like crap."

The corner of his mouth lifted, and she recognized a hint of the fun-loving, sweet man who'd existed two days before.

"Where have you been?" The last stream of dark brew filled the cup and she placed it in front of him. Black. No sugar. He took his caffeine at full octane.

Lucas stared down at the steam rising from the cup and lifted it with shaking hands.

This had to be bad.

"Are you dying?" she blurted, because holy shit, how would she be able to handle another person she cared about battling illness? This was too much.

He stopped midway to taking a sip and his mouth flew open. "Not anytime soon, I hope."

Darcy exhaled and plopped on the opposite chair. "Then what's going on? I've left you messages for days now. I assumed you were out of town or something. Our set is on its way to being built, by the way. I wanted to share the good news."

Lucas took another sip then absently ran his finger along the rim of his mug. "Good job," he replied with a nod, almost on autopilot, but the praise didn't reach his eyes. He seemed more than a little distracted. As if something weighed heavily on his mind.

Good job? "Thanks," she said faintly, then watched as he guzzled the hot beverage in two long pulls. "You remember that guy who I mentioned about his mother's obituary?"

Lucas dropped the now-empty cup on her table with a thud, and she recoiled.

She squared her shoulders and decided to explain anyway despite his weird actions.

"Luke Christianson's his name. Turns out he's a carpenter and he agreed to build our set. It's coming together nicely. That's what…I called to tell…you." Her voice drifted off for he'd shot up, bumped the small square table, and toppled her chair over in the process. His mug wobbled on the table.

"He's staying here in town?" he asked, visibly agitated.

"Yes, of course. He's building our set. I thought you got that part of our conversation. Lucas, what in the world is going on? This is the second time you've become frazzled at the mention of Luke."

"Marines don't get frazzled." He sounded offended and started pacing her small space. A glimpse of the old, steady, strong Lucas unleashed. Good. The Lucas who'd more than once handled a drunken patron at Royce's when they'd got a bit too touchy-feely with her.

She smirked, grabbing his coffee cup before it went flying. "You sound like him. Luke's a former Marine, too. You and he would get along great."

A strangled sound emitted from his throat and he rubbed a hand over his head. His breaths were measured, as if he struggled to control them.

Her eyes fixated on his clenched fists.

"He's not costing the Revelers much in terms of his

carpentry fees. In fact, Ina at the Historical Society thinks so highly of him that she offered to pay the fee."

Again silence.

"Enough small talk. What's wrong? Did you bathe in a brewery? Frankly, I've never seen you this way before. I'm concerned, Lucas. Talk to me." She held her ground for she cared about him, and he obviously had something grave to tell her.

"I think Luke's my son."

Chapter Seven

"Mr. Christianson, that should be fine," the park ranger said when Luke had presented his request to scatter Mom's ashes. "I appreciate your letting us know of your plans." Her green uniform matched her kind green eyes. The Havenport Park, HPP, patch on the left pocket included her name—Ranger Wilson. The park's main offices had been easy to find, and thanks to Darcy's information, all was set for tomorrow.

"Thank you, ma'am." He smiled and they shook hands. "I just wanted to make sure I do this legit. May I also put flowers at the bottom of the tree?"

She nodded. "Of course you can. There's a florist in town, too. My niece, Frannie, runs things."

She opened her desk drawer and pulled out a business card. "Just ask for her and she'll be thrilled to help. She's quite *unattached*." Ranger Wilson winked then slid the card across her desk.

Luke stifled a chuckle of disbelief. This small town was something else. Sure, once upon a time, he might have been curious about the "unattached" florist, or figured, what the hell, swing by, buy a bouquet, and if Frannie proved to be reasonably attractive, ask her to dinner.

Now? *Yeah, no.*

Darcy's long hair, sweet smile, and penchant toward citrus weaved its way into his psyche and refused to vacate.

That made things damned complicated. Royally messed with his plans to vamoose.

When she'd spoken about Mom's ancestors, he had to admit it'd piqued his interest. Made sense that someone military had been a part of his family tree. This General Sullivan gave his life for freedom against a tyrant nation, not unlike the current war on tyrants, the terrorists.

He'd joined the corps to escape.

The thing was, Darcy embodied the complete opposite of escape. She'd confided when he'd taught her to hammer a nail straight...err...well, almost straight, her motive for coming back to Havenport was her folks. Although Luke suspected she'd moved back because some ex had hurt her. Why? Too many of his corps buddies were of the love-'em-and-leave-'em variety. More than once he'd consoled a buddy's crying girl because they'd screwed someone else with no remorse. Call him Mr. Nice Guy.

He'd never established a liaison longer than the occasion hookup on short-term leave. Most women he'd slept with understood those parameters from the get-go. But Darcy wasn't like those women, and it scared the shit out of him. From her openness, to the way she reveled in history and her role in the reenactment group, she made the best of things.

She'd come home and *stayed* for duty purposes. There they were similar. Unfortunately, that *duty* triggered her deepest, darkest thought about wishing she'd died instead of her brother. Yeah, he could relate. He'd lived that sentiment every single day.

Their differences: he'd run from his family and from survivor's guilt, whereas she vaulted toward hers, no matter if they appreciated it or not.

Would you look at that? He'd become a regular Sigmund Freud. His corps buddies would piss themselves laughing. As soon as Mom was laid to rest, he'd leave. The reenactment set was ninety-nine percent complete. The Historical Society lady had already paid him.

He had to go. Run, as was his pathetic MO.

No matter how much anticipation built in his skull and traveled lower with the thought of seeing Darcy, spending hours or mere minutes with his gorgeous Shakespeare-loving friend, he wasn't ready or equipped to be someone special to anyone. Everyone he'd ever cared about eventually left him.

Friend? Talk about kidding himself. His desires for Darcy were hardly of the *friend* variety, and she'd responded in kind. He hoped his willpower would win out, for the last thing on his to-do list in Havenport was to hurt Darcy.

♥ ♥ ♥

Of all the things Darcy guessed Lucas would say, those anguished words would not have made the top ten.

"How is that possible?"

Lucas's nostrils flared, his pregnant pause a mechanism to consider her question carefully. Jumping into action, she righted her poor thrift-store chair and gestured to it.

"Sit while I call Adam and tell him I'll be late." Her shift at Royce's was supposed to start in half an hour, but she knew the owner of the tavern would understand her delay.

"You don't…" he started, but she held up a hand to stop his protest.

A quick call and another two piping dark roasts in hand, one for herself this time, and they settled on her couch. Lucas shed his jacket and stretched out his long legs. She regarded him, his mannerisms, the shape of his nose and color of his eyes, and a light bulb illuminated like a flare in her brain.

Their resemblance surfaced immediately. Now that she'd kissed Luke, peered into his face up close and stared at his hands, his body, and those amazing depths of his icy blues, the clarity struck her.

Oh shit. He and Lucas shared the same genes in height, eye color, and long limbs. Hell, they both loved to run, too. And both were corps veterans. *He was Luke's dad after all.*

"Start from the beginning," she prompted when he considered resisting, but didn't.

"We were in high school and fell in love," he confessed, and Darcy's heart melted at the wistful tone of his admission. "Mary became everything. Love at first sight, if that exists. We shared a birthday."

Darcy gasped, and it clicked. The reason Mary wanted her ashes spread on that very day. She held on to that revelation.

"We couldn't have been more different. I the jock, and she the artist. Many nights she'd sneak out of her house to paint people's fences and render murals on buildings. I couldn't let her go it alone, of course, so I became her accomplice."

Darcy couldn't help but smile at his protective tone, and imagined a young Lucas, hunky jock defending his eccentric girlfriend.

"The town called her the 'phantom artist.'" He made air quotes and grinned. "I recall an article in the *Herald* at some point. Everyone knew it was Mary painting the murals. She became quite the legend in terms of her creative genius. Her art won awards in school. What a brilliant and free spirit—everything I wasn't."

He smiled, as if a treasured memory surfaced. "Mary insisted I photograph each creation to leave our children her legacy to Havenport. We had such plans. You know some of her artwork remains on display? It's bittersweet when I drive past the images."

Before this moment, Darcy hadn't connected the dots to the vintage building murals around town and the woman behind them.

An idea hatched, but it wasn't the time.

"You two had a soul connection," she whispered, and wondered what that felt like. Or maybe she already knew? *With Luke?*

Lucas turned to face her and the couch cushions shifted. "We'd meet under the massive oak tree in Havenport Park whenever possible and celebrated our birthdays there. It was all so clandestine but exciting. Hell, her art friends thought I was a dumb jock and my friends thought she was weird so we didn't do the affection thing at school. But I loved her."

Darcy's eyes blurred. "Is that why you...I mean...you're not married..."

Lucas's shoulder lifted and he blinked. "No one ever compared."

How romantic.

"Back then, times were different. The town frowned on unwed pregnant girls. It wasn't the nineteen fifties different," he clarified, "but small towns can be vicious. Girls more than guys were ostracized. Hell, my own football team had called her loose."

"That's disgusting," Darcy commented, feeling more than a little pissed for Mary.

His eyes hardened. "Mary didn't care. She gave it back in spades. It always amazed me how confident and strong she was. Her parents were shitty, horrible people. So were mine, now that I've discovered their lies." He let out a disgusted snort and sipped his coffee.

Darcy considered offering Lucas a dram of whiskey for his coffee, but figured he'd had more than enough of *something* alcoholic last night.

"We found out she became pregnant and I was fully prepared to do the right thing and marry her."

"Why didn't you?" Darcy prompted.

"Our parents wouldn't allow it. They both were pillars of Havenport, the perpetual *upstanding socialites*. My mother told me Mary had changed her mind and decided to place the baby for adoption. I suspected her parents had forced her. Mom lied about Mary going to live at an unwed mothers' home and about Mary's refusal to see or speak with me."

Darcy frowned and toyed with the handle on her mug. "Why didn't you reach out or try to find her?"

He looked stricken with guilt and grimaced. "It was impossible. There was no social media or Google search engines. Plus, I guess I'd somehow believed them. She'd disappeared without a goodbye. I left for college in the fall, but I despised it. I missed her too much and had nightmares about what had happened to our baby."

"Oh, Lucas, I'm so sorry." What else could she say? How incredibly tough it must have been for an eighteen-year-old Lucas, who she suspected wasn't nearly as strong a man as he'd grown to be.

He patted her hand. "I survived. God, you've got such a good heart."

He let out a long breath. "I rebelled. Quit the university and joined the corps. I'd figured, why not get the crap beat out of me to add to my misery and pain. I don't know." He placed his cup on her coffee table. "I *needed* a purpose, I guess. I sure as hell wasn't man enough for Mary…"

His voice broke, and Darcy wanted to weep as well. She squeezed his hand.

"When you mentioned that obituary, I *knew*. I fled like a bullet out of the library. I'm sorry I worried you," he said with an apology.

"It's okay," she whispered through tears.

"I drove to Connecticut, to my mother," Lucas said between gritted teeth, "who's still a mean-spirited eighty-year-old broad. She confessed, with coercing of course," he said with a determined glint. "Verna knows who pays for that ritzy home. She'd lied about everything. Mary hadn't obeyed her parents' orders. She ran away. They'd all lied to Mary, too, saying I'd abandoned her and believed the baby wasn't mine. Mary had been a virgin. Hell, so was I," he managed through clenched teeth. "If my old man was alive, I'd punch his ever-smug face."

"What about the Sullivans?" How could they treat their only child so wretchedly? But then again, considering her own twisted parentage, nothing surprised her.

"Those pretentious assholes never even tried to find her. I thought my child had been raised by strangers, possibly by a man, a father I didn't have the balls to be."

He covered his face with his palms and his chest shuddered.

"I guess I was right." His bunched shoulders shook in despair.

His stricken expression smashed into her heart, and she forced herself to not look away.

"Mary's *dead*. I ache as much as I did when she left me. But maybe I've been given a second chance. Christ, I don't deserve it. Perhaps this coincidence—you taking the obit, us being acquainted—means it's meant to be?" His eyes implored her to respond, but she honestly didn't know how.

Darcy's mind raced. Had Mary's forcing the *duty* on Luke become her final gift to them?

But how could she help Luke, whom she'd grown to care for, and Lucas, who was like a surrogate father to her, find each other? To make things right? Could they become father and son?

And what about Luke's father, or the man who'd raised him? Mr. Ben Christianson noted in the obituary? Granted, Luke hadn't mentioned him. Did Luke know about Mary being pregnant and unwed?

It wasn't her place to let that whopper of a cat out of bag, was it?

Before Lucas departed, he implored she keep his secret from Luke, which didn't sit well, but she'd agreed. Worse, though, he intended to meet Luke tomorrow at that old oak tree for the last time.

She was no psychic, but she imagined it wouldn't end well.

What a mess. Secrets had a way of coming back to bite the holder, and she had a feeling it might be her.

Chapter Eight

Darcy wiped down the bar, the ritual quite soothing—*swipe, ring out cloth, repeat*—and tried to ease her mind of the craziness. She polished the taps until the chrome gleamed, shut the water faucet, arranged the napkins in the square plastic bins, and righted the bottles on the shelf. The closing checklist duties helped distract her from stealing glances down the bar. Luke sat on the last stool nursing his IPA and staring into the huge mirror hanging behind the massive bar. Every once in a while he bit his bottom lip in deep thought.

"Jane needs me at home, Miss Darcy. Shall I tell him to leave?" The question took her out of her daydream, and she hoped her face wasn't the shade of the ketchup bottle she'd just wiped. Adam, the owner of Royce's Tavern—a hunky man himself and one thousand percent in love with his wife—tilted his head at Luke.

Darcy figured from the way Luke's shoulders tensed he'd heard Adam's question. She gave the subject a sideways glance before focusing on Adam. "Um, he's fine. I know him. I'll close up when I'm done."

Adam hesitated, eyeballing Luke when he took a swig then placed his glass down on the bar.

"I'm perfectly safe," she stated. Adam acted more than just a bar owner and boss; he protected the women who worked for him. Seemed old-fashioned, but they all appreciated him.

"Go home to your wife." She swatted his shoulder and steered him toward the kitchen doors. Adam nodded curtly then left.

Darcy swung into the kitchen and heard Adam lock the back door before she grabbed a rack of washed glasses out of the industrial-size dishwasher. Normally, Adam took care of carting them, but it seemed Jane needed him in a hurry. She hauled her load through the swinging doors and pulled up short. Luke had relocated to this end of the bar.

"Oh, hey. Are you done?" *Damn.* The rack felt like fifty pounds while she stood there stuttering like a nitwit. She peered to the bar's surface and groaned. She forgot Liz left the stack of trays on this end of the bar and asked her to put them away. *Stupid, stupid.* She'd been too preoccupied by the man in front of her to remember.

"I'll settle up with you in a second, okay?" It wasn't really a question, but a plea for him to wait or the glasses were toast and Adam would not be happy. Luke frowned down at her arms, now shaking under the weight.

"Why didn't you call out for help?" In a blink he scooted over the bar. *Over.* It was a high bar. He commandeered the rack as if it weighed nothing.

"No need. I had it."

"And now I do. Where do you want these?" he asked, but she couldn't help but be transfixed by his bulging biceps and the way his shoulders bunched under his T-shirt.

"Darcy." Luke's mouth quirked.

Her eyes shot up to his face. "Right there." She rustled the trays and extra condiment bottles to the sideboard. Luke set down the rack and stepped back. They stood almost shoulder to shoulder and she was dwarfed. A dwarf wearing a stained apron, hair shooting out of her ponytail all troll-like, and smelling like she'd worked a long shift. *Great, just great.*

"Why didn't that big guy carry these out for you?" His lips flattened after the question.

Big guy? "Oh, you mean Adam?" When he didn't react she explained, "He usually does, but his wife needed him home right away. It's no biggie." She shrugged and wiped her hands on the towel sticking out of her apron pocket. "But thanks all the same."

Luke peered down silently. Was there a smudge or something on her cheek? "Can I get you anything else?"

He craned his neck toward the kitchen door and frowned. "You all alone here, or is there someone else in the back?"

A tingle of nervous awareness seeped into her scalp. His sheer maleness and the heat radiating from his cut physique made her tingly with a desire to abandon her good sense. Yes indeed, they were quite alone.

"I don't mind closing up on occasion. Besides…"

"Besides what?"

Do *not* tell him.

Instead of answering, she seized two newly washed glasses from the rack and stacked them behind the bar for tomorrow's opening. She pivoted back to snatch another glass, but he already held one out. She tried to retrieve it, but he wouldn't let go.

"Besides what?" he insisted, and one of those sandy, perfectly shaped eyebrows arched.

She chewed on the corner of her lip and contemplated the answer. "I enjoy the solitude when no one is here. Sometimes I fire up the old jukebox and imagine how it used to be."

That sounded dumb.

"No it doesn't."

Oh shoot, guess she'd whispered out loud.

Luke tipped his head back to the exposed beams of the ceiling. "This place has to be pretty old. The molding design is definitely authentic."

The line of his neck lay exposed. He swallowed and his Adam's apple bobbed under the tanned skin. How could a man ooze such masculine sexuality? A hint of sandy stubble, almost auburn, disappeared into peach fuzz along his jaw. She wondered how good he tasted.

Whoa.

She clunked two glasses together by accident. He pinned her with a stare, as if he knew she'd been salivating over his neck, for crying out loud.

"The building dates back to the 1800s, and it was a speakeasy in the twenties or thirties, I believe. I bet if these walls could talk we'd hear tons of the history of Havenport."

"You love your history, don't you?" Luke teased.

Darcy ducked her head and studied the water stain on a glass. "It's my guilty pleasure, I guess."

"The best kind. The dates make sense in terms of the architecture." He helped her stack the rest of the glasses.

They worked in silence. It felt nice to have company, but he sure wasn't very talkative. "I appreciate the help. Otherwise this would have taken a lot longer. I'm about done, so you can, you know, go."

His left eyebrow arched. "I don't think so. I'll walk you out," he said, and the timbre of his declaration made her insides melt. It was kind of nice having her own personal US Marine bodyguard, even though Havenport wasn't the crime capital of Rhode Island.

"I usually have a nightcap. Just one," she added quickly, "so I can still drive. It's sort of my ritual. Do you want? My treat."

His upper lip quirked. "*I'll* buy."

"Suit yourself." Darcy shrugged and swiveled to reach for the bottle of Jack from the top shelf, then palmed two shot glasses. She poured twin inches and handed him one.

"Coffee-and-whiskey girl, huh? I'm impressed."

A blush crept into her cheeks. "I can't stomach any kind of fruity, girlie drinks and I'm not a fan of beer. Jack and I do get along occasionally."

"My kind of lady. Cheers," he said, then threw back the shot before she could say anything. She, on the other hand, nursed hers as their gazes collided.

She looked away first before he figured she had something to hide. Crap.

"I'll shut off the kitchen lights and grab my stuff," she told him, and pulled off her crappy apron. At least her Royce's T-shirt underneath was still in pretty good shape. No pit stains, and the lacy bra she had on underneath peeked over the V-neck.

Kitchen back to rights, Darcy stepped into the main restaurant area and came up short. Luke leaned against the jukebox, ankles crossed and dripping of casual, sexy dangerousness. He reached behind his back, and she heard the click of the button before Adele's version of her favorite Bob Dylan song started. Her heart thumped with nervous anticipation.

"I thought you were walking me out."

He tilted his head to one side. "I thought you'd wish a few more minutes of solitude."

"Solitude usually means alone."

He pushed his body off the machine and stalked her. Her breath caught at his predatory scrutiny. "The way I see it, solitude isn't necessarily how many people are present, but what's in your head. I used to be surrounded by twenty farting guys and solitude to me meant zoning out and meditating into myself."

She grimaced but then laughed. "Um…you lost me at the farting part, but I sort of see your point. I guess it's how you accept quiet and introspection."

He smirked. "Exactly. Dance?" He beckoned with an outstretched arm.

Gliding like liquid, she slid into his arms. His hardness, the planes and angles of his incredible chest and abdomen, grazed her upper body. Closing her eyes, she pressed her nose into the hollow of his chest and breathed in.

What a coward she was.

Here, dancing, enjoying this moment, and within the next day Luke's world would be turned inside out. Could she waylay it? Could she ease the way for this crazy discovery? The burden on her head felt like an iron anvil, heavier than the load her parents stuck her with.

"Easy," Luke whispered against her hair. His heart beat under her ear, and it was like floating in a pool, weightless. Cool on the underside, and hot on the top against the flatness of his torso. Whether he stayed or not, whether he hated her for keeping this secret, at least she could grant herself this miraculous moment, maybe even this one night.

Darcy brought her hands up to lay flat against his chest and the muscles under her palms flexed. They were solid, warm, and good. Lord, he smelled of fresh laundry in the sunshine.

He didn't ever dress fancy, usually sporting a T-shirt and jeans. Not overly tight, though enough that the outline of his thighs strained against the denim, and the back pockets hugged his muscular butt. He loved the carpenter jeans, which, in truth she'd never noticed before were the sexiest cut of jeans on a guy. Especially on Luke, who had zero body fat and the flattest stomach on the planet.

She sucked in her own, fearing he felt her rolls under his shirt.

"Quit fidgeting and enjoy." He chuckled, and the rumble of his laugh vibrated into her sternum and below. That shot of Jack triggered a slow, warm sensation igniting into a burn, like embers on a campfire. Only this time, all it would take for a full flame would be to kiss him.

Should she be so bold or wait?

"Sorry," she mumbled, and forced her arms and torso to relax into him, but it wasn't working. Her mind raced, unable to get into the moment. His *everything* affected her. His slow sway, the buzz of the fan overhead, the lyrics of Bob Dylan's, so poignant.

Luke would soon leave, and if she didn't grasp the moment before all hell broke loose she was a complete fool.

She glanced up as the song faded. "You hungry?"

"I'm starving, Darcy," came his husky reply.

Well. Cue the quivering in her nether regions. She cleared her throat and stepped out of his embrace. "I sometimes go to Mellie's after my shift. I highly recommend the Reuben."

The corner of his mouth lifted. "The Reuben?"

"Yeah. So you want to come back to my place...for a bite?"

He stilled, and she swore she heard him swear under his breath, something about willpower, but she didn't catch it.

"I'd be honored."

♥ ♥ ♥

Darcy opened the door to her apartment. Oedipus meowed but didn't vacate his plush bed. She hoped Luke wasn't allergic.

Her apartment could never be described as huge, but it worked for her. Renting one of the places on top of the stores lining Main Street proved affordable. Plus, she didn't have to walk far to get any type of food. It was also a short drive to work. When she'd come back to Havenport, her folks asked her to live at home, but after being with sleazeball, the thought of sharing a bathroom with anyone held little appeal. And Brett had wagered she'd kill her mother before a month.

"Thanks for the lift."

"No problem," she answered. Ironic how they'd discovered his tire had gone flat in the parking lot. Another twist of fate, she supposed. Either way, Luke was here, in her place with no way to get back to the Inn.

Her pulse shot up, but she tried to keep it together.

"I'm sure Mac can fix your tire in the morning. He's a great guy and the best mechanic in town. Plus, he's a former Marine."

"Okay," Luke commented, and shut the door for her.

Big, hot man. Small apartment. Sharon and Brett would be proud.

"Mellie's makes the best Rueben." Darcy focused on the food, instead of what might lie ahead, and held up the paper bag before heading to her kitchen.

Luke trailed, and when she turned and plopped their dinner onto the orange Formica counter, she found him looking around the place.

"All I have is a white," she announced, and opened the fridge. "Or whiskey if you prefer? Sorry, no beer."

"Wine is good."

Darcy grabbed two glasses from the cabinet near the sink and uncorked the bottle. She handed him a crystal goblet, and they each took a long sip in silence. The cool, crisp Pinot hit the back of her throat and she was thankful for it. He was rather large and looming in her small kitchen. Downing the glassful in half a second, she leaned against the sink and crossed her ankles.

"I like your decor." He chuckled, and she narrowed her eyes at him.

"Yeah, well, the landlord is stuck in a time warp. And I don't have the time or money to redecorate." She'd actually grown accustomed to the foil wallpaper with its large orange-and-brown circle design.

"These crazy colors remind me of my mom's art studio," he said with a tinge of sadness in his voice, then ran a hand along the surface of a cabinet. They were the best part of the kitchen—a deep mahogany with lighter shades and swirls in the center. "They're sturdy and well-made cabinets. It's hard to get this type of wood now without spending a fortune."

His left hand caressed the cabinet door closest to the fridge and his index finger traced the notched design. She stood fascinated by the movement and pondered how his fingers might feel upon her skin. She visualized him building the framework on the set. His shoulders had bunched and contracted. When he'd bent over, half the older ladies who worked at the Historical Society offices nearly peed in their Depends at the view of his perfect ass. A few ladies had given him catcalls. They were ridiculous.

Luke found pleasure in working with his hands.

"You're staring, Darcy."

Cripes. He truly needed to stop saying her name in that sexy, take-me-to-bed tone. The bedroom door hung a few feet away, and it'd been a dog's age since she'd been satisfied, at least not without her own means.

"You know your wood." *Good choice of words, idiot.* She nearly groaned. His eyes flared and he advanced, his boots covering the short distance between them in a nanosecond.

Dinner apparently forgotten, Luke backed her up against the sink. The heat of his body enveloped the tiny space. He'd shed his jacket on the way inside, and the soft cotton of his T-shirt meshed against hers. His every contour seared into her chest. He placed his hands on either side of the counter and sandwiched her, forcing her head to tilt back to see his face, he was *that* close. Close enough to observe the sandy tips of his eyelashes and the stubble on his chin. Between his intensity and the glass of Pinot settling in her stomach, her senses ignited.

One corner of his lip rose. She yearned to kiss the exact spot, but she didn't have to imagine how he tasted, because suddenly she knew and it was better than she'd imagined. Lips to lips, his flesh was so smooth and warm that she gasped. He tilted his head slightly to the right and molded their mouths together. God, he tasted like a mixture of the tart wine and pure sex.

He still gripped the counter, and she yearned to feel his hands around her waist, in her hair, everywhere. He seemed to be in measured control mode, and that just wouldn't do. She needed to get closer. To crawl up into him and fuse.

She moved her hands up the sides of his torso, and he jerked and growled into her mouth. A throaty, deep rumble that gave her courage in continuing to explore his amazing body. She trailed her fingertips up then down his sides before wrapping her arms round his back and flattening like a pancake against his heat. Even those muscles were defined.

"You're killing me," he groaned into her mouth, then leaned his forehead against hers. His breath sawed in and out. The fact that his control faltered made her stomach flutter.

She darted out her tongue to lick then nip at his bottom lip, fueled by her blossoming desire and the wine. "You're a tough Marine. You can handle it."

He growled, turning her legs to jelly.

"But the question is, can you?" In one fluid movement, he lifted her as if she weighed nothing, wrapped her legs around his waist, and strode out of the kitchen.

"Directions. Bedroom?" A question, yet not. Luke had to know this felt so right that of course it was going to happen.

"Second door. On the right," she said between kisses to his lips, his chiseled cheeks, his perfect earlobe.

"Having trouble walking if you continue that."

Darcy threw her head back and smirked. "Luckily I have a small apartment. You don't have to go far."

"You are in so much trouble." The threat held promise, and she sucked in a breath.

Yes!

Luke kicked her bedroom door closed and a picture on the wall rattled, but Darcy couldn't give a hoot. She unwound her legs and placed her feet on the floor, then resumed kissing him. He cupped her head in both his hands, and when they finally came up for air his nostrils flared.

"I am so taking my time with you."

"Yeah, okay. Maybe on the second round." Jeez, when had she become so bold? There was no way she could wait and take this slow. Pulling his T-shirt out from his belt, her hands made contact with the skin on his stomach. His six-pack twitched. In one motion he grabbed his shirt behind his neck and whipped it over his head.

"You're stunning." She blinked and drank him in.

A large tattoo of an intricate cross ran from his shoulder to his elbow. She'd wondered about the design peeking from his short sleeves. The combination of blues and slashes of reds popped out with each flex of muscle. She gulped at the indentation where his pecs met, so defined, and the baby-fine hairs smattering over his chest and downward.

On his torso in cursive letters was "for my brothers." It took her breath away—so simple and yet so profound. By its own volition, her index finger traced the words. He'd shared a special bond with his fellow Marines.

The same way David had.

The sentiment touched her soul.

Darcy bent and placed a kiss on the tattoo. He sucked in a ragged breath. His large, calloused yet soft hands rested on her hair, then wound into the waves. She looked up to see his eyes hooded with desire, and a shot of pure feminine desire gave her the strength to continue her onslaught of his ink.

"That is so beautiful, Luke," she whispered between kisses.

"*You're* beautiful when you do that. When your eyes shine. Bring that luscious mouth up here. Now." He tugged her back up and sealed his mouth to hers again.

"You have entirely too many clothes on." He stepped away, and the loss of his warmth made her shiver. Her lips felt swollen and tingled.

He raised both arms above her head and rolled up her shirt, deftly yet gently pulling it over her hair before smoothing her tousled locks over her shoulders, almost reverently.

He made her feel worshipped.

Darcy trembled, even though Luke's body radiated more heat than the old coal stove in her folks' basement. Thankfully, she'd had the foresight to wear her new matching undies set. Thank goodness for the Victoria's Secret website. The see-through lace bra, with its bit of padding, helped add a bit of cleavage. Until it came off, that was. And the hip-hugger panties made her ass look good, too.

His smile reached his eyes. "How'd you know purple is my favorite color."

"I have the set in pink, too."

"My second-favorite color," he teased. "But you know what?" His lips made a trail down her neck and nipped at the hollow where her shoulder met her neck.

Her head fell back. He'd better not stop. "What?" she asked, all breathy.

"Skin color is my ultimate favorite, and yours is the color of cream. Hmm…tastes sweet, too. I hope you're ready for senseless."

Before she had time to think or be self-conscious, they were naked and horizontal on the bed, warmth to warmth. He called her gorgeous and worshipped a few places on her body with much intense attention. There were a few "Oh Gods," and "Yes, Luke, that's it," and she lost herself in him.

Chapter Nine

The alarm felt like a jackhammer in her brain. Darcy blindly reached over the bed and her arm hit a wall of warm muscle.

"Why would you choose a polka music station for your alarm?" The question came with a strained grunt, and she smiled with closed eyes.

"Because it's the most annoying sound on the planet."

"Roger that."

With that, the mattress shifted and Luke smacked the alarm button.

"Oops, I may owe you a clock," he said after her cheapo clock hit the carpet. It didn't matter, for soon thereafter blessed silence filled her bedroom.

She groaned and stretched her arms overhead, reveling in the relief by cracking her neck. Muscles she hadn't used in a long time—and not nearly as thoroughly—screamed.

"I have to get up, anyway."

Strong arms held her shoulders into the down comforter while he nuzzled her neck, and she relaxed into the pressure. She glided her hands up his smooth back and over his hard biceps. How could he feel and smell so delicious at 7:00 a.m.? And especially after a night of sweating and straining—*phew*.

"Play hooky," he suggested between kisses to her neck and collarbone.

"Excuse me?"

"You heard me," he said, not letting up, then massaging her outstretched triceps, making her moan with the pressure.

"I *could* take a personal day." She hadn't taken a day off in forever.

"Yep, take a Luke day," he announced, propping himself on one elbow and smiling down at her. His tousled hair, grown notably longer the few days since he'd arrived, stuck out in a few places and resembled a spiky ball of sun-kissed yarn. A shadow of a beard caressed his cheeks and jawline. That scratchiness triggered a memory of where he'd tickled her with it.

"What will we do?"

His smile faltered a bit as he peered into her face. "I'd be honored if you'd help me spread Mom's ashes at some point today."

Darcy pasted her smile in place, instead of losing it and jumping out of bed with anxiety. Omigod, how could she forget? *Stupid, stupid.* Today would have been Mary Sullivan's fiftieth birthday, and it was *still* Lucas's fiftieth birthday. And Lucas would be lying in wait for Luke in Havenport Park.

Darcy's eyes misted. Oh, God, what the hell was she going to do? "Are you sure? It's kinda private."

A vee creased the skin between his perfect eyebrows. "Hey, if it's too creepy, I won't insist. I just thought…well, you've been so great and getting me the info, and it's actually a bittersweet thing. Hey," he said, gently pushing the massive mess that was her hair away from her forehead, "don't be sad. You know I thought a lot about what you said."

She sniffed. "Oh, what was that?" Her gaze bounced between Luke's inquisitive gaze and her cell phone on her nightstand. *Cripes*, she had to call Lucas. There must be a better way to broach this subject instead of on this monumental day.

Luke lay back on the pillow with an arm behind his head, resembling a Greek god, perfectly sculptured yet so vulnerable. "About Mom coming home. And, well, I'm glad I could do that for her. At first I was more than a bit annoyed at having to come here, but not so much now. This place shaped my mother. Thanks for helping me understand. And for the job…and of course, last night." When he winked a flush hit her entire body like a blast of summer humidity.

"You're welcome." *He won't be thanking me when he finds out I know who his father is.*

Suddenly the confident, perfect lover and strong Marine seemed uncertain, and it melted her heart even more. "So will you come with me, Darcy?"

Shame pierced at her insides. She should tell him about Lucas. Right here, right now. To soften the blow. To *not* blindside him. But she'd promised Lucas.

"I will, but first you have to see some things, okay?"

♥ ♥ ♥

"Where are you taking me? I look ridiculous," he griped.

"Oh, stop. This is going to be a surprise."

"You're lucky you're cute and sweet, and know how to kiss." He held on to her hand as she led him out of the front seat of her car, which he'd somehow screwed himself into. Oh, his poor knees.

Darcy withdrew the large, fluffy pink scarf from around his head and stepped back.

She threw out her arms wide. "Behold."

Eyes adjusting to the midmorning sunlight, he blinked a few times, then squinted at the house and shook his head in disbelief.

"Way to go, Mom." He laughed, and Darcy relaxed.

Her plan was to take Luke to all the places Mary had bestowed her artwork around town: Mrs. Franklin's house and the infamous magical mystery fence first. The images of the Fab Four and their rainbow colors presented a startling psychedelic sight.

"I know, right?" Darcy clapped like a two-year-old, but she didn't care. Luke's excited expression made her awkwardness worth it. She rose on her tiptoes and pecked his cheek. He grabbed her waist for a squeeze.

"Mrs. Franklin's long gone, but her son, Matt, lives here and he *loves* the Beatles. So much so, he's in a revival cover band. He's Ringo, by the way. Matt kept the fence as is, said it was all because of this fence he caught the Beatles bug."

Luke shook his head with an incredulous expression. "How in the hell would you know all that?"

Darcy blushed and used the toe of her flats to kick a stray white pebble from the walkway. "I made a few calls about your mom, mostly for the piece in the *Herald*, but also for you."

"What am I going to do with you?" He pulled her in close and rested his chin on the top of her head. He towered over her, but somehow they fit. She hadn't felt self-conscious about her height or her curves with Luke.

She broke away and tugged on his hand. "Let's go. Next stop."

"Let me stretch my legs a bit more before I get back into your clown car," he quipped, and she laughed.

"It's a short drive. You'll survive."

"You're worse than a drill sergeant."

They explored Havenport for the next few hours. The side of the municipal building, with its lady of justice mural, and the old animal shelter, including the new service dog school which sported a portrait of puppies piled atop a rotund ringmaster. The man's face bore an uncanny resemblance to old Mr. Washburn, who used to own the property and the majority of the real estate in Havenport, but no one ever dared to say so.

Darcy brought Luke to the library to see the myriad of abstracts hung there, all with the initials MS for Mary Sullivan.

"The retired librarian told me your mother used to drop off paintings practically every week. Free."

♥ ♥ ♥

"This day has been incredible."

They sat on the pier in front of Corky's Café enjoying two steaming cups of coffee, a bag of gourmet popcorn, and basking in the late-afternoon sunshine.

"I'm thrilled I could do this for you." Darcy bit her lip. It was closing in on three o'clock, and Luke mentioned he wanted to go to Havenport Park by four, then grab dinner. They'd swapped vehicles for his truck at Mac's garage then picked up his mom's multicolored urn and a bouquet of purple and pink roses—apparently her favorite—which sat on his back seat.

Luke stretched his long limbs and crossed his worn work boots at the ankles, turning his face into the sun. His chiseled profile never failed to make her want to fan herself.

"You're the most unexpected surprise I've ever had, Miss Darcy Prentice. Thank you for making my bleak life more sunshiny, if that's even a word." He leaned over to place a kiss on her hair.

She'd miss him. *That stunk.*

How could she possibly resume battery-operated after experiencing Luke? After getting a taste of a real, exciting man? His departing would hurt her heart.

"Can I tell you a secret?" he asked, and her stomach lurched.

"Um, sure."

"I considered *not* doing this for Mom, for maybe two-point-three seconds. There were days in between shipping home from a long, shithole deployment, and when I got the letter from Mom's friend, Barb, that I figured who would know, right?"

The question didn't require her to answer.

"It ate me up—the stress of coming here, facing her death again—more than any mission overseas. You always worry about acclimating back into civilian life, being normal again."

She nodded. "David used to tell me that when he'd return home on leave. Normal didn't exist anymore." She missed David something fierce. He would've liked Luke.

"He had a point." He kissed her temple and caused a flood of tears to well, but Darcy held them at bay. Luke threw an arm on the iron and wood bench behind her back and gently ran his thumb along her shoulder. Their casual closeness felt so natural.

Too bad he's leaving. Do it. Tell him.

"So," they blurted together and laughed.

Angst hit her sternum and she squirmed on the bench. The breeze intensified and a lock of hair stuck to her lips. *Coward.*

"You first," he prompted.

She tore away the wayward strand, downed her coffee for liquid courage, and expelled a ragged breath. "I have to ask you something."

He tossed their empty cups in the nearby trash can before turning to face her.

"Uh-oh, sounds serious. No, I do not have any communicable diseases or a woman in every country."

The idiotic words she'd blurted to Brett what seemed eons ago came back to haunt her, but she wasn't going to back down. She had to know in order to help Lucas and Luke.

"Did your father die before your mom?"

He blinked a few times and frowned. "Um, okay, that's out of left field. Why?"

She twisted the rubber band on what was left of her neat braid and trudged on. "You haven't mentioned your father, and given my own father's what I call semi-demise from his awful disease," she said with a wry laugh, "I just wondered if you had other family somewhere and why they hadn't come with you."

A tic materialized in his jaw and he lifted his arm away from the bench to lean forward. He bowed his head and rested his elbows on his knees. The corded muscles in his forearms flexed, the blue veins contrasting underneath his tanned skin. His clenched fists transfixed her until her ears caught his next words.

"Ben died when I was seventeen. There's no one else."

"I'm so sorry."

He shrugged and sat up straight. "I never knew my birth father, or the *sperm donor*. Mom married Ben when I was fourteen, and before that it was just the two of us. Ben's the only father I *ever* knew or needed, and when he died a part of me did, too."

The blood left Darcy's face. *Shit*. He hated Lucas without ever meeting him.

Yet.

She wrapped her arms around her waist and shivered.

He gazed out at the water, a stream of sunlight illuminating half his face.

"You asked why I joined the Marines last night in the dark. Remember?"

She shut her eyes. Of *course* she remembered. She remembered every single touch and word they'd spoken. Curiosity always got the best of her. She nodded.

"I left out a huge part."

"Go on," she said, repeating the words he'd uttered when she'd unloaded about her parents.

He exhaled in a long puff. "Ben was a carpenter by trade. They met at one of Mom's art exhibits when he'd built her display, and they clicked. I was a fucked-up kid," he admitted, but Darcy had a hard time believing it so she snorted.

He grinned and tossed pieces of popcorn at a blue jay perched on the edge of the trash can watching them. Despite the sun beating down on her face, Darcy grew chilled. Luke detected her discomfort and put an arm around her shoulders again, pressing her into his warmth.

"Believe me, I wasn't born a Marine."

She rolled her eyes. "Ha!"

He tickled her neck, and she swatted his hand.

"I cut school, got detention, and smoked weed. All kinds of stupid shit. You name it, I did it. We moved frequently." He scratched his chin and licked his lips, eyes narrowing at the memory. "God, I must've switched school seven times by the fifth grade. I didn't mind at the time, but then I did," he whispered.

Wow, Darcy thought. What kind of crazy mother had Mary been? Maybe she'd been searching for something, too, and taking Luke along for the ride.

The waterfront bench afforded a view of the harbor and the boats, some recently taken out of dry dock for the season, gleamed spotlessly clean. The yachts were enormous, but some of her friends owned smaller fishing vessels moored there.

Havenport was a peaceful place and her home. Darcy couldn't fathom living anywhere else again. Despite how her parents acted now, she'd had a stable household growing up.

"Ben saw something in me I couldn't."

"What?" Darcy asked, hoarse with emotion. The way he spoke made Darcy want to hear it all, to unearth Luke's history. Her fingers inadvertently made circles on his faded denim.

"My imagination," he stated. "Ben showed me it wasn't just Mom's gig. I, too, could create."

He chuckled and shook his head, perhaps remembering a good and bad memory at the same time.

"By high school we'd settled in California, right outside San Francisco. He'd opened a business building custom furniture, theater sets, and Mom painted."

He stopped speaking, and she lifted her head from his shoulder. He'd crumpled the empty popcorn bag and his brows slashed low.

"An ideal life," she carefully ventured a guess.

He swallowed hard. "He bid on a huge job for the local theater company. The sets were enormous for a production of Shakespeare. Mom was stoked for free tickets. I promised I'd help, but I never showed up. There was this girl—hell, I can't even remember her name—who my buddies said was a *sure thing.*" His lips flattened. "Who was I to pass that up? A skinny-shit squirt ready to have my cherry popped at seventeen? *Ooh-fucking-rah.* By the time I'd cared to head home, the police were at my door."

She covered her mouth with her hand. "What happened?"

His throat worked over a swallow, and their eyes collided. "A heavy facade fell on him," he stated flatly. "The EMTs said he'd lain there for at least an hour bleeding out from the head."

There was no way to stop the gush of tears streaming down her cheeks. "You cannot blame yourself. It was an accident."

His eyes softened. "How did I know you'd say that? You're too sweet for this crazy world."

A thought dawned. "Did your mother blame you?"

He glanced at her, the grooves between his sandy brows deepening. "What? No. It wasn't her style. *I* couldn't live with the guilt. Couldn't abide the desolation on her face every day, so I joined the corps to escape the pain and join the ranks of the unfeeling. I ran. It's what I do, Darcy."

"You're not running now," she said, and hugged him close.

"I will. I know it as sure as my own name," he announced against her ear, and her heartbeat skipped.

"Maybe your mom sent you to Havenport to discover her artwork and how it, and she, shaped the town. Maybe she sent you to find a home, or a *family*?" she said, hopeful.

A shot in the dark, but she had to try.

The past years of grief—over David, then Dad, then the slow deterioration of her mother—had sucked her confidence. Why shouldn't she fight for Luke? She was sick of having no useful purpose. Sick of existing, or not being able to control the shit show her own family had become. Luke and Lucas both deserved to heal.

He ran a finger along her cheek. "I have no family besides a few of my corps buds, and to be honest I've grown accustomed to that. But I do want to thank you for giving me the best few days I've had in a long, long time."

Oh, shit, that sounded like *adios*.

Sure, fall for the Marine who's allergic to family, and suffer heartbreak—again. Regardless of this thing between them, which Luke just basically called off, Lucas warranted a second chance to explain he wasn't just a sperm donor.

Darcy hoped it wasn't too big a task.

Chapter Ten

On the ride to Havenport Park, Luke silently berated himself. He'd hurt Darcy. *Goddammit.* Sure, she'd played it off smooth and unbothered. She'd dusted off her jeans, pasted on a smile, and prepared to give his mom, whom she didn't know from Adam, a proper send-off.

She'd laughed with him, cried for him, and dammit, he couldn't stay.

She deserved better than a scarred, commitment-phobic idiot. Christ, she'd lost her brother, and her folks sucked. This incredible woman needed someone with hope and a permanent address, and a credit card at the very least.

Mom's urn in the back seat, along with the flowers he'd bought, pulsated as if she still sat there. Luke imagined Mom glaring at him in his rearview and shaking her head in disgust.

Aw, hell, Darcy handled his big ole whopper of Ben's accident saga and still she stayed in his truck. Again, a testament to the bright light he'd discovered in this sleepy town.

The town. Good God, Mom's strokes of personality still existed after all these years. The librarian, the Beatles guy, they'd all benefited from her creativity.

And sadly, he was an expert at lying.

The thing was, he didn't really *want* to run. He wanted to stay and explore the unknown he'd missed all these years, but he had zero idea how to start.

♥ ♥ ♥

They pulled into Havenport Park. Darcy sat as still as stone on the drive, and he couldn't blame her. Their night of bliss had rocked them to the core, and he'd thrown a bucket of ice on it.

Yeah, maybe he deserved to be alone after all.

"I'll have to park here, then we can walk to the tree." She turned with a nod and a faint, desolate smile.

She tossed her long hair over her shoulder, and he sucked in a breath. He'd never forget how the soft tresses felt trailing over his skin in a blanket of orange bliss. Ever.

"I'll grab the flowers." She leaned over the back seat to snatch the foil-wrapped roses.

He stopped her movement with a hand to her forearm and brought her palm to his lips. "Thank you." Then he leaned down and captured her lips.

She pulled away, and something he couldn't discern crept into her gaze: sadness, determination, nervousness? Maybe a little of each.

"I hope you will," she said with flattened lips before opening the door, hopping down off the running board and trudging toward the massive oak tree.

He frowned at her back. What did she mean by that?

When they reached the base of the tree Luke spotted a guy sitting on the bleached bench. *Crap.* So much for doing this in private.

The grass crunched under his boots as he stepped over a rabbit hole, but gripped Mom's urn tight. Didn't want to drop it on the home stretch. Her ashes had made it from California to Georgia and now back home.

As she'd wished.

Darcy stopped a few feet away from the guy, who'd shot to his feet when he'd noticed them advance. His face flushed crimson when Darcy got there ahead of him. He also had a bouquet of purple and pink roses.

What the hell?

"Darcy," Luke heard the guy say.

Darcy whispered something in the guy's ear, then he patted her on the shoulder. "Thank you," he told her.

Luke felt his whole body tense, and a trickle of annoyance sliced into his head.

"I'm sorry, sir, this is a private matter. Can I ask you to give us a moment, please?" Yeah, he couldn't help being polite. It'd been drilled into him from the corps, and Mom and Ben, too. But damn if he wouldn't forcefully remove this guy, big as he was.

"Son, I'm here for you," the man said with conviction.

Luke respected his no-nonsense reply, but he still had to go.

"And for Mary."

Luke's mouth dropped open and he glanced over at Darcy, who remained silent through the whole exchange.

She placed the bouquet at the base of the tree then walked slowly toward him. She reached out a hand and caressed his cheek, and he noticed her mouth trembled.

"That man is Lucas Cameron. Listen to what he has to say, please. And know I wish you nothing but happiness, wherever that may lead you."

"Wait…I don't understand." But she stopped his words by raising her hand.

"Listen to him."

Then she turned and walked out of his line of sight.

♥ ♥ ♥

Darcy plopped onto her stomach on her bed, and Oedipus vaulted off in protest.

"I'm not in the mood," she growled, then checked her phone for the hundredth time in the past twenty-four hours.

Luke had left. That was agonizingly obvious. And Lucas, the pain in her butt, was also MIA.

Talk about plans backfiring in a monumental way. The only saving grace was her installment of the Havenport Historicals column had run and earned accolades from her boss, the staff, and the readers.

The town apparently gushed over her *brilliantly executed* idea to publish all of Lucas's photos of Mary's works. Dozens of images: black-and-white, color, sketches, with the caption "The Legend of the Phantom Painter revealed."

Someone had even posted yearbook photos of Lucas and Mary on the *Herald*'s Facebook page.

She was also in talk with her boss about Darcy's Deductions. All in the plus column, right?

But not even a call or a text from Luke or Lucas. Had they killed each other under the oak tree among Mary's scattered ashes? No one on the crime desk had reported such an incident. Had Luke stormed off and made Lucas feel like shit? Called him the sperm donor?

He'd better not have. Lucas was one of the most upstanding, courteous men she'd ever met…same as his son.

"This stinks," she muttered, then catapulted off the mattress to lumber into the kitchen. Ben and Jerry's made everything better, a known fact. Chunky Monkey and a large espresso and she'd be ready to face the day. She still had Darcy's Deductions to map out for her editor.

Move on and move up.

So she'd tried to do her good deed for the century and failed. No matter. Mom would be calling in her grocery order any minute now. But you know what? She'd just have to wait for the fiftieth can of creamed corn.

Pulling on a hoodie over her boxer-brief pajamas, she placed her steaming mug on the coffee table, headed back to the freezer, and sunk into the couch.

Open lid, check. Spoon in hand, check. Do *not* look at the carbohydrate count on the carton.

Oedipus eyeballed her spoon but she shooed him away. "No chocolate for you, Mr. Chunky Kitty."

She heard a knock at the door and froze, then found the wherewithal to gradually rise from the couch and open her door. Identical icy blues stared at her, one with a wry smirk at her spoon and half-eaten carton, and the other, younger version ogling her bare legs.

"She's eating carbs. This cannot be good," Lucas said.

"She's a closet carb eater," Luke fired back, but kept his gaze homed in on her eyes. She could not look away.

"You two want to come in?" she finally asked. Polite was the way to go, even though the ice cream threatened to make another appearance as a result of her nerves.

They *seemed* on good terms.

"I'm not staying," Lucas announced before crossing her threshold. He leaned down, kissed her forehead, and smiled. "Our photo shoot is at eleven thirty. Luke's set was wheeled out of the society's warehouse and is all ready for us. Don't be late."

Wait, what? Oh shit, the New Englander photo shoot.

"Thank you," he whispered in her ear, gave her hand a squeeze, then pivoted back to the door. "Second chances do happen to old salty dogs such as us."

"Speak for yourself," Luke said, and thumped Lucas on the back before closing the door behind him.

Darcy gripped the carton so hard she was afraid the melted confection would start to ooze onto the floor. "Things went well?"

"You're the reporter; what do you think?"

Her eyes widened. "What I mean is, you and Lucas…do you know?"

"That he's the sperm donor?"

Anger crept into her scalp. "Do *not* call him that. It's rude and he doesn't deserve it!" The stress of the past few days surfaced, taking her control.

Luke backed up because she hadn't realized she was brandishing her spoon at his nose.

"Whoa, my fierce, pretty Hermia."

Pretty? Hermia?

Luke grinned. "He didn't take offense to my label. Just ask. In fact, he admitted he'd have thought the same thing or worse without understanding the history."

His arms encircled her waist and he kissed the tip of her nose. "And, yes, we spoke. For the entire night. I'm dead tired, but I know everything. Shit, talk about being blindsided. But surprisingly, I'm okay with it. He's an honorable guy. And Mom, well, they both got screwed over. We have a long way to go. We can't predict what the future holds, but there's nothing to lose by getting to know him, right?"

Darcy sighed and relaxed in his embrace. A wave of relieved tears leaked out. "Are you angry with me for not telling you?"

Luke smiled a bit ruefully. "Kinda a moot point. You kept your promise to Lucas."

Her shoulders released all the tension built up for the past days.

"Get dressed and I'll treat you to coffee at Led Zeppoli," he suggested, and directed her to the bedroom. "Ice cream is no kind of breakfast."

Darcy nodded, her eyes filling again. "Wait, are you staying in Havenport?"

He rubbed the back of his neck and a blush stole into his chiseled face, making him seem vulnerable. "Seems the Historical Society needs a new carpenter. And I'd be willing to try settling here—that is, if you don't mind having me around?"

Her breath caught. "I'd love that."

He jerked her back into his embrace and let out a long sigh as his lips descended.

♥ ♥ ♥

Two months later…

The blast of an air horn from the fire truck made Darcy jump backward, bumping into a solid, warm, and sweaty chest. Arms shot around her waist.

"That was loud," came a sexy voice tickling her left earlobe.

"Was it?" She feigned ignorance, which earned a deep chuckle against her back.

"This parade is crazy," Luke commented.

She twisted at the waist and tipped back her head, focused on the strong jaw in her line of sight. That fuzzy two-day stubble of his was too irresistible not to kiss. Luke growled, and the sensation of the low hum against her spine traveled straight to her toes. Thank goodness a soft breeze blew through the leaves on the tree they'd parked themselves under, for her temperature spiked—and not only from the humidity.

They watched group after group of townspeople, local businesses, Mayor Henry, and others march along the main drag of Havenport with a sea of American flags in their hands, waving and bobbing along to the sound of laughter and patriotic music.

"Yeah, the Fourth of July Havenport parade is always a sight to behold."

And it was. For as long as she could remember she, her parents, and David had attended the annual holiday celebration. For the first time since David's death, the void of his absence lessened from an acute stab of pain to a dull ache. This year's parade included honoring members of the community who'd made a difference for town and country. Mary Sullivan's name hung amongst those displayed on a huge banner at the beginning of the parade route, along with David's and many others.

Darcy glanced over at her parents a few yards away, seated on folding chairs at the edge of the curb, also waving flags. In the past couple months, Dad's mental state had further deteriorated, and it was quite painful to watch. However, today he'd remembered a few familiar faces in the crowd and called them by name. Thank Jesus. Even Mom had mellowed in the past two months since Luke had made his fateful drive into Havenport and into their lives. She only went shopping once a month for her folks now, miracle of miracles. And the nurse's aide Luke had suggested turned out to be a godsend. Ironically, the woman also shared Mom's penchant for collectibles.

Darcy sighed and sank into his embrace. Luke rubbed a calloused palm over her bare arm, and she shivered. Things were good. She felt cherished by him more and more every day. This time next week, they'd move into a newly renovated, more spacious apartment, complete with a full bathroom and sunken tub.

Together.

It was a huge and exciting step in this crazy whirlwind romance. And she wouldn't have it any other way.

"Look, there's the Historical Society float."

Darcy's gaze flew to where Luke pointed. It really was a work of art with its detailed woodworking and mini town square complete with the gazebo. Some of the staff waved to Luke as they passed.

"Oh, Luke, it came out amazing." The society had hired Luke as a full-time custodian and resident carpenter. His birth father, her dear friend Lucas Cameron, sat in the middle of the float in period costume. He winked and gave them a million-watt smile.

"Way to go, Lucas."

"Good job, Dad."

Darcy's breath caught at the endearment. In a short period of time, Luke and Lucas had truly become father and son. Miracles happened, and good things happened to good people. Both Luke and Lucas deserved joy and peace in their lives.

"What do you say we duck out and christen our new place?"

She arched an eyebrow and gave him a sideways glance. "Now? We don't take possession until next week."

He dangled a key chain in front of her nose, and she laughed. "Pays to be a handyman in this town and know the landlord." He turned her fully in his arms, and she almost incinerated on the spot at the mischief and heat in his gaze.

"I've got a couple of surprises in store for you, Miss Prentice, which include our new tub and a bottle of champagne." Her stomach fluttered. "You game?"

"Always, and anything with you." She grabbed his hand and they headed to their new home.

About Nicole S. Patrick

NICOLE S. PATRICK has always loved to read, and in her teenage years, she "borrowed" her mom's books to sneak away and become lost in the world of romance. After more than ten years in the corporate world of tech recruiting and HR management, she decided to stay home and raise children. But with so many romantic stories and characters floating around in her head, when the kids napped, she was compelled to put those words on a page and pursue this crazy dream of becoming published. Nicole writes romantic suspense and her heroes are those alpha males in uniform. She lives in New Jersey with her real-life hero, her husband, and her two sons.

♥ ♥ ♥

For more information about Nicole, please visit her online at
www.NicoleSPatrick.com

Also by Nicole S. Patrick

Timeless Tales – Short Stories
Letter From St. Nick featured in Timeless Keepsakes
Poseidon's Strength featured in Timeless Escapes
The Colors of Courage featured in Timeless Treasures
From This Day Forward featured in Timeless Vows

♥ ♥ ♥

Havenport – Novellas
White Christmas
Hometown Hero
A Spirit's Bond
Say Yes

♥ ♥ ♥

Echoes of Betrayal

by Ruth A. Casie

♥ ♥ ♥

Ryan Livingston thinks she has the perfect career as an attorney and campaign manager for her brother, Peter Livingston, the up-and-coming Senate candidate. But when an ex-con is murdered and gives a deathbed accounting of secret incriminating evidence, she teams up with longtime boyfriend Police Chief Jim Kanter, determined to find the documents and the truth behind them.

Jim Kanter has a good life. He's respected for his unwavering integrity and fierce devotion to his job. Ex-military, he's haunted by his failure to save his team from an Iraqi sniper.

Their investigation leads them to a well-entrenched drug ring, forgers, blackmailers, and a bombshell, a betrayer targeting them both. In this game of betrayer and betrayed, Ryan is the killer's next target. But Jim is determined to not let any of that happen.

♥ ♥ ♥

Dedicated to ~

Olivia, Alex, and Caylee for their limitless smiles, hugs and kisses.

DM Comfort who really makes my words sing. I'm so glad you're back on the east coast!

My writing partners Emma, Lita and Nicole, who has the wine?

Chapter One

Havenport, Rhode Island — May 2018

Police Chief James Kanter headed out of the Havenport business district with his lieutenant, Brian Taylor. No sirens—rather a peaceful ride down Washington Avenue past the hospital. Seventy-two hours ago, Jim was anything but calm and composed. Three days ago, he left Brian at the crime scene while he kept vigil in the back of the ambulance beside his longtime friend, Simon Farrell. Lights flashing and horn blaring, the ambulance had rushed down the same avenue toward the emergency room.

Now, each time Simon came to mind, the ache in his chest returned. Hard to believe Simon was gone, and harder still to believe someone killed him.

"It will be strange not to catch sight of Simon at the police academy. Everyone packed into his class. Even big brass enjoyed his digital forgery lectures and the war stories of his life before incarceration," Brian said. "His memoir, *Coming Clean: A Forger's Story*, was an eye-opener. Some only saw a brilliant digital investigator who could make digital protégés look like wimps. No one expected the publicity and recognition he received from his book would elevate him in everyone's eyes. An asset to the department."

Jim didn't know how to respond, so the two policemen rode on in silence. Everyone loved Simon's old stories, the samples he showed, and the hands-on class where people tried to create their own document duplicates. No one would use the word *forgery*, but the excitement he created and the discussion that followed was amazing.

"Ancient history," someone said. It didn't surprise him that once document forgery became a crime of the past, Simon went digital. Jim chuckled silently. The old likable geezer always had a story, each bigger and better than the last.

"It's an amazing story why and how he became a forger, a World War II hero," Brian said.

"He was very brave for a fifteen-year-old in Paris in the 1940s. In those years an ID card was the difference between life and death. He worked in the French underground and developed a talent for copying documents. His first test was to make an exact copy of an ID card in the handwriting of a particular clerk. He practiced and practiced until he could reproduce it exactly, even in his sleep. Then the real test began. He had to create a card for himself and pass through various Paris checkpoints without getting caught."

"He was very low-profile. Who would have thought the old, unassuming man was awarded the French Resistance Medal? His passports, train tickets, and ID cards saved fourteen thousand lives. Who knew?" Brian said.

Jim knew. He spent hours with Simon, listening to his old stories, heroic ones. Simon would be angry if he'd heard that. *"I broke the law,"* he would say. *"Forget about me."* But he wasn't forgotten. His funeral proved that.

"You couldn't find a place to stand with all the Newport, Providence, and Boston police departments paying their respects. And the eulogies. I had no idea he was a concert violinist, but when I thought about his artistic creativity, his nimble fingers, it made sense. And the stories from the people he helped and kept in touch with all these years. I wish I knew him better. If a funeral could be good, that was it," Brian said as he paused at a stoplight.

The intense past couple of days had taken their toll on Jim. He rubbed a small brass key between his thumb and forefinger.

Three days ago, he found Simon sprawled on the beach, his life seeped away amid the swirling papers of his empty folio. The man was barely alive. Trixie, his cat, kept watch over him like a stoic Egyptian statue.

An early jogger found Simon in a desolate area, the zone between the public beach and the elite yacht club. The Good Samaritan tried to stem the flow of blood but the makeshift tourniquet loosened.

With his friend's life leaking out and soaking into the sand, he went into action. He placed his knee on Simon's femoral artery and leaned into him with all his weight. The flow stopped. He had to work fast. He took the emergency kit from his service pants, put on the trauma gloves, and had the tourniquet open in a matter of seconds.

Working quickly, Jim wrapped the belt around Simon's thigh, well above the injury. He threaded the strap through the buckle and pulled it tight so no more than three fingers could get between the belt and Simon's thigh.

"How you doing?" he asked as he twisted the rod. Simon was awake, but drowsy, probably from the loss of blood.

Thankful the pumping blood stopped, he clipped the rod in place, then took out the gauze. Carefully he packed the wound.

"Jim." Simon grabbed his shirt and pulled him close. Trixie mewed and brushed against Jim, encouraging him toward her friend.

The look in Simon's eyes, the color of his skin, and the ever-spreading bloodstain on the lower part of his body told him Simon had only minutes to live. He gave the rod one more twist. A wave of grief tinged with eminent loss rippled through him and left him empty.

"Right here, Simon. The ambulance is on its way." A quick glance at the feeder road produced no ambulance or hint of a siren. Jim opened his clenched fist, curled his fingers around the rod, and gave it another twist, then reached for Simon's ankle. There shouldn't be a pulse if the tourniquet was doing its job. A breath escaped his lips. No pulse. He checked the wound. No bleeding. For now. Where the hell were the medics?

He swung back to face Simon and cursed his helplessness.

The distant wail of an emergency siren reached his ears. "Finally," he murmured, and sucked in a deep breath, the first one he'd been able to manage since he'd got the emergency call from the jogger.

The ambulance came to a stop near Jim's cruiser. Bob and Val, volunteer EMTs, hurried out of the cab and raced to the back. The rear doors flew open and the EMTs pulled out their emergency kits.

"We got here as soon as we could. All the equipment is at the multicar crash on the outskirts of town by Killer Curve," Bob said as he reached Simon and Jim.

The medics made a quick assessment of Jim's handiwork.

"Great job, Chief." Bob turned to Val. "We'll need the stretcher."

"You two go get it. I'll stay here with Simon." Jim had no intention of leaving his side.

"Jim." The urgency in the old man's voice startled him. Nothing fazed Simon Farrell. Always calm and cool, even all those years ago at his trial.

"Easy, Simon. I'm right here. Everything's going to be fine." He smiled through his growing concern.

"Don't sugarcoat it. I know what's happening. Where's Trixie?" Simon struggled to his elbows.

"Whoa, not so fast. That cat of yours has nine lives. You, I'm not so sure." Jim gently pushed on Simon's shoulders, but the old man wouldn't move. Simon put something in his hand.

"What's…" Jim searched Simon's face.

"They think they took it from me."

The old forger chuckled. "Nothing, they have nothing. Don't let anyone find out I gave this to you. Don't give it to anyone, and more *importantly don't tell anyone anything. The proof. Ownership. I tell you I have the proof you need." The man's eyes went wild, his breathing rapid.*

Simon fell back onto the sand.

"Relax. I'll keep it safe. No one will take it from me. Please, Simon, stay calm."

A dark spot started to spread. Shit. The tourniquet must have slipped again. Jim gave the rod another twist.

The medics hauled the gurney through the sand and finally reached him and Simon.

Bob and Val eased Simon onto the stretcher. Trixie hopped on and curled at Simon's feet. Val gave Bob a glare, but the senior EMT nodded. Val shrugged and wheeled their patient off the beach into the waiting ambulance. The medics started an intravenous line and hooked Simon to the equipment. Amid the activity inside the makeshift triage center, medical machines came to life while Jim stood by the door helpless.

Police sirens blared as cars rushed down the road and pulled up next to the ambulance. Brian got out and hurried to Jim.

"How bad is the accident in town?" Jim asked.

"A three-car pileup. Witnesses said some nutjob floored it coming out of Killer Curve. At least ninety miles an hour. I'll check out the surveillance tape when I get back to the office. I can't imagine how anyone would go that fast coming out of that curve without ending up on the beach."

Brian stared at the stretcher, then back at Jim. "Is he going to be…"

Jim shook his head slowly.

"I can take care of things here. Go with Simon," Brian said, his hand out for Jim's car keys. "I'll bring your car back to the station."

Keys in hand, Brian motioned to his men and led the way to the beach.

"Chief." Val peeked out of the ambulance. "He's all hooked up. You can ride in the back with him."

Jim climbed into the vehicle. Afraid his friend would die before the ambulance reached the hospital, he didn't want Simon to be alone. "Just get us to the hospital."

Bob closed the doors. In seconds, the ambulance moved out, sirens blaring.

The cat hobbled up the stretcher and cuddled next to the old man.

"Trixie, go to Jim," Simon whispered. He glanced at the cat, then at Jim.

"Don't worry. I'll take care of her."

Somehow Trixie made her way to him along the edge of the stretcher as the ambulance bounced down the road.

Jim stroked the feline, who nuzzled his hand and purred.

"She's a good companion, quiet and independent. Can't tie her down, likes to come and go. Make sure you leave a window open for her at night."

Simon smiled in a fatherly way. Thank goodness the man quieted. Jim bent close to the old man's ear, more to help Simon than to keep the conversation private.

"Who attacked you?"

"I've waited a long time for him." He let out a labored breath. "Maybe I can stop looking over my shoulder now. I can lie quiet next to my Nancy and be at peace."

The ambulance pulled into the emergency bay at Havenport Medical Center. Simon looked at Jim with a touch of sorrow before his eyes clouded over and the machines let off a cacophony of sounds. The doors were yanked open. Bob and Val made quick work of getting the stretcher out. The triage nurse climbed onto the gurney and administered CPR as Bob and Val rolled Simon away. Jim stood in the ambulance and stared as the automatic doors closed, sure he would never see Simon alive again.

That was three days ago. Now, Jim sat in the police car and stared at the small brass key. Numbers or letters stamped into the metal had been removed without a trace.

"You never told me how you figured out what the key opened," Brian said. "Did I miss something?"

"No, you didn't miss anything. Simon told me before he died. Simon said he could lie quiet next to Nancy and rest in peace, except Simon was buried here with his family in Havenport. Nancy is buried in Scotland, Connecticut.

He knew he wouldn't be buried with her. Aside from the fact she is in a single grave, her family would make sure of that.

"What a pity. He married very late in life. I think Nancy and Simon were mad about each other, but her children would have nothing to do with him after his trial. They either convinced or coerced her to divorce him. It doesn't matter what happened. In the end, the marriage was over. Simon didn't speak of Nancy after that, but he mentioned her in the ambulance. My gut told me the key fit a safe-deposit box at the Scotland Savings Bank or a box at the post office. It couldn't be a safe-deposit box. I would have to be with Simon when he rented the box. It had to be the post office."

Brian nodded and drove on in silence.

Scotland, Connecticut, was a rural town where everyone knew one another. Jim and Brian planned to stop at the police station and say hello to Police Chief Brown. This wasn't a courtesy call, but a necessary one. In Scotland, Jim stood out like a sore thumb. Scots didn't like intruders. The town still remembered the upheaval caused by Simon's trial when the media flooded their paradise and trampled everyone's gardens asking questions about Simon. And the Mulligans. Nancy's parents kept her away from it all. The trial, too. Simon grieved her loss more than his freedom. That was a long time ago.

Brian drove to the back of Scotland City Hall and pulled to the curb in front of the police department. Jim got out of the car, then leaned in the window.

"I shouldn't be too long."

Brian didn't say anything. He took out his cell phone. Jim shook his head and walked into the building.

"Thank you for the call about Simon. I alerted my boys, but things are quiet here," Nathan Brown said. In his fifties and balding with a stocky build, Brown was an easygoing man in an easygoing town. He sat behind his desk with a cup of coffee in his hand.

"Think nothing of it. You'd do the same for me." Jim left the police station and went next door to the post office.

He was firing on all cylinders today. He told the clerk he had his key, but forgot his box number. The clerk took his ID and brought out a card with his box number clearly printed in the upper-right corner. He had to laugh. Simon Farrell had opened a post office box and signed Jim's name. Even he couldn't tell the signature was not his own. He glanced at the date on the form. Four weeks ago.

Jim went over to the wall of boxes, slipped in his key, and opened the door. For a moment he stared at the manila envelope waiting for him, unable to take it out.

"Okay, Simon. What did you leave me? Your will? Or did you keep an old list of clients after all? That would be sweet."

The prosecution really wanted to get their hands on his list. Simon insisted he didn't keep a record of his clients—bad for business. He rattled off eight to ten names from memory, but no one believed that was everyone, not even him.

Jim took out the envelope and quickly eyeballed the contents. There were three items inside. The first was a newspaper article from two years ago. The second was an old document dated 1774, and the third—a doodle—was clipped to it.

He swept his hand around the box. Empty. He closed the door.

Jim walked out of the post office and into the waiting cruiser. He placed the envelope on his lap.

"A message from the office came in while you were inside. The fire department was called to Simon's place. The house was fully engulfed. The fire department did everything possible, but nothing was left. The fire chief suspects arson. There was no sign of Trixie." Brian pulled the cruiser onto the highway.

"Ryan's taking care of her," Jim said. "The cat is a constant visitor at her office. It seems Trixie likes Ryan's treats better than those we dole out."

Murder. Fire. Jim took in the information. Nothing left. A man's life reduced to the papers in his lap.

"Success, I see." Brian pointed to the envelope. "Any idea when he opened the box?"

"The card said four weeks ago."

"Do you think it's a coincidence that Simon rented the box shortly before he was killed?" Brian asked.

"It would have been if he hadn't forged my signature to rent the box. No, Simon did all he could to protect these papers. He knew he was in trouble. He said something about watching over his shoulder for years."

Jim focused on the envelope. The preliminary murder investigation had come up empty. Other than the early-morning jogger who'd found Simon, there were no leads. These papers were all he had.

"You and Simon were good friends. Why didn't he tell you? We could have kept him safe," Brian said.

Sure, keeping people safe was his job. Too bad he'd failed. The acid in his stomach rose, and he fought to beat down the voice inside his head. He'd failed Simon just like he'd failed his friends in Iraq during Desert Storm. Simon's murder brought back the days and months of shame and self-loathing. He let out one strangled breath, then another. *That's right, calm down.*

Echoes of the past surrounded him, and he was back in the desert. The kid had no idea he'd given away their position. He closed his eyes to deny the shadows that crowded around him. *I did what I could, I did what I could, I did what I could,* he repeated over and over. The team was gone, but so was the fucking sniper with a hole in his head for each of Jim's men he'd killed.

"Protect your own" was his mantra. Nothing would stop him from finding the bastard who'd killed Simon and bringing him to justice.

"Who wanted Simon dead?" Jim whispered the rhetorical question he didn't expect Brian to answer.

"Precisely. Who?" Brian kept his eyes on the road. "Could it be related to his trial?"

"The trial was almost ten years ago."

Jim was at a loss. "The parole records show he's been clean. The only thing I can think of is someone from his past, maybe from prison."

The answers had to be sitting on his lap. His fingers absently drummed a steady beat. Why else would Simon have made sure he collected these papers?

He opened the envelope and fanned through the pages.

Item one: a news article taped to a sheet of white paper. Two years old, the article covered the drug bust he and FBI Agent Matt Lyons had worked. Handwritten on the back of the paper were the names of prominent Havenport citizens who weren't associated with the drug bust. What was their connection to Simon? Was this the list the prosecution had been hunting for?

Item two: a tourist souvenir, a reproduction of the 1774 bill of sale of the Emersons' waterfront property to Zachariah Emerson's daughter and son-in-law. Over the years, reproductions of the famous manuscript had improved from a poor paper copy to one on high-quality parchment. This was definitely the parchment version.

Item three: a doodle of sorts, with *caenn cadha* handwritten in three-dimensional block letters sitting in a sea of clover. He screwed up his eyebrow and shook his head. The phrase rang a bell, but he couldn't place it.

The bill of sale interested him because his girlfriend studied old documents. Her hobby wore off on him. Calligraphers used raised marks as guidelines to align the letters. He ran his fingertips over the page as she had shown him in order to make sure the marks were printed, then pulled his hand away as if burned. The tangible feel of pricks and score marks were evident. If he was right, this wasn't a reproduction. His heart pounded in his ears. Why did Simon have an original document? Again, he ran his finger over the document, this time the entire document. It was consistent. It may not be authentic, written in 1774, but it wasn't a photocopy. He blanched at the idea. Had Simon created a forgery and hidden it away? If so, why had Simon directed him here? Nothing was getting clearer.

He put everything back into the envelope, emptied his mind, and stared at the scenery without seeing a thing as Brian continued on toward Havenport.

♥ ♥ ♥

Brian pulled to the curb an hour later. "You want me to wait, or can you find your way home?"

"Thanks. I left my car in the lot. See you tomorrow." Jim got out of the car and waited until Brian pulled away, then headed for the twin glass doors of one of the few upscale office buildings in Havenport.

On the third floor, the brass plaque affixed on the polished mahogany doors read *Livingston and Livingston, Attorneys at Law.* Ryan Livingston shared the suite with her older brother, Rhode Island State Assemblyman Peter Ryan Livingston.

Jim and Ryan had a comfortable relationship. He'd met her in court seven years ago when she'd done a favor for Mayor Henry's son.

"I didn't know Livingston and Livingston represented traffic violators," Brian said as he stood with Jim in the back of the courtroom. Jim scanned the defendant's table.

"I thought the law firm was more high profile," Jim said. "You go on to the office. This should be quick. State the facts and leave. I want to be on the road to Providence as soon as possible."

"Thanks for your support, but there's no need for you to come to the police academy. This is not the first time I'm teaching the class. I can handle it," Brian said.

"I'm well aware you can handle the class. If I thought otherwise, I wouldn't have recommended you as an instructor. You better leave. I'll meet you there later."

As he hurried past the defense table, he sent some papers onto the floor. He and the attorney reached for them at the same time. When he looked up, papers in hand, he stared into the most compelling ice-blue eyes he had ever seen, serious and playful at the same time. He recognized intelligence mixed with understanding and a softness that took his breath away. Short and cropped almost boyish platinum-blonde hair framed her oval face. He wondered how it would feel in his hand, and how she would look with long hair, way past her shoulders.

"Are you going to give those to me? I promise I'm not hiding anything." Her lips curved into a smile that went all the way to her eyes, which warmed into a more fantastic blue, if that was possible.

All thoughts of meeting Brian in Providence faded.

He smirked at her playful tone and handed her the papers.

She stood next to him, her expression all business. "Chief Kanter, would you consider a bargain? My client has a clean record. A young boy with his first car got carried away on the very tempting straight road right after that awful curve."

"The speed limit on that part of the road is forty miles an hour. I clocked him going thirty-five miles over the speed limit. That section of road is deadly at the marked speed. I'm sure Mayor Henry would rather I speak to him about a traffic ticket than about a funeral. Listen, I'm not here to scar the kid for life, just protect him from himself, if necessary."

"Would you recommend community service?" The attorney's blue eyes held him captive. He had a reputation of recommending work in lieu of a hefty fine. It pleased him she asked rather than expected him to be in favor of fifteen to twenty hours of service. He liked her more by the minute.

"All rise," the bailiff said. Jim went to the prosecutor's table as the court was called to order.

"Will the attorneys please approach the bench," the judge said.

Jim admired the confidence in the defense attorney's stride and took her in from his place at the prosecutor's table. She wore a dark navy suit and crisp white blouse with a red print scarf. He noticed her reasonable high heels. It wasn't just one thing about her he found attractive, it was the whole package. This woman was sexy as hell.

At the end of the day, the boy paid his adjusted lower fine and was assigned to work fifteen hours at the animal shelter. He took the defense attorney to dinner. It didn't take long before he was head over heels in love with her.

Chapter Two

Ryan Livingston sat behind her desk, her back to the large palladium window. She wore a simple black dress, her grandmother's sixteen-inch string of pearls, and classic open-toe black pumps she'd put on hours ago to attend Simon's funeral. The outpouring of people and uniforms at the chapel and cemetery was impressive for a superstar or politician. It was remarkable for a reformed convict.

She took a break from the photocopied pages of an antique journal she analyzed. She loved working with old documents. But today, concentration was an issue. She looked up to give her eyes a rest and caught a glimpse of her wall of recognition. Ryan had a passion for—and an advanced degree in—diplomatics. The corners of her mouth pulled into a smile every time she glanced at the citation hanging next to her law degree. After all these years, the stupefied expression on her brother's face still flashed across her mind and made her chuckle. It was difficult for Peter to understand not everyone wanted to follow in their dad's political footsteps. The conversation six years ago with Peter before he'd left with Dad on a campaign circuit came to mind.

"We can use you on this trip. We're meeting with the opposition on several sticky topics. You can get some mileage out of your new degree," Peter said as he prepared for a two-week political junket.

Ryan sifted through the papers and put the ones he needed in his briefcase.

"What are you talking about? I received my law degree two years ago. You and Dad exploit it as often as you can."

She waved the papers at him, the results of grueling analysis and research that had taken up her past three weeks.

"No, diplomacy."

"Diplomacy? What would I do with that? My certification is in diplomatics, an auxiliary science of history."

She reveled in his priceless blank stare. He didn't know everything after all. "The science of research and authentication of old papers."

She shook her head to clear it. It was a challenge being Peter's younger sister. At times, he coldly shut her down and ordered her around as if it was his God-given right. But then, the other Peter would show up, her knight and savior, the one with a sense of humor, the one who took as good as he gave. That was the Peter she liked. Her knight.

"I can't believe the summer is over." Eight-year-old Ryan walked with a group of girls from the Minnehaha teepee where she spent her summer at Camp Thunderclap in Maine and headed for the camp store to wait for the bus home.

Last night's steak dinner and the end-of-camp party was dampened by a rainstorm. The fireworks fizzled, but Mother Nature provided her own light show. The remnants of the downpour had the girls maneuvering around the few remaining deep puddles. The hot August sun was working overtime. By the end of the morning you would never know it had rained last night.

Peter trotted up and whispered in her ear. "Ry, give me some money. I want to buy a soda."

"No. You never give the money back." She kept walking. He strode by her side.

"Give me the money, Ryan Dorcas, or would you rather I stand in the middle of your friends and broadcast your full name?"

She stopped mid-step, so angry she wanted to kick him, but doing him bodily harm was a sure way to make him yell at the top of his lungs.

Mother told her to let him shout. Ryan Dorcas was a beautiful name. Sure, as long as it wasn't yours.

"Fine." She dug in her pocket and took out a ten-dollar bill. He snapped it out of her hand.

"Thanks," he called over his shoulder halfway to the store.

"Is your brother going on the bus with you?" her counselor asked. The girl was nice, but got all weird when Peter was around. And Peter? Puh-lease. He was a junior counselor across the lake at the boys' Hiawatha Camp Ground. He was just as bad around girls, all smiles and polite. If these lovesick girls only knew him as she did.

"I guess." Ryan sat on the bottom of the split-rail fence and wrinkled her brow at the stupid question. How else would he get home?

"Nice jeans." Ryan turned and forgot about the counselor. Her friend's eyes widened at the cascade of rhinestone sparkles down her pant legs. "I haven't seen these before."

Her bunkmate, Grace, stared at the jeans with a hungry look. No, she didn't let Grace near the package from home, although she did find and eat the cookies Mom sent. Ryan didn't really mind about the cookies, but she didn't want to share the jeans.

"I didn't want to get my new jeans dirty, so I saved them for the ride home." The other Indian princesses from the Minnehaha teepees reached the area. Everyone milled around shouting goodbye to people in other groups, chattering amongst themselves, some admiring the spray of bling down her jeans.

A baseball dropped into the middle of the clucking princesses. The startled girls shrieked so loud the camp director ran to investigate what had happened.

"Boys, careful where you throw that ball. Go play in the field. It's a miracle the ball missed everyone," Murray said. One of the boys ran over and retrieved the ball.

Murray was famous for confiscating sports equipment, never to be seen again. There were rumors that at night when everyone was asleep, he rowed into the middle of the lake and gave whatever he had to the great water god as payment for no one drowning. She was pretty sure he rowed out into the middle of the lake to drink beer where no one could see him—except the great water god, of course, who he paid homage to by pissing in the lake.

Back on shore, the goodbyes continued and the exuberant boys played the last round of catch for the season.

"Can't you throw a fastball?"

One of the boys taunted Peter. Peter wound up and let the ball fly. The boy caught it and thought to do Peter one better. He wound up and threw with all his might, but his aim was off. The ball headed for the split-rail fence.

"Ry, look out!" Peter shouted.

Before she could turn he slammed into her, and she flew off the fence, hitting the ground hard. The sound of a snap caught her by surprise, but not as much as the gut-wrenching pain shooting up her arm. She lay screaming in the dirt and mud.

She tried to focus on what people were saying but their voices buzzed in her head. Breathing through the pain the way her field hockey coach had taught her didn't work. The droning morphed into snippets of words. She couldn't make out any of it, and nor did she care.

"Breathe, Ryan. Come on, in and out. That's it." Murray and his assistant kneeled by her side. The edge of the pain receded and was replaced with cold chills and an overwhelming need to throw up. She kept her head down. She couldn't get close enough to the ground. It was the only thing that made the swirling stop.

"Okay, Ry, stop the playacting. You're all right."

Peter tugged on her shoulder. She screamed as the pain spread like liquid fire deep in her arm.

"Don't touch her," Murray yelled, squatting next to her and dialing his cell phone.

"Ryan, can you sit up?" Murray's voice echoed in her head.

Ryan's teeth chattered. The pain subsided, and she glanced at Peter. He stood over her and looked at the blood on his hands, then at her. The pain started to build again. She glanced at her arm lying at a funny angle. Her stomach revolted at the sight of blood and fragments of bone that poked through her skin.

"No," she whispered.

"A compound fracture," Murray said into his cell phone. "No. Don't send an ambulance. The bouncing ride down this gravel road will be torture. I'll bring her to the emergency room."

With Peter's help, she sat up and cradled her arm. The blinding pain returned with a vengeance. Any movement made the agony worse, and without much encouragement her stomach gave up the pancakes and bacon she had for breakfast all over Peter and her new jeans. She closed her eyes and cried.

"Ryan, I'm taking you to the hospital." She looked at Murray through her tears, then at Peter.

"I'll go with her." Peter held her tight. She had never seen him so determined.

"No. Clean up and go on the bus. I'll call your parents and take care of things here." Murray punched numbers into his phone.

"No, Murray. You drive. I'll hold Ryan. I won't leave her alone." Peter stood with her in his arms and eased into Murray's Jeep with her on his lap.

"I'm sorry," she said to Peter.

"You'll be fine, Ry."

She didn't say anything. She couldn't. Another wave of pain built to a crescendo.

Murray fired up the Jeep and started out. The rutted road was the only way out of camp. Everyone enjoyed the bumpy ride when they went on outings. But now, each jolt was torture.

"There's no other way. I'll go as slow as I can, but it's going to hurt like hell."

She nodded as Murray inched their way down the road. The ten-minute ride took almost half an hour.

She winced at the memory and rubbed her arm. The ten-inch scar down her left arm gave her bragging rights when she'd returned to school a few weeks later. Those quickly wore off when she realized the scar came with consequences.

She was an active field hockey and soccer player, but there was no way she could continue any of her sports. She was relegated to the sidelines to cheer on her teammates.

As an adult, long sleeves were always in style no matter the occasion—or the heat.

Over time, the scar faded and the pain became a distant memory. She never went back to sports. What remained was Peter holding her and protecting her. That bond never faded.

The alert on her cell phone startled her out of her musing.

On my way. See you at the office. I hope you're not doing something for Ina. I need you to sign some papers for the Art Society, Peter's message read.

Ryan shook her head. She'd been back for hours. Peter had stayed at the cemetery with some state official, then went off somewhere for an impromptu meeting, which usually meant follow-up work for her.

Peter didn't hide his impatience. He hated the work she did for the Historical Society—another reason to finish the transcript for Ina. Peter really wanted her to concentrate on their law practice.

No, he didn't.

The truth: he wanted her full attention on his political career.

Throughout her three years in law school, her brother spoke of opening a law office together. The conversation continued after graduation and went full-tilt when she'd passed the bar. True to their competitive nature, each wanted top billing.

Peter's choice for a business name was Peter Ryan Livingston and Ryan Dorcas Livingston, Attorneys at Law. He still taunted her with her middle name. Rather than tell him she'd legally changed her middle name to Doris, her mother's name, she came up with another solution. Although Peter claimed the idea was his, they named their company Livingston and Livingston. Simple and straightforward without first names or initials. A clever tactic. This way, either could claim lead attorney in the office. The new partners drank an entire bottle of champagne to celebrate the decision.

He poured the last drop into her glass.

"You finished the champagne."

"You know I want to run for a state office." His announcement hung in the air, the room deathly quiet.

"Yes. You've been at the party's beck and call. I assumed you'd run for something, just not here in Havenport." She added a splash of crème de cassis and turned her drink into a Kir Royale.

"This idea of you working for the Historical Society is a waste of your law degree. Why not work with me and do that on the side? I've been around Dad and his political allies long enough to know I need someone I can trust in my corner. I can count on you to tell me the truth." He bent forward in his seat and took her hand. "I can't do this without you, Ry. You'll be with me every step of the way."

The bachelor politician painted a picture of her driving his campaign, being his hostess when needed, participating in strategy meetings, and getting him elected.

It was hard to believe that was six years and three terms ago. So far everything had played out according to Peter's master plan. She did her job well. Behind the scenes, she made sure everyone in the media and state politics recognized and respected Peter Livingston. With hard work and a lot of coaching, she'd made him the media's go-to person for commentary and analysis. Was it wrong she welled up with pride as rumors ran rampant of a spot for him on the national ticket? His dream was within his grasp. One more campaign.

Ryan was satisfied. Her diplomatic credentials qualified her to work with the Havenport Historical Society, and the Historical Preservation and Heritage Commission in Providence. An attorney with her expertise was invaluable to both organizations.

As soon as Peter secured a national position, she could concentrate on her life and career. One last campaign. She gave her shoulders a shake.

Enough nostalgia. It must be sitting through eulogies and reminiscing on a life turned from the dark side to the light that put her in this mood. She let out a sigh. Her fingers played with the corners of the pages in front of her.

Havenport was in the midst of preparing for the 250th anniversary of the Havenport Hostilities, a significant part of the Revolutionary War Reenactment Series. Heroic Eoin Kincaid and his wife, Catrina Emerson Kincaid, were at the center of the Havenport event.

Catrina's diary was on loan to the Historical Society from the Kincaid family. David Kincaid, a descendant of Eoin and Catrina, brought the diary with him from the family home in Stirlingshire, Scotland. After reading portions of the journal, Ina decided to change up the annual event. She planned to read Catrina's own words at the reenactment event, but found reading from the diary difficult. Ryan agreed to transcribe the text for two reasons.

One, holding history in her hands and reading someone's words made the person and the period come alive. The combination of their handwriting and word choices was so personal, so expressive, that with a little imagination she could step back into their time.

Two, the bittersweet Havenport Hostilities legend was shrouded in controversy. Over the decades, a lack of documentation led to speculation on the events. Whole courses were given at the local community college on the topic. While there were many theories on the series of events, no one questioned the outcome. Eoin warned of an imminent British attack and led the people of Havenport to victory, but at the cost of his own life.

She moved her magnifying glass aside and read through the translation she prepared. Content she had the transcription correct, she edited Ina's introduction.

"Welcome to the 250th celebration of the Havenport Hostilities. It's also the anniversary of Eoin Kincaid and Catrina Emerson. This year, we are honored and excited to have a direct descendant of Eoin and Catrina with us. David Kincaid joins us from the family home in Stirlingshire, Scotland. He brought some wonderful artifacts to share with us: our Eoin's sword, as well as Catrina's diary. Rather than

read the Historical Society's account of the Havenport Hostilities, I will be reading select pages from Catrina's diary. We want you to hear the events echo in her own words.

"The pages tell how Eoin and Catrina met, the origin of the well-known Havenport bagpipes, the young couple falling in love, Catrina's escape from Havenport, and finally, the tragic end of their story."

Ryan put the introduction aside and took up her transcription.

Last month, two men arrived in Havenport looking for work, Lachlan Sinclair and Eoin Kincaid. Papa put Lachlan to work at our farm, and Eoin went to work with Papa and Bennett at the trading company in town. With Bennett taking longer on his trading trips, Papa needs help at the office. Papa said all the girls walk by his office for a glimpse of Eoin. Bennett told me to stay away. The man may be a Scots, but he served the British. My brother is so protective. I would never parade in front of the man, although when I walked past the office today he smiled at me and, well, I smiled back.

Ryan turned to the second excerpt.

I brought Papa, Bennett, and Eoin their afternoon meal. Before I reached the trading office, I heard the most haunting music. I joined others and followed the sounds to find the source. The stream of people headed to the field behind Papa's office. Spellbound. There is no other way to explain it. Lachlan and the children danced to the music. Eoin held a strange pouch that sprouted sticks. He told me about his bagpipes, but never have I seen such an instrument or heard such music before.

I looked at the children's faces, startled by their expression. It was as if the sound had captured them and made them speechless. I looked around me. The children were not alone. I tried to understand why the strange music was so…appealing. It had to be the combination of the piped melody along with a droning bass that set the music in flight. I stood there enthralled like the children. I, too, didn't want Eoin to stop.

Ryan turned to page three.

It's been six months since Lachlan and Eoin arrived. I tried to listen to my brother and stay away from Eoin, but he is everything a woman could want in a man. It goes beyond his handsome face and fit body. He is loyal and trustworthy. Thank goodness Bennett relented.

How special Eoin makes me feel. I wish I was a poet so I could put it to paper. Tonight, we walked in the garden. The May evening was warm, the flowers fragrant, and the moon full. Neither of us made a sound. With my hand on his arm, he kept clearing his throat.

"Would you like to go back? I can make you hot tea with honey for that cough," I said.

When he didn't answer I thought perhaps he hadn't heard me.

He covered my hand with his own. My heart pounded against my chest. I didn't know what to do, but I put my other hand on top of his so he wouldn't take it away. It was a brazen move. I didn't care.

He coughed again.

"Eoin, let's go back. If you don't want honey in your tea I can put a splash of whiskey instead."

He stopped and turned me to face him. My heartbeat quickened, if that was possible. He was the man I wanted. I think I knew that the first time I saw him.

"No, no whiskey. The cough won't go away until I get this out." His strong yet soft hands held both of mine. A flash of worry crossed my mind. Was he going back to Scotland? Was he saying goodbye?

"I love you, Catrina Emerson."

His eyes twinkled and the softness of his voice made me giddy. He took a step back and for a moment I panicked. He coughed again.

"Catrina, I don't know the pretty words to say. All I know is I love you and want to spend the rest of my life with you."

Tears welled up in my eyes. I couldn't see the garden or anything else, only him.

"Oh, don't cry." He stood holding me, a tremor in his voice. "I'm asking you to marry me."

"Yes," I said softly in his ear. His arms tightened around me. I would love him forever.

His eyes had a misty look that made me feel warm in places I can't admit. He lowered his head and brushed his lips against mine. His lips were soft, like velvet. I didn't want him to stop. When he did, he rested his forehead on mine.

"We should tell the others," I said, and pulled away, but not far enough to leave his embrace.

"They know. I asked your father for his permission last week. He told me if I didn't ask you soon he would withdraw his consent. But that was earlier today, before we had the fourth glass of whiskey."

His whole face spread into his smile. He kissed my nose, grabbed my hand, and we ran back to the house.

Ryan grabbed a tissue and blew her nose. How sweet. How innocent. How she remembered that feeling of first love. She cried for Catrina's joy as well as for her sorrow.

Today is our first anniversary and our monthly visit to the chasm. Eoin grieves for Lachlan. Our friend plans to return to Scotland when father's ship, the Sea Hawk, *leaves in the next few days. Eoin said he had no interest in returning to Scotland, not with our child due in three months. Eoin played his pipes for me. Ah, the pipes sound grand here, echoing through the chasm. It reminds my Eoin of his valley in Scotland. This is his favorite place. My favorite place is wherever Eoin is.*

Ryan turned the page.

I write this entry on the Sea Hawk, *the ship taking me to Eoin's family in Scotland. I go with Lachlan, not my Eoin.*

Eoin was forewarned of a British attack on Havenport. The men and women of Havenport valiantly stood at his side as he organized and helped defend the town. Many called him their leader, but someone betrayed him.

He feared for my life and the life of our unborn child. The British knew him well from his prior service. He had seen it before. My Eoin played his pipes as we sailed out of port, but not before promising he'd pipe me a song when we were together again.

Ryan stared at the last page not wanting to feel Catrina's pain. This story did not end well.

Two years ago, I left Havenport and my beloved Eoin. I tried to return to him with our son six months ago when Lachlan went back to Havenport. Father Kincaid wouldn't allow it. Instead, Mother Kincaid and I sent Lachlan off with messages to Eoin. The Kincaid family took me in as their daughter and love my young David as they would their Eoin. His mother told me about every year of Eoin's life.

Together, we've been planning for his return. Today, Father Kincaid gave me a letter from Papa. I was so excited I could hardly read it.

I took the missive to the window seat and opened it. Papa had much to tell me. I savored his words. Some made me smile. Others were so difficult, I cried for him as well as for me. Six months ago, skirmishes with the soldiers escalated. 'I'm sorry to tell you that your beloved brother, Bennett, who fought so bravely, was among the casualties, killed by a traitor." I reread Papa's words. A traitor? I know everyone in Havenport. Some were Royal sympathizers but no one would betray a neighbor. With Bennett gone and me in Scotland, Papa wanted to protect his assets. Rather than bequest his holdings, he sold the property to Eoin and I. The bill of sale was enclosed with his letter.

The fighting wasn't without other causalities. Papa said Eoin was a driven man. He, Lachlan, and a group of other patriots were gone for days at a time fighting the British and hunting for the traitor. After weeks of fighting, Eoin returned wounded, beyond any treatment.

There was a second letter in Papa's envelope, a message from Eoin in his own hand. My heart broke when I saw his handwriting. I ran my fingertips over each letter. I read his goodbye. His words for our son tore at my heart. I clutched our David to my chest, grieving that he would never know his father and vowing that I would keep Eoin's memory alive. For me, I'll hold Eoin's letter close to my heart until I hear him play the pipes and be with him once again.

Father buried him in the chasm, the place he loved, the place that reminded him of home.

Tears stained Ryan's cheeks. She slowly lowered the papers and rode out the swell of emotion. There was magic in the handwritten words, a connection between her and Catrina.

Everyone was familiar with Eoin's story, but no one was aware of a traitor. Over the past week, she'd researched every piece of information available. Resources at the Havenport Historical Society and the Historical Preservation and Heritage Commission turned up no information. She reached out to other Revolutionary War research sites, but there was no mention of a Havenport traitor. On a whim, she searched British records. One man's traitor was another's hero. Nothing.

"Miss Livingston," the receptionist called on the intercom. "Police Chief Kanter is here to see you."

Chapter Three

A soft smile spread across Ryan's face. She pushed the pages aside, closed her laptop, and pulled a mirror out of her desk drawer. While checking her hair she glanced at the window behind her. Trixie stretched out in the late rays of sun on the wide office windowsill, licking her paw.

Unlike the strays in Havenport, this feline was a thoroughbred Abyssinian. Trixie's rich silky orange-brown coat with hints of black gave her an iridescent sheen. Her expressive almond-shaped green eyes made her distinctive, like a muse for an ancient Egyptian painting or sculpture. An energetic animal with a lean, muscular body. The cat usually didn't sit and sunbathe, except when draped on Simon's shoulder. A pang of loss hit Ryan.

The poor thing had limped and cried when Jim brought Trixie to her. They both assumed the animal suffered over the death of her constant companion. Bloody from being with Simon, Jim helped Ryan clean Trixie and found a torn claw. After wrapping her paw, she settled the cat for the night. In the morning, Ryan brought her to the veterinarian. Dr. O'Brien assured Ryan the cat would be climbing trees in a few weeks, but overcoming her loss would take a bit longer.

Ryan turned back to her mirror, fluffed her long hair, and gave herself one more critical look. It would do. "Send Jim in, please."

Jim was a one-woman man who prized brains and authenticity over high heels and lipstick. He was the right height, a shade over six feet. Her head fit like a missing puzzle piece in the crook of his neck. Underneath his uniform was a powerful, well-muscled body trained in combat but made for comfort. His long, dark crew cut was neatly brushed back. She loved his eyes—brown speckled with flecks of gold that could be menacing, deadpan, or twinkle just for her.

Handsome on the outside, he was beautiful on the inside. When the world explodes, James Kanter was the man she wanted next to her. His broad shoulders would absorb the shockwave, and after the dust settled, he'd still be standing. He'd focus on every angle, stay until he was sure one could put two words together in a meaningful way. Other men helped one through a calamity, but Jim was unique. After the crisis, he would stand down, never to mention it again.

Trixie leaped to the floor at the sound of the doorknob turning.

A warm heat of anticipation flushed Ryan's face. The cat brushed against Jim's leg, turned, then pranced back to her perch and slithered out the window. She nearly had a heart attack the first time the cat navigated down the fire escape, leaped gracefully the last dozen or so feet to the ground, then strolled down the street as if she owned it.

Jim, in his full Havenport police dress uniform, stepped inside her office and filled the space in a good way. She got up from her chair and met him in the center of the room, content to rest against the warm lines of his hard body. Like Trixie, Ryan declared Jim belonged to her.

Jim tossed the manila envelope on her desk, took her in his arms, and kissed her nose.

"My nose thanks you, but my lips are jealous. What do you plan to do about it?" She lowered her head and gave him her most sultry peek from under thick lashes.

He pulled her closer and kissed her forehead.

"I wouldn't want your forehead to be jealous." He kissed her cheeks. "Or your cheeks."

She tried to turn her head and capture his lips, but he put his hand up.

"No, not yet." He kissed her chin. "You wouldn't want your chin to be jealous, would you?"

He pulled away and she gasped at the devilish look in his eyes that had her girlie parts bursting into flames.

Slowly, deliberately, Jim bent his head toward her, their lips a breath apart. A deep sigh escaped her chest as his fingers combed through her long hair.

"Silk," he murmured, and moved closer. "You want to go to your place or mine? We could cut costs and move in together."

"And miss all the mystery of what you're cooking for dinner? I love your surprises." Her voice dropped to an intimate whisper.

That was an outright lie, but one they both encouraged.

He let out a low, deep chuckle, the kind that drove her crazy.

"My lips are getting jealous, and not for grilled cheese sandwiches," she said, her mouth a breath away from his. She waited.

"Now," he whispered.

Her arms snaked around him, eager to move past the playful teasing. His hands slipped around her waist, bringing her closer. He claimed her mouth and sent every nerve in her body into a wild swirl.

"Ryan—" Her brother barged into her office. "Chief. I didn't see you come in. When did you arrive?"

Unwilling to leave Jim's arms, she turned toward Peter, her lips warm and wet from his kiss.

"I hope I'm not interrupting anything."

State Assemblyman Peter Livingston posed at the door, one hand on the knob. Tall with a well-developed physique, Peter resembled the Ken doll she once owned. Silver threads streaked his white-blond hair, an older man's look but on a young man's face. His azure eyes held an intensity that spoke of honesty, gentleness, and made him appear noble. She had worked long and hard hours for him to establish this persona and make it his own. He had to look the part inside and out. That's what his constituency needed to see.

Ryan loved her brother. Ten years older than her, it was only the two of them now with their parents gone, victims of a highway accident.

As much as she loved to work with old documents, he was the true artist who thrived on creating fine art. His paintings and pen-and-ink pieces drew a sizable following from the Havenport Art Society. The Society, instrumental in selling his work, also convinced and funded the artistic attorney to follow in his father's political footsteps and run for a state assembly seat. Now, they encouraged him to investigate a national campaign.

This next election cycle didn't make it to the top of her list. There were major differences between a national and state campaign. Peter still had charisma, that magnetic charm, but would that be enough for this challenge? And for her, she questioned her ability to maintain control of a national campaign. She had no illusions. As much as women made strides these past years, the national arena was still an old boys' locker room.

"In your capacity as the Society's legal adviser, you need to sign these papers." Peter held a folder in the air. "It's an affidavit for the valuation for one of my paintings and must be postmarked tomorrow."

"You should have given them to me sooner or at least warned me of the deadline. Leave the folder on my desk. I'll look everything over and bring the signed documents to the post office in the morning."

"Ry, sign the papers, and I'll be out of your way."

Peter oozed friendship on the outside, but his honest, gentle eyes hardened and told a different story.

"After I read them." She tried to hide her annoyance, but only barely succeeded. Peter's new tactic of putting Jim in the middle of a family tiff bothered her.

"I'm wounded. My own sister doesn't trust me." Peter slammed his hand over his heart and dropped the papers on her desk. "Chief, when are you going to put a ring on her finger? Maybe then she'd be more amicable." Peter's words were playful, but not his intent. The assemblyman's smug smile set off a warning.

She stepped away from Jim but not before she noticed his jaw muscle tighten. Neither spoke. Peter knew better than most that engagement and marriage were forbidden topics. Besides, her personal affairs with Jim—or anyone else, for that matter—weren't any of his business.

Her anger settled, but roiled below the surface. Two years ago, Jim proposed and she watched the sparkle in his eyes fade to disappointment when she didn't accept his ring. His expression was etched in her mind forever. Yes, she loved him. Very much. But she trusted no one. She'd done that six years ago and left a relationship with nothing. Her then-fiancé, Mitchell, on the other hand, walked away with her best friend. No. Not again.

"Shouldn't you be on your way? You'll be late for your meeting in Boston with Soren Cross."

Her defiant smile beamed at him. Peter shot her a quizzical stare.

"I thought you were coming with me? Soren wants to talk about buying the old Emerson waterfront property. The three of us can eat dinner at the Greek restaurant you like." Peter leaned over and pushed his folder next to the envelope on her desk, then moved away.

"Thanks for the late invitation, but no. Jim and I have plans tonight." She moved to her brother and kissed him on the cheek. "The Emerson property is a historical site and not for sale. The parcel is part of a trust funded by the Kincaid family. You and Soren have a good time. I'm not the cigars and whiskey type."

"Soren can be quite persuasive. With no place to build on the waterfront, that property is worth a fortune. Come on, I need your help to keep control of the discussion."

Ryan opened her mouth.

Peter held up his hand before she responded. "All right, I can see you're otherwise occupied, but you have no idea what you're missing."

Peter turned toward Jim. "Any news about Simon's murder? My neighbors are concerned. I assured each one there would be patrols in the area."

"Nothing to report. It may be that Simon was in the wrong place at the wrong time. You can assure your neighbors we've increased security in the area," Jim said, his voice deep with authority.

Peter nodded, then strode toward the door. He grasped the doorknob and turned.

"Your last chance, Ry." A flash of humor raced across his face.

"I'll suffer the consequences," she said with a pleasant smile she didn't let reach her eyes.

"Okay then, carry on where you two left off." Peter chuckled and left the room.

Ryan exhaled in annoyance. While her brother enjoyed keeping his political associates off balance, she didn't appreciate the tactic used on her or on Jim.

♥ ♥ ♥

Where they left off? Nothing would please Jim more. He easily imagined the two of them intertwined on her office sofa wearing little to nothing, Ryan's long, blonde hair spread out. Bare legs intertwined. The friction of their naked torsos rubbing against each other on her sofa flashed like lightning in his mind. His body ached for her touch, but thanks to Peter she was all business now. There would be no carrying on where they left off. He coughed and shivered as if he'd been doused with ice water, and the image switched off.

"You all right? There's water unless you need something stronger," she said, motioning toward the credenza against the wall.

"I'm fine." He walked to her desk, took the papers out of the envelope, and handed them to her. "I'd like you to look at these."

She gave the pages a cursory read. It didn't take long for her to become engrossed. He smiled at the way the world around her vanished and she threw herself into the document. He wished he could be as enthralled. The more immersed she got in the document, the more her brow wrinkled. She bit the side of her cheek and her eyes brightened as she moved from the document to pen and paper, recording her findings.

Ryan moved to her desk, oblivious to everything but what was in front of her. With an adjustment to her lamp, she bent over and scrutinized the item with her magnifying glass.

"This is dated 1774. The handwriting is…typical for the period." Ryan took her time inspecting the parchment. Her fingers flew over the computer keys as she accessed information, then returned to the manuscript. At last she sat back, her brow furrowed.

"Where did you find this?" Her hand covered the papers.

"In a post office box in Connecticut."

"No, Jim, I need you to be serious. Where did you find this? Who does it belong to?"

"I found the pages in a post office box in my name. Since Simon gave me the key I'm assuming he rented it under my name."

"You have to sign for one of those." She gave him a puzzled stare.

"Yeah, well, it was my signature, but I never rented the box. Let's just move on." Her eyes widened as he motioned toward the document.

"How could he?" Ryan closed her eyes as if she were in pain, shook her head, and focused on the papers.

"This is the bill of sale for the Emerson waterfront property. It may be authentic, but I need to do more analysis to be sure."

"Did solicitors in the 1700s make multiple copies of their work?" Jim asked.

"Two copies make sense, one for Zachariah and the other for Eoin. I compared this to the electronic version the Historical Society has online. The documents are not the same. A paragraph is missing from this one." She motioned toward her desk.

"Missing?" He peered over her shoulder. "Let me see."

"The quick answer—"

"Do lawyers do anything quickly?" he teased.

She let out a soft chuckle. "In order to keep the land in the family, should the Eoin-Catrina line end, the property reverts to the Emerson family. Property ownership was important in the 1700s. I always equated this sale to Catrina's dowry. Without the paragraph, the land can be sold at any time, to anyone.

"The bill of sale may be authentic, but with the document in Simon's possession, it creates a doubt whether it's authentic or a forgery." Her words hung in the air. She glanced up at Jim with her elbows planted on the desk, her hands clasped. "I can't rule out forgery. I'm sure you want to know if the document is authentic, why Simon had it, and why he gave it to you."

"Hell, when I saw the paper I thought the worst and hated myself. I knew Simon. The man did his time, yet the minute I suspected forgery—" He waved dismissively and turned away. "Simon mentioned something about ownership. This must be what he meant. I came here for you to confirm this is a high-quality souvenir copy."

His gut told him this was going to be messy as hell, and he didn't want to get her involved. Jim paced in front of her desk and rubbed the back of his neck.

"Who gains if the bill of sale is a forgery? David Kincaid is Eoin and Catrina's last direct descendant. He may not be married now, but he's not at death's door," Ryan said.

"Currently, if David Kincaid died, the property would revert to the Emerson family. But according to what I found in the post office box, the property doesn't necessarily revert. The Kincaids can dispose of the property however and whenever they choose. The loss of the property could be a major blow to Havenport and Havenport economics," Jim said. Shit, *mess* didn't begin to describe this predicament.

"But David is very much alive," Ryan said.

Jim lifted his head, a lethal calmness in his eyes.

"This could put a target on his back."

"Wait, we have no idea if this is authentic. This"—she held up the papers—"may be nothing at all."

"I don't plan to find out after an attempt has been made on David's life. Do you?"

"Oh, I didn't think about that." Her eyes widened.

Jim pulled out his cell phone and dialed.

"Brian… Whoa, wait a minute… I want a detail assigned to David Kincaid. No, nothing confirmed. I want to be safe rather than sorry. Around the clock. I'll give you the particulars when I'm back at the office. Ask him for a copy of his itinerary for the week and set up a meeting tomorrow with him… Okay… What were you going to call me about? Where did you find it?"

He covered the mouthpiece. "A patrol found the car from the Killer Curve accident." Jim went back to his phone. "Yes, go on. Yes. Thanks." The call ended.

"They found the car on the road to Providence hidden in the tall beach grass. The front end took the brunt of the damage. The car turned up on a stolen vehicle list. Brian found interesting evidence on the front seat." He bent his head toward her. "An envelope with a souvenir copy of the Kincaid-Emerson bill of sale along with pictures of Trixie."

"Trixie?" Ryan's eyes went wide.

"Yes, Trixie."

A flash of humor crossed his face. "The old geezer arranged a delivery and made a swap instead. Why didn't he come to me? If he had, he'd still be alive."

"Then whoever he met thought he had what he came for and—"

"Silenced him. But Simon had the last laugh. We have the bill of sale, but I wonder what pictures the killer expected. I doubt he wanted pictures of a cat."

"Anything else in the envelope besides the news article and old document?" she asked, rummaging through papers on her desk.

"Just this doodle. Any idea how to decipher it?" Jim asked. He leaned over her shoulder and pointed to the small scrap of paper.

Ryan turned her face toward him. He kept his eyes on the document while she stared at his profile.

He glanced at her without turning his head. "Are you going to help me here or stare at me? What does *ceann cadha* mean?"

"Let me see that." Ryan took the note from him. Doodles and an emphatic circle around two words covered the page.

"*Ceann cadha* is Gaelic. It means 'This I'll defend,' the Kincaid motto. The Kincaid family sent a plaque for the Hero's Chasm. I researched the phrase for the Historical Society last year. They wanted more information on the motto. Where did you find the paper?"

"Clipped onto the old document."

Jim picked up the bill of sale and read aloud. "'To all people to whom these presents shall come, greeting. Know ye that I, Zachariah Emerson of Havenport in the county of Kings within His Majesty's Colony of Rhode Island and Providence Plantations, Yeoman for and in consideration of the sum of one shilling to me in hand before the ensealing hereof, well and truly paid by Eoin Kincaid.

"'Have given, granted, bargained, sold, aliened, conveyed, and confirmed unto him, the said Eoin Kincaid and his heirs forever assign the parcel of land known as the Emerson Trading Company, lying and being in said Kings comprised of two acres.'"

"Here is the missing paragraph."

Ryan turned the screen for him to read.

The land is to be kept within the family and as such until the line of Eoin Kincaid ceases. At that time, the Emerson family shall have full rights to do with the parcel as they see fit without any interference from the Kincaid family of Stirlingshire, Scotland.

He turned the screen back toward her.

"It's too late to make calls," Ryan said, glancing at her watch. "I'll start my research in the morning."

"Why don't you take a break?" he whispered in her ear. "We can eat dinner at the café in Newport you liked or we can go to my place. I'll make dinner."

"Oh, I'm aware of what you call dinner. Grilled cheese or frozen meatballs and sauce. Thank goodness the leftovers from the seafood restaurant we went to are still in my fridge."

"If we lived in the same house we wouldn't need to decide which one had the better food choices."

"How did dinner decisions turn into a change in living arrangements? Things are fine the way they are," Ryan said, a finality in her voice.

Was that so bad? He watched the blood drain from her face, leaving Ryan as white as chalk. Something had set her off, but what? Because he wanted more? Shit. He always wanted more.

"Please don't ask. I love you, but I'm not ready. I…I need more time."

Jim looked at Ryan from under his lashes, his mouth hanging open. Her eyes darted around. She was avoiding him.

"I don't understand." Shit. Everything he felt for her bubbled to the surface. *Put a ring on her finger.* Damn. He still carried the ring box in his pocket. "How can you tell me you love me and in the same breath tell me you need more time? Listen, I know that attorney you were engaged to hurt you."

Shit. Keep your mouth shut, dumbass.

"Hurt me. What makes you say that? Because he called the night before our wedding to tell me he eloped with my maid of honor, my best friend? The coward didn't face me. He called. Called!" She screamed the word at him. "Mitchell's was a betrayal of the worst kind. I fell apart. I will never be vulnerable or deceived again."

She shook so badly, but he couldn't stop what he said next.

"So you paint me with the same brush you do him?"

"No, of course not. I love you. I need more time. You've told me time and again to trust my instincts. That's what I'm doing."

Jim put the papers down. How many times had he listened to her try to find the reason why the son of a bitch left her?

Peter had spoken to him about it one night over a bottle of whiskey. He couldn't figure out Mitchell's actions, either. She had it in her mind that the breakup was her fault and mentioned more than once that if she didn't understand the cause, how could she prevent a breakup from happening with someone else? With him. *Take her word for it. Stop pushing her, making demands.*

"You getting hungry?" His neutral question got her attention.

"With so much that needs to be done—Peter's contract reviewed, the Historical Society transcription, and now this—would you mind if we canceled dinner tonight?"

He studied her, not in that playful-sexy way, but in a professional tearing-you-apart way. Judging. Deciding. He didn't doubt her love for him or that she knew the depths of his feelings for her. He wondered if it was enough. Six years ago, he gave Ryan silent support to get through her ordeal. She had healed and overcome the loss and grief Mitchell had caused. Sometimes the scars tore loose and opened wounds she had to work through. He was there for her and usually able to see the trigger. This time he was at a loss.

He picked up the contents of his new post office box. "I'll drop you off at your place."

With the office locked and closed, he led the way across the street to his car. Neither spoke a word. Jim pulled the car out of the lot and the awkward silence persisted. Her mouth formed a rigid grimace, and a muscle twitched at the corner of her right eye. With her arms folded tightly across her chest, Ryan stared out the window.

What was she thinking? That he loved her and didn't care about why Mitch left. What should he say to her? He concentrated on the road as if nothing was wrong. One minute he wanted to pull over and let her out of the car, and the next he wanted to jump on her and make her his forever.

Jim pulled up in front of her house. He helped her out of the car. She placed her hand on his arm.

"Come in for a drink or cup of coffee," she said, a hint of a pleading tone in her voice.

Jim gave Ryan a warm smile. "Honey, I don't want to be in the way of your deadlines. You…"

The tears trembling on the rims of her eyes stopped him cold. He drew her close and waited several heartbeats before whispering, "What's wrong?"

"I love you," she said into his chest. "More than anything, but I can't—"

"No need to do anything you don't want to. Listen to me, Ryan. I'm not going anywhere. You're all I want, whether you wear my ring or not." He held her tight until the shaking stopped. Once she calmed, he walked her to the door, his arm around her shoulders.

"You sure you won't come in?" she asked.

Her fragile voice killed him, but he knew what he had to do. He kissed her forehead. She'd been here before and come through. This bout of anxiety was tougher than the others. Ryan could handle this setback. If he thought otherwise she wouldn't be able to keep him out.

"Not tonight. We both had busy days. I'll see you in the morning, your coffee in hand." He kissed her nose and walked to his car, forcing himself to not turn. He knew her eyes were on him wishing he would change his mind.

Keep walking. Give her some space. That's easier said than done. It'd been some time since she'd had a severe bout of nerves.

In the car, he checked his rearview mirror and watched Trixie slip inside the house before Ryan stepped inside and closed the door. A sigh of relief escaped his lips.

He waited. Once her bedroom light went on, he drove away. "Stay calm. She's fine. You're only a phone call away."

Chapter Four

"Good morning," Ryan said the next morning, standing at the patio door in her bathrobe. She took the latte out of Jim's hand. She had a perfectly good espresso machine sitting on the kitchen counter. Jim had his allegiances, though, with the local doughnut shop.

Trixie pranced out of the door, brushing against Jim's leg before she swished her tail and left the house.

"Did you make sure everyone saw you at the doughnut shop?"

"I know the pastries at Led Zeppoli are wonderful, but when Fogell retired from the department and opened up a doughnut shop we all laughed. When he put up the sign, Doughnuts and Cops, we fell off our chairs. How can I not support him? Besides, the tourists love the parade of police."

Jim headed for the kitchen, but she steered him to a set table in front of the fireplace in the breakfast room. She hoped with all her heart he would welcome the intimate meal and cozy atmosphere as a good sign after last night's disastrous end.

"Eggs and hand-cut bacon. It's a bit thicker than usual.

For the life of me, I couldn't find my knife. I must have taken it to the office."

"Heaven," Jim said with his eyes shut, sucking in a deep breath.

She laughed. "If you are anything, you're predictable. I could serve you burned toast and you would say the same thing."

"If you made it." Jim wrapped his arms around her, and she cuddled closer.

The night had been cold and empty. She kicked herself for the way the evening ended, afraid she had pushed him away one time too many. The moment she heard his car door slam and the back gate open, her body warmed.

"Sit. I'll be right back. I put a pot of coffee on the sideboard if you want more." She squirmed out of his arms, sashayed into the kitchen, and left Jim shaking his head.

"I hope you're hungry. I slaved over a hot stove for you," she said, carrying a tray filled with eggs, bacon, toast, and everything that went with it. With breakfast on the table, she sat across from him and poured him a morning cocktail.

"To Simon," he said, toasting the day with a champagne Bellini.

"Thank you for—"

He put his finger on her lips. "Shush. We have ground rules. You needed space. I went home. End of story." He raised his glass and touched the rim of her flute with his. "Now, drink up."

Satisfied that last night's crisis was over, she took another sip of champagne.

"I looked over everything last night. Simon clipped the doodle to the bill of sale for a reason. It's been bothering me all morning." She spread the neatly stacked papers across the table.

"I thought about the picture last night, too. All I can make out is a doodle with lots of clover and two foreign words." Jim loaded his fork with some scrambled eggs and a piece of bacon.

"Clover? If I drew clover, there would be four leaves, not three. This looks more like a spade, the ones you find on a deck of cards." Jim shared a quizzical look with her.

"Cards?"

"Trust my instincts. Spades, clubs, diamonds, hearts. Card suits. This looks nothing like clover. Clover leaves are heart-shaped. These are round. And the stem is different, too."

"Yes, I see what you mean," Jim said. "This isn't a picture of clover at all." He put down his fork. From the wrinkle in his forehead she knew breakfast was forgotten.

"What do spades have to do with the Kincaid motto?" He ran his hand through his hair. "Something is staring us in the face, and I can't figure out the puzzle."

She continued to study the note, turning the design in different directions. "Simon had an artistic quality. In a cluster, like he's drawn, they appear to be in a bush with the motto growing out of the middle. Take a look at how he made the letters three-dimensional." She slid the paper across the table.

"*This, I'll defend*, is the motto. It sounds easy enough, but Simon must have used another meaning. Defend, protect, support, represent, back, stand up for. I'm not good at word association." Jim got up. "Want more coffee?"

"No, thanks."

He went to the sideboard and refilled his cup. "Are you sure this isn't clover? Perhaps he's trying to tell us something is going to happen on St. Patrick's Day."

"Maybe it's not the motto we need to analyze, but where he's put it. It's not a clover. I'm sure it's a spade. How do you use a spade? Shovel, dig, scoop…" She stopped midsentence, excitement bubbling. "Jim. Is he telling us to dig up something? By the historical plaque in the chasm? It's the only place in town where the motto is displayed."

"I hear what you're saying. Do you think it's possible? Could Simon be that devious?" Jim asked. "Perhaps it's a holdover from his French resistance days."

She loved to watch him put the pieces of a puzzling problem together. He gave off a sense of command and control with his wrinkled forehead and intense focus. The way he organized and thought through each piece of evidence front, back, and sideways not only fascinated her, but added to his appeal.

"You may be on to something. The more I think about the note, Simon, and the bill of sale, the more your explanation makes sense."

"We'll need a good reason to dig at a historical site. Doodles by an ex-con and a list of verbs from word association won't be enough. We don't have any idea what we're looking for," she said.

"Could this lead us to the pictures the murderer expected to get from Simon? The ones he really wanted, not pictures of Trixie? And what part do the pictures play in the story?" He picked up the news article that had been with the bill of sale. "Did you look at this?"

"I read the names on the back of the newspaper and did a quick search to see if I could link these people to the drug bust. I didn't find anything," she said.

"The newspaper article needs more research. The evidence in the car, the bill of sale, and the doodle are just too weak. I don't think you have enough to convince a judge to issue a court order."

"You were alone with Simon before he died. Tell Judge Daly he told you something that leads you to believe there may be evidence regarding his murder at Hero's Chasm. If he agrees, he'll tell you the preservation society's permission to dig at a historic site is also needed. I'll show the society the court order and use the investigating-a-murder story. Let's be objective and look at this. No one wants to catch the leader of the group of drug dealers more than me. I don't like the fact they're targeting our kids, but this must be done within the law, or any case we might have will be destroyed," she said.

"Will you put together the paperwork for the court order?" Jim kissed her. His moist, firm lips demanded a response.

"Yes," she said against his mouth. "When the judge laughs, don't say I didn't warn you." She gave him a slow, drugging kiss.

He nuzzled her ear. "I think you better put on your clothes before I have other ideas."

Shivering from the touch of his hot breath, her body warmed all over. She jumped away from him, smiled, and hurried into her room. Jim followed behind and grabbed the door before she closed it.

"About those ideas." He stepped into her room and closed the door behind him, just as she planned.

♥ ♥ ♥

Ryan sat at her desk with an afternoon cup of coffee and a dish of kibble. Trixie graced the windowsill and licked the bandage on her paw. The glow of the morning's encounter lingered.

Peter peeked into Ryan's office from the doorway. He stood with his slim navy slacks, tailored blue pinstripe shirt, and red power tie. Would the man ever knock before he came into her office?

"Morning. How was Boston?" she asked.

"Not as good as I expected. I've been thinking about a vacation. I told you months ago, between your clients here and the Historical Society, you work too much."

"Vacation? Is vacation your code word for a political meeting? You go ahead. I have some projects for the Historical Society I can finish while you're away."

"No, I need you with me. I don't want you here." He walked into her office.

"Why? What's going to happen?" She let out a heavy sigh and crossed her arms. Couldn't he see she was busy? No, of course not. This was Peter.

Ryan gave him her full attention and hoped he'd leave quickly. She hit the keyboard shortcut and sent the court order to her printer.

"I didn't want to tell you, but the talk about putting me on the national ticket is gathering momentum. The Art Society said the position required some international savvy. I thought in a short three-week trip we could—"

"Three weeks? Peter, I do a lot for you, but I have my own clients. I can't be gone for three weeks."

"Yeah, I thought three weeks might be too long. How about two weeks?" He sat on the corner of her desk and hovered. She lowered her computer screen. That made him sit straight.

"Not now, Peter. In a few months perhaps, but not now."

"I have a meeting in London next week. Give me five days." He played with the pencils in the holder on her desk.

She shot him a withering stare. He had no intention of relenting. "Five days. After the reenactment. We can fly out on Wednesday and be back on Sunday."

"You drive a hard bargain, Ms. Livingston. I'm glad you're on my side of the courtroom. What case are you working on that you need a court order?" With the pencils abandoned, he got off her desk.

The door to the reception area opened. No need to look at the time. Jim was better than an alarm clock.

"Based on information Simon gave Jim before he died, we believe some evidence concerning the drug cartel that infiltrated Havenport is hidden in the chasm. I'm putting the finishing touches on a request for a court order to excavate."

"Dig at the chasm? What information?" An element of irritation entered his tone, and she wasn't certain why he would care one way or the other.

"Good morning, Jim," she said, looking past Peter.

Peter glanced at Jim as he entered.

"Are you sure you want to dig there? Or will this be like the big Capone ruse? The national newscaster was made a laughingstock. With the reenactment a few days away, the disturbance could detract from the big celebration the town has planned. This can wait until after the festivities are over." Peter fidgeted with his tie and stretched his neck, as if the collar was binding.

Jim picked up the court order from her printer and read the first sheet. He looked over the top of the page at her and moved closer. She could use an ally.

"I don't think Mayor Henry is going to want to put the town's reputation at risk. He has some important guests attending the celebration. Soren Cross a big international developer interested in buying some waterfront property, and David Kincaid is visiting from Scotland. I also don't think you have a snowball's chance in July of getting Judge Daly to sign the court order or obtain approval from the preservation society to dig at the memorial."

She stood, determined to convince Peter she and Jim were on the right track. "But Peter—"

"Why are you against investigating the chasm?" Jim asked as he tucked the papers into his pocket. "For the past two years, my department has worked alongside the FBI trying to put an end to the drug trafficking. You were with us last winter when we caught Russian mobsters trying to set up shop in Havenport.

"If we can find information to put a big dent in the drug business, perhaps even stop it in Havenport once and for all, you and your Health and Human Services committee would be credited with the takedown. I would think you'd be eager to act since this is an election year." Jim's declaration hung in the air for several seconds.

"With all the media here for the reenactment, if nothing comes of the dig, you'll look foolish. Is that what you want for Ryan? Her business is built around her hard-won reputation, both for her private practice and the party. She can't jeopardize that for some foolish notion." Peter turned to his sister. "Wait until the press is gone. Better yet, Ryan, distance yourself from this. On a recent call, the party leaders talked about appointing you the Assistant to the State Attorney General. I don't want you to put all your hard work in jeopardy for this treasure hunt that may come to nothing but embarrassment."

"One moment you say wait until the press is gone and the next you tell me to forget about it entirely. Which is it, Peter?" she asked.

Peter ran his hand through his hair. Jim didn't move.

Peter turned toward Jim, his hands placed belligerently on his hips. "How can you let her be exposed to such ridicule? You both know you have nothing here to command a court order."

She straightened her shoulders and cleared her throat.

Before she said anything, Jim walked up to Peter. "Let me be clear. First and foremost, I'm investigating a murder and will follow up any and every lead no matter where it takes me. Do you understand?"

Her brother stood motionless in the middle of the room, his expression a mask of stone.

She kept her eyes on Jim, willing him to back down. There was no need to make this a big issue, or be exposed if it were a hoax. After the press was gone, she would work by Jim's side to search the chasm. The minutes ticked by. Neither man moved.

"Jim, Peter may be right. Now may not be the best time to dig in the chasm. I'll be overseas with Peter next week. We'll get the court order and preservation society approval ready so we can start excavation once the celebration is over and I'm back. By then, the newspeople will be gone and things back to normal." She stared at Peter and waited for him to say something.

"Ryan," Jim said. Something in his tone made her straighten up. "Are you sure about this?"

No, she was anything but certain at the moment, about Peter or him. *Trust yourself.* Jim's words echoed in her head.

A deep breath. *That's it. Now another.* Little by little, she pushed down the building panic. In silent gratitude she patted Jim's arm.

"I need to concentrate on Peter's trip. I'd hate to start this investigation and leave the work unfinished."

Ryan looked at the calm, cordial smile painted on Peter's face. It didn't match with her brother's inability to hold eye contact and keep his hands from fidgeting. She'd conducted enough interviews to know the signs. Peter hid something, and not only from her.

She turned to Jim and watched him rein in his anger with a lethal calmness she wished she could master.

"I need to take care of a few things before I leave with Peter," she said in a sensible voice as she sat at her desk. "This shouldn't take too long. I can call you when I'm done."

"Sure," Jim said in the same matter-of-fact tone.

Peter hurried out of her office and across the reception area into his suite.

Jim turned back to say something. She kept her head down and pretended to be lost in her work. He said a soft goodbye and left the room.

Ryan looked up at the click of the door closing and rested her head on her hands. Trixie jumped down from her perch onto Ryan's desk, then curled into a ball and closed her eyes. She stroked the silky coat and let her racing heart return to its natural rhythm.

She loved Peter, but Assistant to the State Attorney General? Only wishful thinking on his part. Not because of her ability—she was more than qualified. No, because she was the candidate's sister.

Peter's reason to delay any excavation was sound. Given an opportunity, the media would turn the dig into a circus. No, she didn't want any part of that fiasco.

But Jim had a point. He was following a lead from a murder investigation.

She raised her head and drummed her fingers on the desk. An idea burst in her head like a soap bubble. She could take a look and see if anything was hidden at Hero's Chasm. Just look around. If she found something of interest she, of course, would share it with Jim. And without the media around there wasn't any chance of a circus.

"I can take care of this alone."

The chasm closed at dusk, but without a fence it was more the honor system. All she had to do was avoid the park ranger.

Judge Daly was in court until 4:30. If Jim saw him and if the judge signed the court order, he wouldn't be able to get to Providence for the preservation society approval until tomorrow.

She had to go tonight. After dusk.

♥ ♥ ♥

For the umpteenth time she checked her watch. It was only 5:30. She had another two hours before she went to the chasm.

She was too antsy to stay at the office. Instead, she used her pent-up energy putting together her treasure-hunting kit: garden shovel, small lantern, and her illusive pink floral garden gloves she kept for weeding the garden. A quick search and she found them on the patio next to the large flower pot. Satisfied she had what she needed, Ryan changed into jeans and a sweatshirt.

Dressed with her treasure kit in hand, she stood at the patio window. The sun was sinking and the sky streaked purple and gray. It seemed to take forever for the last edge of the sun to slip below the horizon.

As the sky darkened, she put her things in the car and left for the short drive along the coast to the chasm. There was little vegetation and no sign of life along the serpentine road she took to the top of the cliff. Here, she got a clear look at the vertical rock that faced the water. Below the cliff were rocky beaches. In the distance, a spur stretched out into the water. At its far end, a lonely lighthouse.

There was no way to drive directly to the chasm from the coast road. From here, the only way in was either a seventy-foot dive and a hundred-yard swim through the narrow opening to the chasm's pool, or a trek through the winding path in the forest. Ryan was a good swimmer, but timing a jump with the swells did not appeal to her. She'd trek in.

Parked near the edge of the lot where her car would be hard to see, Ryan took her tools and followed the footpath through the forest to the field and the shoreline beyond.

She knew the area well. The Parks Department kept the lush, worn trail in good repair. Most people weren't divers. Together with her good friend Ina Emerson, she'd walked this path every year on her way to the annual private memorial at the hero's grave.

Ryan was honored to be one of few non-Emersons invited to the private family event. The service was an emotional one of remembrance without any fanfare. The final portion of the ceremony was breathtaking. The bagpipes played to commemorate Eoin and Catrina's anniversary.

Ryan traipsed out of the forest, came to the edge of the field, and stopped. The deep purple dusk reflected off the stone palisades that surrounded her as she walked to the other side of the field. Eyes closed, she took in a deep breath of clean air with its tang of salty brine. In the distance she could still see the narrow opening to the ocean that protected the chasm from the onslaught of crashing waves.

Pine trees and a gate built by Zachariah Emerson surrounded the small graveyard on three sides. New

England had many Revolutionary War cemeteries, but this one was special. Everyone who came here walked away with the same feeling: they'd been to a sacred place.

Ryan entered the graveyard and looked at the carved headstones. The markings were worn away, almost unreadable. In contrast, Ryan found the bronze plaque in a place of honor, at the foot of Eoin's grave. The memorial the Kincaid family erected would last forever.

The purple sky had turned gray. She stepped closer to the plaque for a better look. Her foot sank into the ground. The ground was soft. She lit her lantern for a better look. The earth had been turned not long ago.

Breathless, she couldn't believe her luck. Her heart pounded until she talked some sense into herself. An animal could have been digging here. Erosion may have softened the ground, but deep down inside she knew this was the place Simon sent them to. *Calm down. Take it slow.* She slipped the gloves on her trembling hands, took the small shovel, and stabbed the ground.

Fifteen minutes of digging and her confidence withered. Simon's message deteriorated with each shovel full of sandy soil. Twenty-five minutes later, she had dug a three-foot-square by one-foot-deep hole in front of the plaque. Nothing. She sat back. This was ridiculous. What did she expect to find?

"No wonder Peter cautioned me," she said to no one. "This whole thing is laughable. Thank God Jim isn't here." She let out a dry cackle and with all her strength, directed her frustration into one last jab into the dirt. A metallic scrape sent a vibration up her arm.

Stunned, she dropped her shovel and brought the lantern close. She tore away the dirt with her hands. A few inches more and she uncovered the corner of a metal box. Her heart raced. The treasure was right where she and Jim thought it would be.

She spent the next few minutes working the box loose and dragging it out of the hole. It was a simple metal box, nothing extravagant. *Okay, you hauled the thing out of the ground. Now what?*

Ryan turned the box around looking for the lock, but she couldn't find one, only a small latch. Curiosity pushed her. Before she lost her nerve, her fingertip worked the clasp.

A shiver scurrying across her shoulders made her uneasy and alert. She tried to convince herself the sensation meant nothing, her mind playing tricks, but she knew better. More and more, her body warned her of danger until she felt eyes boring into her back.

A quick scan of the grave and area beyond confirmed she was alone. But she couldn't shake the sensation.

Now was not the time to admit she shouldn't be here. Trespassing in a public park after hours and destroying a historic landmark? Her head hurt with all the laws she'd broken.

The wind picked up, carrying the briny aroma of the ocean. The sky was now inky black, shrouding everything from her sight. Even with the lantern, it was difficult to see.

Her shoulders were still chilled. Ryan stared into the darkness and jumped at two almond-shaped pale-green eyes staring at her.

Trixie strutted into the lamplight. Her tail switched left then right, broadcasting she was a feline ninja to anyone who dared to disturb her space. To Ryan, the rumble of the cat's deep purr brought her down from a high alert.

"Thanks for the support." Ryan relaxed her clenched hand and looked at the marks her nails made in her palm. She flexed her fingers to get them working and opened the box.

Chapter Five

Unable to grasp the contents wearing garden gloves, she took off one glove and lifted out an old worn notebook. Two folders lay underneath. She brought the notebook closer to the lantern, opened the cover, and stopped. A sea of three-leaf clovers and the words *ceann cadha* in three-dimensional block letters covered the inside page. In the bottom margin, the numbers 062013 were written.

The notebook's first entries started in 2010, two years prior to Simon's time in prison. The last entry was dated last month. Notable names from Havenport society, as well as local and state politics, jumped off the pages as she leafed through them. The list of familiar names made her shudder until she came to one that had her gasping for air. She looked at the name again, but refused to admit it.

She remembered this case well. Simon swore he never kept names. She lowered the book to her lap. The names on the pages swam in her head, and her heart sank.

A soft rain began to fall. She stuffed the notebook and folders into her bag. She put her tools away and looked at the mess she'd made. Removing the box left a recognizable crater next to the memorial. Big fat drops splashed around her.

Ryan stood trying to keep control, but sheer black fright washed over her. She searched for something to fill the hole. The rocks littering the area were either too large or too small. Frantic for something to hide her illegal excavation, her gaze landed on the metal box. She worked fast and put the empty box back into the ground, covered it with dirt, then patted down as much of the grass as possible. She got up, stomped on the area, and focused the lantern on the ground for a closer look. Satisfied, she picked up her things.

"You coming?" she said to the cat. Trixie trotted alongside her. Together they traipsed down the forest path that protected from the rain. Ryan put her bag with the notebook and folders on the passenger seat. Trixie curled on top of the materials and closed her eyes just as the downpour began.

Ryan grasped the steering wheel with both hands. *No, he can't be involved in this.* She rested her forehead on the wheel. Maybe he'd tried to clear Simon. That had to be the answer. Why else was his name listed so many times?

A flash of lightning in the distance shook her out of her trance. She started the car and made her way back into Havenport.

Trixie didn't move. She guarded the treasure like her feline cousin, the lion. It was late, but too many things ran around in Ryan's head. She needed to ride out the adrenaline. She turned down Main Street and headed toward her office.

The rain let up as she parked her car. She and Trixie made their way to her office. Ryan put out a dish of kibble and brewed herself a cup of strong coffee.

Simon's book needed more than a cursory review. Ryan made herself comfortable at her desk and opened the notebook.

Ready for a long night, she pored over each page and noted each name. She recognized some people only by name, others she spoke to often, two were on the town council, a bank manager, and—

Ryan slammed her hand over the next name. His name. *Peter Livingston.* Her heart ached to read it among these…these monsters.

Don't jump to conclusions. Read everything. Understand why his name is listed. Investigate first, draw conclusions afterward. Could she, though? Be objective?

She took her hand away from the page. His name shouted at her.

Reading through the last pages was difficult. Each time Peter's name popped up, her heart sank. She compared the dates in Simon's book to Peter's appointments in their joint calendar. Only the past two months were kept online: his hairstylist, staff meetings in his Providence office, followed by meetings with the assembly's committee on Health and Human Welfare. The committee worked on the new bill concerning the opioid epidemic and fought hard to pass legislation. The committee built an airtight case for Peter to present. But a drug lobbyist named Soren Cross, the same man who wanted to buy Havenport's waterfront property, remained one step ahead of them.

Soren Cross. His name appeared here, too. She sat back, angry and confused. What the hell was going on?

"This is ridiculous." She picked up her phone and speed-dialed Peter's private number. He would straighten this out.

"Sorry, I'm not available. Leave a message and I'll—"

Ryan ended the call more agitated than she'd been.

The ring of an incoming call from her phone startled her. At last.

"Peter?"

"Sorry to disappoint you." Jim's morning voice, even though it was late evening, was soft and deep. The sound made her want to roll over in bed with him. And she was sure he knew it.

"Jim." Her shoulders relaxed a click. "I'm sorry. I thought you were Peter returning my call."

Should she tell Jim what she found? Aside from getting the information illegally, what if Peter represented

Simon? She rubbed her arms. Peter could never represent Simon. As a state assemblyman, he didn't take cases. No. She couldn't hand this information to anyone. Best she keep this to herself for now.

"You okay?"

"I'm fine. I tried to reach Peter but had to leave a message. I still had the phone in my hand when you called. The sound startled me." She put her hand over the notebook, as if Jim could read the pages over the phone.

"You sound busy. I'll say good night. See you in the morning."

"I'm glad you called, and sorry I'm preoccupied. Peter told me about the trip right before you arrived at the office." A stifled moan built in her chest. *Stop blabbering and giving him excuses*. Her temples pounded. If she didn't take control soon, the pounding would grow into a full-blown migraine.

"I love you," she said.

"Yeah, I love you, too. See you in the morning." He ended the call.

She closed her eyes. Where was Peter? He'd get an earful when she spoke to him about this list. A chill went up her spine. What did she expect him to tell her? He's paying Simon to keep quiet, or he's secretly paying Simon's legal expenses? Neither scenario rang true, not with the names of the others on this list. She looked at her door, his office beyond the reception area. Best to speak to him face-to-face tomorrow.

Tired, she put the phone down next to the folders she found in the box. Without much thought, she opened the first folder and removed incorporation papers and bank account opening materials. She methodically laid out everything on her conference table, then opened the second envelope.

"Pictures." Her back straightened and her heart raced. "These must be the pictures the killer wanted."

Ryan laid out the pictures on the table one at a time.

Thirty pictures in all. Her stomach sank with each one. Peter's subcommittee and the FBI had these people under investigation for drug trafficking. One face stared at her from every picture. Hers.

Trixie brushed up against her legs, then in a graceful leap jumped onto the conference table. A wave of nausea built until it hit her hard, along with a numbness that kept her immobile. *Peter.*

After sitting down and examining each document, she drew her conclusion. She was one of the owners of an offshore laboratory and the only signer on the company's bank account.

An account she'd never heard of.

No. This had to be some sort of joke. Her chest heaved. She tried to take in air, but her lungs wouldn't move. All she could manage were short bursts. "No," she said in a low murmur. The cat's ears perked up.

Her anger grew. "No," she said in a hoarse voice. The cat stood, her tail twitching.

"No, no, no," she shouted in a scalding fury as she slammed her hand on the table, sending Trixie scampering to the floor.

She looked at the door, the bank document still in her hand. She forced herself to settle down. The thought of Peter…the idea he would… She had to have it all wrong.

The past six years were a lesson in political duplicity and stretching the truth. But Peter? She paced in front of her desk. Her chin jutted out. He didn't operate that way. Appearances could be deceiving. Although he may have gotten his hands dirty, at the heart of the matter he… Ryan lowered her chin to her chest. *Oh, Peter. We had such plans.* She looked at the papers and pictures strewn over her conference table. There had to be an explanation for all this. There must be.

Trixie jumped onto her desk and sniffed at the drawer. The sobering revelation pricked like a hundred needles under her skin as she lowered herself into her desk chair.

The cat pranced toward her, brushed up against her arm, and purred.

"Okay, girl." Ryan opened the drawer and stared at the office keys next to the bag of cat treats. She gave Trixie a handful. Ryan's hand rested on the keys. Her gaze fixed on her door, as if touching the keys would summon her brother—or better yet, give her an answer.

Trixie rubbed her head on Ryan's hand. She gave the cat another treat, curled her fingers around the keys, and pulled them out of the drawer. She needed to know what side of the truth her brother was on.

She looked at the doorknob in her hand, not remembering walking to Peter's office. *Go on. Look for yourself. There is no reason for these doubts.* She'd feel foolish when Peter gave her a simple explanation. How could she doubt him? According to the campaigns she crafted for him, he was the epitome of truth and honesty.

Ryan opened the door and threw on the lights. She knew this office as well as her own.

Now, though, his space appeared strange and foreboding, almost frightening. Were all these thoughts real or a product of an overactive imagination?

No use looking at his office files. If he had confidential ones, they wouldn't be in plain sight.

Instead she went to his bar and moved the wineglasses on the second shelf. She slid the panel to the side and dialed the safe.

She and Peter kept their important papers here: deed to the building, life insurance, as well as some heirlooms and her expensive jewelry. She pulled the handle. The safe didn't open.

Stunned, she tried the combination again, and again, and again.

Her heart hammered. Her breath came in uneven spurts. She held back tears of disappointment that turned to fury that almost choked her.

Ryan closed the slide, put the glasses back, and returned to her office.

He must have changed the combination and forgot to let her know. He'd done it before. She'd straighten everything out in the morning.

Sure, chalk it up to him forgetting. He lies so close to the truth that it passes under the radar, or lies so big you'd never dream he could make it up. She knew the truth.

"Peter deceived me. How could my own brother… He stood by me after Mitchell."

It had taken her years to get over her fiancé's betrayal. The grief of the broken relationship hurt like hell.

How she hated Mitchell—all men—but the worst part was she doubted every friendship. She would not let anyone into her life. She'd never go through that kind of pain again.

Doubt had become her constant companion and tainted every decision, from picking her clothes to being with Jim.

She slammed her hand on the papers and crushed them in her fist. *This is all circumstantial evidence you've misinterpreted.* Yes, misinterpreted.

A small voice in her head echoed. *Look at the evidence. Don't be naive just because he's your brother. Don't deny the truth.* She didn't see the signs with Mitchell. Could she have missed the signs with Peter?

Ryan opened the crushed ball of paper and ironed it with her hand. She glanced at her signature.

There were public sources at her disposal she could use to investigate the papers. A person just needed to know where to search and what to look for. Ryan started with the corporate papers, Imprevin Laboratories.

♥ ♥ ♥

It was three in the morning. The lights in the parking lot across the street went out. Ryan got out of her chair and paced the office. Checking the company name led her to a small pharmaceutical started in 1954. George Imprevin, the laboratory owner, learned about paracetamol, an aspirin-like compound not marketed in the United States. The drug was effective at reducing children's fever. A large firm bought Imprevin in 1960 in a multimillion-dollar deal. Two years later, Imprevin Laboratories closed. For the past five years, George Imprevin Jr. had been the chairman of the Rhode Island Joint State Committee on Drug Addiction.

She found no other information until four years ago when, according to the papers, she'd represented George Jr. as legal counsel when he resurrected the company. Bank instruments, all held in the Cayman Islands, also appeared to be signed by her. The problem was she had not signed any of these documents. She'd never been to the Cayman Islands, nor would she ever do business with a bank or company there. Did someone forge her signature? Peter? Simon? *For God's sake.*

Her brother had her deeply involved in Imprevin. Her insides twisted. If prosecuted, she faced being disbarred, even jail time.

Her head swam with facts, assumptions, documents, and pictures. She sank into her chair. A crushing anger morphed into calm acceptance.

Everything she'd worked for was at stake—her livelihood, her reputation. She didn't have time to feel sorry for herself. She needed to understand how Peter used her and decide how to move forward. There was a slim chance she had it wrong, but that small voice kept telling her that was a fantasy.

And Jim. Tears slid down her cheeks. He would stand by her to the end. No, she couldn't let that happen.

"Peter, what have you done?"

Chapter Six

Judge Miles Daly sat reviewing the day's cases, a morning cup of coffee on his desk. An overflowing folder labeled Traffic Violations filled the inbox. Daly had a casual, homey way about him on the outside, although Jim had witnessed one or two court cases that riled the sixty-five-year-old judge. It was not a pretty sight.

"You're here early, Chief. What do you have for me?"

Jim handed over the court order request to excavate by the chasm landmark.

Daly browsed through Jim's court order. "Why do you want to disturb poor Eoin?"

"There is good reason to believe some evidence regarding the recent Simon Farrell murder and a possible connection to a drug cartel may be hidden in the chasm."

Daly stopped reading, lifted his head, and looked at Jim. The laid-back mask was gone, replaced with an edgy cold stare. "What type of evidence?"

Daly's sudden clipped speech held Jim's attention. He put on his best poker face. "Someone said they witnessed some activity by the landmark. I suspect we'll find nothing, but every lead must be followed. If something is found, I want to be prepared to take immediate action. Once you sign the court order, I'll be off to Providence for the Historical Preservation and Heritage Commission's approval."

Daly's stare didn't waver. Neither did Jim's. It took another three heartbeats before Daly picked up his pen and signed the order.

"You still need the Commission to approve this." Daly put the papers in an envelope and shoved them at him.

"I will. Thanks." Jim closed the door behind him and took his time putting the envelope into his pocket.

"Daly here," Jim heard through the door. "Kanter came to see me to sign a court order. To do some excavation at the Hero's landmark. Kanter said he's following a lead involving Simon's murder and drug cartel involvement. Yes, I signed it. What did you expect me to do? You make sure the preservation society doesn't give him a permit."

Jim wanted to march back in and confront Daly. Demand answers. Simon's words echoed in his head. *Don't tell anyone anything.* Cold sweat ran down his back. Shit. This was not his brightest move. Whatever Simon hid at the monument would be long gone by the time he arrived.

His thoughts turned to Ryan. Damn, if she decided to go and nose around she'd walk right into the crooks' hands. No way would he let that happen.

His phone was out before he left the building heading for Doughnuts and Cops.

"Hello." Her voice never sounded so good.

"Hey. Regular or a light latte?" His face split into a wide grin. He'd called her landline. She was safe at home.

"I think I'm going to sleep in this morning." Her voice was all silk—smooth, rich, and sexy.

"Okay, I'll be there in ten minutes," he said, his voice deep and husky. "We can skip the coffee foreplay."

Ryan let out a sleepy laugh that made him want her more. "Not this morning."

"I was concerned you'd go to the chasm alone."

"You have nothing to worry about. I'm too tired to go anywhere."

The deep rumbling of Trixie's purring reached his ear. He could imagine Ryan curled up in the covers in the large queen-size bed. A subject change was needed before walking became too painful. "You worked on Ina's translation all night, didn't you?"

There was a hesitation. "We need to talk." A ring of finality replaced her warm and sultry tone.

"Talk?" That stopped him midstep. He had similar conversations with Ryan early in their relationship when she was fragile and unsure. *Talk* was her code word for separate, isolate. He thought she was past that.

"About us, our relationship. I like you—"

"Where did that come from? Yesterday you told me you loved me, several times." *Fuck...Peter.* The state assemblyman didn't impress him on a political or personal level. Peter manipulated Ryan to prove he controlled her. Her brother's abuse drove him crazy. Ryan didn't need to be controlled. She needed to be loved.

"Is Peter with you?" *Shit. Slow down. Deep breath. No need to bark at her.*

"No. He's in Newport this morning. I understand you think he's overprotective, but he's been taking care of me since before our parents died. Besides, Peter has nothing to do with this. I've been thinking about us for some time. Our relationship isn't going anywhere, and I don't want to hold you back or be in your way. You deserve more."

Protective, no. Manipulative, yes. He discussed this with Ryan before, but now he sensed something different in her voice. Conviction. This time she scared him.

His first instinct was to go see her, but that wouldn't work. He needed to give her time. A few days. No, he couldn't risk that. A few hours. If he could wait that long.

"Jim, I don't want to draw this out any more than necessary."

Silence hung in the air thick and heavy. He waited.

"It will only be more difficult for both of us." Her voice was a mere whisper. That, and the small bit of hesitancy, gave him hope he could still help her, help their relationship.

"I have to follow up some leads on Simon's murder. I'll call you later. If you want to talk, great. If not, we'll see what happens." His breath burned in his throat. Every nerve in his body said to go to her, but his head said to give her room. Trust her.

The call ended. He started his car and headed to his office, his mind racing a million miles an hour.

No need to go to Providence now. Daly's call took care of that. Now that he told Daly and his cronies where to find the evidence. He pulled into his parking spot behind the police department.

Perhaps if he kept his relationship with Ryan all business, he could find out what bothered her. He was glad she wasn't going to the chasm. She had been so adamant before. Yet it wasn't like her to give up when she had a bone to chew. Ryan saw things through to the end. Just like she did for Ina's project, working all night. He reached for the station's front door and froze. Wait a minute. Hold him back or be in his way. How? Something bothered him, and not just the conversation with Ryan. If Peter wasn't manipulating things then what had her so determined she had to save him?

Not from Peter. From her? The idea brought him up short. It sounded weird, but very plausible. She was sacrificing their future for what? His career. No, his life. What did she have? What did she find?

He dropped his hand from the door. The thought that flashed through his mind startled him. Ryan had searched the chasm and took the evidence. The pieces of the puzzle had to fit. It was the only way anything made sense.

He hurried into the station and went to the left of the lobby to the dispatcher.

"I want someone tailing Ryan Livingston."

"Sure, Chief. I'll call it right in." Jim tried to figure out what Ryan might have found. The pictures were the first thing that came to mind.

"Get me Brian." The dispatcher raised the lieutenant and gave the radio-phone to Jim.

"Where are you?" Jim's voice was clipped, his tone controlled, his question a command.

"I'm on Manor Road heading toward the station. Is everything all right?"

Back off. Don't bite his head off. "I just got a lead on Simon's murder and we need to act quickly. Go to the chasm memorial and wait for me."

"Am I looking for anything in particular?" Jim heard Brian's car siren begin to wail.

"I don't expect the area to be too crowded this early in the morning. Cordon off the memorial. I want to know who is up there. We're going on a treasure hunt. I'll see you within the hour."

Jim left dispatch and made his way across the lobby to his office. When he arrived, Agent Matt Lyons was leaning over the counter, giving all his attention to Jim's young receptionist. The men knew each other well and had worked together putting a dent in a drug ring that had infiltrated Havenport.

"Sorry to pull you away," Jim said as he walked toward his office.

"Duty calls. I'll be at Royce's Tavern at eight," Matt said to his receptionist. Jeez, did the guy turn it on all the time?

"Any calls?" Jim waited by his door for her reply. She shook her head, obviously unable to put two coherent words together. Matt had that effect on women.

Matt preceded him into his office. Jim brought up the rear, then went to a supply closet in his office and picked up a shovel.

"What brings you here?" Jim eyed the envelope tagged

062013 in the agent's hand. "I haven't got a meeting on my calendar." He enjoyed Matt's company, but he had no time to socialize now. He had to get to the chasm.

"I wanted to speak to you after Simon's funeral but you left in a hurry with Taylor," Matt said, stretching out in one of the chairs in front of Jim's desk.

Jim and Matt knew most of the players in the drug ring and were close to bringing it down. But the leader eluded their dragnet.

"I ran an errand for Simon. He left me some old papers." Without having to think twice, he showed everything to Matt.

"The papers appear to be a bill of sale for the Emerson waterfront property. I asked Ryan to look at it. A crucial paragraph is missing. This version allows the property to be sold by the Kincaid family at will. Simon also left an obscure note."

"*Ceann cadha*. This I'll defend." Matt handed the note back.

"You can read Gaelic?" Jim asked, impressed.

"I would say yes, but the Havenport Herald published an article today that mentioned the Kincaid motto and its placement by the memorial in the chasm. The only other Gaelic word I know is *sláinte*. It comes in handy at Royce's Tavern. You have no idea how many would-be highlanders are in Havenport. So you thought I spoke Gaelic. I had you going for a minute." Matt had a cat-ate-the-canary grin on his face. "Your expression was worth it."

Jim let out a quiet sigh. "Ryan thinks she figured out the note. All the spades—"

"Clover?" Matt asked.

"I thought so, too. No. Spades. Like a garden shovel. We think the picture is a message to dig by the motto's plaque. Simon may have hidden something. Ryan and I planned to search the area, but Peter convinced her to wait until after the reenactment celebration when the media is gone. Ryan didn't want to bring any attention to the excavation."

"You didn't agree," Matt said, his arms crossed.

"This isn't an educational exercise. I'm working a murder investigation, but I made a big mistake. I went to Judge Daly and got a court order to excavate near the memorial."

"You'll also need approval from the Historical Preservation and Heritage Commission."

"Yeah. That's not going to happen now. When I left Daly's office, I overheard him tell someone not to approve my request and explained I was searching for evidence about Simon's murder and possible drug connection at Hero's Chasm. Taylor is guarding the memorial now."

Matt glanced at the shovel. "Looks like you're going treasure hunting. Do you have room for one more?"

Jim nodded. The men walked toward the door.

"What did you bring?" Jim dipped his head toward the envelope Matt held.

"I met up with Simon at Royce's Tavern last week. I think I know what we're going to find."

Jim looked over his shoulder as he led the way to the parking lot.

"I'll drive while you look at what's inside." The men got into Jim's personal car.

"What are you holding back from me?" he asked as he pulled out papers. Matt picked up speed as he rushed down Manor Road.

"Bait." Matt's blank expression put him on high alert.

"What's the bait?" he asked. Matt's chest heaved. He didn't have a good feeling about this. Matt drummed his fingers on the steering wheel at a stoplight. His fingers went silent. Matt turned and faced him.

"Not what. Who. Simon got his hands on incriminating evidence. The legitimacy of the document was questionable, and he understood the damage it would cause in the wrong hands. We convinced him to play along and not give anything away. He didn't like the idea, but he wanted to protect her."

"Her?" Jim asked. Alarm rippled along his spine. Fear knotted his insides as he braced for the answer.

"Ryan," Matt said, accelerating.

Jim's heart hammered madly as the agent confirmed his worst nightmare.

"Go on. Why did Simon need to protect Ryan?" A swift flare of anger raced through every cell of his body. Protecting Ryan was his job.

"Her name is all over the papers and bank account for a shell company, Imprevin Laboratories, created by Peter. Peter did it as a joke after he took one of Simon's classes. His teacher was not impressed and told him to destroy everything.

"Except years later, Simon noticed that Imprevin Laboratories was a large player in the opioid market. He told me, and I investigated further. The company bank account is in the Cayman Islands and it made sizable contributions to Peter's campaign.

"We took Simon's deposition and decided to leave things as they were, for now. As Peter became more politically active, he distanced himself from Imprevin, but he made no move to protect his sister. We suspected a setup to let Ryan take the fall. Simon 'borrowed' the papers. We needed time and needed to protect Ryan. That's the transcript from Simon's interrogation along with a transcript of his trial."

"She knows everything," Jim said as he browsed through the pages.

"Are you sure?"

Jim glanced at the FBI agent. "I knew something was wrong when I spoke to her today. She's trying to keep me away. Simon hid the papers from Peter to protect Ryan, and I handed him the information on where to find the documents on a silver platter. Aren't I the smart guy?

"I love and want to protect her. So what do I do? I directed her to information that will expose her most trusted person as a traitor, implicate her in a drug cartel, and get her killed. Talk about a switch in positions. She wants to end our relationship to protect me. I don't know whether to laugh or cry. Right now, the only way to protect her is to get her away from Peter."

Matt pulled into the lot next to Taylor's cruiser. After getting the shovel he and Matt hurried down the path.

"Chief, someone's been digging here and I don't think it's an animal."

Jim and Matt examined the ground and the loose dirt. Jim kicked the dirt aside with his foot. He took out his pen and fished out one pink floral-print cotton garden glove.

Ryan wore the same gloves when she weeded her garden. The coincidence was too strong for the gloves to belong to anyone else.

The loose dirt made it easy for Brian to dig out the hole. The metallic click of his shovel hitting an object made him stop. With latex gloves on, the police lieutenant knelt and carefully brushed the dirt away. Minutes later, he pulled out a metal box and handed it to Jim.

"I can't believe we deciphered Simon's message." Jim fumbled with the latch and sprung the lid open. Empty.

"Ryan," Jim murmured her name, dropped the box and took off up the path. Matt and Brian followed. "She emptied the box. We need to get to her now. She's foolish enough to sacrifice herself for her brother."

"Brian, is there any report from the stakeout?"

"Two men entered Ryan's house five minutes ago. The license plate of the car is registered to Peter Livingston."

Dread owned him. It pushed against him, plastering him against an invisible wall. His lungs locked up tight, nothing in or out. *Breathe*, he commanded his lungs. *Protect her*. Shit. He should have gone to her house after he spoke to her this morning, not here. What was he thinking?

"What coverage do we have around the house?"

"An unmarked car in front," Brian said.

"Come with me," he said to Matt, and doubled-timed to the cars. "You and Brian pull into the park at the top of her street and take a position on the south side of her house. The north side is all windows. I'll go to the back. No one moves without my say-so."

"Peter whittled down her self-esteem and made her dependent on him. Is she strong enough to confront him without falling apart?" Matt asked.

"She's stronger than you think," Jim said. He hoped he was right. If anything happened to Ryan, someone would pay.

Matt went in Brian's car and pulled out of the lot. Jim followed in his car. The policemen raced along the coast and through town. He didn't slow until he got close to Ryan's house.

Matt and Brian peeled off and pulled into the park. The two would make the rest of the way on foot.

Jim slowed as he turned the corner and continued down her street. In the distance, a car with a distinctive government license plate sat in front of her house. He drove on and parked a dozen or so yards farther down the street.

His radio crackled. "In position," Brian reported.

"10-4," Jim replied.

Chapter Seven

With the same stealth Jim used in the desert to seek out a murderer, he stepped into the backyard adjacent to Ryan's house. Staying close to her neighbor's home, he moved to the corner and peeked around the edge to survey Ryan's yard. Everything was quiet.

That was the easy part. Her windows were open and the sliding door to the patio stood ajar. There was little cover. No large bushes or trees. Jim estimated her house ten yards away.

He pulled out his gun and centered himself. A few deep breaths and he looked around the edge. He picked his path and moved as quietly and quickly as he could. When he reached the side of Ryan's house, he plastered his back against the wall and lifted his gun.

"What was that?" said what sounded like Peter's voice.

Out of the corner of Jim's eye, Trixie slipped through the open sliding door.

"Calm down. It's just a cat." *So, Soren is with him, too.*

Jim stretched and peered through the sliding door. Ryan stood in the living room. Her brother held what looked like Simon's document. Soren stood close by. Trixie sat as silent as an Egyptian statue at Ryan's feet.

"You found the papers." Peter flipped through the clipped documents. "That SOB has been holding this over my head. I'll take care of it. And you thought Simon was your friend. Look at this. Look what he did. I've been trying to take it from him and expose it for the forgery it is. Now we can both breathe easy."

A hearty laugh escaped her lips.

"Peter, Simon didn't forge this. You, my artistic brother, forged my name."

Peter's mouth hung open. Not a sound came out.

"Growing up, you teased me about my middle name until I cried. How you laughed at my law school graduation when the dean, a good friend of yours, called out my name, Ryan Dorcas Livingston. I heard your roar all the way across the auditorium floor.

"I hated that name. After Mom died, I went to court and had my middle name changed to Doris, Mom's name. Everything I've signed since I was twenty-four, I've signed Ryan Doris Livingston. These are all signed by Ryan Dorcas Livingston."

♥ ♥ ♥

The raw look of resentment stained Peter's face. The brother Ryan trusted and loved morphed into a monster. It hurt like hell, but she had to face facts.

"It was your brother's idea, to prove his loyalty. Frankly, it was to protect his own ass," Soren said. "I thought it was very clever of him. We needed to create a company and had no time to make arrangements, if you know what I mean. Peter couldn't put his name on anything, not if we were going to make him a senator. Your brother called Simon Farrell, but he wouldn't accommodate us. Peter had a solution: use his old homework assignment he created years ago. Simon had given him high marks at the time. But enough about the past. I want the list of names you found."

She took a deep breath and she concentrated on Jim's words. *Trust yourself; you're strong.* He was right. The hurt was still there, but so was her strength.

"Here, take the list, but that won't help you. I sent copies to Jim Kanter and Matt Lyons."

She hoped she sounded convincing. Ryan held out the list to Peter. Soren reached over and grabbed it from her.

"I doubt that," Soren said, and tore the list to pieces. "The authorities will do what they do best, follow the money and the pictures. Everything leads back to you. I can see Peter now, the poor victim, betrayed by his greedy sister who used her position and contacts to orchestrate a drug business. Imprevin will be taken down. The money—what's left of it—confiscated. And you, ah, you will go to jail. And Peter? The votes will pour in." He took a knife out of his briefcase and set it on the table.

"Why did you nose around? Why didn't you go on vacation when I told you?" Peter said through clenched teeth.

Ryan had no doubts. Soren spoke the truth, but Peter's confirmation hurt as bad as if Peter grabbed the knife and cut out her heart.

Trust yourself. Anger churned deep in the pit of her stomach, but instead of falling apart, she vowed to seek justice for Simon and herself. She looked at the bloody knife on the table, her kitchen knife. The murder weapon. Fear quickly morphed into anger that strengthened her resolve.

"I can't help you." Peter's emotionless and unapologetic voice rang in her head. "Only your fingerprints are on the knife and your name is all over the Imprevin papers. You'll go to jail and never practice law again."

"How could you? There is still time for you to tell the truth." Pain squeezed her heart. She had to quit fooling herself. Peter was too far involved to find his way back to the truth.

"You have no idea, do you? Our dear parents. They taught me everything. Involved with Soren and others you don't want to know about. A heartbeat away from becoming a senator and Dad decided, no more."

"Is this *True Confessions*? Do you think your little sister will love you if she knew you were involved in your parents' deaths?"

Ryan swung around and stared at her brother.

The Livingston 2012 campaign headquarters brimmed with excitement as they anticipated her dad's return. Her mom called, stating they were on their way and would arrive in forty minutes.

The celebration ramped up as everyone waited for the senator-elect and his wife. Peter walked around with a bottle in each hand, pouring wine into everyone's glasses.

"Congratulations, Ry. You did a wonderful job." He poured champagne into her wine flute.

The three monitors around the room that weeks ago displayed the results of each precinct now replayed the swearing-in ceremony.

"Hey, quiet down," Peter shouted from the middle of the room.

Everyone followed Peter's stare and turned toward the monitors. Their faces fell at the sight of the mangled wreck of a state car.

Ryan stepped forward for a closer look, and the bottom fell out of her world. Her mother banged on the side window. Helpless, she, Peter, and the staff stared at the monitor as those at the scene ran toward the vehicle. The newscaster said something about a tractor trailer, but all she saw was her mother's hand pounding on the glass.

Fire licked from under the car. Her heart raced. She didn't want to look, but couldn't pull her eyes away. Someone hauled the newscaster away. The camera focused on the fire trucks coming down the highway.

What were they doing? Someone must have gotten her parents out of the wreck. The flash of an explosion followed milliseconds later. The camera swiveled back toward the car as a ball of flame rose into the air. Gray smoke shrouded the area. When it settled, fire engulfed the car. She combed the screen for any sign that her parents were safe. The activity at the scene made it difficult to see, but the tension from the accident poured through the screen into the office. Nose to nose at one of the monitors, she searched every face.

A moment later, a second explosion rocked the area. Her hand tightened around the stem of the crystal glass.

The snap of the glass stem echoed in her ear. Gut-wrenching pain shot through her and left her disoriented. She dropped the remnants of the glass and turned away from the pictures, unable to scream. The edge of the pain receded, replaced with emptiness and overwhelming loss. Woozy, she searched for Peter.

Where was everyone?

Only she and Peter remained. She calmed and took a step toward him, but he turned away, walked into his office, and closed the door.

Alone. In the middle of the empty room littered with streamers and confetti, the three monitors continued to flash pictures of her parents and the remnants of the fiery debris.

She wrapped her arms around herself and cried.

"I had no idea the Art Society fronted for Imprevin. They bought my artwork and gave me money for my campaign. Ry, I had no idea. Dad found out. He was going to turn me in, use me as an object lesson. The Art Society thought otherwise. I was just as shocked when we watched the accident."

She stepped away from him, staring as if he was a monster. Everything about him was a lie.

Peter grabbed her by the shoulders, shook her, and screamed, "The enterprise is bigger than you and your desire for the truth! The truth didn't pay your law school bills, for your pretty clothes, or this house. Who else took care of you after Mom and Dad died?"

Something inside Ryan snapped. She shoved him away. "My school bills?" She stepped forward. "I worked my ass off through school and got scholarships through undergrad and law school. Don't give yourself any illusions here. You didn't pay a cent for my schooling. And as for my clothes, I paid for them, too."

The words ripped out of her as she stepped closer to him. Her index finger poked his chest as she made each point. "And the house."

Her fury almost choked her. "Mom and Dad left the house to both of us, and I bought you out. You were a spoiled little boy who became an even more spoiled man."

"I thought that over time you would join us. I never meant to hurt you, not even when I pushed you off the fence at camp to get your sexy counselor's attention."

Camp? "What are you talking about? You took me to the hospital. You wouldn't let Murray near me."

"I couldn't let him near you. Murray knew I pushed you on purpose. I played the dutiful older brother and it worked to my advantage. I wanted your counselor's attention, so I carried you to the car. When I went back to camp, she said I acted like a knight coming to your rescue. The girl was all over me. Coming to her rescue was easy after that."

For a moment, Ryan was back at Camp Thunderclap, lying in the dirt and mud. The impact of falling off the fence knocked every wisp of air from her lungs. Sprawled in the mud, she struggled to inhale, to exhale, to do anything. Now the pain hit her, but not from remembering her broken arm. No, from Peter's betrayal.

"You idolized me no matter what I did. Right after Mom and Dad died, everyone asked me who was going to take care of you. I had been your knight before; I could do it again. I even found a spot for you in my campaign to show others how I took care of you. I never expected a one-woman campaign organization, and you never complained. I took care of everything and kept you safe. You have no idea how many creeps I had to keep away from you."

With each statement his voice got louder, his face redder, his eyes wider, and the veins in his neck pulsed faster. He spat out his words in rapid fire. Peter couldn't stop, and she didn't want him to. She wanted to hear it all.

"Who protected you from Mitchell and his great plans to open a law office with you? The man was a liability that needed to be neutralized. Getting rid of him was best all around. He would have taken you away from me, and you were the brains behind my campaign. No one could do what you did. You knew who to speak to, what to say, and how to say it. You didn't need Mitchell, so I did you a favor and got rid of him. I introduced him to the right people and helped him when he needed funding. His ambition did the rest. I kept you busy with my campaign. Your best friend was more than eager to console him."

Her eyes and mouth froze wide open. He was behind Mitchell's betrayal? Ryan tilted her head and got a clear picture of her brother. He'd lied to her at every turn. Stunned, she couldn't bear to be with him a moment longer. Ryan headed toward the sliding glass door.

"Ryan," he said, and stepped in front of her. "Where do you think you're going? I won't let you destroy everything I've fought for, everything that's mine."

She stood nose to nose with him, hands on her hips.

"It's always been about you. I understand that now. All the time you consoled me, you were the cause of my pain." Her eyes closed. How could she be so blind? "And Jim. You manipulated everything so I would break it off with him, too."

Ryan turned away. She couldn't stand to look at or be near him.

"You disgust me in your righteousness to save yourself at the expense of others, to sacrifice me to save your skin. I've got to get out of here. The stench is toxic."

Peter grabbed her. His fingers bit into her arm. Ryan looked at his hand, then at him. She squeezed the fragile bones on his wrist until he released her. "Don't touch me. Don't talk to me. Don't come near me."

"You're not going anywhere," Soren said. "I thought

Peter could reason with you. You take the fall, and we can save you. Do anything else and we'll kill you. I promise."

Peter stared at Soren. The emotion that raced across his face made her angry. Not denial. Not protecting her. Agreement. Soren pushed her back and drew his gun. Trixie stood, her tail twitching from side to side.

"Is that supposed to scare me?" Ryan turned toward Peter. "He'll have to kill me to stop me."

Soren leveled the gun and aimed at her head. Ryan stepped toward the door and heard the metallic hiss of the slide as he cocked the gun.

A hissing, spitting, and snarling cinnamon-brown streak leaped at Soren. Trixie's thornlike claws stretched out in front of her. Fearless, Trixie bared arrow-tipped teeth as she lunged at Soren's neck.

The gun dropped to the floor as Soren struggled to rid himself of the cat. Ryan and Peter grappled for the gun. He pushed her to the floor, but not before she'd kicked the gun away.

As she rose to her feet, Peter drew a gun from his pocket and pointed the weapon at her.

"Ryan, don't make me do this." Peter's panicked voice faded into the distance even though he stood a foot away from her.

Time progressed in slow motion. Peter's mouth moved as Soren struggled with Trixie, but the thundering beat of her heart echoed in her ears.

Her gaze swept from Peter's hand to his eyes, which were filled with determination and purpose. She had no doubt her brother would pull the trigger.

That didn't mean she would be his victim. A white-hot anger boiled inside her, melting away the barriers she hid behind. The situation made her laugh. For the first time since Mitchell's betrayal, she felt free. No, she wasn't Peter's victim. Instead, she would be his albatross.

Trixie screamed as she continued to claw at Soren's neck, and he struggled to get the cat off.

This was Ryan's chance. She started to rise, but before she got to her feet Peter shouted.

"Don't move, Ry. It didn't have to be this way. All you had to do was be quiet. Worst case, you plead guilty, and Daly would commute your sentence. But no, you had to go digging."

"Go ahead, Peter, but I'm not going to look away or close my eyes. You'll have to watch me and see what you're doing. How you cursed Mitchell for his betrayal. Well, Peter"—she spat his name—"here's my curse. Every time you look in the mirror, you'll see me. Do you hear me? When you brush your teeth, shave your face, even straighten your tie, it's my face that will stare back at you. You'll see me and what you've done."

Ryan hoped with all her heart her curse would plague him the rest of his life. His wavering arm steadied and straightened. With a deep breath, her mind focused on Jim. How she wished she could project her thoughts and tell him she was sorry for everything, but never for loving him.

Peter closed his eyes.

No, he had to watch. "Look at me!" she shouted at him.

His eyes flew open.

Soren pulled the cat off his back and tossed Trixie out the sliding door. Somewhere in the distance, Trixie screamed.

A wave of panic flashed through her. Behind Peter, Soren picked up his gun. Did he intend to kill her brother? She saw a red laser beam aimed at her head.

That's when the guns fired and she slid to the floor.

Chapter Eight

Ryan struggled to open her eyes and focus on the dark shadow next to her. Her vision cleared. She was in bed, with Jim at her side.

"Welcome back."

The concerned expression cleared from his face. Yes, if she was going to die, his was the last face she wanted to see.

Disoriented, she looked around the room. Trixie was curled up at the foot of her bed, asleep. The cat didn't appear any the worse for her experience.

"You thirsty?" Jim poured a glass of water and handed it to her.

"Thanks."

She coughed to clear her throat, which set off jackhammers pounding in her head. She raised her hand toward the pain.

With a gentle touch, Jim pulled her hand away. "You were collateral damage. I'm sure Matt will nominate you for the Purple Heart."

"Don't make me laugh. It makes the pain worse."

Jim bent close to her. "The bullet grazed you. You

may have to part your hair a different way until it heals. The doctor said there'd be no scar."

"What happened?" she whispered.

"Trixie's attack on Soren gave Matt and Brian time to get in position. Matt disarmed Soren and I shot Peter."

Her heart pounded, but her head hurt more. She closed her eyes, but in the darkness, Peter's frightened face stared at her. If it didn't hurt so much she would laugh. Her curse backfired.

"The medic said Peter will be fine. They're ready to take you to the hospital. As a precaution."

"No. I'm fine. You said it wouldn't scar. The hospital won't be necessary."

♥ ♥ ♥

"I shot Peter. I'm not sorry." No, Jim wasn't sorry, but he wasn't happy, either. He held her shoulders and pulled her closer. "I would do anything to protect you. Anything."

"I know." He could barely hear her voice. She looked into his eyes. A smile touched her lips.

"What about Soren?" She eased into his arms.

"Soren backed up Peter. I think he was afraid Peter wouldn't shoot you. But when I saw the laser from Soren's gun aimed at you, I went into action. I smashed the flower pot on the patio. Soren swung his gun toward me. I still didn't have a clear shot at him. Matt shot Soren. I shot Peter.

"Soren's shot went wild. It grazed your head. The medic attending Soren's wounds found old claw marks on Soren's arms and neck. I put two and two together. I think Trixie attacked Soren when he killed Simon. It could be how she lost her claw. Brian told me Val, the EMT, gave him a cat claw he found on the stretcher."

Jim had almost lost her. The sound of the smashing

flower pot distracted Soren enough to make him turn toward the noise. He didn't doubt the man's aim. He had never been so afraid of failing her than when she'd stared down Soren.

"Even though we'll never know if Peter intended to shoot, you need to understand that he is going to stand trial. The charges against him are serious." He held her tight, stroking her back, and for a moment wondered if he was trying to soothe her or himself.

"I'll be indicted, too," she said in a choked voice. "It seems my brother wanted his illegal enterprise to be a family business."

She moved away. "There are pictures of me with some scary people. Simon was the only person who had all the information about when and how those pictures were created. With him gone, I have no way to clear my name."

Her chin trembled as she struggled not to cry.

Jim moved closer and gathered her into his arms.

"Peter was manipulative," she whispered in his ear, "in keeping us apart, but now… It may be best we don't see each other."

"We'll worry about that later." He tried to draw her closer, but she escaped his grasp.

"No. When this mess hits the papers, I'll be a liability to you and your career. I don't want to do that, ever."

"I'll worry about my career. What did you find in the metal box at the memorial?" he asked, his soft voice coaxing her away from her topic.

"A list of Simon's accounts and two manila envelopes, one filled with pictures."

"The ones Soren wanted?"

"See for yourself. They're on my dresser. There are pictures of me with known mobsters at shady locations. One picture with Soren looks like we're intimate friends. The other envelope was filled with papers that show I'm on the board of directors of Imprevin Laboratories."

"I know. Matt let me read the papers."

Jim pulled the envelope Matt gave him from his pocket. Docket 062013. "This is the transcript from Simon's trial. Read the third page."

Ryan turned to the page. Her lips formed the words as she silently read. Done, she looked at him with new understanding.

"This number, 062013, was written in Simon's notebook," she said.

"It's all there," Jim said. "Simon took the blame for the Imprevin forgeries even though Peter created the documents. The FBI decided to leave Imprevin up and running in order to avoid tipping off Soren and his cronies. So Simon came through for you. You're safe with nothing to fear."

"Where is Peter now?"

"He and Soren are in the living room. The medic should be finished by now, and Brian should have read them their rights," Matt said, standing in the doorway. "We heard enough while we were outside. One of my men is paying Judge Daly a visit. You should control this message before it gets to the media or else it will be a nightmare. We've been able to keep it quiet, but as soon as we bring Peter and Daly in everyone will know."

"You're right. Can you give me about fifteen minutes? What are the charges against Peter and Daly?" She took a pad and pencil from her nightstand.

"Matt's team gathered a dossier on Peter and Soren. Peter's name came up two years ago when the drug dealers were using the kids as mules. His position as the state drug czar put him in a vulnerable position. Soren and his team, the Havenport Art Society, used him. Peter thought he was safe with Soren and his kind, but that's not how these guys operate."

"Thanks for the context, but what are the charges?" She tapped the end of the pencil on the pad of paper, waiting for his answer.

"The charges are fraud, money laundering, drug trafficking, conspiracy, and accomplices to the murder of Simon Farrell, and attempting to murder you," Matt said.

Jim had his arm around her. Matt hadn't been gentle, but Jim saw no other way. Besides, she could handle this. He was serious when he told her he would face this with her.

The three made their way into the living room.

Matt took Jim aside. "Listen. I'll take Soren to the car. Give Ryan time with her brother." Jim nodded.

"Okay." Matt put his arm under Soren's and dragged him to his feet. "In the car."

Matt and Brian led Soren out of the house. Peter remained handcuffed on her sofa, his head down. He didn't try to make eye contact with her. Ryan went to her desk and dialed the phone.

"Hello, Governor. This is Ryan Livingston. I need about fifteen minutes of your time." She took the phone and went into her bedroom.

"I'll need you to take care of a few things," Peter said.

Jim raised an eyebrow and said nothing.

"I can pay you—"

"Peter," Jim said, and bent close to the man's face, "you can't pay me to do anything for you."

Peter lifted his chin. "I would never hurt her."

"Don't go there. Even you don't believe that lie. I'm opening up an investigation into the vehicular death of your parents. Soren mentioned some interesting facts."

Ryan returned and put the phone down.

"He took that as well as could be expected," she said. "He'll inform the others. The party wants to prepare a press release."

"Ryan," Peter said in a small voice. She and Jim turned toward him. Matt came in through the sliding doors.

"There's money in the safe for bail. There won't be an arraignment for a day or two. I could stay here…" His voice trailed off at the utter look of disgust she gave him.

"That won't be possible, Peter," Matt said. "The arraignment will be later this evening, and the recommendation is no bail. Aside from being a flight risk, your closeness to Soren makes you a likely cartel target. To keep you safe, I'll be taking you to Providence."

"I...I know too many people in Providence." Peter gave Ryan a pleading look.

"You can commiserate with Judge Daly and Soren," Ryan said, her voice ice cold.

Ryan came up next to Jim and slid her hand in his. He turned toward her and reveled in her control, determination, and resilience. Disappointment and sadness touched her eyes, but she didn't shrivel up or withdraw as she did in the past. No need to ask if she was all right. She glowed with self-confidence and determination that made her more beautiful, if that was possible.

"It's the best way for us to protect you," Matt said in a matter-of-fact tone, and turned to Jim. "You take care of Ryan. If you don't mind, Brian and I will see to Soren and Peter."

"Thanks," Jim said as the men left.

"Jim, would you mind if we stayed in for dinner? I'd rather it just be the two of us tonight. I want to talk through what will happen tomorrow when this all hits the papers."

"Would you like me to make you a grilled cheese sandwich, or do you have frozen meatballs and sauce?" He glanced at the kitchen.

"Only you could make me smile right now."

She looked up at him, and his heart skipped a beat. Silence. With Peter and Soren forgotten, she and Jim stood transfixed, lost in each other's eyes.

♥ ♥ ♥

Ryan sat in her bathrobe and fuzzy slippers at her kitchen table, her landline and cell phone going right to voice mail. The phones started ringing at 6:00 a.m. She took a cup of coffee from Jim and read the *Havenport Herald*. She had no idea how Candy Apples got the news about Peter before the political reporter, but Candy was on the front page rather than the usual place her gossip column graced, page three.

Good morning, Havenport. You won't need your cup o' joe this morning. What I have to tell you is a real eye-opener. While we were sleeping, our friendly neighborhood would-be senator, Peter Livingston, was indicted on several counts of fraud, embezzlement, conspiracy, money laundering, and drug trafficking. My sources tell me that the righteous Senator Livingston fraudulently implicated his sister and legal partner, Ryan Livingston. This is like a Mickey Spillane novel. For those of you too young to know who that is, ask your digital assistant.

Less than a week since the murder of Simon Farrell, our own Chief of Police Jim Kanter and Special Agent Matt Lyons—that hunk every woman in town is trying to attract—cracked the case. Soren, the international businessman snooping around the Emerson waterfront property and head of the New England drug cartel, was indicted for Simon's murder and the attempted murder of Ryan Livingston.

There is an unlikely heroine to this thriller—Trixie, Simon's cat. That's right. Trixie attacked Soren and saved Ryan Livingston's life. Rumors are flying that our fearless feline has the evidence needed to convict Soren of Simon's murder, as well. It seems there are recent claw marks on Soren's arms. Dr. O'Brien—be still my heart—treated Trixie for a torn claw retrieved by the EMT at the murder scene and handed it over to Lieutenant Taylor as evidence.

Matt Lyons and James Kanter worked together for the past two years to crack the drug ring plaguing Havenport and preying on our kids. Like the Royal Mounties, they got their man. So wake up, everyone. It's a new day where our kids are safer and the garbage is weeded out of our state assembly. All is well with our corner of the world.

Jim sat next to her. She fluffed and straightened his sleep-matted hair.

"I finished the analysis of Catrina's diary for Ina while you were sleeping," she said. "Catrina wrote about her father selling the building and land to Eoin and her, and she mentioned the terms of the sale. That, and Simon's record of the forgery, confirms the document in Simon's safe-deposit box is false. I'm not sure how I'll be able to explain the pictures I found are fake."

"Did you examine the pictures closely? I mean really closely?" he asked.

Ryan gave him a curious stare and took the envelope he handed her. One by one, she pulled out the pictures and spread them on the table. Her face stared back at her from each picture.

"I don't know what you see that I don't."

"All the pictures are summer shots."

Her face morphed from mystified to enlightened. "Sleeveless."

She checked each picture and sat straight in her chair. "No scar on the left arm. I never thought the incident at camp so many years ago would ever be a blessing."

"We better get ready. I want to be at the chasm to support Ina. She's worried about this celebration, especially with David Kincaid in from Scotland. She mentioned he brought Eoin's sword for the reenactment. I had to call her this morning to let her know Peter would not be able to attend. To say she was shocked is an understatement."

She folded the paper, got up, and sat in his lap.

"I also called campaign headquarters. Peter was telling me the truth. My name is being considered for assistant attorney general. I told the governor I was honored, but not interested and asked that my name be withdrawn from all political committees."

She looked into Jim's eyes. "I'm reducing my case load at the office, too."

She was glad he didn't ask her to explain, although the question was clearly on his face. "Politics and the law were

Peter's dreams, not mine. I think being out of the public eye for a while would be best and give me time to work with the Historical Society."

He kissed her nose, then her forehead. "I think that's a very good plan."

"My lips are waiting," she said.

"Patience. I'll get there."

They walked toward the bedroom. "We should get ready for the celebration. Ina is waiting."

"Soon." She grabbed his face and kissed his lips hard and deep, then eased up. "Maybe not so soon."

♥ ♥ ♥

Jim stood beside Ryan at the celebration with one arm at her back and the other in his pocket, like any other couple at the event. Her close friends approached her, not knowing what to say. She made small talk and tried to ease their discomfort.

"How are you? I've worried about you since we spoke," Ina said. "The family was excited with the transcript. They would like you to transcribe the rest of the diary. If you can, join us for the family memorial and bagpipes."

"I appreciate your concern. I'm glad you want to transcribe the rest of Catrina's story. I'll pick up the diary tomorrow. Now, go ahead. Break a leg. I know everyone will be thrilled to hear Catrina's words and what really happened."

Ina took her place with David at the podium and nodded at Ryan. The mayor started his introduction.

Ryan listened to Catrina's words with a new understanding. She felt the woman's anguish and pain, but also her strength and determination. Ryan stood next to the man who silently gave her the strength to take the steps she needed to make her life whole and complete.

The reading ended to a loud applause.

"Do you mind hanging back?" she asked Jim. "I'd rather not get crushed by everyone going into town for the reenactment."

Jim didn't ask any questions. He stood with her and watched Ina and the rest of the Emerson family gather around Eoin's grave for their private memorial.

His hand never left her back. He maneuvered her away from the crowd toward the upper road along the cliff. With the area to themselves, he steered her to the lookout to savor the view over the ocean. The clear sky and crisp sun gave her hope for a new beginning.

"Do you need to meet with Matt?" She stared out at the sea. Jim stood with her watching as waves built speed and height in the distance, rose in peaks above the water, and crashed against the base of the cliff. The methodic sound, salty air, and his nearness were all she needed, all she wanted.

"No. Matt and his team are the cleanup squad. They'll take care of Soren and his illegal claim."

"The story of Eoin and Catrina is one of betrayal," she said.

"Shhh. You don't need to explain."

"Thank you for that, but it's not an explanation as much as it's a release. You taught me not to bottle things up, rather let everything out and deal with it. I spent much of the night thinking about things. Lots of things, and people."

She turned to face him. "Can you ever forgive me for thinking you would—"

"Betray you."

She laughed. "You are the one person I trust most, who would never let me down. My own flesh and blood betrayed me."

"Are you saying you trust me?"

"I always knew I could trust you. Mitchell was a convenient excuse."

♥ ♥ ♥

"You doubted that I love you?" Jim held his breath waiting for her answer.

"No. Not that, either. I thought I was damaged goods and when I saw no way out of being indicted, I didn't want to hurt you. You deserved better. I love you." Ryan raked her hand through his hair, brushing the strands out of his face. "I fell in love with you when I looked into your eyes that day in the courtroom when you conveniently knocked the papers off the desk."

"That was six years ago. Look at all the time we've wasted." He smiled, his chest expanding at the words. He pulled his hand out of his pocket, took hers, and slipped an engagement ring on her finger.

"I fell in love with you that day, too. I tried to talk myself out of it, but I kept coming back to a plain and simple fact. You are the woman I want to spend the rest of my life with. Ryan Doris Livingston, will you marry me?" He took her in his arms and held her close. "I love you. And I always will."

He ran his fingers through her long, blonde hair, reveling in its silkiness and in her strength.

"With all my heart, I love you. Yes, I'll marry you." She leaned her head against his chest. "I never doubted your love for me, but I was so afraid I lost you."

"I was prepared to keep asking you until you said yes. Now, let's go home."

As they left the cliff, they passed the opening to the chasm and heard the plaintive sound of the bagpipes.

Epilogue

Havenport, Rhode Island — August 2018

Ryan carried a tray of iced tea to Jim on the back patio and placed it on the table. Trixie stretched out in the sun not far away.

"Ah, Mrs. Kanter. Iced tea. You read my mind." Jim took the offered glass and sipped his Rhode Island iced tea.

Ryan Kanter. She loved the sound of her new name. Two weeks since their wedding, and she said her name or wrote it down every chance she got. Mrs. Kanter snuggled next to Mr. Kanter, who read the paper. She dreamed she was in heaven.

"It seems our Candy Apples may have missed her calling. She'd make a good investigative reporter." He folded the paper to a neat two-column spread. "Someone asked why the Emerson waterfront property was so important. Our girl figured out that since the town council has banned any additional building along the waterfront, it was the only place that Soren could get dock access to the bay without construction and a lot of questions.

"But more importantly, how's the diary coming along?" Jim asked as he unfolded the *Havenport Herald*.

"I finished the transcription and came across an interesting section."

Jim lowered the paper. "What does Catrina have to say?"

Ryan pulled the typed pages from her pocket.

At the bottom of Papa's letter, he said he and Mama wanted to see me and my David. My family is coming to Scotland on the next ship. For weeks, Mother Kincaid and I planned for their arrival. I was busy during the days getting their rooms ready, deciding where to take them, but at night, after I put David to bed, I was alone and mourned for my Eoin.

After waiting eight weeks, Father Kincaid rushed into the drawing room with news.

"The ship. The Sea Hawk *has arrived from Havenport."*

We all hurried into the carriage and left for the dock. In the distance, I saw my father's ship and my heart pounded at the thought of seeing him and Mama.

I picked up my David and rushed toward the pier, searching the gangway for them. There. At last, I saw my father lead my mother and an injured man. It must have been Lachlan. My eyes filled with tears of joy at seeing my family.

Mother Kincaid took David and told me to go to my family. She followed behind. I squeezed through the throngs of dock workers and people by the ship and made my way to the end of the dock. Mama and my wee sisters rushed toward me and held me tight. Mama didn't stop kissing me. Laughing, I pulled away and introduced her to Mother Kincaid and her grandson, David.

My boy reached for Mama. The look on her face made me cry. I turned to Papa, but I didn't see him even though he was there. Eoin stood in front of me.

With a shaking hand, I touched his face to make sure he was real. He took my hand. I almost collapsed. He held me in his arms, and I cried for joy that he was with me. Mama handed us David and the three of us stood in the center of the turmoil but saw only each another.

Later that evening, Eoin told us what happened. The British hunted him like an animal. The Redcoats tormented our friends and neighbors. Someone played the traitor and told the British that Eoin was the leader of the Havenport insurgents.

I asked about Bennett. Eoin held my hand. Bennett was killed in a skirmish in Newport, fighting for the British. They promised him Papa's land and ships once the rebellion was put down. He was naive enough to believe the British would honor their pact.

After much prodding, Eoin told me it was Bennett who betrayed him. I think I knew all along, but didn't want to admit it.

He and Lachlan were wounded. While Eoin recovered, Lachlan's wound turned grave. Before he died, he devised a plan with Papa that would save Eoin and send him back to Scotland. When Lachlan died, his grave marker would have Eoin's name.

The British still harassed Papa's ships, inspecting each one for contraband. It is the reason Papa sent me the letter about Eoin's death. He knew they read all correspondence. Papa's message was for them more than for me. As hostilities progressed, the British became involved in Boston and had little time to waste in Havenport. The time was right. My family and Eoin sailed for Scotland.

My husband held me close. I mourned for Bennett and Lachlan. After months and years of sorrow, it was difficult to believe I was in my husband's arms.

I fiercely love my Eoin and have learned to honor each hour and each day we have together.

Ryan put down the pages. "I called Ina and read her the rest of the story. She's going to recommend that the full story be told at the annual celebration, but the grave and memorial not be altered. It will be Havenport's tribute to a Revolutionary War legend.

"My story is so much like Catrina's. Betrayed by her brother. I know how she felt. I was glad to read that Eoin was alive."

"Does that make me the handsome Scotsman?"

"You're my handsome, wonderful police chief who I love more than anyone." Ryan let out a yawn.

"Let's go back to bed where I can show you I'm your sexy, handsome, wonderful husband."

About Ruth A. Casie

RUTH A. CASIE is a *USA Today* bestselling author of historical swashbuckling action-adventures and contemporary romance with enough action to keep you turning pages. Her stories feature strong women and the men who deserve them, endearing flaws and all. She lives in New Jersey with her hero, three empty bedrooms and a growing number of incomplete counted cross-stitch projects. Before she found her voice, she was a speech therapist (pun intended), client liaison for a corrugated manufacturer, and vice president at an international bank where she was a product/ marketing manager, but her favorite job is the one she's doing now—writing romance.

♥ ♥ ♥

For more information on Ruth,
please join her newsletter or visit her online at
www.RuthACasie.com
Ruth@RuthACasie.com

Also by Ruth A. Casie

Medieval Romances
The Druid Knight Series
Knight of Runes
Knight of Rapture
Knight of Redemption – Coming Soon
The Druid Knight Tales A Short Story—Expanded

♥ ♥ ♥

The Stelton Legacy
The Guardian's Witch
The Highlander's English Woman
The Maxwell Ghost
The Pirate's Jewel — February, 2019
The Guardian's Sword — Mid 2019

♥ ♥ ♥

Collections

Timeless Tales – Short Stories
Mistletoe and Magick featured in Timeless Keepsakes - Medieval
Whispers on the Wind featured in Timeless Treasures - Medieval
How to Marry a Stuart Brother featuring Second Chance by the Sea & Forsaking All Others

♥ ♥ ♥

Havenport – Contemporary Novellas
The Witching Hour
Never Say Never
Happily Ever After featuring I'll Be Home for Christmas & The Game's AFoot

♥ ♥ ♥

You're Invited!

We hope you enjoyed your time in Havenport, Rhode Island. If you're like us, and didn't want to leave our small town, we have great news!

Despite the snow, things are heating up during the holidays. Come join some of Havenport's favorite citizens as they celebrate **Christmas in Havenport**.

Havenport is having a July fourth celebration and you're invited. Revisit old friends and meet some new in **Welcome to Havenport**.

If you're not afraid of ghosts, visit Havenport for Halloween. You'll be sure to run into one or two friendly spirits at the annual Halloween ball in **Haunted Havenport**.

A blizzard is coming to our small town, so be prepared to snuggle up and stay warm while everyone is **Snowbound in Havenport**.

Mystery and romance are sure to brighten your day when **Love Letters from Havenport** are discovered. Coming October 2019.

We'd love to know what you think of our stories. Please consider leaving a review on the site where you purchased your copy, or on a reader site such as Goodreads.

Thank you!